HEARTBREAKER

HEARTBREAKER

TANIA
CARVER

Sphere
An imprint of
Little, Brown Book Group
Carmelite House
50 Victoria Embankment
London EC4Y 0DZ

An Hachette UK Company

sphere

www.littlebrown.co.uk

SPHERE

First published in Great Britain in 2015 by Sphere
This paperback edition published in 2015 by Sphere

1 3 5 7 9 10 8 6 4 2

A CIP catalogue record for this book
is available from the British Library.

ISBN 978-0-7515-5788-6

Typeset in Plantin by M Rules
Printed and bound in Great Britain by
Clays Ltd, St Ives plc

Papers used by Sphere are from well-managed forests
and other responsible sources.

MIX
Paper from
responsible sources
FSC
www.fsc.org   FSC® C104740

To Christabelle, research assistant extraordinaire

Acknowledgements

There are a whole load of people who deserve to be acknowledged for the part they play in putting these books together and never get the recognition. Time to remedy that.

To my agent Jane Gregory and the rest of the team at Gregory and Company: Claire, Steph, Terry, Irene, Ruth and Mary.

To my editor Jade Chandler and everyone else at Little, Brown in Team Tania: Thalia, David, Jo, Vicky, Andy, both Sarahs and I'm sure I've missed out loads for which I apologise.

To Beth - the next one's for you. Promise.

To all the booksellers who've got behind Tania. Thank you. I really appreciate it.

To Mark Billingham, not only a brilliant writer but also a real friend, even when I didn't deserve one. *Truth or Dare* should have been dedicated to him. In my head it always will be.

To Jamie-Lee for holding me upright.

But mainly for the readers who continue to buy and (hopefully) enjoy the ongoing exploits of Phil and Marina. Thank you. Seriously. You make everything worthwhile.

PART ONE

ITCHY FEET

1

Gemma Adderley had had enough.

She had taken everything she possibly could, endured everything that had been slung at her, and was scared, humiliated, broken, hurt. Hurt above all. In so many ways.

As the front door slammed, shutting out the outside world once again, Gemma looked round the house. At her possessions. At her life. What was it Robert De Niro had said in that film she had watched once when Roy was out? Never get attached to anything you wouldn't walk out on in thirty seconds if you had to. Something like that. She sat at the kitchen table and looked at the walls, the floor. The cooker he had wanted her chained to. The fridge he had told her to keep fully stocked, even if she didn't always have the money to do it. They weren't her possessions. He had bought them. Had tried to make them possess her. There was nothing in the room – the flat – she wouldn't be able to walk out on. That she didn't want to walk out on.

Except Carly. And that was why she was taking her daughter with her.

Heart thumping, Gemma stood up, went into the living room. Thought once more of Roy. What he would say to her if he knew she was planning this. Do to her. The sins she would be committing. The punishment he would inflict – no, not him, not his punishment, God's, for daring to go against His will. And knew she wouldn't face that again. Never again. She

3

opened the door, gripping the handle, trying not to notice how much her fingers were trembling.

Carly was lying on the floor watching TV. Some unreal reality show. The kind she could only watch when Roy was out. She turned as Gemma entered, her eyes as usual wide, head and body flinching. Expecting God's wrath. Expecting to go straight to hell. Gemma's heart broke every time she saw her daughter do that. She had wondered where she had seen eyes like her daughter's before and the answer had come to her one night when she was watching the news. They'd shown footage of some war zone in the Middle East, tortured refugees making their way slowly out of the city, trying to forget what they had seen, trying to carry on, and she'd seen the same things in the children's eyes that were in Carly's.

A war zone. Just about sums it up, thought Gemma. Straight to hell. How could you fear going there when you were already living in it?

'Hey,' she said, trying to keep her voice light, 'we're going out.'

Carly sat up, looked round nervously. She had heard the door slam shut as well. It was usually a sign for them both to relax. Get together, find a shared strength to keep them going. But this was new. This was unheard of for the little girl. What her mother was proposing was against the rules. And she knew there would be punishments.

'But . . . ' Carly's eyes darted to the door. 'We can't . . . '

'We can,' said Gemma, hoping she sounded calm and in control, fearing she didn't. 'And we are. Come on.'

Carly stood up, dumbly obeying, even if it was against the rules. 'Where . . . '

Gemma summoned up a smile for her daughter. Only for her daughter, she thought. It had been a long time since she had smiled for herself. 'Somewhere nice. Somewhere safe.'

Carly said nothing.

'Come on,' said Gemma, holding out her hand for the girl to take.

Carly, clearly not happy but not wanting to go against her mother's wishes, walked towards her. Then turned back to the TV. 'I'd better turn it off. If I don't turn it off . . . '

'Leave it on,' said Gemma.

Carly stared at her.

'Yeah, leave it on.' Gemma smiled. That little act of rebellion had emboldened her. With Carly she turned, left the room.

She had already packed their bags, hidden them under the bed. She pulled them out.

'Are we . . . are we going on holiday?' asked Carly.

'Yeah,' said Gemma, 'that's right. A holiday.'

'Where?' asked Carly, excitement building despite her fear. 'Somewhere hot and sunny? Like Benidorm?'

It was one of the seven-year-old's favourite programmes. Something Gemma let her stay up and watch if Roy was out. Which was most nights.

'Not Benidorm, petal, no. But somewhere nice. Somewhere we'll feel . . . ' What? What could she say to her daughter, tell her about where they were going? 'Safe. Happy. Somewhere happy. Come on, get your coat on.'

Carly turned to go to her own room, stopped, came back. 'Can I bring Crusty?'

Her toy bear. She took it everywhere.

'He's already packed. We won't forget him. Now come on, we've got to go.'

But Carly didn't move. A thought had occurred to her. Gemma stood, waited. She knew what the child was going to say. Had her answer prepared.

'Is . . . is Daddy coming with us?'

5

'Not, not just yet, petal. D'you want him to?'

'He's Daddy.' Her voice flat, monotonous. The words like something learned by rote at school. 'We're his family. He's the head. In charge. Just like God. He has to know what we're doing all the time.'

'That's right. He's Daddy.' Not dwelling on the rest of her daughter's words. Hoping she was young enough to forget all that stuff in time. 'Well, look. We'll get going and he can come and join us later if we want him to. How does that sound?'

Again those wide war-zone eyes. Carly nodded.

Gemma knew she didn't mean it, knew she had done it more out of fear of disagreeing than because she wanted him to join them. She knew also the conflict that would be raging inside her daughter, tearing her apart. But it had to be done. It had to be.

'Good,' she said. 'Right, just a couple of things to do before we go.'

She took out her phone, dialled a number she had memorised. Waited.

'Gemma Adderley,' she said when someone answered. 'Safe Haven, please.'

The voice on the other end of the line asked her where she was. She told them. She was given directions, told where to be.

'The car'll be with you in ten minutes. Is that okay?'

'Yeah,' said Gemma, hardly believing that she was actually doing this. After toying with it for years, wanting to but not having the strength, the courage to actually do so, she was leaving Roy. And with him would go all the pain, hurt and suffering that she and her daughter had endured for so long.

'Yeah,' she said again. 'That's fine.'

'The driver needs to give you a word so you know it's from us. The word is strawberry. If they don't give you that, don't get in, okay?'

'Okay.'

'See you soon.'

Gemma ended the call, looked down at Carly. Her daughter had her coat buttoned up and was staring up at her, trying to be excited but unable to hide the fear in her eyes. In that moment Gemma thought it wasn't possible for her to love another person more.

'Come on, petal,' she said. 'Let's go.'

They reached the front door.

'Oh,' said Gemma, 'one more thing.'

She went back into the living room, took the book – Roy's only book – from pride of place on the shelf. The Bible. The family Bible, a source of guidance and prayer. A template to live your life by. She felt the edges. Hard leather, scuffed and indented where it had struck her and her daughter. A weapon of anger, of fear.

She felt rage build inside. Wished she had a fire so she could throw the book on it, watch it burn away to nothing. Instead had to content herself with opening it up at random and ripping out pages, throwing them round the room in a frenzy.

Eventually she wore herself out, dropped the book on the floor, knowing it would serve as a goodbye letter, and went to join her daughter.

She looked at the front door once more. He never locked it when he went out but she knew she was expected to remain inside. Imprisoned not by lock and key but by fear. Of what would happen if she dared to be out when he returned. If she dared to even think about leaving. Well, now she was. Leaving for ever. And it had taken her longer than she could remember to build up the courage to do that. To walk out of her open prison, never to return.

Gemma and Carly held hands as well as they could with their bags; left the house together.

As Gemma closed the door behind her for what she hoped would be the last time, another Robert De Niro quote sprang to mind. Something about life being short and whatever time you got was luck. That was what she was having now. Luck.

She had been given this chance for a fresh start, and from now on, Gemma Adderley was going to create her own luck.

2

Nina felt the air on her face, cool and welcome. Closed her eyes and kept walking.

The club had been good, she had to admit. Itchy Feet night at Lab 11. Just one room with bare brick walls and a bar, kind of damp-smelling, but it played good music for a club night. Not the usual stuff all the other places played. Fifties music, swing. Retro. Just what she liked. And she'd enjoyed herself, mostly. It hadn't been her idea to go but she didn't want to seem like the odd girl out or the killjoy who held all the others back. Especially as they hadn't known each other long and were still bonding as a group. The first uni semester was like that. Just as she'd expected it to be. She wanted to make friends with the rest of the group she had been put in halls with, and this seemed to be the best way of doing it. Also, she suffered from serious FOMO. She hadn't heard the phrase before she had arrived at uni, but it had stuck in her mind ever since. FOMO: Fear of Missing Out. And now that naming it made it officially a thing, she was relieved to admit it was pretty strong inside her.

She opened her eyes, still walking, looked at the others she was with. Andrew was from Manchester, gay and mouthy. She'd had a friend like him in sixth form. She hoped he could be her surrogate. Every girl needed a gay best friend, she had decided. Laura was the other girl in the group. Nina could see herself gravitating towards her too. They seemed to have lots in common and they were on the same course. The other two boys were Mark and John. Lads. That was all she could think of to say about them. They were good fun; bright, funny, but not really on her wavelength. Good lads, though, happy to be seen out with girls and didn't stigmatise Andrew for being gay. A great bunch to be with and it seemed like they all got along together. Early days, but that was a good sign.

Mark and John were clowning as they went. Loud, laughing like everyone was watching.

'Oh,' said Andrew, 'you and your laddish fun ...'

This seemed to be a pattern, fooling around as soon as they got a drink inside them. First time away from home, experiencing that nervous, giddy freedom. Nina wasn't like that. She was cautious, careful. Took everything as it came, in her stride. Tried not to have fixed expectations. That way she wouldn't be disappointed. That was what she'd always told herself. But she smiled at them. They were funny.

'Did you see that guy?' asked Andrew.

'Which guy?'

'Looking at you. That guy. Dark hair. Big eyes. Like Jared Leto.'

Nina knew exactly which guy he meant. She had fancied him but didn't want to admit it. Not in the game plan, she'd told herself. Do the degree, have fun, get out. Don't get lumbered.

'Nah,' she said. 'Must have missed him.'

Andrew's eyes rolled and widened in stage shock. 'Missed him? How could you? My God, if you didn't want him, I was going to have a go.'

Nina smiled.

Her ears were still ringing from the BPMs in the club, but she let Andrew go on, not really listening to him, pleased with the constant buzz. It was light now, early Saturday morning.

They had gone into town quite late and Nina had paced herself with her drinks. Always bottles, always in her hand, making sure she knew who had bought them, ensuring no one could have tampered with them. Always in control. The way she liked it.

'Where are we?' asked Laura.

'Digbeth,' said Nina. 'Birmingham.'

'Yeah, I know that. But where are we? How do we get back home?'

Nina looked round. All the streets looked the same in Digbeth. Run-down warehouses and factories supposedly having had the cultural magic wand waved at them. The new hip and edgy part of town. All cool bars and vintage clothes shops. She could see the silver-spotted undulating form of Selfridges in the city centre off in the distance. Like a massive science fiction slug had just died there.

'Head for that, I suppose,' she said. 'Get a cab.' If we've got any money left, she wanted to add. She had budgeted carefully for the night. She hoped the rest of them had. She didn't fancy walking all the way to Edgbaston.

'Nah,' said Andrew, 'let's—'

'Guys.'

They stopped talking. Up ahead, Mark and John had stopped walking, John turning to them, serious expression on his face.

'Guys,' he said again, gesturing towards a doorway, suddenly no longer drunk. 'Come here, guys, come here . . .'

Nina moved forward, caught up with them. The other two followed. She looked to where John was pointing. There, huddled in the doorway, was a little girl.

The child looked away from them, curled herself into a foetal ball, eyes screwed tight shut; if she couldn't see them, they wouldn't see her. Her clothes were dirty but not rags, her face

11

equally grimy; tears and snot had left tracks down it. She clutched hard at a teddy bear in her hands, pulled it towards her chest. She looked like she had been living rough on the street. She looked, thought Nina, like the kind of kid you saw on the TV news from a war zone.

Looking round to see what the others were doing – nothing – Nina knelt down in front of the girl.

'Careful,' said Andrew, 'she might have something—'

Nina turned, gave him a hard stare. He said nothing more.

'Hello,' she said quietly. 'What's your name?'

The little girl didn't reply, just screwed her eyes up tighter.

All sorts of thoughts tumbled through Nina's head. She'd been trafficked, she'd run away from somewhere, she'd been abandoned. She might not even speak or understand English.

'I'm Nina,' she said. 'What's your name?'

The little girl started to cry. 'Go away,' she said, clutching her toy like it was a life raft.

Nina edged forward. 'What's your name? Look, we can help you.'

Nothing.

Andrew knelt down next to Nina, wanting to help. The little girl flinched, seemed as if she was about to cry again. Wide-eyed, he moved back. Nina stayed where she was.

'Where's your . . . your mum? Where do you live? Do you know?'

The girl shook her head.

'Look, we'll get help. We won't leave you, okay?'

The girl still said nothing. Held on harder to the bear.

'Can you tell us anything?' said Nina, sensing that words were now futile and they should phone the police. 'A name? Anything.'

The little girl looked up at them, her eyes wide with ghosts.

'Why are you here? What happened?'

The girl seemed about to answer but stopped herself. The enormity of what was behind the words too much for her. She looked away from them again, eyes down.

Whatever she had been about to say was now locked up firmly within her.

3

'Hello.'

Psychologist Marina Esposito smiled, sat down on a chair that was way too small for her. She looked at the little girl in front of her.

'I'm Marina. What's your name?'

The girl looked up briefly, eyes wide, then away again. Back to the bear in her hands. Clutching it tightly.

Marina kept her smile in place. 'You've had a horrible thing happen to you, haven't you? I'm here to help you get over it.'

The girl didn't look at her. Marina looked at the bear in her hands. It was filthy but she knew the girl wouldn't give it up. Hadn't given it up since she had been found.

'What's your bear called?' asked Marina.

'Crusty,' the girl replied.

'Crusty. Nice name. And has he been with you all the time?'

The girl nodded.

'And what's your name?' Marina knew – it was in the report – but she still had to ask.

The girl kept staring at the bear.

When she had received the call, Marina had told them this wasn't her area. She didn't usually deal with children, no matter how traumatised. 'I'm a criminal psychologist,' she had said on the phone. 'Unless she's committed a crime, I don't think I can be of much help.'

14

'She's been the victim of one,' said Detective Sergeant Hugh Ellison, 'or at least we think her mother has. She's disappeared. And the daughter's the only witness.' He paused, letting that sink in, went on. 'Normally we would go with a child psychologist, but your particular skill set makes you a better fit for this. And you come highly recommended.'

'Right.' Marina nodded even though he couldn't see it. She knew who had recommended her. Her husband, Phil Brennan, was a detective inspector with the West Midlands Major Incident Squad based in the centre of Birmingham. She had worked with him on cases before. Helped.

A shiver ran through her as she thought of him. He couldn't help her now. Not any more. And that was a wedge driven between them, because she doubted he ever could again.

And she couldn't give him the chance.

'Anyway,' DS Ellison had continued, 'she was found on the street in Digbeth. Said she'd been going on holiday with her mother but her mother had gone off without her. Thrown out of the car, left on the street. Found by some students.'

'What's happened to her mother?'

'That's what I'm hoping you can find out.'

And the call had ended.

Marina had agreed – with some reluctance – to try and help the girl. She had read every report presented to her. The girl had given her name – Carly – but little else. She wouldn't tell them where she lived and she looked terrified at the prospect of talking about her mother. Marina suspected that the two things weren't connected, but the responses suggested some kind of trauma related to each. There had been no missing persons report answering her description, so that was all she had to go on.

Now she found herself at the special reception centre where the girl was being treated and cared for. The walls were bright,

15

colourfully painted with murals of cartoon characters. But even that didn't disguise the institutional feel of the place.

'You're Carly, aren't you? I got your name from Lesley who's been looking after you.'

The little girl nodded.

'How old are you, Carly?'

'Seven.'

Marina nodded. 'Good age. I've got a little girl. She's a tiny bit younger than you. Her name's Josephina.' She looked at Crusty. 'She's got a favourite teddy she never lets go of.'

The girl just stared at her. Marina wasn't sure, but she saw the beginnings of interest, a tentative kind of trust building within, reaching out to her.

'So where's your daddy, Carly?'

Something dark seemed to flutter over the girl. She had almost made eye contact with Marina. Instead she looked away.

'At home,' she said.

'And where's home?'

'Home.' Her eyes guarded, downcast.

'Do you want to tell me how to get there, Carly?'

She kept staring at the bear. Shook her head.

'Why not?'

'Mummy said we were going away. On holiday. Not Benidorm, but somewhere nice, she said.'

'Benidorm? Why Benidorm? Did you want to go there?'

Carly nodded. 'Like on the telly.'

On the telly? Marina thought, puzzled. Then it came to her. A comedy. Of sorts. All bright sun and broad acting. She smiled, nodded. 'The programme. You like that, do you?'

Carly nodded. 'Mummy lets me stay up to watch it. When Daddy's not—'

She stopped herself, eyes scared, guilty, once more.

16

Marina studied her. 'When Daddy's not what? Home?'

The girl said nothing. Clutched the bear, knuckles white.

Marina leaned forward. Just enough to be seen, not enough to invade the girl's personal space. 'You want to know something, Carly? About your teddy? And about my daughter Josephina's teddy?'

The girl looked up once more, wary but interested.

'They protect you. You hold on to them and they protect you. When things get bad, they're always there for you. Sometimes you have to do things you don't want to do. And you have to be strong to do them. That's when teddies help.'

Carly kept staring at her. Marina, sensing she had the girl hooked, continued. 'My little girl, Josephina, when she was even smaller, she ... she had to be brave. She had to be strong.'

'What happened?' asked Carly, interested despite herself.

'Well, she ...' *Was kidnapped. Held to ransom. And I had to go after her, hunt down the kidnappers and bring her home.* 'She ... there were some bad people. And they wanted me to do something for them. So they took her away from me.'

Carly's eyes widened. 'Did ... did she come back?'

Marina smiled. She hoped it was reassuring. 'Oh yes. I got her back. She came back home with me. But you know what? When things got bad for her, really bad, she had her teddy to cling on to. All the time, all the way. And he protected her. Made her feel strong. Just like Crusty is doing for you now.'

And it was me that got her. Brought her back. Not Phil, me.

Carly looked at the bear, back at Marina.

'So no matter what happens in here,' and to emphasise the point, Marina gestured round the room, 'you're safe. Whatever you say, whatever you do, you're safe. Because your teddy's with you. He won't let anything bad happen to you.'

Carly gazed at Marina, her eyes wide, desperate to believe, to trust. Not yet able to take that final step.

'Is . . .' She glanced down at the teddy, looked once more at Marina. 'Is Josephina safe now?'

Marina smiled. Hoped it was convincing.

'Of course she is.'

Hoping the girl wouldn't notice the lie. Hoping she wouldn't be able to read her mind, know that nowhere was safe for Josephina – or Marina – now. Not any more. Not since . . .

She put those thoughts out of her head. She would deal with them later. She knew what she was going to do. But now she had to concentrate on Carly.

'So we're safe in here, Carly. You're safe. And we can talk. That's all. Just talk. Would you like to talk? To me?'

Carly took a long time to make up her mind. Then nodded. 'Yes,' she said.

Marina smiled. 'Good,' she said. 'That's good.' She arranged her posture into her least threatening, most open and responsive pose. 'So tell me what happened.'

Carly looked at the teddy, studied it for a long time, as if it was relaying information to her, giving her the will, the strength, to speak. Eventually she looked up. Said one word.

'Strawberry.'

PART TWO

SATURDAY BRIDGE

4

Rain lashed down, incessant and hard, washing away the life from the city, draining the colour from the afternoon, turning daylight to premature dusk. It was borne on a chill wind that when it swirled and strengthened made the cold wet drops into razor-ice projectiles, reminding everyone, if they needed it, that summer was only a distant memory and autumn was on its last legs.

Not the best kind of day to be out for any length of time.

Not the best kind of day to discover a dead body.

Detective Inspector Phil Brennan of the West Midlands Major Incident Squad stood on Saturday Bridge in Birmingham, looking down on the nearly drained locks of the Birmingham and Fazeley Canal from underneath an umbrella, waiting to be given the signal to approach. The two-tone crime-scene tape stretched across the footpath, demarcating where the normal world ended and the other world – the dangerous, murderous, tragic and brutal other world – started. Phil stood with his back to the tape. He had been here enough times. He knew which world was his.

The rain kept all but the most persistent rubberneckers away. The white plastic tent erected on the bank of the canal ensured that those who remained wouldn't be able to see anything anyway. Phil ignored the watchers, avoided eye contact and feigned deafness with the few reporters and TV crews who had braved the elements to chase a story. Shut out everything that was taking up valuable real estate inside his head, just concentrated on what was before him.

The hand holding the umbrella barely shook. That was something. His unshaven look could be explained away as fashionable stubble. His clothes, never very smart, might just look particularly shabby because of the rain. The sunken red eyes with the sleep-deprived black rings around them were harder to explain, though. He just hoped no one noticed. He sucked on an extra-strong mint, focused.

Even with the white tent erected, he knew that the chances of preserving the crime scene in the face of this whipping rain were, unless they were miraculously, religiously lucky, slim to none. But procedure had to be followed. He walked down the raised metal squares of the common approach path, stood at the entrance to the tent.

'You ready for me yet?' he called in to Jo Howe, a short, round, middle-aged woman and the leading crime-scene investigator.

Jo was kneeling on the ground, checking all around, careful not to touch the body in front of her. 'I'll call you when I'm ready. Get in the pub with the others,' she said without looking up.

He wanted to say, *I just want to be doing something. I* need *to be doing something.* But didn't. Instead he turned, walked away. Doing as she had suggested.

His wet jeans moulded themselves to his legs like a second skin, constricting his movement in the most unpleasant way possible as he walked back up to the bridge. His leather jacket kept out most of the water, but it still ran down his umbrella-holding hand and up his sleeve, down the back of his neck. He should change his clothes as soon as possible. Might get a cold or flu. Part of him didn't care.

He pushed through the small crowd, dodged the media, crossed the road and made for the pub. The Shakespeare had been on the same spot in Summer Row for years. Victorian and resolutely old-fashioned, it maintained a sense of tradition beside the more fashionable bars and kitchens that had sprung up next to it.

Phil went inside, flashed his warrant card at the barman, who beamed back. 'What can I get you?' he asked.

Phil knew the type. Eager to get bragging rights for assisting the police and hoping that some of the glamour of a major investigation would rub off on him. Glamour. *Tell that to the dead person on the canal towpath*, thought Phil.

'Coffee, please,' he said. 'I'll be in the back room.'

They had temporarily taken over the pub. Uniforms, plain clothes and SOCOs gathered around, sheltering from the rain until the temporary incident unit arrived. Phil saw two members of his team, Detective Sergeant Ian Sperring and Detective Constable Imani Oliver, sitting silently at a table underneath a bust of Shakespeare. He went over to join them.

'Heard somebody in here once asking if they were brothers,' said Sperring, pointing to the bust above his head, then to an identical one on the other corner. 'Shakespeare. Wondered if one did the writing and one did the, I dunno, acting or book-keeping or something.'

'And what did you tell them?' asked Imani, a glint of humour in her eye.

Sperring shrugged. 'Told them what they wanted to hear,' he said, expression liked a closed fist.

There was no love lost between the two officers, but Phil had insisted that since they were part of his team, they had to work together. Detective Constable Nadish Khan, the other immediate member of the team, was away on a training course. Sperring, ten years older than Phil and many pounds heavier, was ensconced in the corner, his bulk at rest, looking like he was going nowhere. Imani, keen and alert, was on the stool opposite.

Phil had been settled in Colchester, happy with his position with Essex Police. But when events had taken a near-terminal turn for the worse, the area hadn't seemed as welcoming, so he and Marina had decided on a change of scenery and picked Birmingham, the city of Marina's birth, as a destination. It had taken Phil some time to be accepted by his team. And for him to accept them. But out of that animosity had evolved a way of working they could all accept. The team had even begun to respect Phil's methods, even if they weren't in a hurry to adopt them.

He took off his leather jacket, slung it over the padded chair and sat down beside them. The pub was warm. He could almost feel the steam rising off his soaking legs. The front of his plaid shirt was wet through, the T-shirt underneath likewise.

Phil never wore a suit for work. He dressed as he pleased. A combo of Red Wing boots, heavy Japanese selvedge denim, a Western shirt and a leather jacket was the nearest thing he had to a uniform. This approach had brought him into conflict with other officers over the years, most recently his own team. He believed that creativity in dress led to creativity and intuition when it came to the job. His views weren't embraced, but he was tolerated. As long as he kept getting results.

'They ready for us yet?' asked Sperring, barely glancing up from the mug of industrial-strength tea he was stirring.

'They'll call us when they want us,' replied Phil.

'Why you been standing out in the rain?' asked Sperring, looking up.

Phil looked at his junior officer. Sperring had been stabbed on a case a few months previously and it seemed to have aged him. Not that he would admit it; he had wanted to come back to front-line duties the first opportunity. Phil admired his tenacity.

'Just . . . waiting,' he said.

Sperring studied him, eyes unusually compassionate. About to say something else. Thinking better of it.

Phil's coffee arrived. He thanked the barman, put his hand in his pocket.

'On the house,' the barman said.

'No,' said Phil, 'let me pay.'

'Won't hear of it. Anything I can do to help our boys in blue.'

The barman loitered in front of them, grinning, hoping to pick up some titbit of information, something he could tell his mates about. Or more likely a reporter.

'Well, thank you,' said Phil, dismissing the man. Once he was out of earshot, he turned to the other two. 'Hate it when they do that.'

'What?' said Sperring. 'Hang around trying to eavesdrop?'

'No, not let us pay. Like we're trying to get something for nothing.'

Sperring shrugged. 'Precious few perks in our line of work,' he said. 'A free cuppa now and again's neither here nor there.'

'That's how it starts,' said Phil. 'Anyway, who called it in?'

'Uniform,' said Imani. 'Got a call from a dog-walker this morning.'

'Not a dogger?' said Sperring. 'Get our fair share of those round here.'

'Must be committed to be out in this weather,' said Imani. 'Or need committing. No, this dog-walker saw the body in one of the locks. Supposed to be drained. No chance in this weather.'

'Did they give a statement?' asked Phil.

Sperring nodded, thought about having a sip of his tea. Thought better of it. 'Yeah. Don't think we've got much there.

Didn't see anyone else, anyone acting suspiciously, running away. Nothing. Spotted something in the lock. The dog almost went in looking at it. A woman. Mid to late twenties, as far as we can tell. That's all we know at the moment.'

Phil nodded. 'What else do we know about this dog walker?' he asked.

'Office worker in the city. Little dog, yappy kind, lives in those posh flats over there by the roundabout. Exercising it so it doesn't crap all over the carpet while she's out at work. Didn't seem the kind to be involved.'

'They never do,' said Phil.

At that moment his phone rang. Phil jumped, his heart skipping a beat. He took it from his jacket, almost dropping it in his haste to look at the display. He sighed. *No*, he thought. He put it to his ear, listened, nodded. Ended the call.

'That was Jo,' he said to the other two. 'She's ready when we are.' He stood up. 'Come on.'

The other two did likewise, Sperring not without difficulty.

Phil felt the wet denim tightening against his legs once more as he moved towards the door. Even worse than when he had entered. The wall of cold air hit him as he stepped outside, but he was chilled from more than the weather. He crossed the road, not looking forward to the sight that was waiting for him.

5

'So what have we got?' asked Phil.

Jo Howe straightened up, stared down at the body in front of her. The rain high-hatted on the plastic-sheeted roof, a never-ending irritating drum solo, especially inside Phil's head. 'Look for yourself,' she said. 'Ask Esme. Her department.' The way she phrased the words told Phil she was glad she didn't have to deal with that side of things.

Kneeling beside the body was the pathologist, Esme Russell, arrived while Phil had been over the road. Young, pretty, her hair scraped back into a ponytail, she looked and sounded to Phil more like a debutante at her coming-out party than a professional corpse-prodder at a crime scene.

'Hey, Esme,' he said. 'Good to see you.'

She glanced up at him, nodded, went back to examining the corpse. 'We'll have to stop meeting like this. Someone will talk.' She gestured to the body in front of her. 'Not this poor creature, though.'

Phil came over, his paper-wrapped boots already threatening to dissolve, clanking wetly on the raised metal CAP. He knelt down beside Esme, as near as he dared to go to the body. His first instinct, even after all his years as a front-line detective, was to look away. Not out of horror. Perhaps decency. But he knew that wasn't the correct approach, the professional one. Resurrecting this person as a living, breathing human being would come later. Right now, whoever this had been was, just for a few moments, not as important as who – or what – the body was now. A mass of clues. A way in, The climax to a story that he had to write the beginning to. A whodunnit for him to solve.

'Jesus,' he said. 'She didn't go easily . . .'

'No,' said Esme. 'Let's see what we've got. Female. Perhaps in her twenties, thirties, judging by what's left of her.'

Phil studied the body as dispassionately as he could. 'Yeah,' he said. 'What's left. Not to mention what the water's done to her.'

'And the things in the water,' said Esme. 'Where exactly was she found?'

'Just outside. In the lock, floating. Someone called us.'

'Good job she was lying face down,' said Esme, 'or whoever found her would have lost their breakfast.'

'Can you work out what's been done to her pre- and post-mortem?'

'Do my best,' she said. 'But it'll take time.'

Phil nodded in agreement, studied the body. It was difficult to differentiate between what her killer had done to her and what had happened in the water. Difficult but not impossible. He made some preliminary judgements.

The woman was white, or had been. Death had discoloured her, the water bloated her. Her face looked bruised and purple. Small chunks of flesh were missing, ragged holes all over.

He pointed to the marks. 'Rats?'

'And whatever else was in the water with her.'

Phil shuddered, tried to convince himself it was just the cold and the damp.

Her legs and arms were cut and scored. He peered closer. Small round patches on her skin.

'What are they?' he asked Esme.

'Look like burns to me,' she said examining them. 'See here, on her thighs and arms. Mostly her inner thighs.' She looked closely. 'I'll run some more tests later, but it looks like they've been allowed to scab over then been burned open again. Hard to tell, everything's so wet.'

Phil felt his stomach lurch. He swallowed it down, concentrated on the professional, analytical part of his brain.

'So this was done, what? Over time?'

Esme shrugged. 'Looks that way.'

'Can you—'

Esme smiled. 'I know what you're going to ask me. And no. I can't give you a time of death. Not yet. I couldn't even hazard a guess.'

'Worth a try,' said Phil.

Another smile, equally as grim as the first. 'You should know better than to ask by now.'

'I know.' He turned his attention back to the body. 'What d'you think caused those?'

The other wounds on her arms and legs were deep, straight slices.

'A knife, I would say. Straight blade, sharp. No serrated or jagged edges. Swift cuts. All done with force, and judging by the depth of the wounds – that one cuts right down to the bone –' she indicated the right arm, 'there was a degree of emotion behind the thrusts.'

'I can guess what kind of emotion,' said Phil. 'And what about that?'

Finally. He had kept the biggest till last.

There was something about the body that neither of them had yet mentioned, but it was the one feature they couldn't ignore. The defining one of the woman's fatal injuries. The gaping hole in the centre of her body.

'Well,' said Esme, 'I'd say her heart's been removed.'

29

'Yeah,' said Phil, distracted by the sight. 'I agree. And it certainly wasn't the rats.'

'No,' she said. 'Not unless they were strong enough to crack open her ribs, bend them back and cut the heart out.'

Esme sat back, exhaled. Phil kept staring at the body, hoping it would give up its secrets. He became aware that Esme was watching him. He turned to her. She smiled.

'Any news?'

Phil frowned, surprised. 'How did you . . . '

'Oh, come on. It's all over the station. Everyone knows, I'm afraid. Sorry.'

Phil said nothing.

'How are you?'

Phil felt another shudder inside him that was definitely nothing to do with the cold or the body. 'I've got my work,' he said. 'I'm fine.'

She straightened up, face just beside his. 'If you want to . . . ' She sighed, almost shook her head, but continued. 'If you'd like a drink one night, or . . . I don't know, dinner . . . just as, you know. Just as friends. Or . . . ' A shrug. 'Friends.'

Phil dredged up a smile. 'Thank you, Esme, but—'

'Can we come in yet?'

They both turned. Sperring and Imani were standing at the flap of the tent, getting drenched. The umbrellas they held seemed ineffectual.

'Sorry,' said Phil, standing up as if he had been caught doing something he shouldn't. He was aware of Esme moving swiftly away from him. 'Got caught up. Careful where you stand when you come in.'

They entered, saw the body.

'Jesus,' said Sperring, 'Deep breaths all round.'

'Oh my God . . . ' Imani screwed her eyes tightly closed.

'Look at it out of the corner of your eye,' said Sperring. 'Like stargazing at night. That's the way you see constellations and that.'

They all stood in silence, taking in the sight before them.

'Suppose ID's a bit too straightforward to hope for,' said Sperring.

'There are a couple of tattoos on the body,' said Esme, 'One looks like a name. Perhaps her? Or a child?'

'We'll check with MisPers,' said Phil. 'See if they've got anything outstanding that might fit.'

'So,' said Imani, 'what kind of person we looking for? The man that did this?'

'You think it's a man?' asked Phil. 'Jumping to conclusions.'

Imani shrugged. 'Well ... if it is a man, it's a man who ...' She couldn't finish.

Phil kept staring at the body. Nodded. 'Yeah,' he said, eyes never moving from that gaping wound. 'Whoever they are, they certainly hate women.'

6

Janine Gillen took a seat slowly, lowered herself carefully. She failed to quell her shaking as she crossed her legs and placed her hands on the armrests. Then she quickly, jerkily smoothed down the front of her blouse. It was Primark but good. Clean, well looked after. She always liked to look her best coming here. Liked to have something to dress up for, to take pride in her appearance. Even this. She took a couple of deep breaths. Tried to relax, or at least look relaxed. Failed.

The man in front of her, Keith Bailey, smiled. Janine relaxed slightly, finding the smile comforting.

'Just you this time?' asked Keith.

Janine nodded. 'I . . . I tried to . . . ' She snuffled, drew in a ragged breath through her nose. 'Just me.'

'Okay then.' Keith nodded, smiled once more. Casually dressed, a soft plaid shirt and chinos, blonde hair nicely styled. Glasses. He had notes on his knee but he didn't consult them. He was familiar enough with Janine's story. She had been seeing him for a few weeks now. Mostly on her own, which wasn't ideal, but . . . that was the way it went sometimes. Unfortunately.

'So . . . ' Keith paused, allowed Janine to gather herself before the talking began in earnest. 'How are things with Terry?'

Janine sighed. The shaking in her hands began again. 'The . . . the same. He . . . ' She took her hands off the armrests, uncrossed her legs. She hugged her arms close to her body, aware of the increasingly violent trembling in her hands, especially the left one. Always the left one. 'He . . .' She sighed. 'I . . . I thought things would get better. After, you know. After he came here.'

Keith nodded. He had heard these words – or similar ones – before. Too many times.

'But he . . . he . . . Well, things were okay for a few days. After, you know. The first time. He was . . . mindful of things. Of me and the twins. He . . . would think before he . . . he did things.'

Keith nodded, shifted slightly in his seat. 'And did he ever seek counselling on his own? Contact the therapist I gave him the number of?'

She shook her head. 'No. He, he said he would. And I think he meant to, I really do. But he . . . he didn't.'

'Right.' Keith nodded, made a couple of notes on the pad in his lap. 'Right. And how is he with the twins?'

The trembling in Janine's left hand increased. She pushed it tight against her body. 'He . . . he started to get angry with them again.'

Keith leaned forward, professional concern in his eyes. 'Has he hurt them? Attacked them in any way?'

She shook her head. 'No. Not . . .' Another shake of the head, more emphatic this time. 'No.'

'You sure?'

She nodded, not making eye contact.

Keith sat back. He had been a marriage counsellor long enough to know when someone was lying to him. And not just lying, covering something up. Something unpleasant. 'Are you sure, Janine?'

Still she couldn't make eye contact.

'Janine?' Again Keith leaned forward. His voice dropped. 'Has he hurt the boys?'

She shook her head. 'No.'

Keith sat back, understanding. 'Has he started hitting you again, Janine?'

She nodded. And that was when the tears, long dammed, erupted.

Janine Darvill had thought she had found the perfect man when she met Terry Gillen. Tall, dark and handsome, with a glint of the roguish bastard twinkle in his eye. As she eventually found out, it wasn't just a twinkle. And she wasn't the only one to fall for it. Unfortunately, she was married and pregnant by then.

It had sounded quite romantic, or at least she had made herself believe it was. Meet a handsome man, have kids, be happy ever after. Her friends had stayed on at school, got A levels, gone to college or even, in a few cases, university. And Janine had intended to do that, or something like that. Go to college. Learn hairdressing or beauty, whatever. Get trained. Get a job. Meet a man, have kids ... She had done that all right. A mother at seventeen, married at eighteen.

Terry was the first real boyfriend she had ever had. He was a few years older than her and had been around a bit, but she knew that. Liked it even; it made her feel special that such a man of the world had chosen her.

Except he hadn't. Once the twins were born, he was back out at nights, drinking, disappearing for days on end sometimes. He was a roofer by trade, when he was working, and he sometimes 'forgot' to leave her housekeeping money.

Janine was spending more time on her own. Or rather on her own with two squealing babies that she didn't know how to look after, barely more than a kid herself. And no friends to turn to. They were all in work or at college.

Her mother would help when she could but she also had to look after her stepfather, who was on long-term sick. Janine knew it was alcohol and obesity-related diabetes but her mother insisted he had been injured at work.

Janine couldn't cope. She had told Terry he had to stay in more, take more responsibility. And that was when he first hit her.

She didn't know what had happened. He had smacked her across the face, told her to shut her whingeing fucking mouth. She was so stunned that she burst into tears and just lay there. Terry had stormed out. Later, when he returned, he was drunk and tearful. Told her he didn't know what had happened, that he had never hit a woman before and that he never would again. That men who did that were the worst kind of scum. He begged and begged her to forgive him. So she did. And things got slightly better.

Until he did it again.

And again.

The same treatment, the same drunken remorse afterwards.

And as everything spiralled downwards, Janine tried to work out how her life had come to this. How her romantic ideal had come crashing down around her. She wondered what she had done wrong, how she had displeased him. Couldn't find anything but knew there must be something. Eventually she told her mother, who said she had to leave him.

She tried. Told him she was going, taking the kids with her. He hit her again, even harder. Told her that she was his, and not to forget it. And hit her again, harder than ever this time. That was the first time the police were called.

After that, things changed. For a while. Knowing that the police would be keeping an eye on him, Terry agreed to marriage counselling. He started to come with Janine to see Keith. And things seemed to be better. But deep down Janine knew it wasn't peace. It was just the pause before reloading.

And then he started getting angry again.

*

35

'So . . . ' Keith was saying, 'he doesn't hurt the children.'

She shook her head.

'Is that because he's taking it out on you instead?'

She felt that she could tell Keith anything, that he would understand. He was a reasonable man, a *good* man. She wished all men were like him. Or at least the one she had married. She nodded.

'Right. And is there a pattern to this behaviour of his? Is he drunk when he does it?'

'Usually.'

Keith sighed.

They talked for nearly an hour, the whole of the session, Keith being as professionally concerned as he could, Janine sobbing over what had happened to her life. Eventually he opened the file on his lap, took out a card, handed it over.

'Here,' he said. 'Take this.'

Janine took it, looked at it. Safe Haven, it said. And a phone number.

'Legally I'm bound to tell the police. And social services. There's a crime being committed and your children are in danger.'

'No, please . . . ' she said between sobs. 'Please don't. That'll just . . . just make things worse.'

'Perhaps in the short term, but in the long term it'll make things better. In the meantime, you need to get out of that house. It's a toxic environment for you and the kids.' He looked straight at her, steel in his eyes. 'You don't have to put up with this. You deserve better. You've got your whole life ahead of you.' He sat back. 'Think about it. Think about it hard.'

She nodded, clutching the card close to her.

It was time for her to go. They both stood up. Janine was reluctant to leave the room, to go back to her life.

'Call that number,' Keith said. 'They can help you.'

'Thank you.' Almost sobbing again.

'And do it straight away. Things aren't going to get better with Terry. He's not going to change. Get out of there as quick as you can.'

Janine nodded once more and the tears started again.

She waited until they had subsided, then, aided by copious amounts of tissues from the often-replenished box in Keith's room, made her way outside, the card clutched tightly in her hand.

Terrified, but ready to make a positive change to her life.

7

Seedy. It was a word that Phil had, of course, often heard and often used. He knew its original meaning – gone to seed, no use any more – and its more recent connotation – the above but with an added layer of sleaze – but he had never seen such a perfectly apt example of both definitions sitting in front of him.

Short and round almost in proportion, Detective Sergeant Hugh Ellison looked like he came from a planet with a denser gravity than Earth. Despite being younger than he looked, he appeared to Phil like the kind of detective who was waiting for the seventies to return, with all that decade's swagger, corruption and political incorrectness. A relic of a bygone age he was too young to remember. Amongst other things, the moustache – clearly not grown ironically for any charitable purpose – gave him away. He was thinning on top, his suit a remnant from when he was a couple of sizes smaller, his shirt collar unable to meet round his neck, his tie overdue for a clean. Eyes darting, shifting. Gambler's eyes, always calculating the odds, working an advantage.

Seedy.

It had been relatively easy to find out the dead woman's identity. That was one thing Phil felt he should be grateful for. He had phoned the Missing Persons Unit, asked if they could run a search on women, twenty to thirty, missing fairly recently, with tattoos, one saying 'Carly', one an inscription in a foreign language, possibly something Arabic. That in turn led him down to Digbeth nick on the High Street.

When he had first arrived in Birmingham, Phil had been sent to Steelhouse Lane, the main station. Backing on to both the magistrates' and crown courts, it looked like a faux-Gothic castle. He wasn't naive enough to think they would all look like that but had nevertheless been surprised at the differing stations in the city. He had been amazed to find that Digbeth was actually a functioning police station. It looked from the road like a closed and shuttered mansion or private school, litter and street detritus gathering in its main doorway, faded posters in the wall-mounted glass display. The blue lamp still hung outside, seemingly never lit since the fifties. But a quick walk round the side showed how deceptive first appearances could be. Patrol cars, vans, people carriers and unmarkeds were all parked up alongside. He had gone in asking for the name of the person he had spoken to on the phone.

Now, in an office that boasted the best of office-surplus chic, Phil was shaking hands with Detective Sergeant Hugh Ellison. The man sat at his desk surrounded by detritus, making Phil think of a spider at the centre of a dirty, cluttered web.

'Sit down,' said Ellison, pointing to a black object that had been an office chair in a previous life. He noted Phil's trepidation. Smiled. His teeth matched the rest of him. 'Budget cuts,' he said. 'Not that glamour boys like you would know anything about that.'

Phil was slightly taken aback. Was that meant to be an insult? Or maybe a test, to see how he would react. He kept a straight face, didn't rise to the bait. 'Nothing glamorous about finding dead bodies. Thought we were all on the same side.'

Ellison just shrugged, like he didn't care if Phil was offended or not.

'So you want to see me about Gemma Adderley,' said Ellison.

'That's the name I was given.'

Ellison nodded. 'Think it's fair to say we're thinking of the same person.' He reached forward, grabbed a folder from the desk. 'Could have just emailed you all the stuff, but here's a copy of the file. Nice to do it the old-fashioned way sometimes.' Another smile, another reminder for Phil to book a dentist's appointment.

Phil took the folder. 'Thank you. Sure it's her?'

Ellison nodded. 'Worked the case myself. Stuck in my mind. Course, the tattoo's the thing. Soon as you mentioned that, I knew.'

Phil skimmed the notes in the folder. 'What can you tell me about her?'

Ellison shrugged, looked at the Tesco Value sandwich on his desk. Phil presumed it was a signal for him to leave so the two of them could spend some time alone, but he hadn't finished so he stayed where he was.

'Went missing from her home in Hollywood,' said Ellison when he realised Phil wasn't going anywhere. 'About a month ago. Exact date'll be in there. Without her husband. Disappeared.'

'Right. Okay.' Phil was already formulating plans, means of approach.

'Don't you wanna know the rest?' A glint in Ellison's eye now.

'The rest? Yeah. Go on.'

'There was a daughter.'

'Carly?' asked Phil. 'The tattoo?'

'That's the one. Found wandering the streets in Digbeth by some students coming out of a club. Couldn't get much out of her, poor kid. In shock. Had to bring in a professional to help.'

'Right,' said Phil.

Ellison grinned. 'Your missus.'

Phil stared. Said nothing.

Ellison laughed. 'Yeah, I know who you are, mate.' He nodded. 'Your DCI, Cotter, recommended her. And she was good, too, Marina.' The look on his face and the relish in pronouncing her name indicated that he was making more than a professional appraisal of Phil's wife.

'Good?' Phil barely got the word out.

'With the kid. Carly. Got her talking. But then when you've got kids yourself, you know how to talk to them. I've got three.' He gave a guttural laugh. 'That I know of.'

Phil didn't join in.

'That's how we found out so much about Carly's mother. And the father.'

Phil swallowed back everything that the thought of Marina had put into his head, concentrated on Ellison's words. 'Tell me.'

'The kid said they were going on holiday. Just her and the mother.'

'And were they?'

'Dunno. Nothing was booked. At least not in her name. Her mobile never turned up either, so we don't know if she made any arrangements on that.'

'Just her and the mother?' asked Phil. 'What about the father? You questioned him, I take it?'

'Yeah, we liked him for it. But . . . ' Ellison shrugged once more. 'Couldn't get anything to stick. And we tried. By God we tried. The kid was thrown out of a car. Didn't get a good look at the driver, didn't hear his voice. She didn't think it was her father but we didn't rule it out. She was in shock. Memory plays tricks.'

'What about—'

'Him hiring someone, were you going to say?'

Phil nodded.

'Nothing in his bank account. But again, that doesn't rule it out.'

Phil looked at the file in his hands, suddenly anxious to leave. The cramped room was becoming oppressive. He felt like he couldn't breathe.

'Well, thanks. I'll be—'

'One more thing,' said Ellison. 'About the husband.'

'What?' Phil waited.

'Still reckon it was him, but . . . ' Ellison brought his hands together in prayer, looked heavenwards, mock piety in his eyes. Then he looked at Phil, laughed. 'God on his side. Good luck, mate.'

Phil took that as his cue to leave, and turned, walked down the corridor away from Ellison.

Feeling sure eyes were boring into his back all the way out.

8

Birmingham Airport sat outside the city centre on a flat suburban stretch of land, a collection of huge metal and glass huts with added overhead noise pollution.

Phil Brennan flashed his warrant card on the way in and parked his Audi in the staff car park. He and Sperring asked for directions, then made their way to the administration building.

'I'm looking for Roy Adderley,' he said to the woman on the desk. 'Is he about?'

The woman, small, round and Afro-Caribbean, with perfectly made-up hair, stared up at him, eyes wide in alarm. He knew what she was thinking. Police. Terrorist.

'Can I ask what this is concerning?'

Phil gave her what he hoped was a reassuring smile. Reassuring, yet hard enough to stop her asking any further questions. 'I'm afraid it's a personal matter.'

Head down, the woman began pressing keys, checking her screen. Eventually she looked up. 'He's working at the moment.' Like that was an end of it.

'Could we see him, please? This is important.'

Again she looked down, then back up. 'I'll need to get you an escort.'

'Thank you,' said Phil.

A security guard came to take them across to where Roy

Adderley was working. First he checked their warrant cards again and asked the nature of their business. Phil wasn't very forthcoming.

'Just take us to Mr Adderley.' He was losing patience.

The security guard stared at him, clearly not used to having his authority questioned. 'I don't have to, you know. If you want to be unpleasant, I can just refuse. We take security very seriously here. Can't let just anybody wander about.'

Phil turned to him, glared like he wanted to do him some damage. 'And I take having my time wasted even more seriously. We're on official police business. We're doing our job. You do yours.'

The guard reluctantly backed down, led them out of the admin block and across the tarmac, never speaking once, striding so quickly they had to almost run to keep up. Eventually he came to a stop, gestured towards another low-level building, this one with less glass and more metal, of the corrugated variety.

'He'll be in there.'

'Right,' said Phil. 'Thank you for your cooperation.'

'I'll tell him you're here.'

'We can mange,' said Sperring, wheezing from the brisk exercise.

Phil joined him as the security guard walked away, muttering audibly under his breath.

'You all right?'

'Fine,' said Sperring in between gasps for breath.

'Don't exert yourself. Remember what the doctor said. Give your body time to heal fully.'

'Nothing wrong with me,' said Sperring. 'Fuck's the matter with you?'

Phil bristled. He knew what was coming. 'What d'you mean?'

'You know what I mean. Talking to that security jobsworth the way you did. Thought you were going to leather him one.'

'Officious little twat,' said Phil. 'Deserved it.'

Sperring frowned at Phil. 'What happened to Mr Liberal? Sorry, Detective Inspector Liberal? Usually it's me doing the bad cop routine and you telling me not to be so hard on him because he's on minimum wage and his mum didn't buy him a pet dog when he was little, or some such bollocks.'

'Yeah, well,' said Phil, looking straight ahead and not wanting to be drawn into conversation. 'Just the way it is.'

They approached the hangar. It had huge double doors at the front, a glass-fronted entryway beside them. They went into the reception area. Beyond the window was a small room with uniformed people sitting round on worn-out easy chairs. A sink area in the corner. Through another door Phil could see that the main part of the building was full of buses. This was where the passenger transport was coordinated from.

'Roy Adderley,' he said to the woman behind the desk, showing his warrant card once more. 'Detective Inspector Brennan and Detective Sergeant Sperring.'

'Is this about his wife?' asked the woman. She was quite young, white, heavily made up, with a figure that had crossed the line between curvaceous and morbid obesity.

Here we go again, thought Phil. 'Just get him, please.' His tone perhaps more brusque and irritable than usual.

She turned to the room behind her, gestured. 'He's in there.' She looked between the pair of them, eyes wide, looking scared. She stood up. 'I'll go and get him.'

'No thanks, we can—'

But the woman was off her seat and straight through to the other room. Phil and Sperring followed. They arrived while she was still speaking.

'Roy,' she said, 'it's the police. They want to see you . . .'

A uniformed man on the other side of the room stood up. Medium height, medium build, sandy hair, he had once been good-looking, but various forms of self-abuse seemed to be taking care of that.

'The police, Roy,' the receptionist said again.

Roy Adderley looked between the three of them.

Then turned and ran.

9

Marina Esposito checked her watch. It was nearly time. She looked out of the window, up and down the street, both sides, stayed there until she was sure no one was loitering, hiding. Scanned the windows opposite for signs of movement, sudden or otherwise, light glinting off anything behind them. Any unfamiliar cars that she hadn't seen before, number plates that didn't match those on the lists she had already made. She repeated this procedure once more before she was satisfied that there was no one in the street who shouldn't have been there. Then she picked up her keys, checked her pockets and made her way out, making sure she triple-locked the door behind her.

It was her routine, her system.

Still in her gym gear – she barely seemed to be out of it these days – she ran down the road, knowing that the blade was in her pocket, hoping she wouldn't have to use it but knowing that if she did, she would do so without a second thought. Scanning all the time, alert for any signs of danger.

She reached her destination, stopped running. She was barely out of breath. Her time at the gym and her regular self-defence classes had left her in good shape.

Her route was timed; she knew exactly how long it would take. She also knew how long she would have to spend there – at least roughly; there were always fluctuations that she couldn't control – and how long the walk back would be. She didn't speak to anyone else, had nothing to say to them. Sometimes she offered a smile so as not to draw attention to herself. To look as normal as possible. But mostly she just did what was expected of her. Her job, almost.

She stood by the gate until the noise level on the other side began to increase, then readied herself. Another glance round – behind her, to the side, nothing out of the ordinary – and then she turned her attention straight ahead. Locked on, focused, determined to let nothing and no one come between them.

The afternoon school run.

'There you are, precious.'

'Hello, Mummy!'

Josephina Esposito-Brennan ran towards Marina, smile on her face like she didn't have a care in the world. Marina knelt down and hugged her, as she always did. Then straightened up, holding her hand and glancing round, checking. Like she always did.

'You had a good day, sweetheart?'

Josephina began to tell her mother about her day while they walked. Marina listened, eyes alive for threat all the while.

'Can Krista come round to play?'

'Sorry, sweetheart. Not today.'

The little girl looked momentarily sad. She was used to being given that answer but it didn't stop her from asking. She glanced up at Marina, face expectant.

'Is Daddy home tonight?'

'No, sweetheart, I'm afraid he isn't.'

'Why not? Why do I never see Daddy any more?'

'Because . . . ' Marina sighed. *Because he can't protect us, sweetheart. He can't keep us safe any more. Not like I can.* It wasn't the first time that question had arisen and it wouldn't be the last.

Marina tried to be honest with the little girl, but there were still some things she couldn't tell her.

And hoped she would never have to.

'He's . . . still busy. Sorry.'

'Is he still away?'

'He is, yes.' She hated lying but knew she had no choice. She changed the subject. 'Shall we bake some biscuits when we get home? You and me?'

The disappointment at not seeing her father slid off the little girl's face, to be replaced by a tentative excitement at what lay ahead when she got back to the flat. She nodded vigorously.

'That's my girl. Come on, I've got everything we need ready in the kitchen.'

They hurried back to the flat, Marina scanning the streets constantly.

They made it to the front door without mishap. *Dodged another bullet*, Marina thought, and went inside, checking the lock for signs of tampering. Everything looked fine. Thankfully.

She ushered Josephina into the kitchen, gave her some juice, got her set up for baking.

Always busy, she thought. That was the best thing. Always keep busy. Something to do, someone to protect. Work. Push herself. Don't stop to think. Because if she did that, she might just fall apart.

'Right,' she said, summoning up a smile, 'chocolate or peanut butter? Or both?'

Before Josephina could answer, Marina's phone rang.

She excused herself, went to answer it. Checked the display. Work.

'Marina Esposito.' Her voice strong, capable.

'Afternoon,' said a voice she had come to know quite well in the last month. Know, but not necessarily like.

'Hello, DS Ellison, what can I do for you?'

'Hugh, please, I've told you. No need for such formality when we're work colleagues.'

She could imagine the leering smile as he spoke those words and felt a nausea in her stomach.

The Carly Adderley case. Marina had talked to the girl, managed to coax facts out of her about her mother's disappearance. Comforted her when she had broken down repeatedly in tears. Then tried her best to put her back together again, even arranging treatment to hopefully minimise what she had gone through. If that was possible.

Ellison had been impressed with her work. And, Marina strongly suspected, impressed with her in a less than professional capacity. It happened from time to time. She just ignored it, carried on. Let Carly Adderley break her heart.

'So what can I do for you, DS Ellison?' Ignoring his exhortation.

A pause, then he continued. 'Just wanted to give you a heads-up, that's all. You might be back on the case.'

'Which case? Carly?'

'That's the one. Her mother's turned up. Well, her body, anyway. Or what's left of it.'

A shudder ran through Marina. 'Oh, God.'

'Yeah, I know.' Ellison's voice sounded anything but empathetic. 'Murder, they reckon. So I just wanted to let you know that you might be asked for your thoughts.'

'Right. Thanks. Well, I have—' She stopped short as another thought occurred to her. 'Who's . . . who's investigating?'

Ellison could barely keep the relish out of his voice. 'Your ex.'

'He's not my ex,' she said quickly, heatedly. 'We're . . . separated.'

'Right,' said Ellison, with some degree of disappointment. 'Well, like I said, I just wanted to let you know.'

'Thank you.'

50

'And if you ever want some ... assistance or—'

'I'll let you know.'

She hung up as quickly as she could, threw the phone on to the sofa as if it were contaminated.

Shit, she thought. *Shit, shit, shit.*

'Are we going to make biscuits now?'

Marina turned. Josephina stood at the living room door, concern on her face.

'Yes,' she said absently. 'Yes, darling, we are.'

She ushered her daughter into the kitchen. Tried to find a smile for the child. One that told her everything was all right, that her mother was there for her and everything was going to be fine.

Hoped she succeeded.

10

Straight through the inner door, out into the main bus hangar, Adderley ran, Phil right after him.

Adderley knew his way round better, knew which corner to duck round, where to run ahead. He ran between parked buses, doubled back, down the other way. Phil, fast but often wrong-footed, kept chase.

Adderley broke into the open, made for the main doors. Phil could sense him flagging, saw him trip, stumble, but keep going. He reached the doors, went outside. Phil after him. Immediately all sound was taken away by the roar of a departing plane, right overhead. Adderley kept running, down the tarmac, towards the perimeter fence. Phil felt anger burning inside him. Who the hell was he to run? Who did he think he was?

Adderley was weakening. He stopped ahead of Phil, bent double, hands braced on his thighs, back heaving with heavy, deep breaths. As Phil approached him, he turned, looked up. Shaking his head slowly from side to side, he began to speak.

Phil was on him. Head-butting him right in the middle of his face, knocking him flat on the ground. He bent down, grabbed Adderley by the front of his uniform, pulled him up. The man had trouble breathing, the fall having knocked all the air from his lungs. That didn't stop Phil from his task. Neither did the blood that was now spurting from Adderley's nose.

He set him on his feet, ignoring his protestations, his waving arms, the wheezing, groaning sound he was making.

'Roy Adderley,' said Phil, 'I want a word with you.' He looked at the damage he'd caused. Smiled.

'Right, boss, I'll take it from here.'

Phil barely heard the words. It wasn't until he felt a forceful hand on his shoulder that he turned round. Sperring was behind him, the woman from reception next to him. Another plane boomed overhead. The rain poured down.

'Let's get back inside that hangar,' said Sperring, 'shall we?'

The room with the worn-out chairs had been cleared. Roy Adderley sat hunched over, the majority of a roll of toilet paper applied to his face. The paper was more red than white. The receptionist sat next to him, her hand on his arm, concern in his eyes. She kept firing darts of pure anger at Phil. Until she saw his expression. Then the looks became more fearful and her eyes would flutter and drop.

'Can I have a word?' asked Sperring at Phil's side.

Phil turned to him. 'Not now,' he said.

Sperring kept staring at him, clearly with plenty to say.

'Later,' said Phil. He turned his attention to Adderley. 'Mr Adderley. You ready to talk now?'

Adderley looked up, eyes as fearful as the receptionist's. 'What did you do that for?'

'Why did you run?' asked Sperring, lowering himself into an armchair opposite Adderley, then instantly regretting it as he wondered how he would get out of it again, 'We only wanted to talk.'

Adderley's eyes darted from side to side. Getting ready to lie, Phil thought.

'I didn't know who you were,' he said. 'I thought . . . thought you were . . . I don't know.'

'We identified ourselves as police officers, Mr Adderley. There was no doubt as to who we were.'

Adderley just shook his head. 'What did you want to talk about?'

Phil glanced at the receptionist. 'Might be better if you hear this on your own.'

Adderley shook his head. 'You can say what you want in front of Trudi,' he said. 'I don't mind.'

'And if I'm not here as a witness, you might hit him again,' said Trudi, feeling braver now.

'I didn't hit him,' said Phil. 'Force was used but it was used proportionately and appropriately.'

She didn't reply.

'Mr Adderley,' said Phil, sitting down. 'It's about your wife. About Gemma.'

Adderley took the red-crusted paper away from his face. The blood had dried on his skin, giving the appearance of an all-over birthmark. 'You found her?'

'We have, Mr Adderley.'

'Where is she then? Where's she been? She left me, you know. Ran off and left Carly too.'

'She didn't, Mr Adderley.'

Adderley leaned forward, feeling braver now. 'Oh yes, she did.'

'No, Mr Adderley, she didn't. She was murdered.'

Adderley looked from one to the other. 'Murdered?'

'I'm afraid so.'

Phil studied the two of them. Trudi seemed the more upset. Adderley blinked hard and fast, like his eyes were doing calculations behind his eyelids.

'We'll get a family liaison officer to contact you,' he said. 'In the meantime, we're going to need you to answer some questions.'

'What, here? Now?'

Phil raised his hands, looked around. 'Why not? If you don't mind doing it in front of Trudi, of course.'

A look of cunning entered Adderley's eyes. Cunning interlaced with fear. 'No,' he said. 'Not here.'

'Why not?' asked Sperring.

Adderley's eyes darted once more. 'Because ... I'm not going to say anything without a solicitor present. That's why. Not going to answer anything.' He sat back, looking quite relieved.

Phil scrutinised him. 'Why did you run?' he asked again.

Adderley said nothing.

'In my experience,' said Sperring, 'only guilty people run. Why did you run, Mr Adderley?'

'I'm ... I'm not saying another word until I speak to a solicitor. I know my rights.'

'I'm sure you do, Mr Adderley. And I'm sure you have a solicitor handy.'

Adderley narrowed his eyes. 'What's that supposed to mean?'

'We checked your file before coming here,' said Phil. 'Seems you have quite a history where your wife was concerned.'

'Nothing was ever proved,' Adderley said.

'No,' said Phil. 'Complaints were made against you by Gemma, but she always dropped the charges, didn't she?'

'What's this?' asked Trudi.

'Lies,' said Adderley. 'Said I was ... hitting her.'

'And were you?' asked Phil.

'We had arguments, yeah. Like all couples. But that was it, that was all. I'm not ... not like that. Not that kind of person. I'm born again.'

'Right,' said Phil. 'And does your God know you go about hitting women? Or was he the one who told you to do it?'

Adderley reddened, looked angry. Phil stared at him. He didn't reply. Silence fell.

'Don't you want to know any of the details?' asked Sperring. 'About your wife?'

Adderley glanced between the pair of them like it was a trick question and he didn't know what the right answer would be. 'When my solicitor's there,' he said.

'And that's that, is it?' said Phil.

'Yeah,' said Adderley. 'That's that.'

Phil and Sperring exchanged a look. 'Well,' said Phil, 'in that case, we'll be off.' Behind him, he heard Sperring noisily trying to extricate himself from the armchair.

They made their way to the door. 'We'll see ourselves out,' said Phil.

Sperring paused before leaving. 'I hope you'll be very happy together,' he said. 'And that God approves.' He followed Phil out.

The rain was easing, the clouds thinning. But no sign of the sun. Dark soon.

Sperring stopped walking, stared at Phil, mouth open. 'What the bloody hell was all that about?'

Phil tried not to make eye contact with him, keep walking. Sperring wouldn't let him. 'Nothing.'

'Nothing? Nothing? You nutted that bloke. He could sue you.'

'Let him try. He ran. Had to stop him somehow.'

'If it is him, and if this case somes to court, a good brief could have it thrown out. Jesus Christ, what's the matter with you?'

Phil looked at Sperring. Really looked at him. 'I'm fine,' he said.

Sperring studied his boss's features. He seemed about to say

56

something but thought better of it. The anger was draining from him, to be replaced by something else. Compassion, Phil thought. The last thing he wanted.

'I said I'm fine.'

Sperring stepped back, still looking at him. 'You'd better be.'

They reached the car and drove away. Phil thought about the lies he was telling people. The lies he was telling himself.

11

Janine Gillen could barely breathe. She was on the verge of a panic attack, she knew it, recognised the signs from the previous ones. And it wasn't her fault. None of it. *None* of it. But she knew she would get the blame. She always did.

The Metro train was stuck on the track. Hadn't even reached The Hawthorns yet. No word from the driver other than an apology for the delay and a hope that they would be on the move shortly.

Janine glanced round the carriage, checking everyone else's expressions, trying to find answers. Clues as to how long they would be there, comfort that it wouldn't be long till they were moving again. All the while trying not to let her terror show, communicate to the others. She didn't want any of them asking if she was all right. She didn't want to answer that question.

Her twin boys were with her sister. They always went there when she was in town. Terry didn't know she was still going. No idea. He had told her what he thought of the counselling sessions, of Keith, in no uncertain terms, and that was that. End of story. He wasn't going again, therefore she wasn't going again. And she knew what she would get if she defied him.

Yet still she went. She didn't know how or where she had found the strength to defy him, but found it she had. And she kept going because she drew comfort from the sessions. Keith made her think of her life before she met Terry. The silly, romantic girl with her hopes and dreams. Thinking that she didn't need an education, not if she had a good man to love and take care of, and who would love and take care of her in return. Keith didn't make her feel stupid for thinking those things. Like he said, he gave her permission to feel like that, to think like that.

There was one other thing the sessions had taught her, and it was something she couldn't stop saying to herself: *It's not my fault.*

Because it had been. For years. Her fault. Always her fault. Whatever happened. If it was bad weather and Terry couldn't work, her fault. If one of the twins was ill and off school, making a noise coughing while Terry was sleeping off a hangover, her fault. If she herself was ill and couldn't make Terry his dinner exactly the way he wanted it, when he wanted it, her fault. Everything. Her fault.

She would hurry home – like she was trying to do now – and if she was late for some reason then it would be her fault. And Terry would punish her for it. Sometimes it would just be a slap to the face or a punch to the stomach. But the punishments crept up depending how late she was. Sometimes he had taken off his belt and lashed her across her back with it. Sometimes he had just contented himself with banging her head off the dining room wall.

And then he would sober up and the apologies would start. And she would look at him, cringing, weeping, begging, and something would be touched inside her. That spark of emotion – of love, even – that she used to feel for him would be slowly fanned back into life. And as the pain subsided and the bruises and welts healed, she began to feel hope for the future.

Until the next time.

After a while, Terry hadn't even bothered to beg for forgiveness. Hadn't even been drunk – or not too drunk – when he hit her. He had told her it was what she deserved, what she should expect. She was worthless. Ugly. Stupid. And after a while, she had started to believe it.

She shook her head, looked round the carriage once more. Still no sign of movement.

How had she got to this point? How had it happened? If it hadn't been for the counselling, she didn't know where she would have ended up. *It's not your fault.* Her personal mantra, said over and over in her head, every day, so she wouldn't forget it. Not her fault. It was Terry's. No matter what he said, how forceful he was, it wasn't her fault. Keith had told her about some cases, strong, independent women who'd ended up in her situation. And they couldn't believe what had happened. How the man they had loved – still loved, in most cases – had turned out to be the way he was. And turned them into the person they were. But it wasn't the end. It could be stopped.

She felt inside her pocket once more. Her fingers curled round the card that Keith had given her. The refuge. The phone number. All she had to do was call.

So why hadn't she? Why didn't she just do it?

Because . . . She didn't know. Not really. She found reasons, although she thought they were probably just excuses. The twins needed her. That was a lie. They loved their father. Probably more than her. She could see it in their eyes. The same look he had. Growing up, growing up into two copies of him.

Maybe that was it. Maybe she should stay, fight him. Make sure they turned out all right. No. She knew that was stupid. So why was she going back? When she knew what was waiting for her?

Because . . .

Because.

Because she didn't have anywhere else to go.

She kept hold of the card. Yes, she did. She did have some-where to go.

But it wasn't just that. It wasn't easy to walk out on a mar-riage even when it was going as horribly wrong as hers. It was admitting defeat. Telling the world – and yourself – that you were wrong all those years ago. That you'd made a huge mis-take with your life. It was inviting ridicule and laughter. Hatred, even. That was how she felt. Keith had insisted that it wasn't like that, that no one would be judging her. But still the feeling persisted.

And she was also inviting her children to hate her. If she took them with her, they would resent her for leaving their father; if she left them, they would grow up hating her in her absence. And that was a horrible burden for a mother – any mother, she thought – to bear.

But she had to do something. She had to take that leap of faith Keith was always talking about. She had asked him once about his own life. She knew she wasn't supposed to, but she couldn't help it.

'You're married,' she had said, looking at the gold band on his finger.

'I am, yes,' he said almost shyly.

'What's your wife like?'

He had hesitated before answering.

'Sorry. I know I shouldn't ask.'

'No, no,' he had reassured her, 'that's all right. My wife's . . . ' He had smiled to himself. 'Lovely. A strong woman. A great person. Great mother, great wife, the lot.'

Janine nodded. Jealous of their relationship. 'Not like me, then,' she'd said, trying to smile.

Keith had leaned forward then. 'She'd been in an abusive relationship before she met me. Very bad, had to escape. Like I said, it can happen to the strongest of women.'

'And you saved her.'

Keith had shaken his head. 'She saved herself. One of the things I love her for.'

With a jolt, the train started moving again.

Janine sighed. Looked out of the window. It was still raining. And she knew what that meant. No work. Terry would have spent the day in the pub with his mates. Roofers can't work in the pissing rain, he had told her on many occasions. Except he could, she had thought. If he wanted to badly enough. But she had never dared to say it.

So that meant he would be home already. Waiting. Angry. And she knew what would be in store for her.

Her stomach turned over in dread at the thought.

The train stopped. The Hawthorns. Two more stops and she would be home. Home. Or whatever she called it.

She looked at the open space beyond the door.

She felt the card once more.

So easy. She could just get off the train now, call that number. She could ...

The doors closed.

One last chance, she thought. She owed it to that romantic girl who had believed in everlasting love. One last chance.

The train moved forward.

Janine tried to have hope, to be strong.

Tried to ignore the terror that gripped her.

12

'That was quick,' said Phil into his phone. 'Must be a new record.'

'Oh, you know how it is,' said Esme Russell in reply. 'Sometimes we have quiet days.'

There was a pause. The silence threatened to become deafening until Esme said, 'You coming over, then?'

Phil checked his watch. It was almost time to call it a day. Shift's end. He looked round the Major Incident Squad office. The team were working on the murder of Gemma Adderley: writing reports, checking and cross-referencing databases. They knew their jobs. There didn't seem to be anything more that he could do at present. If he went to see Esme he couldn't claim it as overtime. He checked his watch again. That was fine. It wasn't like he had anywhere to be.

Anyone waiting at home for him.

'Yeah, okay,' he said.

'I'll hang on for you.'

He hung up, leaving the day's earlier awkwardness between them hanging in the air. Ignored. Or perhaps just unacknowledged, even welcome.

Phil, getting up and heading for the door, wasn't sure which was better and which was worse. Which he wanted and which he didn't.

Just a post-mortem report, he told himself. That's all.

He left the office.

'It's only preliminary,' Esme Russell said once Phil had arrived at the mortuary, deep in the bowels of Birmingham's Selly Oak Hospital. 'But it seems quite comprehensive.'

The air in the mortuary was chill, but still carried on it the ghosts of spoiled meat with an underscore of preserving chemicals and a faint dirty copper tang of blood. The smell always reminded Phil of what a butcher's shop would be like if it set up in a hospital. Which, he thought wryly, was exactly what it was.

The body was no longer in sight. He knew its fate. It would have been rendered down to its base components, organs removed and weighed, measurements and samples taken. Gemma Adderley's death reduced to a series of chemical and biological puzzles to be answered.

Music was playing. Something Phil didn't know. Something classical. A bottle of chilled white wine was open on Esme's desk. Two glasses. One almost full, sipped from.

Esme saw him looking. 'I always do this at the end of the day. Little ritual. Care to join me?'

Phil looked at the bottle of wine, condensation running down the glass. He didn't want to think about what had been in the fridge with it.

'No thanks,' he said.

'Still on duty?'

'Not much of a white wine drinker, that's all.'

'Right.' Esme smiled, took a sip.

Phil looked at the report she handed him. 'Talk me through it,' he said. He had seen enough reports to know what they meant, but he always asked for a description too. His eyes weren't as well trained as those of a pathologist. He couldn't pick up what was important as well as she could.

'Well,' she said, putting her glass down, moving close to him and looking at the report he held in his hand, 'it's pretty much as we surmised. Tortured: burnt with cigarettes, as far as I can make out, cut. The knife was sharp. Kitchen knife, medical blade, perhaps, although the size of the cuts would suggest something large.'

'Any degree of medical accuracy?' asked Phil.

'Not really. Just random cuts, it seems. Deep, though. Lot of weight behind them.'

'Man or woman?'

'If it was a woman she would have to be huge. No, the angle and weight of the blade suggests a man. Left-handed, too, I think.'

Phil wrote that down. 'Pre or post?'

'Pre. She was very much alive when this was happening.'

'Jesus. Raped?'

'No evidence of semen or DNA but some degree of vaginal tearing. Either he was very careful or he used substitutes. Large ones.'

'Punishment? Humiliation?'

Esme smiled. 'Your department, I think. Ligature marks on the wrists and ankles. Had her tied up somewhere for quite some time.'

'Right. Did he know the woman?'

'Your department again.'

'No, I meant are there any signs of what you could infer to be intimacy? Would a stranger have done this, or would it be someone she knew? Like I said earlier, it's clearly someone who hates women. I'm just wondering if he hates all women, or just this one.'

'I don't know. Good question, but I really couldn't say.' She pointed at something in the report. Phil noticed that she was wearing perfume. And make-up. 'She wasn't killed at the scene. And she'd been in the water for some time.'

'Time of death?'

'Can't say. She'd been in there long enough to have attracted rats but not long enough to have any flora growing inside her. Lividity and decomposition suggest she was dead for a while before he put her in the water. Stomach contents back that up. I don't yet know what kind of place she was kept in.'

'She'd been missing a month, how does that sound?'

'About right.'

'The hole in her chest,' asked Phil. 'Pre or post?'

'Post.'

'And no sign of the heart?'

She shook her head. Phil was aware of her perfume once more. He was getting used to it now, even quite liked it. 'None. I checked the area. Jo and her team did likewise. But we didn't really expect to find it there.' She looked at the report once more. 'The injuries, the torture, although they're extreme, I can't find any evidence of one fatal blow. Maybe she just died of shock. Or of the cumulative effects, even.'

'He still killed her, though.'

'Undoubtedly. Any suspects?' she asked.

'At the moment, the husband. History of spousal abuse. Got a new girlfriend. Ran when I tried to question him. Won't talk to us without a lawyer.'

Esme took the report from his hands, put it down on her desk, turned to him. Faced him. 'Quite a day.'

'You're not wrong.'

Another silence fell between them. Of awkwardness or anticipation, Phil didn't know. He couldn't read his own emotions at the moment , never mind anyone else's.

'Look, erm . . . '

Phil waited.

'I'm sorry about what I said this morning. About . . . I didn't want you to get the wrong . . . Oh, you know what I mean.'

'I know,' said Phil, not altogether sure if he did.

'But ...' Esme shrugged. 'I know you've not had a good time of it lately. With everything that's happened. I just thought ... Are you free tonight? A drink? Dinner? Just a chat.'

He looked at her. Thought of all the times he'd done the right thing for the wrong reasons. And the wrong thing for the right reasons. And sometimes just the wrong thing for reasons he couldn't even explain to himself. Or didn't want to explain to himself.

'Okay,' he said. 'Where did you have in mind?'

13

He opened the box. Looked inside. Stepped back. Feeling pride, or something like pride. He wasn't sure what the exact word was, the exact emotion. But pride would do until he could think of a better one.

He kept staring. At it. Beyond it. Back. Doing what it was supposed to do. What he had collected it for. His ritual. His exorcism. Cleansing the past. Enabling the present to become the future. A clean future.

Back. He kept staring. It started to work. He started to see. To hear.

I don't know where you think this is going. There it was. Her voice, back again after all those years. Lorraine Russell. He'd never forgot her name. Never.

What d'you mean? But he knew what she meant. Had known she was going to say this all along. This or something like it. The end result would be the same.

You. Me. This. Looking around, gesturing, taking in the city. He had never understood that bit, when she did that. It hadn't been about the city. Never about that. Only the two of them. Only ever the two of them. Down by the canal. The lock. Saturday Bridge. Before the gentrification, years ago, when it was still run-down, dangerous. The only ones who ever went there. *I mean, it's not like this is it, is it? Forever.*

The words piercing like an arrow through his heart. It must

have shown on his face. She responded with an expression that looked compassionate yet contained hints of a mocking smile. Yes, both. He had thought about that for years, gone over it in his head. Over and over it. And yes. Compassion, yet a mocking smile. He was right. Remembering it like it was yesterday.

The autumn air. Cold. Brown leaves blowing. Summer dying. She was wearing his denim jacket, the collar turned up. The room was cold but it was the memory that made him shiver.

What? she said next. *You thought it was?*

Yes. The only world he could think of. His words had dried up. Before that, before they had stopped, he had said plenty. Told her his plans for the future. Their future. He had thought of nothing else. Worked the whole thing out. And now this. Compassion, yet mocking.

Sorry. No.

Why not?

This was . . . never meant to go anywhere. It just got out of hand, that's all. I know what you want. Marriage and kids and that. But I'm still at university. I've got my third year coming up. I can't do all that.

I'll . . . I'll wait.

That look again. Compassion, yet mockery. He tried once again to work out the percentages.

Look, I'll . . . I'll come with you. When you go back to Exeter. It's not far.

I'm a student. What will you do while I'm at uni?

I'll . . . I'll get a job. Work. Find . . . find our home. You need never have to . . . I'll take care of you. You . . . you won't need to work or anything. I'll do that. I'll look after you.

A sigh then. A shake of her head. And in that one movement his heart split open once more. The pain that was always with him, buried somewhere, came bubbling to the surface like dark, black, bad blood from a fatal injury.

I don't need looking after. I'm doing a law degree. It looks like I've got a job lined up at the end of it. A career. Why would I give that up? Especially for someone here, without a job. That's what I've worked towards all these years, that's what I want, more than anything.

Anything? Unable to keep the pain from his voice.

Anything.

He walked away then, three paces, three and a half, then turned back to face her.

And that's . . . that's it. We were just fun, were we? Something to fill the time before you went back to uni. Anger tingeing his voice now.

She shrugged. *It was fun, though, wasn't it? You have to admit that.*

He waited a while until his words, his breath, were under control. Then spoke. *So this is . . . it? The end?*

She laughed. *No need to be so melodramatic. God, it's not like we're the love of each other's lives or anything. I'll see you at Christmas. We can go for a drink, maybe.*

And that was when the split happened.

The reality, remembered. He looked at her. Really looked at her. Saw her for the first time, what she really was. And there was no compassion. Only mockery. That was all there had ever been. Mockery. And pity. That was all he had been to her. A pity fuck. A common kid to occupy her time with until she went back to uni and surrounded herself with her posh friends. Something to tell the others about over drinks in the union bar: *Well, I had a common kid this summer. That's one thing ticked off the bucket list . . .* Rage rose up inside him, threatened to spill out. He wanted to grab her, shake her, hurt her. He wanted her to love him. But he did nothing. Just accepted her words. He mumbled something and walked away. Left her there.

He never saw Lorraine Russell again. He spent years twisted

up by the pain of her rejection. He attempted suicide, needed therapy to sort him out, just get him functioning again.

The reality of what happened.

But now, standing in front of the box, came the exorcism. The chance to make things right after all those years, those long, painful years. A time of atonement.

He closed his eyes.

In this version, Lorraine Russell never sees the knife. Neither does anyone else. It's like they're apart from everyone else. Alone. What few passers-by there are are just ghosts. They don't stop to interfere.

Her eyes widen, her mouth falls into a rigid O. Like a long-haired Munch *Scream*. Then she goes to scream herself. No one hears her. Nothing comes out, like a dream scream. He grabs her. Pushes her against the heavy wooden lock gate, holding her by the throat, bending her over backwards. Smiling all the time. Knife glinting.

You know what you've done? he screams at her. *You know?*

She tries to shake her head. She's about to speak. He stops her.

Shut up. Listen. I'll tell you. You've taken my heart. That's what you've done. My heart. I gave it to you. You've got it. And you've fucking killed it . . .

She just stares at him. He's aware of her breathing becoming restricted. His hand on her throat, her body bent backwards.

So now . . . He shows her the knife. *Now I'm going to take yours . . .*

He gets to work. Rips open her jacket – his jacket – then her blouse. Then snaps her bra in two with a swish of the blade. Her breasts are exposed. Her beautiful milky-white breasts. How he loves those breasts . . .

The knife goes in. Blood bubbling up and over the blade, covering those magnificent breasts. He pushes it in further. More blood.

The look of terror on her face is exquisite.

He gets to work. Hacking, cutting, sawing. The blade is sharp, never lets him down. And it's easier than in real life. His hands, arms, body, are covered in her blood. He luxuriates in it. Imagines he is bathing in it. Eventually he throws the knife aside, plunges his hands in. Finds what he is looking for.

Her heart.

He pulls. It's reluctant to leave her. But he is stronger than she is. And soon he stands over her, her heart in his hands. He smiles. But she is already gone.

He was back. In front of the box. Looking into it. Seeing his latest trophy. The heart.

He breathed deeply. In, out again. Smiled. Tried to place himself back in his room. Tried to work out how the exorcism had made him feel. Good, he decided. Centred. Calm. At peace.

The exorcism had worked. Lorraine Russell was gone. Forever. All he had to do was close the lid and that part of his life was over. All that hurt and pain, all those wasted years gone. Banished.

He closed the lid.

And felt a warmth spread throughout his body.

He looked at the other boxes. All empty. All soon to be full.

He pulled off his gloves. Heard voices calling.

'Daddy . . . Daddy . . . dinner's ready . . .'

'Coming.'

He took one last look at the box. Smiled. Left the room.

14

He couldn't protect us. He just couldn't protect us.

The words ran laps round the inside of her head, over and over, again and again, a mantra to keep the rhythm going.

Josephina was in bed. Asleep, hopefully, but Marina knew from experience that wasn't always the case. She was worried that taking Josephina away from her father might damage the child, but it was a risk she had had to take. She spent as much time as she could with her daughter, made her feel as loved and wanted as possible. Since Ellison's phone call, she had done that even more, keeping busy, trying not to think about what she had just heard. Or anything else. And she had just about succeeded. She had become so lost in the world of her daughter that – just for a short while – she forgot why she was in that house and what she was supposed to be doing and allowed her guard to drop. Just for a while. But, like a terminal diagnosis or incessant pain, she could never relax for long.

Nights were the worst. That was why Marina was working out. The house belonged to a work colleague from the university. He had taken a year-long sabbatical accompanying his much better renumerated wife on a business venture abroad, and let her stay for as long as she liked. The house was beautiful; detached, so anyone approaching it could be seen, with alarms and security systems, in a discreet part of Edgbaston. But the thing she liked best about it was the home gym. Small, but useful. Very useful. Physical activity that would tire her out, make her able to sleep. But not only that: exercise that would build her muscle, sharpen her reflexes. Keep her prepared. Ready.

No matter what she did, though, she knew that as soon as she closed her eyes, that face would be there again. Those eyes. The smile. Those taunting words:

Goodbye. Although it isn't really. I'll be seeing you again very soon.

And when Marina had countered that:

You're wrong, Marina. Very wrong.

And then the words that had chilled her then and still did so now:

Give Phil my love.

Fiona Welch. Or the woman who had called herself that. The woman who had split Marina and Phil up.

She had engineered the murders of several women in East Anglia and escaped from a high-security hospital for the criminally insane, killing one of Marina and Phil's closest friends in the process. She wasn't really Fiona Welch. The real Fiona Welch was a twisted, murderous, insane individual whom Phil had watched plummet to her death several years previously. They didn't know who this woman really was. But she had behaved just like the real Fiona.

Then there was that night. Never far from Marina's mind. The night she came home and found Phil unconscious on the floor, beaten. He had come round, in pain, and told her what had happened. The woman who called herself Fiona Welch had been there. Except she wasn't calling herself that any more. She wanted to go by another name.

Marina's.

She had been in their bedroom. That was bad enough. But she actually been in their bed, waiting for Phil to return home. And after the fight she had gone, taking some of Marina's

74

clothes with her. Leaving Marina feeling violated in so many ways. And leaving that final message relayed to Phil:

I'll be seeing you again very soon.

A description of the woman had gone out to police forces all round the country. But any reported sightings of her had turned out to be false. They still didn't know who she was or what her motivations were. And they were no nearer to finding her. It was like she had just vanished into thin air. All they had was the threat that she would return. And that had been more than enough.

In the aftermath, Marina and Phil had talked. Marina was terrified that the woman would return. Phil had to be too, but Marina decided he was better at keeping the fact hidden.

'Look,' he had said, 'I'll call in some favours. Get the house watched. Bodyguards for Josephina. I'm police. There's things we can do.'

And she had to admit he had sounded convincing. But things still gnawed away at her. 'You can't keep that up. If she doesn't show up any time soon, the threat'll be downgraded. And Cotter has to balance the books. We won't be guarded for ever. And when all that's gone, when we're alone and vulnerable, that's when she'll come back.'

'And we'll be waiting for her.'

They had agreed to face whatever was coming together, and that worked for a while. But when the unmarked car was no longer watching the house and Josephina had no bodyguards to escort her to and from school, the unease that she had initially suppressed began to resurface.

She told Phil. 'It's fine,' he had said. 'We're aware. Both of us. Let's not show that she's got to us. Let's just live our lives. Get on with things. We can't live in fear of her all the time.'

But Marina wasn't convinced. She *was* living in fear. Over

the last few years their work had brought them – and their daughter – into danger. Real, life-threatening danger. And she had dealt with enough criminally unhinged people to know that this madwoman couldn't be easily dismissed.

Once again she confided her fears to Phil. Once again he tried to manage them. 'Don't give in to her,' he said. 'That's what she wants.'

'What she wants?' Marina could contain herself no longer. 'I know what she wants, Phil. She wants *you*. She wants *my life*. Phil, she was in our bed. When she left the house that night, she took some of my clothes with her. She's insane. No, beyond insane.'

'And that's your professional opinion?'

He had only been trying to make a joke, lighten the tension. She knew that. She had thought about it long enough afterwards. But the months of living looking over her shoulder, of dreading stepping outside the door, of fearing what she might find when she picked Josephina up from school, all of that had taken its toll on her.

'I can't do this any more,' she said, tears coming as they so often did.

He hugged her. 'It's okay. We'll get through it. We'll be fine. She might never—'

'She will, Phil. She will.' Pulling away from him as she spoke. 'And if she doesn't? I don't want to spend the rest of my life looking for her. Seeing her everywhere. Terrified to move in case she's there. I can't stand this any more. I . . . I'm heading for a breakdown.'

He tried to hug her again. She stopped him.

'No,' she said. 'No. We have to . . . have to do something. We can't keep on living like this.'

'What do you suggest? I'll try to take some time off, maybe we can go away somewhere.'

Marina shook her head. 'Run away? And what if she's there, waiting for us? No, Phil. That won't do.'

Phil stepped back, looked at her. Like he was seeing her for the first time. 'What, then?'

She regarded him the same way. As though a naked, truthful light was shining on him. 'You're . . . you can't protect me, Phil. You can't protect our daughter.'

'What d'you mean? Of course I can. Of course I will.'

The conversation she had had with Carly Adderley came back to her. The look on the child's face when she'd told Marina how her mother couldn't protect them. And what had happened as a result. Then the image of Phil lying there outside their bedroom, defeated, broken, almost paralysed. The sheer helplessness in the face of something greater, something darker.

'No, Phil,' she said, her voice small but firm, 'you can't.'

He tried to speak again. She didn't let him.

'I'm going away. I . . . It's better if I'm not here.'

Phil stood there, stunned. Waiting for her words to sink in. Eventually he tried to speak. She stopped him.

'No. Don't say anything. Don't try to talk me out of it. Phil, I love you. More than anyone else I've ever known. But I can't keep going like this. Every time I look at you, I see her. What she did. What she'll do again.'

Again he tried to talk. Again she stopped him.

'It's all arranged. I'm taking Josephina with me. She doesn't deserve to be put in danger. She's been through enough over the years. Don't ask me where I'm going. I'm not going to tell you. Don't try to contact me.'

She couldn't say any more. The tears had started again. She ran from the house.

Soon she had run from his life.

*

77

Marina counted reps in her head, reached the number she wanted, put the weights down. She slumped to the floor, exhausted, sweat covering her whole body. She stretched out a still-shaking arm, admired it. The sinew and muscle. The leanness of it. She made a fist, pulled it back, let it go. Hard. Imagined Fiona Welch's face on the end of it, connecting, breaking.

'I'm ready for you, bitch,' she said, her voice a hoarse whisper. 'I'm ready.'

15

'So is this your local?'

Phil took a sip from his pint of San Miguel, looked round. The Plough in Harborne was a neighbourhood boozer that had gone the upscale gastropub route. Not the kind of place he would usually come to, but he had to admit he liked it.

Esme Russell took a sip from her wine, sat back, looked round also, then back at Phil. 'I suppose so. If I have a local. I like it here. Good place to meet friends.'

'Harborne. Nice.' Phil was being polite, looking for things to say. And things to avoid saying. 'I wonder who decided that all pubs should now be full of mismatched rustic furniture and bits of industrial salvage? It's like the back room at an auctioneer's.'

Esme laughed. 'Don't you like it?'

'I do, actually. Bet they've got craft beer, as well. A hundred and forty different varieties that all taste the same.'

Esme laughed again and he enjoyed that feeling. Making someone laugh. Pleased to be with him. He had missed that.

'I like it here,' she said. 'Harborne. Like a village, almost. It's got that feel. You can forget you're so close to the city centre.'

'And so close to work, too.'

Esme smiled. 'With what we do? You know as well as I do that it can happen anywhere.'

'True.' Another mouthful of lager. Phil settled back in his

metal chair. It was surprisingly comfortable for something that looked like it had come out of the canteen of a fifties steelworks.

'So.' Esme replaced her drink on the table, leaned forward.

Phil said nothing.

'How are you?'

The good feeling of a moment ago dissipated. 'Fine,' he said, almost cutting off her question in his haste to answer.

Esme looked down, toying with the stem of her wine glass. 'I mean . . . everything.'

'This a professional enquiry? Has Cotter put you up to this?'

Esme pulled back, removing her fingers from the stem of her glass. 'No. I . . . I'm just concerned about you. That's all.'

Phil looked at her. Esme couldn't meet his eyes. He studied her. She was a very attractive woman. Not really his type, if he was honest. Tall, slender; long, straight blonde hair. An accent so posh it could cut glass. But attractive. He had never really noticed it when they had met professionally. Or if he had, he had subjugated his feelings. For obvious reasons.

And maybe she was concerned about him. For professional reasons. But he didn't think so.

'I'm . . . coping,' he said. 'I'm sure I'm not the first man whose wife has left him.' But I might be for the reasons she gave me, he thought.

'I know. But you seemed so happy together. So . . . '

'Yeah, well,' said Phil, reaching for his pint to hide behind, 'it happens.'

Esme nodded. 'I'm just saying,' she said, reaching across the table, 'you've got friends.'

He nodded. Made no attempt to remove his hand.

They sat in silence, each waiting for the other to make the next move.

'Are you hungry?' asked Esme eventually.

'I'm okay,' said Phil.

'No, you're not,' she said. 'You've lost weight and you don't look healthy. If you don't mind me saying so.'

'Thank you.'

She smiled. 'I'm a professional. I'm good at spotting those kind of things.'

She took the opportunity to remove her hand and reach for the menu.

'Their pizzas are very good. And burgers.'

'I'll have a burger, then.'

'Sorted. My treat.'

Before he could say anything else, Esme had jumped up from the table and crossed to the bar to place their order. Phil watched her go, his mind performing emotional somersaults.

Why was he sitting here? What was he doing? Esme was attractive, yes. No denying that. And if he thought about it, if he allowed himself, he was attracted to her. And she laughed at his jokes, which counted for a lot. But he was still married. Even if Marina was gone and he didn't know where she was. And it wasn't just that. He still loved Marina. He didn't want anyone else.

So why was he here? Why was he with Esme? He knew the answer to that. Because he was lonely.

She returned to the table. Smiled at him.

'Thank you,' he said. 'You didn't need to do that.'

She shrugged his words off.

At that moment a waiter appeared with more drinks.

'I didn't . . .'

'I took the liberty.'

'I've got to drive.'

Esme didn't answer.

The food arrived. The burger looked bigger than Phil's head. He started on it, pecking at it, but felt full very quickly. Esme on the other hand devoured her pizza. He wondered where she put it all. Maybe she was the kind of woman that other women hated, who could eat anything they wanted and never put on weight. Or the kind Marina hated, anyway.

Marina. There she was in his head again.

'Not hungry?' Esme looked down at Phil's plate. He had pushed it away. 'You've barely touched it.'

'Sorry,' he said. 'Thought I was. Mustn't have been. I've wasted your money. Sorry.'

He noticed that his second pint of lager was almost gone.

'Thirsty, though,' said Esme. 'I'll get you another.'

'No, I'm fine,' he replied. 'I don't think . . . '

She gestured to the waiter. Another lager arrived. The plates were cleared away.

'You trying to get me drunk?'

Esme sighed. 'Life's too short, Phil. Too short to be unhappy, anyway. I've discovered that from experience. And it's been a hard lesson to learn.'

He said nothing.

'You're not the only one to have a relationship break up. A relationship that you thought was going to last for the rest of your life.'

He nodded. And realised in that moment that he didn't really know anything about Esme. Beyond work, anyway.

'I was married once. And I thought he was the love of my life. He didn't share my feelings, however. Result: one messy divorce. Years of heartbreak, thinking I was unattractive, wasn't good enough to have a man in my life. Years and years of that. And then one day I just woke up and thought, fuck it.'

Phil's eyes widened. It was the first time he had heard Esme swear.

'Yes,' she said, smiling grimly. 'Fuck it. Life's too short. I'm not unattractive and I deserve to be happy.' She shrugged. 'And

82

that was that. It's been my philosophy ever since.' She sat back, wine glass in hand. Looked at him, waiting for a response.

Phil knew what kind she wanted.

He sighed. Couldn't give it to her.

'Thank you,' he said. 'For dinner. And the drinks. But I think I should be off.'

He stood up. She looked at him, sadness in her eyes. 'I'm sorry.'

'No,' he said, shaking his head. 'I am. I'm a . . . bit of a mess at the moment. I don't want to do something tonight that I'd regret. That we'd both regret. In the morning. Whenever.'

She was clear-eyed as she looked at him. 'I wouldn't regret it.'

He nodded. Made his way to the door, weaving as he went.

Not sure if he'd made the right decision or the wrong one.

16

Janine Gillen opened the door as slowly and carefully as she could. As though if she didn't disturb the atmosphere, her actions couldn't ripple out and cause any kind of disruption in the rest of the house.

'Where the fuck have you been?'

Too late.

He came towards her. Terry Gillen, her husband. Angry, as usual. Like it was his natural state of being, his default setting. She wondered whether it was more from habit than anything else, angry with her because that was what he did. What he had always done.

But it wasn't what he had always done. How he had always been. Not at first. Just the way he had become. Or maybe he had always been like that and their courtship was just some temporary blip. Being nice to lure her in. She had been thinking about that a lot lately. Keith had asked her questions and in turn made her question. But she hadn't found the answers.

Whatever, another part of her brain said. That was later. Now she had to think how to get past him, how to make it through another night. How to avoid a beating for something she had either done or not done, or any permutation of the two.

'Hello, Terry,' she said.

He loomed before her in the hallway. The house was small

and he seemed too big for it. Like it was keeping him constrained. A too-small cage for a large wild animal.

'I said, where the fuck have you been?'

'Out. In . . .' She felt her heart palpitate once more. 'In the city.'

His eyes narrowed. Suspicion in them. 'Why? Where?'

'I . . .' This was it. Should she lie or tell the truth? Which would be easiest? 'I . . . went to see Keith. We had an appointment. I thought you would be there. You said you would.'

'I said nothin' of the sort.'

'But you did, you said—'

He grabbed her then, his big meaty hand gripping her neck, pushing her up against the wall.

'I said nothin' of the sort. You deaf? I told you I don't want to see that interferin' fuckin' faggot ever again.' He tightened his grip. 'Ever. Again. And I don't want you seein' him either. Puttin' fuckin' ideas into your head. Fuckin' faggot.'

'But he's not a . . . not gay.'

Terry's eyes became glowing hot coals. His grip tightened further. 'Oh, he's not, is he? And how would you know, eh? You fuckin' him, that it? That where you've been? Fuckin' your gay-boy boyfriend?'

Janine tried to shake her head. Couldn't. 'Terry, I—'

'You want to argue with me, that right? You want to answer me back, do you, you useless fuckin' bitch? Yeah? Do you? You know what that'll get you, don't you?'

Janine felt her whole body start to shake. She knew it was better not to reply. She cast her eyes to the floor.

His grip loosened slightly. 'That's better.' Nodding. 'That's better. Now. Where's my fuckin' dinner?'

'I . . . I'm sorry, Terry. I . . .'

'You brought anythin' in with you?'

She shook her head.

His hand was back at her throat again, harder this time, tipping her head back, pulling it away from her body. She felt her throat being stretched, breathing becoming harder. He moved even closer to her. She could smell alcohol and sweat coming off him. Knew then that he hadn't been to work today.

'What kind of a mother are you, eh?' he said, sour beer breath right in her face. 'What kind of a fuckin' wife are you? You don't have to answer. I'll tell you. A shit one.'

She tried to speak. Could find no words. She felt she was about to piss herself.

'You know what day this is, don't you?'

Janine tried to think, tried to order her mind into something rational. Couldn't. Terry answered for her.

'Stupid cow. It's Monday. The Villa are at home and I'm takin' the boys. I picked them up from your sister's. You forgot that, didn't you? While you were in the city fuckin' that faggot.'

'I wasn't, Terry, I—'

'You'd better fuckin' not have been.' Face pushed right into hers. 'If I find out you have, well. Your life'll be fuckin' over.'

She moved her mouth but no words would emerge.

He relaxed his grip on her. 'Too late to have anythin' to eat now. We've got to go out. I'll have to get the kids somethin' at the ground. More fuckin' expense. And all your fault. That's less money you'll be gettin' off me next payday.'

He turned, walked away from her. Called for the boys to get their things, they were going.

Janine didn't move. Couldn't move. She stood trembling up against the wall, her mind reeling. She watched Terry's retreating back as he went towards the kitchen.. Allowed herself a sigh of relief. At least he hadn't hit her. At least she wasn't physically hurt.

He must have read her mind. In that moment he turned back into the hall, arm raised, so fast she didn't see him coming, didn't have time to think, to move out of the way. He slapped her right across the face, the force of the blow sending her sprawling on the floor, the noise reverberating all round the house. He stood over her, stared down at her prone body. Breathing like he was in the middle of a lengthy fight or a bout of strenuous lovemaking.

'Fuckin' useless bitch.'

The boys appeared on the stairs, stopped dead when they saw the scene before them.

'Come on,' Terry said to them. 'We're going.'

He went to the front door, the boys following mutely. Janine tried to look up at them, plead for . . . What? Sympathy? Help? Support? She didn't know. She got nothing. They just stared at her, expressions blank of anything but contempt, fledgling versions of their father.

Terry turned to her. 'They'd better fuckin' win. Because there'll be hell to pay in here if they don't.'

He slammed the door behind them.

Janine tried to get up. Couldn't move. Just lay there, numb, staring at the ceiling. Trying to imagine that this wasn't her on the floor. That all this was happening to someone else. Someone who deserved it.

It was over a quarter of an hour before she could get up.

It wasn't until then that she noticed the puddle of urine she was lying in.

17

Phil hadn't gone home. Couldn't face going home. Not after what had just occurred. Not now. Not on his own.

But he had nowhere else to go. He had run through a few options in his head: cinema, walk, pub, back to work, even. But none of them worked, nothing grabbed him. He couldn't concentrate on a film, didn't want to be alone with his own thoughts on a walk, couldn't face sitting in a pub on his own and watching everyone else in couples or groups, and he didn't want to go back to the station and just sit there, unable to think clearly enough to do any work.

No. He knew where he wanted to be. And who he wanted to be with.

Marina.

Anywhere, as long as Marina was with him.

He put the bottle to his lips, took another swig. The beer had given him a taste for alcohol, and a mellow buzz that he didn't want to let go of. He had stopped at an off-licence on the Hagley Road, driving back into the city; bought a bottle of Maker's Mark. He wasn't much of a spirit drinker, but he was quite partial to a good whisky or bourbon. And Maker's Mark was his favourite. Expensive, and something he only bought himself as a treat, for special occasions. Well, he thought, this counts as a special occasion. Although there's not much in the way of a treat about it.

He had parked up a few streets behind the row of shops he had bought the bottle from. Next to a tall brick tower. The locals had told him that Tolkien had used it as inspiration for one of his books. Phil neither knew nor cared if that was true. It was just somewhere convenient to sit. And think.

Marina was the love of his life. He knew that. Had felt it almost from the first time he met her. Like there had been some kind of electrical spark between them. Like she knew him, could see him as no one else had ever seen him. And he felt the same with her. Phil had thought the concept of a soulmate was something for trashy supermarket magazines. But meeting Marina changed his mind. Both damaged, both missing something, they completed one another. He had thought he would never leave her. Never lose her. And certainly not like this.

He could understand why she had gone. That was the worst of it. He could understand. After what they had been through together over the years, the threat of this Fiona Welch woman was just too much for her. She had reached breaking point. Something had to give. He just hoped she felt safe now, wherever she was.

Now he was alone. And lonely.

He had been tempted by Esme. He could admit it to himself. Very tempted. Even if it had been for all the wrong reasons. If they were in fact the wrong reasons.

She was attractive. Undeniably. Vivacious, fun to be with. Entertaining. And he had been very close to taking up her offer. Going back to her place. Having sex. Part of him had wanted to. A big part. Just for the connection that being close, intimate, with someone else gave. For the opportunity to take himself out of himself, even for a short while, to let another part of his brain take over. Even just to hold another body next to his.

But he couldn't. Because he was still married to Marina.

I still love you, Phil. She had said that as she was walking out on him. *I still love you.* And he had held on to those words, believed in them, even while knowing that hope was the cruellest of all emotions. One day she would be back. One day they would be together again.

Hopefully.

And he had to keep believing that. *Had to.*

But now, tonight, sitting in his car, hope wasn't enough. He had to talk to her, listen to her. Connect with her. Even though it was against the rules, even though he knew what the response would be, he had to try.

He took one more swig, for courage, and took out his phone. Hit her number. Waited.

Nothing. The phone just rang and rang, eventually going to voicemail. His heart fluttered at the thought that he might hear her voice, even if it was just a recording. But that was denied him too. Her voice was no longer there. She had replaced it with a generic service-provider speech, reiterating the number and asking him to leave a message after the tone.

The tone sounded loud and harsh in his ear. His mouth moved but nothing emerged beyond a couple of strangled, mangled sounds, halfway between syllables and sobs.

He ended the call.

The phone fell from his suddenly useless fingers, slid to the floor. He brought his head down on the steering wheel, slumped and breathless, like he had just run a marathon. Tears racked his frame.

He rode the tide of tears out. Sat back, wiped his eyes. Reached for the bottle, ready to take another swig. Checked the level. Nearly half gone. No. Not the way.

He threw the bottle back on the passenger seat. Thought.

That anger was still inside him. Anger and self-pity. He had to do something, get rid of it somehow. He thought for a few moments.

Then he had it. Just the thing. Yeah. Just the thing. He knew he was breaking all his own rules, not to mention the rules he was supposed to uphold as a police officer, but he had to do something. *Something.*

'Right, you fucker,' he said, and started the car up. 'Coming to get you.'

He drove unsteadily away, Warren Zevon cranked as loud as he could stand it. So he didn't have to listen to his own thoughts.

18

He loves me. I know he does. He loves me. That's why he's doing this, that's . . .

Janine Gillen sighed, closed her eyes. Leaned her head back against the hard tiled wall, her legs straight out, her shoulders against the cold porcelain, even colder in contrast to the hot water she lay in. Tried to let the bubbles soothe and comfort her, her cares and worries rise and disappear like the steam all around her.

He loves me. I know he does. He . . .

Tried not to cry any more. Couldn't.

The tears came again, shaking and shuddering the water, making the bubbles vibrate and quiver. It would have been comical if it hadn't been so sad.

He loves me. I know . . .

She replayed the events of earlier over and over in her mind. The way Terry had touched her. Hurt her. The look on his face while he did so. The humiliating effect it had on her. And the way her boys had looked at her. God, the way the boys had looked at her . . . She shivered, despite the warmth of the water.

And then started crying again.

No, she thought; she might even have said it out loud, *this isn't love. Nothing remotely like love . . .*

Instead of stretching her body, she curled it up as tight as she could. Made herself as small and insignificant as possible.

Like a hedgehog fearing attack. She felt the muscles stretch and contract as she did so, thought of all the times he had hit her, taken out on her whatever had made him angry that day. She kept her eyes tightly closed, imagined all those beatings she had taken, the casual slaps and punches, the everyday abuse, like a map on her body. Leading from where she had started to where she had ended up. Her final destination. It had taken her a long time to realise that that was what it was, a long time to allow herself to actually use the word *abuse*, but she did so now. And she never wanted to stop doing it. Call it what it was, take the power of the word, of the abuser, away. But that didn't stop her crying. In fact, the realisation of who and where she was, of how she had ended up, just made her cry all the more.

Eventually the tears subsided and Janine began to uncurl herself. She stretched out once more, the water now carrying a chill when she moved about in it. She lay back, staring at the ceiling until she could no longer look at it. Then she put a flannel over her face, closed her eyes.

In that moment she could have been anywhere. Lying in a bath in a beach hut in Mauritius, tired from the exertions of a day spent swimming in the purest blue sea, relaxing on a white beach, drinking the finest cocktails and eating the best seafood of her life.

Or in a Russian ice hotel, having a quick soak before heading down to the bar, surrounded by the most exquisite ice sculptures, wearing a gorgeous evening dress, drinking vodka cocktails and making sparkling, charming conversation with the most beautiful and handsome people in the world, all thinking she was so funny and profound, all loving her for who she was.

She moved her legs. Noticed that the water had become even colder. It brought her back to where she was: in a characterless, charmless housing estate in West Bromwich. Each street like the wing of a prison. Each house like a spur on that wing. Each room in the house as small as a cell. And she was trapped in the middle.

Reluctantly she opened her eyes, took the cloth off her face. The bathroom light, cold and stinging, hit her like reality flooding back after a dream. Even more reluctantly she began to drag herself from the bath. She reached for a towel, wrapped it around herself, pulled out the plug. She stood and stared, watching the water flow away, until there was nothing left. Then she straightened up, walked into the bedroom.

It was gone. All of that was gone. Who she was, who she could have been. Who she had ended up as. Gone.

No more.

Her features impassive, eyes set hard, she took the suitcase from the top of the fitted wardrobe, threw it on the bed, opened it. Stared down at it. She turned back to the wardrobe, opened the doors, looked at her clothes hanging there. She suddenly hated all of them, didn't want them touching her skin any more. But she knew she didn't have the money to get new ones and she knew she had to wear something, so she pulled as much as she could from the hangers, crammed it into the case. As she did so, her face barely registered emotion. Like a blank mask in a Greek tragedy.

The suitcase as full as she could make it, clothes and shoes and coats and cosmetics crammed in, she pushed down the top, zipped it closed. It was heavy to pull from the bed and she was glad that it had wheels underneath.

Dressed, she wrestled it downstairs, checked her watch. She had about an hour or so until Terry and the boys came back from the football. A little pre-programmed shiver ran through her: I hope they win. She had always thought that, even praying to a God she had long since stopped believing in. That way,

Terry wouldn't take out the inadequacies of his team on her body like he usually did. She smiled. It didn't matter any more. Because by the time he returned, she would be gone.

She sat on the sofa, having one last look around the place she couldn't call home. Her arm accidentally rested on the remote, turning on the TV. She jumped at the sudden noise. The local news. A woman's body had been discovered. Missing over a month. Janine shuddered. They showed a photo of the woman and her husband. Smiling. They looked happy. Something sank within Janine. Happy and still murdered.

Then the face of a stout, slightly sleazy-looking man filled the screen. He was greasy and sweating, but something in his eyes said his sweat hadn't been honestly achieved. *Detective Sergeant Hugh Ellison*, a caption read underneath. He talked about the case before the screen gave way to a woman police officer, DCI Alison Cotter, who seemed altogether more capable and knew what she was talking about.

Janine turned it off. She didn't want to hear any more.

She stood up, made her way to the coat rack. Pulled on her coat, felt in the pocket. The card was still there. Thank God. She knew, rationally, that it would be, but that still didn't stop her worrying. While she was packing, she had even begun to imagine that she had made the whole thing up. That Keith hadn't given her the card, hadn't given her those all-important words of encouragement, of self-esteem. She had even begun to worry that Keith wasn't real. That she had imagined him as well. That happened a lot to her. Events that she could clearly remember would be contradicted by Terry, even ones that he hadn't been at. When she tried to point out that he was wrong in his recollection, she would receive a smack for her trouble. And if she persisted in pointing it out, she would receive another. And another. Until yes, Janine would agree with him. He was right. She must have been mistaken.

But not this time. She took the card out, took out her phone, too. Dialled the number.

Then stopped. Stared at the screen.

Just one little tap of the button, that was all it would take. One little tap. And she would never see Terry again. Never be hit, never be hurt, never be humiliated again. One little tap. That was all.

And never see her children again. A pang of loss passed through her at the thought. Her children. What kind of mother gave up her children? And then she thought about the boys. What they really were. Not hers. Never hers. They were Terry's. She had just borne them for him. Dispensed food to them, cleared up after them. There was no joy in the relationship, either way. She was nothing to them.

She looked round: the hallway, the kitchen beyond that. The staircase. The door to the living room. Her house. Her world.

And she hit the button as hard as she could.

A woman's voice answered. 'Safe Haven.'

'I . . .' Janine sighed. The voice waited. 'I think I need . . . no, I need, yes, I need to come to you . . .'

And the tears started again.

19

The bottle was now two thirds empty and Phil had the acid burn from his throat to his gut to match.

He picked it up from the passenger seat of the Audi, put it to his lips. Felt the liquid there but didn't open his mouth. *No*, he thought. *No more.* He fixed the lid, tightening it hard, and threw the bottle on to the passenger seat once more, where it settled with a final, atonal slosh.

He looked instead at the house before him. Tried to convince himself he was doing something positive, something good. Something worth risking his licence for – his career, even. He had to squint to see it, covering one eye to throw the house into relief. He bit his lip at the same time, checking. If you can feel your teeth, someone had once told him, when it hurts if you bite, then you're not drunk. Phil bit down on the corner of his lip. Hard. Harder. Ground his teeth, jaw straining with the effort. He felt something in his mouth then. Old pennies. Dirty money. Blood. *Yeah*, he thought. *I'm sure I felt that. Yeah.*

'Fucking God-botherer . . .' he mumbled, good eye on the lighted front room of the house. 'Wife-beating fucking God-botherer . . .'

After his aborted call to Marina, he had driven out to Druid's Heath, driven around until he had found Roy Adderley's house, parked up in front of it. Doing something good, he thought. Yeah. Thanking a God of his own that he hadn't had an accident or been picked up by the police.

Boxy and redbrick, on an estate of identical red boxes, it had probably looked modern sometime in the late sixties. There had been attempts at expansive individuality all down the street. Polite bay windows, Georgian front doors. The inhabitants trying to make the most of their homes, their lives. But the modest back and side conservatories didn't enlarge the houses, just made already tiny gardens look even smaller.

Adderley's house was unremarkable in every way. But Phil was experienced enough to know that a dull exterior was no disguise for what was going on inside.

He had checked Adderley's file; the case of his wife's disappearance, now murder. Adderley had claimed he was out at a church meeting the night she disappeared. However, cursory questioning revealed this to be a lie, prompting him to then become a person of interest. Eventually Adderley had admitted that he was at the flat of his girlfriend, Trudi. She had vouched for him, and with no body, there had been nothing to charge him with so they had reluctantly let him go. Now that Gemma's body had turned up, Adderley was again of interest. And he knew it, which was why Phil could only talk to him with a solicitor present.

But it didn't stop him doing this. Not harassment, though. Just parked up somewhere for the evening. Should anyone ask.

The alcohol had deadened any questions that Phil might have had about his actions. Both the cause of them and the effects they might have. And that was good. The less time he had to think, the more he just had to do, the better.

It was cold, both outside and inside the car. But Phil didn't feel it. Or told himself he didn't feel it. He wouldn't put the heater on in case it ran down the battery. The same for the CD player, although he was in the kind of mood that he could never find music to accurately reflect. Warren Zevon had been fine for driving, but there was nothing in the glove box for just sitting. So he sat in silence, with only an unacknowledged, crystalline anger and the emptying bottle for company. And that, he thought, with a bitterness in his mind to match that in his body, was fine by him.

The curtains of Adderley's living room had twitched a few times while he had been sitting there. Phil took a cruel solace from that. Someone was watching him. Or was at least aware that he – or someone – was there.

'Good,' he said as the curtains twitched again, reaching for the bottle.

The front door opened.

Phil sat immediately upright, attention as focused as it could be. Roy Adderley stepped outside. Scanned the empty street. Spotted the car.

A rush of adrenalin went through Phil. *Come on*, he thought, *come on. Over here, make something of it, come on . . .*

He smiled, gave a little wave.

Even in the darkness, even across the street, he could see how the gesture enraged Adderley. Enraged but, Phil reckoned, scared him as well. Adderley walked over to the car. Phil flung the door wide, tried to square up for confrontation. But the drink had affected his legs, and he found that he had to stagger to his feet.

Adderley stopped before him. 'You're that copper from the airport.'

'Yeah,' said Phil.

'You're pissed.'

Phil managed a smile. 'Yeah,' he said, his words tumbling and slurring, 'but in the morning I'll be sober. And you'll still be a wife-beating little shit.'

Adderley sprang back as if he had been struck. 'I don't have to take this from you. I could have your job for this.'

Phil attempted a shrug. 'Really?'

'This is harassment.'

Phil looked round with what he hoped was a nonchalant swing of the head but was actually a loping drunken swagger. 'Public property here. Can park where I want.' He took a step closer to Adderley, who flinched. 'Why, you got something to hide?'

Before Adderley could answer, Phil saw another figure appear in the doorway. He recognised her straight away. Trudi, from the airport. He turned his attention back to Adderley. 'You didn't waste any time.'

Adderley turned, saw what he was looking at, turned back to Phil. 'Carly needs a mother. A woman round the house.'

'Doesn't your good book say something about living in sin?'

'We've got . . . separate rooms. If it's any of your business.'

Phil gave a snort of laughter. 'Separate rooms? What, till your daughter goes to bed?' He shook his head. 'Fucking hypocrite.'

'You've got no right to—'

'Aw, shut up,' said Phil, waving his hand dismissively, staggering slightly from the effort. 'You're a fucking hypocrite. Admit it. Beating your wife, then going to church and asking for forgiveness. Then coming home and doing it all again. Hypocrite. Weak . . . spineless . . . little . . . hypocrite . . . '

Adderley looked like he didn't know whether to hit Phil or run from him. Instead, he spoke. 'I'll have your job for this. Just you wait.'

Phil pointed a finger, having to squint in order to do so. 'Yeah? Not if I have you first.' He leaned in to him, Adderley recoiling from his lethal breath. 'You're scum, you. You know that? Scum. The kind of man the police hate. The kind that's too fucking scared to attack other men so he takes it out on women and children. Scum. That's what you are.'

Adderley said nothing.

'And I'm going to have you. One way or the other. Fucking have you . . .'

'I'm going to call the police,' said Adderley, turning to go.

'Yeah, you do that, mate,' said Phil, attempting another laugh. 'Tell them what I said and why I'm here. Tell them how handy with your fists you are when it comes to your wife. Sure they'd love to know that.' He looked over to the house once more. 'She know what she's got coming, does she? The lovely Trudi? Is it going to be her we're looking for in a couple of months' time?'

Adderley walked away.

Phil watched him go. Then, convincing himself that his actions had been victorious, he made his way back to his car.

And passed out.

20

'Call the police, Roy, you've got to ...'

Trudi stood in the hall beside Adderley, waiting for him to respond in some way. Instead she saw him do something she had never seen before. He twisted his face, contorting it into several shapes, all of them unpleasant. She watched, fascinated and a little scared, as his lips started moving. He was talking to someone, but not her. Someone who wasn't in the room with them.

He turned away, his conversation going on without her. Eventually he nodded. Mind made up.

Trudi watched him. 'Roy?'

He turned to her, eyes unfocused, mouth curled into a snarl. 'Shut up, just ... shut up ...' He turned away, paced up and down the hallway, a trapped animal in a too-small cage. 'I'm ... thinking ... Got to think ...' He resumed his one-sided conversation.

Trudi stepped back, watched him. She had never seen Roy like this before. Happy, sweet and, she had to admit, sexy Roy. This was a different side to him. Scared. Angry. And slightly unhinged. Watching him, seeing that animalistic snarl, she could suddenly believe some of the things she had heard about him. She felt a frisson run through her. Not an altogether unpleasant feeling.

He stopped walking, went into the living room. She followed. He crossed to the window, looked out.

'He's still there. Just, just sitting there . . . '

He sighed, turned away, shaking his head.

'Got to get out . . . got to get out . . . '

'What, now?' asked Trudi. 'Where you going?'

He turned back to her. And there was that animalistic look in his eyes again. But this time there wasn't anything of the snarling, aggressive beast about it. Just something feral and trapped, ready to spring loose, take out anyone or anything who tried to stop it.

'You questioning me?'

'What?' Something in his voice, his eyes, made Trudi instinctively step back. This wasn't like the aggression of a few moments earlier. This was something else.

His eyes flicked to a Bible on a shelf. It was just about the only book in the house, apart from the Argos catalogue. Though given the scarring and tears on its heavy leather cover, the missing and torn pages sticking out, it looked like it had been used as more than just a book. A shiver went down Trudi's spine at the thought.

At that moment, for the first time, she felt scared to be alone with him.

Adderley reluctantly tore his eyes from the Bible, walked over to Trudi. Faced her, unblinking. 'I've made my judgement,' he said, voice small and hard, like a rock that could crack open to reveal white-hot lava. 'And when I've made my judgement, you don't question me.'

He walked into the hallway, grabbed his car keys from the table, opened the front door.

'But what am I—'

'You're staying here. You're doing what you're told. Know your place.'

'But I—'

'Don't question me, woman . . . '

Another step towards her, his hand raised this time. That was enough. Trudi cowered away from him, really scared now. He stood like that before her, arm raised, heavy but suspended. She closed her eyes, waiting for the blow, anticipating the pain, already flinching away from it.

But the blow never came. Roy let his arm drop, reluctantly, to his side. She studied his eyes. It was like there was something else living inside him, another identity fighting for dominance. He tore his gaze away from her. She wasn't sure, but she might have glimpsed a shudder of fear or revulsion in them as he did so.

'Roy . . .'

He didn't look at her, didn't reply, just strode out, slamming the door behind him.

Trudi stood there staring at the door. From upstairs came the sound of Carly crying; suddenly, like a wound-up air raid siren.

'Mummy . . . Mummy . . .'

Trudi, looking one way then the other and feeling unexpectedly tired, just stood there.

21

Janine stepped outside. The night was cold, dark, the threat of rain hanging heavy in the air. But she didn't feel any of that. All she could feel was the freedom.

She closed the door behind her. It hit the frame with a satisfying final thump. The sound of something ending. She grabbed hold of her suitcase, pulled it along behind her.

As she walked, she felt a pang of regret over the boys. What kind of mother was she to walk out like this? But when she remembered the look her sons had given her as they passed her on the way out with their father, the hatred and contempt, she didn't feel so bad. She would have to hang on to that image, that memory, every time she felt she had done the wrong thing. Put it in the forefront of her mind. Never forget.

Clive Street was deserted. Janine, walking quickly, idly wondered why. Was everyone behind their front doors? Locked away from the rest of the world? The pubs in the area were losing money, haemorrhaging customers, so they weren't there. But she'd read somewhere that TV viewing figures were down as well. So what else was there to do? They couldn't all be at the football like Terry. She felt a pang of envy. They would probably be having better times, better lives, than she had had with Terry. All of them.

Unless . . .

Unless they were putting up with the same thing.

She gripped the handle of the bag, walked faster. Sang a couple of bars of a song her dad used to sing when she was little. Some country song about not knowing what went on behind closed doors. It didn't matter now. Not to Janine. Because that was the old her, the old life. She was about to embark on a new one, a better one.

She walked the few streets to her allotted pick-up spot. The corner of Milton Street and Garrett Street, just by Oakwood Park. How anyone had the nerve to call it a park was beyond her. A tree-lined plateau rising from the road hid a wide, flat expanse of grass and a basketball court held within a chain-link fence. In the centre of the grass stood a small clump of trees. And that counted as a park.

Janine checked her watch. She was early. As she put her arm down, she looked along the street. A car was moving slowly towards her, headlights off, side lights only, hard to make out in the shadow of the trees. Like it had been parked there, waiting for her. She felt giddy, suddenly, stomach flipping, light-headed. This was it, she thought. No going back now. The car crawled closer. Janine readied herself.

It drew alongside her. The driver's window slid down. She waited, remembering what the voice on the phone had said. *Let the driver say the word. Don't prompt her.* She bent down.

'Strawberry,' said the driver, sitting back, features hidden in shadow.

Janine gave a tired, taut smile. 'Oh,' she said. 'Yes. Strawberry.'

'Get in.'

She opened the back door, put her bag on the seat, climbed in after it. The car began to pull away.

Janine looked in the mirror, saw the driver's eyes. Puzzlement crept over her face.

'Wait,' she said, 'you're not a woman. You're—'

'Just be quiet,' he said. 'Everything will be fine.'

Janine frowned. 'But—'

'I said be quiet.' The voice sharp, commanding.

This wasn't what she had been expecting. Not at all.

She looked round, suddenly worried. This wasn't how she had imagined it. She began to feel uneasy.

'I . . . I think I've made a mistake.'

The driver didn't reply.

'I think I want to get out now.'

Nothing.

'I want to get out now,' she said, her voice stronger, louder, tinged with panic.

'Just stay where you are.'

Janine looked round in a panic. The car hadn't got up much speed yet. The driver was still creeping along the side of the park, head going side to side, like he was trying to see if anyone had spotted him.

'I want to get out . . . '

They pulled to an abrupt stop. The driver turned to her. Anger flared in his eyes. He jabbed his finger at her. 'Just stay where you are. Do as you're told.'

Janine sat back, eyes wide. Stunned not only by the words and the tone, but by something else.

'I—'

She didn't finish her sentence. Just grabbed the handle and pushed the door. It opened. A hand appeared over the back of the front seat, trying to grab her. It missed. She managed to get out of the car. And ran.

She didn't know where she was going. Streets that she had lived on or around all her life suddenly seemed alien, unfamiliar. She just ran as hard and as fast as she could. Behind her she could hear the sound of the car turning round in the street, coming after her.

Oh God . . .

Not looking back, she ran even faster.

The car sped up. Not full speed – the driver still didn't want to be observed – but fast enough to catch up with her. Janine looked round. Houses on one side. Park on the other. Her mind whirled furiously. She could knock on a door, ask for help, get them to call 999. If they were in. If they answered the door at night. And what if they weren't, or they wouldn't? Would she be able to try another house? She doubted it. Park on the other side. Without stopping to think, she ran up the tree-lined slope on to the grass.

Once there, on the unlit stretch of dark green, she allowed herself time to get her breath back. But he could run up here, she thought. Run after me, catch me . . .

She looked round. No one. Deserted. Not even the few teenagers who occasionally congregated. For once she would have been glad to see them.

Then from behind she heard a familiar sound. The car. She turned. Headlights made their way upwards and through the trees as the driver managed to negotiate a route for himself. The engine revved, the car appeared over the brow, then on the flat of the green.

Oh shit . . .

Heart pounding so much she feared it would jump from her chest, legs aching and stomach ready to heave from the exertions, Janine ran once more.

The car didn't bother to keep its speed down or its lights low now. It was on a course for Janine. There was no way she could outrun it. She tried to put her hand in her pocket as she ran, bring out her mobile, call 999, but she didn't dare slow down enough to do so. So she ran. Blindly on.

The noise of the car increased and the grass ahead of her was suddenly starkly illuminated. He was on her.

Janine turned. The car hit her, almost breaking her in two, sending her spinning over the bonnet and windscreen.

She landed with a thud on the green.

She opened her eyes, looked down. Pain coursed all round her body like infected electricity. Her legs were the wrong way round.

She looked up once more. The car was bearing down on her.

She tried to crawl out of the way but her body wouldn't work.

The last thing she saw were the headlights hammering towards her.

Then pain.

Then nothing.

He reversed and went over her twice more.

But Janine was long gone by then.

22

Phil only woke up when the near-empty bourbon bottle rolled off his lap and on to the floor, spilling its remaining contents on him as it went.

He looked round, not knowing where he was, or, for a few seconds, who he was. He managed to refocus. He was still sitting in his car outside Roy Adderley's house. He checked the house: darkness. He checked himself: his jeans and shirt front were now soaking wet and stinking of booze. It just added to his disorientation. His mouth felt thick, sickly and sour, his head swirling and spinning like a waltzer, his stomach a combination of the two.

'Oh God . . . '

Groaned more than spoken. A plea more than a prayer.

He sighed. Checked his watch. Nearly three.

He sat back against the car seat. What was it that someone had said about three o'clock in the morning? In the dark night of the soul it's always three a.m. Something like that. And who had said it? Hemingway, Faulkner, Fitzgerald? One of them. Someone like that. Whoever it was, they were bang on.

That was just how Phil felt. The dark night of the soul. Body and mind addled and curdled from so much more than just the booze. And, like a hook in his flesh, drawing his mind away from his problems, drawing the attention of the pain he was feeling, the case he was working on. Gemma Adderley. And her husband Roy.

He checked the house once more. Still no movement. Decided it was time to do the thing he had been dreading most, putting off. Time to go home.

He turned the engine over. Band of Horses immediately began singing about a funeral. He switched it off, head pounding even more. Took a few seconds to steady himself, focus on the road ahead, to see only a single one, and begin to pull out.

As he did so, he became aware of headlights coming along the road behind him.

He checked his own car: he hadn't yet turned on the lights. He still looked stationary. He turned the engine off immediately, checked the rear-view mirror. Roy Adderley was driving back to his house.

Phil stayed where he was. Slumped down in his seat, pretended to be asleep. With one eye open. Watching.

Behind him, Adderley drove slowly to the front of his house. In his wing mirror Phil watched him turn the car's engine and lights off, get out, quietly close the car door and turn in his direction. This was it. He couldn't give himself away now.

Adderley watched Phil for what seemed like hours but was only really seconds, or at the most, minutes. Satisfied, he turned, went into his house. Closed the front door behind him.

Phil waited. When nothing more happened, no lights, no sound, no movement, he knew it was safe to drive away. He did so quietly, not putting on his lights until he was in the next street and on the way home.

He drove slowly, not wanting to attract attention to himself, not wanting to get pulled over. That would be highly embarrassing. He could probably get away with it, that wasn't a problem. Rank saw to that. But the whispers would start, word would spread. Phil's reputation would be compromised. And that was something he couldn't allow to happen.

So he drove as carefully as he could, thinking all the time, wondering just where Roy Adderley had been. Wondering what answers he would give when he was questioned properly.

Anything to avoid thinking about what was most on his mind.

PART THREE

THE SOFTEST BULLET EVER SHOT

23

The room was still spinning. Phil looked down at his feet, immediately wished he hadn't. It spun some more. He looked up. Slowly. Carefully. Tried to breathe, focus. The morning briefing was just about to get under way.

He hadn't slept, just endured a brief state of uncomfortable unconsciousness. He hadn't even made it to bed. Woken by his phone's alarm in the living room armchair, he had showered and changed clothes, but the previous night's beer and bourbon, combined with the stress he was already under, ensured he felt even more tired than previously. Not to mention hungover. Severely, nauseously hungover.

DCI Alison Cotter was standing before the room. Phil's boss and nominally the head of the inquiry, she delegated most of the work to the members of her team. Phil, as the chief investigating officer on the case, would normally be expected to address them. But Cotter had seen the state he was in and decided to take over. He knew she would be having words with him later.

'Okay,' she said to the assembled throng. 'Another day, another chance to get it right.'

Not Phil's words, hers. Her briefing, not his. He sat by her side, tried to fix an expression of intent listening to his features. Hoped he was successful.

'So I suppose I should start by asking, where are we?' She turned to him. 'Phil?'

He stood up, found his legs were made of water. Summoned imaginary ballast to them, strength to stand still and upright.

'Right,' he said, clearing his throat and closing his eyes as the room spun. He swallowed. His mouth was full of putrescent gravel. 'Gemma Adderley went missing over a month ago. We can be a hundred per cent sure that the body found is hers. Esme Russell' – he coloured slightly mentioning her name; stumbled on it – 'has done a preliminary PM. She gave me the results last night.' He paused, realised that what he had said could be misconstrued. He glanced furtively round the room. No one seemed to have picked up on it. Grateful for that, he continued. 'She says Gemma Adderley was kept alive after her abduction. She was tortured before she was killed.'

'Raped?' asked Cotter.

'Looks that way,' said Phil. 'Or at least it was attempted. Either by him being very careful or by using something else.'

'Maybe he couldn't get it up,' chimed in Sperring.

'It's a thought,' said Phil. 'Then he cut out her heart before dumping the body.'

'Was that the cause of death?' asked Cotter.

'Probably not,' said Phil. 'Her body just gave up under all the abuse, it looks like. The heart-cutting took place post-mortem.'

'Find the heart, find the killer,' said Cotter.

Phil nodded, even though he could have done without the interruption.

'So far,' he said, 'we've been looking at the husband, Roy Adderley. DS Sperring and I paid him a visit at his place of work, Birmingham International, yesterday. He ran when we tried to question him. Now he'll only talk with a solicitor present.'

'Feelings?' said Cotter.

'Seems like a good fit. He's got previous for assault and actual bodily harm. There's also been a history of disturbances at the Adderley household, and while there were no charges, he's been cautioned for spousal abuse and domestic violence. But he says that's all in the past and he's found God now.'

Sperring put his hand up. Phil nodded at him. It hurt to do so.

'Now he's just battering for Jesus,' said Sperring. 'I spoke to DS Ellison yesterday, who handled the initial MisPer inquiry, and he fancied him for it too. The daughter was a witness but she was inconclusive as to whether he was the one who drove her mother away. We can't rule out the idea that he could have paid someone to do it.'

'Has he an alibi for the night of Gemma Adderley's disappearance?' asked Cotter.

'Said he was at a Bible study group for his church,' said Sperring again. 'But that was a lie, may God forgive him. He was with his mistress. I'll talk to him today, see if he can elaborate on that.'

'He still looks the likeliest suspect at the moment, but we can't rule out someone else,' said Phil. 'The body must have been dropped in the canal sometime on Sunday night. We've set up a mobile incident room on site, but so far no one's come forward.' He turned to a young Asian woman sitting by a computer. 'How's the CCTV going, Elli?'

Elli looked slightly nervous to have all the attention of the room focused on her. She was even more relaxed in her dress than Phil, taking the laissez-faire he had introduced to an extreme. It was tolerated because she was the team's resident expert on all things computer-related. Today's T-shirt was advertising a 1950s Bela Lugosi movie, *Bride of the Monster*. The garishly rendered monster on the front was a visual representation of how Phil felt.

'Slowly,' she said. 'I've requisitioned all the footage from cameras in the area, but nothing so far. We're still looking for vans.'

'Or a boat,' said DC Imani Oliver.

Phil looked over to her. She was young, local, black and ambitious. But not ambitious in a political, careerist manner, just to be the best detective she could be. Working-class, university-educated. That dedication to the job had made her enemies in the department. But Phil liked her – and more importantly, trusted her – enormously.

'Good point,' he said.

'Thank you,' said Imani.

Phil nodded in acknowledgement, making the room spin once more.

'This sounds like the work of a full-on nutter,' said Imani. 'Ripping the heart out, taking a boat down the canal, or a van, all that. I mean, he must have somewhere he's taken the victim to . . . do what he gets up to. That takes planning, forethought. Would it help to have a psychologist on board to give us a profile, or at least some clues on how to proceed?'

Phil didn't answer. Couldn't answer. He shivered, his stomach tumbling from more than the hangover.

In the silence, Cotter answered. 'Good idea, Imani. Might be helpful, but for the moment we'll keep on with what we're doing.'

Imani nodded in response.

'Right,' said Cotter. 'There is one other thing that I was only made aware of just before this briefing.'

She looked round the room, ensuring she had everyone's full attention.

'There was a killing last night in West Bromwich.'

She paused. Sperring was about to go for a funny remark, so she cut him off.

'And there may be a connection with Gemma Adderley.'

'What d'you mean?' asked Phil.

Cotter drew herself up to her full height, looked at the team once more. 'A young mother. Janine Gillen. Killed in what seemed like a hit-and-run. But the car was used more as a murder weapon. She was chased off the road into Oakwood Park, where the driver seems to have deliberately targeted her. Mowed her down, and then, just to make sure she was dead, ran over the body several times.'

A ripple of disgust went round the room.

'So how does that link in with this case?' asked Imani.

'The on-duty pathologist noticed something odd about the body,' said Cotter. 'Despite the extreme damage, the driver seems to have gone back and removed something. Guess what?'

'The heart,' said Phil.

'Right,' said Cotter.

Phil felt that thrill run through him. He knew this was something, the strands of the inquiry knitting together. His pulse quickened; adrenalin kicked through the nausea. 'A car,' he said. 'Any idea what time?'

'Last night sometime,' said Cotter. 'No more details yet.'

Phil could almost feel his body vibrate with excitement. 'It's him,' he said, barely able to get his words out.

'Who?' asked Cotter.

'Adderley. Definitely. It's him.'

She turned to him, a genuinely quizzical expression on her face. 'Why d'you suppose that?'

'He went out in his car last night,' said Phil. 'Didn't come home until after three in the morning.'

'And how d'you know this?'

Phil looked round the room. The team were waiting for an answer. He paused, thought up a more convincing answer than the one he had been about to give.

'I . . . got someone to follow him. Find out where he went, what he did.'

Silence from Cotter. Phil felt himself reddening once more.

'After yesterday, I thought . . . ' He shrugged, tried to make it natural. 'He was a person of interest. Maybe even the prime suspect. So I got someone to follow him. That's all.'

'Who?' asked Cotter.

'A . . . ' Phil thought quickly once more. 'Confidential Informant. Owed me a favour. Got him to sit outside Adderley's house, see if anything happened. Good job too.'

'What state was the car in when it came back?' asked Imani.

'Don't know,' said Phil. 'We can send someone over to assess it after we bring him in.' He looked at Cotter hopefully.

She returned his look, but it held more questions than answers.

Phil swallowed hard. Like rocks in his throat. 'Shall we, then?' he said. 'Bring him in?'

'Do it,' said Cotter. 'But don't jump to conclusions. And remember, he'll have his solicitor with him. We don't want the interview stopped before it's started.'

'Thank you, ma'am,' said Phil. He turned to his team. 'Right. Here we go. Imani, you go to West Bromwich, see what you can find out about last night.'

Imani nodded.

'Ian, you're coming with me. We're going to pick up Mr Adderley for a little chat. Elli, keep on keeping on. See what you can turn up.' He looked at the rest of the team. 'Right. Let's get this guy.'

'Remember what I said,' said Cotter. 'Find the heart, find the killer. Bear that in mind. And quick. Once the press makes the connection – even if there isn't one – between these two murders they're going to be all over us. The last thing we need.'

Orders given, the team moved their chairs back, made ready to get on with the day. Cotter looked at Phil.

'A word, please,' she said. 'In my office.'

Feeling nauseous all over again, Phil followed her.

24

It was useless. No, worse than useless. There was no connection. It meant nothing to him at all. Nothing.

He held the heart in his latex-gloved hands, stared at it. Crushed and broken, the blood congealed and hardened on its surface. He felt nothing for it at all. Might as well be some butcher's offal.

He scanned the room, searching for the right box, the correct final resting place for the heart. But nothing spoke to him. The one he'd had planned, a dark wooden Indian box decorated with carvings and inlaid ivory, wouldn't do now. He had chosen that box specifically. The right box designed to invoke the desired memories. He had then planned to work as he usually did. Acquire the body, spend the right amount of time preparing it, remove the heart, leave the body in the correct place and alignment, then, once alone, undertake the breaking ritual. And afterwards experience what the ritual intended: the healing.

But not this time.

He looked round his room. The boxes were all in their places on the shelves. All hand-chosen, carefully considered. Some were already filled. But many more were still awaiting their contents. And that was understandable. Because this room held his life, his inner life. His *real* life. All his fears and rejections, his darkest secrets and disappointments. And he hadn't finished dealing with them yet. Hadn't finished working through them.

And now this. West Bromwich. West fucking Bromwich. What had that place to do with him? Ever? Nothing. No connection at all. Totally wrong.

He had panicked, that was what had happened, what he had to admit to himself. He had seen her body lying there and had thought quickly. His car had made plenty of noise, leaving the road and taking to the park, and her screams had been shrill and plentiful. Both those noises would have eventually brought people over, no matter how reluctant most of them were to step outside their doors at night. So he had knelt down and got to work.

A few cuts, some deeper incisions. Wasn't hard this time. Wasn't much of her left. His car had done the job for him. She looked more like a carrier bag of badly wrapped butcher's meat, crushed, dripping and splitting all over the place, than a human being. Her ribs smashed where the wheels had gone over her torso. He had snapped on the latex gloves, pushed inside her body. Her heart, or what was left of it, came out easily.

Then in his car and quickly away before anyone came. He had scanned the windows as he drove out of the park once more. Nothing out of the ordinary, no one watching. Or no one that he could see. He had kept his lights off and driven slowly. Coming quietly down the grassy ridge, finding a space in a row of parked cars. Well away from the street lights, he had parked up, watched.

Nothing. No one. Either he hadn't been heard, or no one wanted to get involved. Knowing human nature, he knew which one he believed.

Once he was certain he wasn't going to be discovered, he simply put his lights on and drove carefully away. The car was a bit of a mess, though. The front bent and bashed where he had hit her, the wheel wells and sides blood-splattered. He would have to get it cleaned. Repaired, even. Or perhaps just dump it, torch it and report it stolen. For now it was garaged, but he'd have to take it out at some point. He needed time to think about that. For now, he had more pressing matters to attend to.

The police, for one thing. What had he left at the scene? No fingerprints, as he was wearing gloves. Fibres? DNA? Could he have done that? He was always so scrupulous, so controlled about every aspect of his work, hated to let anything get out of hand, hated any variables he couldn't account for. Everything was meticulously planned.

Usually.

But last night . . . Had he done the right thing in taking the heart? Maybe he should have just left it there. Let them put her death down to a hit-and-run. Okay, a chase, hit and run, but nevertheless. Had he left footprints in the blood? On the grass? Could they get prints from that? Catch him from it? What about his car tyres? He didn't know. Didn't know anything.

He felt himself becoming agitated. No, he told himself, keep calm, keep controlled. He closed his eyes. Think. No matter what they had, witness statements or DNA, they had to find him first. Make a match. And he wasn't on file. That was the thing to keep in mind all the time. Plus his face had been covered. And his number plate was obscured and unreadable. Precautions. Control. He was all about that. And he had to keep reminding himself of that when the other moods threatened to take over.

He looked at the heart in his hands once more. Then at the box he had prepared for it. He had to do something, had to try . . . He closed his eyes. Tried to summon up the memories, the images, get the ritual started.

Nothing.

124

He sighed, opened his eyes. Felt anger rising within him. This wasn't right. Wasn't right . . .

Closed his eyes, tried again.

Waited, waited . . .

Nothing.

Anger welled inside him once more. Typical. Bloody typical. Just like all women. Leading him on, getting him to make mistakes. Even when they were dead . . .

'You coming?'

The voice came from outside the room. It hit him as swift and hard as a wrecking ball swung into his chest.

'I . . . I'll be along in a minute.'

'Well, hurry up, then. You know what the traffic's like at this time in the morning. Shall we take my car?'

'Yes.' Too quickly. He took a breath, calmed himself. 'That's fine. We'll take yours.'

Reluctantly he placed the heart in the box allocated for it, then stripped off his gloves, dropping them in the bin.

'Mustn't keep her waiting,' he said, feeling that familiar nub of anger inside him once more. 'Mustn't keep that cunt bitch waiting . . .'

He turned off the lights, locked the door and, forcing himself to stay controlled, made his way back into the real world.

25

'Come in. Close the door behind you.'

Phil did so. He eyed the seat before Cotter's desk, but, tempting though it looked, didn't sit down on it.

Cotter seated herself behind the desk, looked up, noticed Phil was still standing. 'Sit down, then.'

He did so.

Cotter had the senior office, the corner office. The room was a reflection of her personality: sleek, uncluttered, efficient. The only traces of a life beyond work were an unostentatious framed photo of herself and her partner, Jane Munnery, a city lawyer, and a squash racquet and gym bag in the corner of the room.

She regarded Phil with the kind of scrutinising stare she usually reserved for the interview room. In his fragile state, he felt himself begin to wilt under it.

'I was going to ask how you were,' she said, 'but I can see that for myself.'

Phil didn't reply. Just looked at his feet. This room wasn't spinning quite so much as the previous one, but it was still enough to make him feel queasy. That and the expectation of what Cotter was going to say.

'You were a shambles out there,' she said, pointing to the main office. 'You stink of booze and you can barely stand upright. And you're white as a sheet.' She scrutinised him further. 'Are you white? Or are you green?'

'I'm sorry, ma'am,' said Phil, as steadily as he could. 'I've . . . had a few personal issues to take care of.'

'I'm well aware of that. And I'm not unsympathetic. You've got some leave coming up. I think you should take it.'

The words, while hardly unexpected, still hit Phil hard. 'But I'm in the middle of an inquiry. I'm CIO.'

'Look at you. Stumbling all over the place—'

'I had a bad night.'

'Don't interrupt me.' Cotter's eyes shone darkly. 'Look at the way you're dressed. I've always given you a certain leeway in regard to this department's dress code, but you've gone too far. A T-shirt and jeans? And when was the last time your face was acquainted with a razor?'

Phil sighed, found he couldn't answer back to anything she had said. 'Sorry.'

'I should imagine you are.'

He held up his hand. 'Could I just say something?'

Cotter sat back, waited. Clearly she had been expecting this. 'Go on.'

'In there.' He gestured to the main office. 'The briefing. Was I out of order? Did I handle it badly?'

'You looked terrible. You smelled drunk. That's unprofessional.'

'With respect, ma'am,' said Phil, choosing his words carefully, 'I'm not the first copper to turn up hungover and I definitely won't be the last.'

'True.'

'So did I handle it badly? The look and the smell aside, of course.'

Cotter thought. 'No. I suppose you didn't. Overall. Other than a little slurring of words.'

Phil said nothing.

Cotter leaned forward. 'Look, Phil. You're a bloody good detective. One of my best. You're unconventional at times and, Ian assures me, a pain in the arse. But I tolerate that because you get results. But not this time. Take time out, Phil. Get some help. We can provide you with someone through the department. Work things through. Then, when you're ready, come back to work.' Her words were straightforward; her voice, while professional, was not unkind.

'But like you said,' said Phil, 'I was all right in there. In the briefing.'

'Yes, all things considered, I suppose you were.'

'Last night was bad. I drank too much. But I'm still focused on this case. I'm still in charge. I can still do it.'

Cotter was about to reply, but Phil cut her off.

'Please. You know what's happened.'

'Yes, I know.'

'I'm pouring everything I've got into this job to try and stop myself thinking of anything else. To keep me going. The job is all I've got. Please.' Phil felt a pleading tone enter his voice. He tried to stop it, but it had crawled there of its own volition. 'Don't take it away from me.'

Cotter sat back, thoughtful. Phil said nothing. Eventually she leaned forward again.

'Who was your CI?'

'What?' It wasn't what he had expected her to say.

'Your CI. The one who followed Roy Adderley last night. Who was it?'

'Erm . . . it—'

'Because I received a complaint from Roy Adderley's *friend*' – she spoke the word in speech marks – 'saying that you were round there last night harassing him.'

Phil felt himself reddening. 'Ah. Well . . .'

'I'm waiting.'

Phil shook his head. No point in lying. 'Yeah, it was me. After the way he was when Ian and I went to see him yesterday, we thought there must be more to him. So I . . . parked outside his house. And he saw me. Came out. There was an argument.'

'And you drove away.'

'One of us did.'

Despite the nature of the conversation, Cotter's copper instincts were still working. 'Where did he go?'

'I don't know.'

'Why not?'

Phil shrugged, apologetic.

'You passed out.'

He looked uncomfortable.

'And presumably his return woke you up.'

'Yeah. Kind of a coincidence, really.'

Cotter sat back once more, shaking her head. A smile almost appeared at the corners of her lips. 'On the one hand, that's good police work. On the other, you were a drunken, angry slob out looking for a fight. And there's no place for people like that in my team. No matter what's happened to them.'

'Yes, ma'am.'

Cotter sighed. 'Not to mention how you got there. Were you driving drunk?'

Phil said nothing. Just looked ashamed.

Cotter shook her head, mouth curling in distaste. 'Jesus Christ . . . One last chance to pull it together, Phil. Otherwise you're out of here until you can convince me you're fit to return. Got that?'

Phil felt something positive stir within him. 'Thank you.'

'Don't make me regret this. The case has been upgraded to high priority. Go on, bring Adderley in for questioning. But Phil, I want you focused. Not fixated.'

'Right.'

'He's the prime suspect, but if it's not him, you keep an open mind.'

'Okay.'

'And if it does turn out to be something more, we may – and I stress may – get some psychological help in. And you would have to be all right with that.'

Phil didn't reply. Just nodded.

'Good.' Cotter sat back. 'On you go, then.'

Phil thanked her once more, got slowly to his feet and left the office. A reprieve. Nothing more than that.

He was standing on the edge of the abyss. He just hoped he had the strength not to be pulled in.

26

'Not much chance it was an accident, then.' Detective Constable Imani Oliver stared at the crime scene in Oakwood Park.

It looked like the garden party from hell. Most of the grassed area had been taped off, giving it an air of exclusivity, while the ubiquitous white plastic tent had been erected over Janine Gillen's final resting place. Instead of caterers, paper-suited crime-scene investigators moved about. Behind barriers at a distance, the usual collection of rubberneckers were watching, along with the media.

'Thought you'd have screens up,' said Imani. 'Stop that lot from getting too much footage.'

'Screens?' Detective Constable Avi Patel laughed. 'Wish we had the budget. Anything beyond the plastic tent has to be begged for.' He looked at Imani, smile still on his face. 'Must be different over in the big city.'

Not being unkind; just banter, thought Imani. That was how she would take it. He seemed naturally cheerful. She hoped she hadn't misread that. 'Big city? We're only down the road.'

Patel nodded. 'Yeah. And we might be handing this one over to you, from what I've heard. Could be a link with that body in the canal?'

'That's what I'm here to find out. You identified her?'

'Janine Gillen. Her wallet was still in her coat pocket. Wish they were all that easy.'

'Know anything about her?'

Patel took out his notepad, read from it. 'Quite a bit. Wife of Terry Gillen. He's been on and off our radar over the years. Bit handy with his fists, that sort of thing.'

A shudder of something like recognition ran through Imani. 'Against his wife?'

'And others.' Patel checked his notebook once more. 'Yep. Cautioned. That's all.' He looked up and the earlier cheerfulness was absent. 'Fucking scum, they are. Wife-beaters.' He realised he had been talking to a woman. 'Sorry. 'Scuse my language.'

Imani smiled. 'You'll hear no argument from me.'

Patel looked relieved, continued. 'I know we get sent for training, go on courses for how to deal with this, but ...' He glanced round at his colleagues. 'Most of them? Not high on their list of priorities. Slap on the wrist, don't do it again, that sort of thing. Or even worse, when uniforms agree with the husband. Women need a smack now and again, keeps them in line. All that shit.' He shook his head, looked like he had something unpleasant in his mouth, wanted to spit.

Imani gave a short laugh. 'You sure you're actually a copper?'

He smiled, slightly shamefaced, reddened. 'Sorry. Bit of a pet hate. Just tell me to shut up.'

'No, I'm glad to hear it.' Imani found herself smiling once more. Maybe there was more to DC Patel than met the eye. 'So what's the husband got to say for himself?'

'He was out last night. First thing he said, wanted us to know it. And he's got a watertight alibi. With his kids. Watching the Villa.'

'Poor bastards,' said Imani, then looked up hurriedly. 'Sorry.'

'Don't worry,' said Patel. 'More of a cricket man myself.'

'That's okay,' said Imani. 'It's just I come from a family of Villa fans. I can remember what it was like at home when they lost. My dad wasn't worth being around.'

'Did you know that when a football team loses, the rate of domestic attacks in that area rises? What does that say about us?' said Patel. He looked at her sheepishly once again. 'Sorry. They told us that on one of our courses. Couldn't get it out of my head ever since.'

'I'll bear that in mind.' Imani looked back at the murder scene. The body was long gone, but the aftermath of the act still hung in the air. Phil Brennan always likened it to a stage set in a theatre after the actors and audience had gone home, and she could see what he meant, but for Imani it was something different. It was as though all the incidents in Janine Gillen's life, no matter how large or small or seemingly insignificant, had led her to this point. Everything. Imani didn't believe in predestination or anything religious, but there was something about moments like this, settings like this, where the forcible absence of life had occurred, that made her understand spirituality, the need for there to be something else, even the desire to take pilgrimages to certain sites in the hope that something mystical might occur. Some answers be found. Even here.

'So this husband,' she said as they walked towards the white tent. 'How did he take the news?'

Patel shrugged. 'Not that bothered really. Maybe he was in shock and it hadn't quite hit him yet. Just moaned that he couldn't take time off work to look after the kids.'

'Where does he work?'

'Roofer.' He smiled when he said it. 'Kind that doesn't bust a gut if the weather's bad.'

'What's your feeling about him? Think he did it?'

Patel stopped walking, gave the question some thought. 'Don't think so. I mean, I know he wasn't all that bothered, and of course he was a bastard to her at home, but I didn't get a murderer vibe from him. Not deliberately, anyway. Not like this. One thing he said, though. They'd started seeing a therapist, a counsellor together.'

'Really? Doesn't sound the type.'

'Don't think he was. Marriage was rocky, though. Apparently his brief told him to do it.'

'So next time he hit his wife he could say he was working on being a changed man.'

Patel gave a grim smile. 'Exactly. Anyway, he didn't last long at it. But I think Janine kept going. Became something of a bone of contention between them.'

Imani gestured towards the white tent. 'Enough to ...?'

Patel shrugged. 'And there's the question of the car as well. Terry Gillen was driving his last night. We looked it over. Not a mark on it. Well, no new ones, anyway. Nothing to match this.'

They stopped walking, in front of the tent now. Imani could see the ruts left by the tyre tracks, deep and muddy. The grass seemed to have almost been ploughed, the driver had gone backwards and forwards so much. She could also make out where the earth was much darker in colour than in other places. She knew what had been there. Or rather who.

'Body was in a right mess when we got here,' said Patel, no trace of a smile now. In fact his mood seemed to have changed the nearer he got to the murder scene, any earlier humour now completely gone. 'Some dog walker just about brought up their breakfast. Body was all over the place. Bottom half on back to front, ground into the ... well, ground, I suppose. Horrible. Horrible way to go.'

Not that there's ever a good way, thought Imani. She liked this young DC. His attitude, his thought processes, his commitment. Or at least that was what she told herself.

'There was one other thing,' said Patel. 'She had a card in her purse. For a refuge.'

'A women's refuge?'

Patel nodded. 'It's been bagged and taken as evidence, but I wrote the details down.' He tore a page out of his notebook, handed it to her. 'Here.'

She read it, looked up. 'Safe Haven,' she said. 'D'you know them?'

'Not my area, really. I'd just started asking around about them. Hadn't got very far.'

Imani smiled. 'Considering what little time you've had, I think you've done a great job.'

Patel blushed, looked away. 'Thanks. You know ... So you think it's connected with your case, then?'

'Could be. Some strong links there. Need to do a bit more digging. But thank you.' She held out her hand. 'I really appreciate the help.'

'No problem,' he said, taking it and holding it for a moment too long after shaking it.

'Why don't you come with me? I want to check out this refuge and the counsellor. And there's someone I want to bring in who might be able to link the two cases together. I'll give her a call on the way. You up for it?'

Patel smiled. 'Off to the big city?'

'If you think you can handle it.'

'Why not? It'll look good. Bit of joint enterprise, if you like. Engendering relationships across the forces. Sharing good practice. All that bollocks.'

Imani smiled. 'Another training course?'

Patel laughed. 'Paperwork'll be a bastard, though,' he said.

'You can deal with that.'

She walked away towards her car, Patel following.

27

The interview room held stories. And the ghosts of stories. They hung in the air like stale coffee-coated breath, clung to the hidden dusty corners where no cleaner could reach. They lay amongst the dead fly carcasses in the strip-light casings. Clung to the walls, refusing to be washed away by paint or paper. And in more tangible form, the table held the marks of those who had sat there previously. The names of the players, guilty and innocent and everything in between, their illiterate litanies recorded forever, biro upon biro, carving upon carving. Threats to the guilty for stitching up, grassing, all violence and horror and bloody retribution. Prayers for the innocent and invocations of despair. Heartfelt and real and often the only honest sentiments ever expressed in that space.

From that side of the table at least.

Phil sat on the other side. The clean, unmarked side. Sperring alongside him. Their story in front of them, hidden in the binding of a manila folder. About to add it to the room's collection.

Opposite sat Roy Adderley and his solicitor, Lesley Bracken. She looked professionally stoic, bored even. Adderley had the look of a man who had gone to hospital to have his bunions looked at only to be told he had something inoperable and terminal. He looked like he was about to melt into a pool of sweat. The closeness of the room amplified it, gave the atmosphere a rank edge.

'Thank you for sparing the time to come and see us, Mr Adderley,' said Phil, unable to keep the smile from his face.

'My client wishes to state that, for the record, he came here voluntarily and of his own free will,' said Lesley Bracken, the words said so often she could probably have recited them in her sleep.

'And we're very grateful,' said Phil. 'Saves us the trouble of doing this under caution. And this way nothing gets put on tape.' He opened the folder in front of him, studied it. Or pretended to. He knew exactly what he was going to say, the approach to take. Before he could start, Bracken spoke again.

'My client would also like it known that as a gesture of good will, and to demonstrate his innocence, he will not, at present, be pressing charges arising from your behaviour towards him yesterday, Detective Inspector Brennan.'

'Kind of him,' said Sperring, finding something on the wall fascinating.

'Your client ran when we identified ourselves as police officers. That what innocent men do?' Before she could say anything further, Phil continued. 'But let's get down to business.'

He stared at the words and pictures before him, playing a waiting game, making Adderley's unease rise even higher.

Eventually he looked up, straight at the nondescript man before him. Didn't look like a wife beater or a murderer. But then they very rarely did. 'Not the first time you've been in here, is it, Roy?' he said, face blank.

Adderley didn't respond. Just gave his solicitor an imploring look.

Bracken jumped in. 'Is that relevant?'

'We'll see when he answers the question,' said Phil. He turned once again to Adderley. 'Do you want to answer the question? Or shall I just tell you?'

137

'That . . . that was different,' said Adderley, voice small.

'Not so different,' said Phil. 'Assault. Bodily harm.'

'I was never charged,' said Adderley. 'It's not relevant.'

Phil smiled. 'That phrase,' he said. 'Never charged. Never proved. Not "I never did it", not "I was innocent". No. Just never charged. The refuge of the unproved guilty, that phrase. Well, you *were* charged. You were cautioned and no further action was taken. Your victims all withdrew their complaints.'

'All women,' said Sperring, before Bracken could raise an objection. 'Your victims.'

Phil leaned forward. 'Like hitting women, do you? Gives you a thrill, makes you feel big? Like a real man?'

Adderley looked down at the table, shook his head. There were things being said that even his solicitor couldn't help him with.

'You've got previous for violent attack as well, haven't you?' said Sperring. 'Against men this time.'

'Years ago,' said Adderley. 'All in the past.'

'Yeah,' said Sperring, looking down at the report in front of him. 'Looks like you always came off second best, an' all.' He glanced up. 'They used to hit you back, the other blokes? Hurt you too much?'

'I . . .' Adderley sighed. 'That was years ago,' he repeated. The words dried up and blew away as soon as they left his lips.

'Right,' said Phil. 'So now you only hit women.'

'That's not fair,' began Bracken.

'You're right,' said Phil. 'Not fair at all.'

'I . . . I'm a different man now,' said Adderley. 'I . . . don't do things like that any more. The Lord gives me strength now.'

'The Lord?' asked Phil.

'God. I worship God now. He gives me strength.'

Phil looked at him, a mocking expression on his face.

'Look,' said Adderley, 'I know I've had problems in the past.

138

Trouble with my temper an' that. But ever since I gave myself up to the Lord I've been a much better person. A much calmer one. At peace. Contented. I've put all that behind me.' He looked at Phil. 'You should try it.'

'I'm not quite that desperate,' said Phil. He opened the folder. 'May I?' Didn't wait for a response. 'Here's a transcript of an interview with Gemma Adderley, your wife. This is from . . . let's see. Two years ago. Nearly three. A complaint she made to the police about you. She gave her statement to a constable while she was in A and E. Remember? Or do they all blur into one after a while?'

Adderley dropped his gaze, bowed his head.

'Here we go. *He would hit me*, she says. *Like this time. He would get angry because I hadn't done something right, or he'd come in from work and the table wasn't set the way he wanted it or I'd made something for dinner he didn't want. Something like that. Or Carly was making too much noise playing with her dolls. Then he'd get angry with me, start to shout. Prayers and stuff. Then he'd get the Bible down. This big old book, massive and heavy, really thick, and hit me with it. All over, my arms and legs, my body. Shouting all the time, bits from the Bible, prayers. Then my head. Sometimes I'd pass out. But this time it's really bad. And he hit Carly this time. So I came down here.* There's a bit more, then she says: *It was always the same. If I go back now he'll be on his hands and knees praying for forgiveness, in tears. It always happens. Every time. And I go back to him because he promises to be better. But not this time.'* Phil looked up, put the paper down. 'But she did, didn't she? She did go back to you. Shame, really, because if she hadn't, she would probably be alive now.'

'So that's the kind of strength your God gives you, is it?' asked Sperring.

'That was a long time ago. I'm a changed man now. He saved me,' said Adderley.

139

'Didn't save your wife, though,' said Sperring.

Before Bracken could interject once more, Phil jumped in.

'Which brings us to last month. October the sixteenth, in particular. The night your wife went missing. The last time anyone saw her alive.' He checked the notes in front of him once more. 'The detective in charge of Gemma's case, DS Ellison, initially interviewed you. You said you had no idea where she might have gone. They tried to talk to her friends, but she didn't have any. You wouldn't let her have any. Apart from the other women at church, and Gemma hated going. Wouldn't go. I'm sure she paid for that. So no one knew if she was going anywhere. And then she was gone.'

It looked like Adderley was fighting back tears.

Phil ignored him. 'So. The night she disappeared. You initially said you were at Bible study. But you were actually with your new girlfriend. Why the lie?'

'I . . .'

'Did you think it would make you look suspicious? Is that it?'

'Something . . . something like that . . . '

Bracken spoke. 'My client was visiting his girlfriend, who has subsequently moved into the family home and is helping him to bring up his daughter.'

Phil looked straight at Adderley. 'Couldn't wait to get rid of one before you moved the other one in, eh? What does the Bible say about that?'

'My client realises this isn't a flattering portrait of him,' Bracken continued, 'but in light of subsequent events he thought it best to tell the truth.'

'Better late than never,' said Phil. 'And where were you last night, Roy?'

Adderley looked up, his expression an angry, hurt sneer. 'You should know.'

Sperring looked at Phil. Phil knew he was frowning.

'Just answer the question, please.'

'You were sitting outside my house. Watching. You should know.'

'That could be construed as harassment, Inspector,' said Bracken.

'No, it couldn't,' said Phil. 'Your client is a suspect in his wife's murder. Having his house watched is proper procedure.'

'But my client says you were drunk.'

'His word against mine,' said Phil, feeling anger rise within him.

'Nevertheless—' began Bracken, but Phil kept going.

'So, Roy, you got in your car and drove away. Came back about three in the morning. Where'd you been till then?'

Adderley looked to his solicitor once more.

'This would be inadmissible in court, Detective,' said Bracken. 'Whatever you're trying to prove—'

'There was another murder last night,' said Phil. 'Another woman, about Gemma's age, build, type. She was killed about the same time as Roy here went out for a drive.' He leaned forward. 'So I'll ask again. Where were you last night?'

Adderley stared round the room, looking for ways of escape. His mouth worked but no sound emerged.

'Janine. That was her name. Janine Gillen. Know her?'

'Inspector, I don't think this is—'

'You know how she died, Roy? Hit by a car. Repeatedly. How's your car today?'

'Inspector—'

'We'll need to take a look at it, of course. See what kind of state it's in today.'

Adderley dropped his head to the table, began to cry.

Bracken stood up. 'That's quite enough, Detective Inspector Brennan. My client came here today of his own free will to assist the inquiry into his wife's death. Instead, you've accused him of murdering not only her but another woman as well. Where's your evidence?' She stared at him. Silence.

'Sorry,' said Phil. 'I thought it was a rhetorical question.'

'I don't appreciate your attempts at flippancy,' she said.

'I wasn't trying to be flippant,' said Phil. 'You want evidence? We'll get evidence.'

'Should you do that,' Bracken said, picking up her bag, 'then we'll be back. But please don't harass my client again, or attempt an illegal seizure of his car. Or we will take matters further.' She turned to the door. Adderley rose as if in a dream, not believing he could actually leave. He meekly followed her out.

Phil sat back, expelled a heavy whisky-soaked breath. Rubbed his eyes. 'How . . . fucking . . . dare she . . .'

28

'Thanks for coming,' said Imani. 'I appreciate that this is short notice, that you've got plenty of other things you should be doing. Your day job, for a start.'

Marina sat back, gym bag next to her work bag at her feet. Listening. 'No problem. Luckily I'm not teaching any classes today. Just admin that I'm glad to get away from. What can I do for you?'

The Six Eight Kafé on Temple Row in the heart of the city. An independent coffee shop, all chalkboards and stripped blonde wood. The antithesis of Starbucks. Marina was sitting opposite Imani and Avi Patel. The police officers sipped various milky coffees. Marina had ordered fruit juice and water. Two manila folders lay on the table in front of them. Unopened.

'Well,' said Imani, 'I'm sure you can guess.'

Phil was her first thought. Something had happened to him. Something bad in a next-of-kin-notified kind of way. The distress must have shown on her face.

'It's work,' said Imani. 'The job you did with the child last month? Carly Adderley? I don't know if you've seen the news, but her mother's body has been discovered.'

'Yes,' said Marina. 'I'd heard. That poor kid.' She remembered the little girl. Lost, abandoned. Literally.

'Right,' said Imani. 'There's more. DS Patel here is involved in the case of another dead young woman and there are similarities.'

'You think it's the same person?'

'That's what I'm hoping you'll be able to tell me.'

'No pressure then,' said Marina, a small smile in place.

Imani returned the smile, even smaller if anything.

'Does Cotter know about this? About you asking me?'

'Not yet. I put it to her and she thinks you should be brought in if you're needed. I'm just sounding you out, getting your opinion. I think the two deaths are related.'

'What makes you say that?'

'I'll give you the files to look at. In the meantime, what d'you think about the husband? Roy Adderley, was it?'

'You mean do I think he did it?'

Imani nodded.

'Gut feeling? I didn't like him. Felt there was something off about him. Carly was returned to him once he was located but I always felt it was too soon. That there was something more the girl could have told us. That she needed more help.'

'Couldn't you do anything?'

'I voiced my opinions,' said Marina, trying to put distance and professionalism into her words. 'I'm sure they were noted down somewhere.'

'What did the CIO on the case say?'

'Hugh Ellison?' Marina suppressed a shudder. 'Tried to push the husband but couldn't get anywhere. To be honest, I don't think he was the most incisive of interviewers. Eventually had to let it go.'

Imani nodded.

Marina leaned forward, her voice dropping involuntarily, face as blank as she could make it. 'I take it Phil's running this one?'

'He is,' said Imani.

'And was this meeting his idea?'

'Definitely not,' said Imani. 'He knows nothing about it. This is all coming from me.'

Marina smiled, relief apparent on her face. 'So you're running an investigation within an investigation?'

'I'm just using my initiative, that's all.' Her features inscrutable. 'Like any good copper would do. I don't think there's any money in the budget for this, not at this stage. But I'll see what I can do.'

'So this is just a favour?'

Imani looked apologetic. 'At the moment, yes. Sorry. I know it's unorthodox, but if I'm right and these two cases are connected, I think it's safe to say you'll be on the payroll. And I wouldn't want anyone else to do it. You're uniquely placed for this. You're already involved in the investigation.'

Marina said nothing. Was Imani abusing their friendship for the sake of her investigation? Trying to look good at Marina's expense? Did she think there was a genuine need for Marina's services? Was she telling the truth? Or the worst option: was this about getting her and Phil back in close proximity again in the hope of a reconciliation?

'What d'you say?'

Marina kept thinking. Weighing things up. Part of her felt disloyal to Phil to even be considering doing this. Especially when she thought of what had happened to him after their separation. How he had seemingly not heard her words, understood her concerns and fears; how badly he had taken it.

But there was another part of her mind whirring away inside her. The part that was thrilled to be engaged on a case, to be active in pursuing criminals, using her skills to stop them. She had always found it difficult to say no, whatever the circumstances.

She looked at the manila folders on the table in front of her.

And suddenly couldn't wait to open them, see what was inside. Phil or no Phil. Money or no money.

'Okay then,' she said, reaching for them.

'Thank you,' said Imani. 'Just look them over, let me know what you think. Similarities, differences. Your hypothesis. I'd be very grateful.'

'Fine.' Marina put the folders in her work bag. 'When d'you need this by?'

'Soon as.'

'Okay. Well, like I said, it's a light work day today. I'll get straight on to it.'

'Thanks.' Imani stood up. Taking his cue, Patel did likewise. 'I really do appreciate it. You know where to find me when you've finished.'

They said their goodbyes and left the café. Marina sat and watched them go, the files burning a metaphorical hole in her bag, her mind. She would get straight on to them.

After she'd had a session at the gym.

29

Sperring turned to face Phil. Both were still in their seats in the interview room. 'So all that about a CI was bollocks, was it?'

'Yeah.' Phil sat forward, controlling the temper inside him. Trying to shake away the near-constant rage he felt. 'After what he did yesterday, the way he ran, his lying, I knew there must be something iffy about him. So I sat outside his house to see if he moved.'

Sperring just looked at Phil, shook his head.

Phil stopped rubbing his eyes, turned to him. The anger was still there. 'What? Like you've never done that.'

Sperring started to answer, but Phil stood up, began walking round the room. His body containing too much energy to remain seated. 'How many times have we had words about you taking off on your own, mavericking about? Doing stuff that's borderline illegal to get information? And now you're taking the moral high ground for what? Because I sat outside his house last night?'

'The difference is, boss,' said Sperring, staying where he was, 'I do it with scumbags who know the score, play the game. I don't do it with suspects who go crying to their solicitors. You knew he was getting his brief in here; why d'you go antagonising him?'

Phil walked round to the other side of the table, placed his

147

fists on it, stood where Adderley had sat, faced his junior officer. 'He was out last night at the same time Janine Gillen was being murdered. In his car. We have to get a warrant, see that car.'

'You heard what his brief said. You've made it impossible now. Might even give him enough time to get rid of it.'

'So there's our proof of guilt. We'll have him then.'

'Yeah,' said Sperring, 'because that's how it works. We always arrest someone with no evidence.'

Phil just stared at him.

Sperring shook his head. 'You think it's him then? Definitely?'

Phil turned away from the table, resumed pacing. 'Course it's him. Who else would it be?' He held up his fingers, counting off. 'Means, motive, opportunity. He's got the lot.'

'And how does he know this Janine Gillen?'

'For us to find out, isn't it?'

'So he was out last night,' said Sperring. 'Right. It's still a bloody big jump for him to be Janine Gillen's killer as well. You're usually spot on, boss, but I reckon you're off on this one.'

'But look at him,' said Phil. 'He gets down on his knees and prays after he beats up his wife. He's got previous. He's got a temper on him.' He shook his head, as if confirming the truth of his words to himself. Gesturing as he walked. 'The bloke's a nutter. A dangerous, violent nutter. We have to stop him from doing it again.'

Sperring didn't reply. Phil, feeling suddenly weary as the withdrawal of adrenalin hit, sat down in Adderley's seat, facing his colleague. Sighed.

'Listen, boss,' said Sperring, his voice not unkind.

Phil looked up. He wasn't used to hearing sympathy or concern from Sperring. Usually the opposite.

'I think . . .' Sperring stopped, unsure how to proceed. 'Why don't you take a bit of time off?'

'I don't need time off. I just need to get this bastard off the streets.'

'I don't mean a lot of time, just . . .' He sighed. 'Look, all I'll say is don't mix the personal and professional. Don't bring your home life to work.'

Phil stood up once more, anger rising with him. 'You're lecturing me? You're fucking lecturing me?'

'Somebody has to,' said Sperring, raising his own voice now. 'You're heading for a breakdown the way you're going. Not only that, but you're going to make a mistake on this job and then the shit's really going to be spread. We'll all be for it.' He stood as well. 'Get a grip. Get yourself sorted. Not later, now.'

Phil stared at him, about to argue. He saw that Sperring was ready to argue too.

'I don't want a fight,' said Sperring. 'Not with you. Not about this. But if that's what I have to do to make you see sense, then I will.'

'You're going to take me on, are you? Really?'

Sperring stood his ground. 'If I have to, yeah.'

Phil stared at him until he could hold his gaze no more. He wanted to charge at Sperring, pummel the anger out of his system. But he didn't. Instead he just sighed. His head dropped. The adrenalin withdrawal was flatlining in his system now, leaving him wearier than he had ever felt. He closed his eyes. As he did so, an image of Marina appeared before him. He smiled at her, his heart breaking all over again.

'Boss?'

Phil opened his eyes. 'Yeah.' He nodded. 'Yeah.'

'What?' Sperring, wondering which way Phil's mood was going, was still ready to fight.

'Maybe I . . .' Another sigh. 'Could you hold the fort for a while?'

'Course.'

'Follow up whatever you can on—'

'I said of course. Do what you've got to do.'

Phil nodded, looking at Sperring once more. He opened his mouth to speak but the first-choice words couldn't make themselves heard. 'I'll be back later,' he said.

Sperring nodded, understood.

Phil left the room.

30

He sat in the toilet cubicle even though he didn't need the toilet. Head in hands, eyes closed tightly. Rocking slightly, backwards and forwards. Hands pressed into his face. Blocking out the world around him, refocusing, repositioning his mind. Thinking. *Thinking*. But it was no good. No matter what he did, what he said, what he thought, he could only think about the previous night.

He was trying to say the right thing, do the right thing. But he couldn't. And he could tell it was wrong from the way it was received. He found himself distracted. Making mistakes. And if he kept on like that, it would be noticed. Normally that wouldn't bother him. He'd just shrug it off. A bad day. Everybody had them. But not him. Not today. Too much suspicion.

He still couldn't stop his mind from drifting back to the night before. He relived it over and over again. The conversation in the car. Janine's unease. Unease that blossomed into panic.

Panic. That was the word. The one he kept coming back to. The whole night summed up in that one word. Panic.

The chase. Then the eventual capture. Over and over again in his mind. He hadn't stopped to think while he had been driving; just acted on impulse. She couldn't be allowed to get away. Not with what she'd seen. That had been his overriding impulse. And then when her body lay there, mangled under the wheels of his car, he had tried to salvage something.

He still didn't know whether he'd been right to do that. In a sense it didn't matter. Not any more. Because he done what he had done. And now he had to deal with the consequences of that.

He kept telling himself what he had thought earlier. No DNA. Nothing on file to make a match even if he had left any. He had got away with it.

And yet . . .

That niggling voice in the back of his mind. Trying to trip him up, pull him down. Put obstacles in the way of his more rational thoughts. Guilt? Was that it? No. He had no guilt about his actions. None whatsoever. It was therapy. And it had been *working*, before this. But it had to go on. Had to. Because it mattered. It was the only way he could be well again. In his mind. Free of everything – everyone – that had been holding him back. Stopping him becoming the person he should be. His therapist had given him the clue.

'You've got to find a way to put all this behind you,' he had said. Sitting in his armchair, dressed casually and relaxed, legs crossed as usual. Calm and knowledgeable. Sun streaming in through the windows behind him. Like a different, better world being glimpsed outside. 'Something that works for you. Take all the individual hurts and upsets, the scars and the tragedies, and box them away. They won't be gone for ever. You'll know they're there, but you won't be tempted to reopen them. Just acknowledge their existence and move on.'

And that was exactly what he had done.

He had thought long and hard about it at first. About who had hurt him, had made him the way he was. And he knew straight away. Women. Not men, never men. Just women. And not all women, either. Just the ones he had been in contact with.

His mother had been the first. But the box he had put her in

152

was so large and complex and so deeply buried that he could never think about her. If he was ever tempted to mentally exhume her, he knew the effort would be so much, the consequences so dire for himself, that it wasn't worth it. So that particular part of his past would have to stay buried. No matter what.

But the others. That was different . . .

All the girls who had broken his heart, had thought him weird, had called him names, shamed him, humiliated him, made him want to kill himself . . . they were fair game. More than that: they were necessary. But he couldn't do it with the actual women. No. For one thing he didn't know where they were, and for another, if he could find them, the police might link their deaths to him. And he couldn't have that. So after much thinking he had settled on his plan. Surrogates. That was what he needed. And he knew where to get them.

It was simple. So simple. Find the right girl. A damaged one, so she would empathise with what he had been through. Then take her. Keep her safe until she was in the correct state of mind and body. Then take her heart. Once he had that, it was a simple matter to evoke the particular memory. They were never far from his mind. Then perform the ritual. Box the heart up. Seal it. And that was that. Another part of his past put firmly away. One step closer to moving on completely. To becoming a full person. To letting his inner man become his outward one too.

His therapist would have been proud, he thought, that he was taking his advice so literally.

And it was working, he could feel it. As each heart was safely boxed away, he felt something inside him lift. A stone, a great weight. He felt he was inching his way to being like everyone else. If not happy, then at least normal.

He heard someone come into the lavatory, try the door to

the cubicle. Heard a mumbled *sorry*, then the retreat of feet. The action brought him out of his reverie. He took his hands away from his face, blinked as the light hit his eyes. Then rubbed his face, like he was trying to wake himself. He stood up. Pulled himself physically together.

Something would have to be done. He knew that. Because he'd panicked last night, because he'd spoiled the ritual and the memory was still stuck within him, he would have to rectify the situation. Sooner rather than later. And the thought of that – the promise of that – would have to be enough to keep him going. For now.

But first, he had the rest of the day to get through.

31

Marina entered her office, closed the heavy wooden door behind her, waited for the click of the lock. She put the overhead light on, then her desk lamp. Checked every corner and shadow in the room. Satisfied that she was alone, she crossed to her desk, sat down in her chair and closed her eyes. Exhaled.

She opened her eyes, sat forward. Her hands were shaking from her time in the gym. Thirty minutes with the bag in two-minute sessions, interspersed with one minute of aerobic jumps and jabs. Hard, pounding. Relentless. Just let anyone try something. She was ready for them.

She reached down into her bag, drew out the two folders Imani had given her. Ran her hands over them, feeling that familiar thrill once more. The sense of delving beyond the surface, turning the academic into the real, slipping out of one world into another. Marina knew that on one level it was probably wrong to feel this way. For the sake of decency to the dead. But she couldn't look at it like that. Despite everything that had happened in her own life, she still had to know, had to dig deeper. Find the skull beneath the skin. And the mind within it.

But she didn't even have time to open the folders before there was a knock on the door.

Marina froze. No one knew she was here today. She stood up, her gym-hardened body ready for whoever it could be.

Another knock.

She waited.

A voice. 'Hello?' Small, timorous. But male. Definitely male. Not female.

'Yes?'

'Could I . . . could I come in, please? I need to see you.'

Marina's body began to relax slightly. A student, that was all. Come to see her about work. Or just to moan about the course and use her as a surrogate mother. The usual.

'Just a minute,' she said.

Leaving the folders where they were, she walked to the door, turned the lock, opened it.

And there stood Phil.

Marina was too stunned even to slam the door.

'Hi,' he said, waiting for her familiar response. It didn't come.

She found her voice. 'How did . . . '

'How did I get in?' Phil edged himself just over the threshold. 'Police ID. Warrant card. Just asked. Can I come in?'

She was still staring as he moved forward. She made to close the door on him, but he was already too far in. It slammed harmlessly against his chest. She began to get angry.

'That your police tactics, is it? What you do with suspects when you call on them? Just barge your way in?'

'Look, Marina, I know you're angry, but please. Stop shouting. Or at least close the door.'

He stepped fully inside. The door closed behind him. She walked across the room to her desk. Once there, she turned to him, her anger becoming fury.

'You just walked in. Just showed your card and walked in. Just like that.'

'Just like that, I suppose, yeah. But Marina, I—'

'Don't you *but Marina* me.' Her voice hissing out like a sudden leak in a high-pressure hose. Before he could say anything more, she started on him. 'If you could do it, she could too, couldn't she? Just walk in here, get into my office when I'm alone. It wouldn't take much, would it? To find a warrant card, do that. She could . . .' She ran out of breath, of words, of anger. Even as she spoke, she doubted it was true. If that woman had found her way in, Marina would have been ready for her. It was one of the places she expected to be attacked. But she wasn't ready for Phil. She was still too raw, too mixed up in her own head about what they had been through, what she was going through now, to have him near her again. Not yet.

'I just wanted to talk to you, that's all. Please.' Phil's voice was plaintive. 'I need to talk to you. To see you.'

He crossed the floor to her desk. She saw him coming, opened a drawer. Took out a letter-opener. The blade glinted under the overhead lights. She pointed it at him.

'Don't,' she said. 'Just stay where you are.'

He did so. 'Marina . . .'

'Don't.'

He looked at the letter-opener. 'I could have you for possession of a dangerous weapon.'

'Try it.' Again her voice hissed. 'I know the law. It's not counted as a dangerous weapon. It serves a purpose.'

'It looks sharp.'

'It is,' she said, 'it has to be. In case I need to use it.'

Phil sighed. 'Look,' he said, 'I'm tired of this. And from the look of you, you are too. Let's talk. Let's . . . find a way through this. Come on, we have to. We need to.'

Marina looked at him then, seeing him properly for the first time since he had entered her room. He was unshaven, his hair greasy and standing up even more than usual. His eyes looked like they had been hollowed out from his face and his clothes seemed to have been slept in. There was also the faint tang of something unpleasant around him. Stale sweat and alcohol.

In that second her heart broke. She missed him so much, wanted him, desired him.

Phil moved forward. 'Marina, you're just causing us more pain ... '

'Shut up. Don't throw all this on me. And stay where you are. Don't ... ' The letter-opener brandished once more.

Phil stopped moving. He stared at her. His eyes fell to her desk. He saw the folders.

'What are those? How did you get them?'

'Something I'm working on for Imani,' she said. 'Unpaid.'

He stared at her, unconvinced. 'That's ... that's my case ... '

'It's from Imani, not you. Nothing to do with you.'

He seemed to be about to answer back, argue further, but his face fell. Collapsed.

'I can't live without you,' he said. 'Or our daughter. It's not right to keep her from me. You can't ... I can't ...' Tears formed in his eyes. 'I'm not right without you ... '

'Stop it,' she said.

'No,' he said. 'You know what I mean. You complete me. I know that sounds like bullshit but you know it's true. You're my missing part. I'm yours. That's how it's always been. Two sides of the same coin, you said. Both damaged in different ways, healing each other. That was our life. But I can't ... I can't function without you ... '

She couldn't bear to see him cry in front of her. She didn't know whether she would resent him for it, think him weak, or whether it would make her want to join in. Either way she couldn't face it. 'Just ... stop it.'

'Please . . . please, Marina. We can face this together. We can. We're stronger together than apart. Just . . . come home. Please, we can sort it . . . '

She sighed. It would be so easy. She knew that. Just to say yes and go. Do as he was asking. Take Josephina. Go forward together.

But she remembered what it had been like before she left. What she had been like before she left. Every day lived in fear, in desperation, just waiting for that woman to turn up, to destroy everything and everyone she loved, everything she held dear in the world. Every time she looked at Phil, she saw the same thing in him reflected back at her. That waiting. And she couldn't bear it any longer. But there was more than that: with it came the knowledge of his inability to protect her and their daughter. That was why she'd had no choice but to leave. To save herself and Josephina, and to perhaps save him as well.

'Please go,' she said, her voice almost breaking.

'Marina . . . '

'Please, just . . . go. Now.'

Phil stared at her, unable to comprehend what he was hearing. 'Couldn't we just—'

'Leave. Now.'

He didn't move. 'So is this it, then? Is this the end?'

Marina turned away from him. Couldn't answer. Knowing that if she did, she might well say yes to him. Return to him, take their chance. And she couldn't. *She couldn't.*

She heard movement behind her, and she knew that Phil was making his way to the door.

She heard the door open and softly close. Even then she hoped he would come back in, that he wouldn't take no for an answer, that he would make her come home. But she knew he wouldn't do that. And really she knew it wouldn't be right. If he did that, she would always feel as if she had been forced. And every time she looked at him there would be the ghost of that decision always between them.

So she stood there. Alone. Her back to the door. Telling herself she had done the right thing, made the correct decision. Waiting until she was sure he had gone.

And then the tears came.

32

'Feeling better?'

Lesley Bracken sat behind her desk. Roy Adderley came back into the office and resumed his seat, hands still wet from where he had washed them in the lavatory.

'Thanks,' he said, absently.

Rage was simmering inside him now. He had run the gamut of emotions since leaving the police station, had tried to sort things out in his head and had thought he had succeeded. But he hadn't. Now he was just left with anger.

'You're breathing rather heavily,' said Bracken, concerned. 'Sit back, take some deep breaths.'

'I'm not going to have a heart attack, if that's what you're thinking,' he said. 'Wouldn't give Brennan the satisfaction.' *And wouldn't want you to not be paid,* of course, he thought sarcastically.

He knew he wasn't having a heart attack. It wasn't his time yet. God had other plans for him.

He stood up once more. 'He has no right, no right . . .'

'No,' said Bracken, 'he doesn't. That's why we . . .'

Adderley tuned out. There were two kinds of law. God's law and man's law. He had seen man's law in action, been at the wrong end of it. And it wasn't remotely concerned with justice. Just revenge. So he didn't answer her, just let her talk. And while she talked, he thought.

'I said,' said Bracken, realising he wasn't listening, 'he was out of order to bring up your past like that.'

Adderley nodded. A plan forming in his mind. God's law. Pure law.

While she spoke, he prayed for guidance.

And received it.

He stood up. 'I'm going now. I've got things to do.'

Bracken, mid-sentence, just stared at him. He ignored her, walked out of the building and drove away. Off to gather the materials he needed for the test that lay ahead.

He sat, arms against the steering wheel, steadying himself with a few words of prayer. He heard God's voice telling him that what would come next was the right thing to do. The *just* thing to do. And he replied saying he wouldn't let Him down. That he would shine like a light in the world.

He felt his breath catch when he thought those words.

He opened his eyes once more, took in his surroundings. The Pentecostal church he attended was right before him. An old converted hall in a poor area of Handsworth, it was where he had found God. Or rather, where God had been waiting for him to enter.

He could remember the day vividly. He still didn't know what had made him walk into the church. He had been out all afternoon with friends, drinking and watching the football in a pub. His wife was at home, Carly was only four. He had thought that married life would suit him, settle him. Hoped it would. But it hadn't. All his life he had felt like he didn't fit in. Not at school, not at home. His father constantly reminded him of that, telling him he wasn't the son he wanted, favouring his brother instead. His father had been the kind of post-war petty tyrant who ruled the home with an iron fist. His mother was almost a ghost, like subservience had worn her away. And Roy had always blamed her for being weak, never forgiven her for that.

He had been, even from an early age, a failure. Not sporty at school. Not intelligent enough to do well either. Not physically robust enough to follow his father's footsteps into factory work. Not like his brother. Never like his brother.

So Roy had played up to it. If he was the idiot son, he would act like it. He got drunk, took drugs. Went looking for trouble round the city centre bars and clubs. Frequently found it. Managed to get a job, several jobs, but never held them down for long. As for women, it was just frustration after angry frustration. And then he met Gemma.

They moved in together when she was pregnant. By the time Carly was born, Roy had a job at the airport and was trying to stay on the straight and narrow. But it was hard. He missed his friends. He missed the fights, if he was honest. The raw feel of fist upon flesh, of grappling muscle on muscle, the crack of bone as his opponent went down. Usually his opponent. Sometimes himself. But he missed it. It was the time he felt most alive.

He supposed that was what had brought him into the church that Sunday three years ago.

He had sat on a chair and listened. And watched. All the people around him had seemed so content. All sharing stories about how good Jesus was, how happy he had made them, the strength they had drawn from him. They made him sound like the best friend a person could ever have. And Roy wanted some of that. When he left to go home that night, there were tears streaming down his face.

He went back. Again. And again. Soon he was asking to be baptised. He had watched them do it to others, a full pool at the front of the church, the person totally immersed in the water. He wanted that more than anything. That cleansing of body and soul. And he got it. And that, he had thought, was that.

163

Except it wasn't.

Yes, he had accepted Jesus into his life. And he now had God to help him cope. But other things hadn't changed. Gemma, for one thing. She seemed to be living her life in a way that wasn't taught at his church. She wasn't showing subservience to her husband, like the Bible said she should. She was arguing with him, telling him when he was wrong, defying him. That wasn't the way she should be behaving. Not her. Not his *wife*.

She was dressing immodestly. When he complained, she looked at him uncomprehendingly. This was how he liked her to dress, she said. How she had dressed when they first met. He told her he had moved on since then. And she would have to as well. He didn't like the way she was bringing up Carly, letting her watch inappropriate things on the television. Ungodly things. Licentiousness and worldliness.

One day he had had enough. Enough of Gemma defying him, answering him back, telling him he was wrong. Just another woman disappointing him. Enough. So he took the Bible down from the shelf and, rage blinding him, let her have it across her head.

Afterwards he was in tears, sobbing and praying and begging for forgiveness. Not only from Gemma but from God himself. Gemma forgave him. God, he felt, did too.

But that was only the first time. There were others. More and more frequent. Gemma needed to be taught a lesson. She needed God beaten into her. And he, God had told him, was the one to do it. To bring her under the obedience of her husband in a Christian manner.

And all that had led him to this.

He got out of the car, went to the boot. Took out the things he had bought, put them on the pavement, closed the car, locked it. Then picked them up, went into the church.

Praying all the while.

33

'Thank you for seeing me at such short notice.' Imani Oliver sat down in the consulting room easy chair, Avi Patel in the one next to her.

'Not a problem. Anything I can do to help.' Keith Bailey sat opposite them, one leg thrown casually over the other.

The two of them had come straight to the Relate office in the centre of Birmingham. Hidden behind a seventies strip mall of cheap clothes and phone shops and fast food outlets just off Colmore Row, it had barely any markings and no advertisements as to what went on behind the shuttered store front. Imani wasn't surprised by that: no one wanted to broadcast their marriage troubles to the world.

She had phoned ahead, checked that Keith Bailey was in. He was. He sounded young on the phone, open and pleasant. Like she imagined a counsellor would be. In person he lived up to his voice. There was something engaging about him. She felt immediately he was the kind of person she could open up to, tell her problems to. The receptionist had said he was popular with the clients. She could see why.

And he looked like she imagined too. Sandy-blonde hair, perhaps less of it than he wanted, swept over his head, parted, falling boyishly to one side. A red plaid shirt and jeans. Some kind of jewellery, metal and leather, poking out from under his right sleeve. Trainers. A heavy silver ring on his wedding finger.

Metal-framed reading glasses. Like his whole wardrobe came from Fat Face or Mantaray at Debenhams. A bookish lumberjack who'd never cut down a tree.

The room was bare. Some pre-school toys in the corner; three chairs. A couple of boxes of supermarket paper tissues sat on a small table between the two police officers and Keith Bailey. Imani nodded to them.

'I imagine they get used a lot, Mr Bailey.'

He smiled. 'Constantly. Should have shares in Tesco.' The smile faded. 'Can I ask what this is about, Detective . . . '

'Oliver,' she said. 'And this is my colleague, Detective Constable Patel.'

Patel nodded, then settled back in his chair. Just like a married couple, she thought. Except we've jumped straight to the bad bits.

'I believe you have a client called Janine Gillen.'

Keith Bailey glanced between the two of them, a slightly worried look on his face. 'Should I be discussing my clients with the police?'

'I'm afraid she's dead, sir,' said Patel. 'And we're investigating her murder.'

Bailey's eyes widened. 'Dead?' He looked at them once more, mouth open in shock, eyes eventually settling on the tissues, as if the answer lay there. 'But . . . I just saw her yesterday . . . '

'It happened last night,' said Imani. 'Very suddenly. Very nastily too, I might add.'

Bailey shook his head. 'Dead . . . Oh my God . . . '

Imani shared a look with Patel. *Get him going*, her eyes said.

'We realise this must be upsetting for you,' said Patel, 'but if you could just give us a few details about Janine Gillen, we'd really appreciate it.'

'Of course, yes . . . ' Bailey still looked like he wasn't listening properly. 'Anything I can . . . '

'What did you talk about at your session yesterday, Mr Bailey?' asked Imani. 'You did say you saw her yesterday?'

'I . . . I did, yes. She was . . . ' He looked up, quizzical. 'Should I be talking about this? Client confidentiality and all that?'

'I don't think that comes into it now, sir,' said Patel.

'Oh yes. Yes. You're right.' He rubbed his chin, eyes staring off into the distance once more.

'So what kind of things did you talk about?' Imani again.

'Well, she . . . ' Bailey shrugged. 'I don't know. I'd have to get her notes. She was . . . unhappy at home. I used to see both her and her husband. Thought they were making good progress together. So did she. But I think her husband had other ideas.'

Imani leaned forward. 'In what way?'

'Well, he . . . ' Bailey moved about, as if the seat had become suddenly uncomfortable. 'He wasn't supportive of Janine seeing me. Of the whole process, really.'

'And he let you know?'

'He did. Very vocally. One session he just walked out. Effing and blinding. Awful. Never came back again.' He shrugged. 'But you get that sometimes. You tend not to see people at their best in this job.'

'But she still came to visit you after that? Janine?'

Bailey nodded.

'Did her husband not mind?' asked Patel.

Bailey's voice dropped, became conspiratorial. 'I don't think he knew. Or if he did, she tried to sugarcoat it somehow. Told him it was good for her. I don't know.' He became silent then, pensive. Shook his head. 'So she never reached the refuge, then.'

'Refuge?'

'Yes, Safe Haven. I could tell she wasn't happy with her home life. An abusive husband, and it sounded like he was turning her children against her too. There wasn't a lot more I could do for her really. It was a toxic environment and things clearly weren't going to get any better. So I suggested a way out. But I was too late. He got her.'

Neither Imani nor Patel answered. Bailey looked between the two of them, his expression quizzical. 'He did . . . do it, didn't he?'

'We're keeping an open mind at the moment, Mr Bailey,' said Patel.

'This refuge,' said Imani, before Bailey could speak again. 'Have you any details?' She took out her notepad, noticing that Patel had done the same.

'Er . . . yes,' he said, and got up, crossed to a filing cabinet behind him. He took out a card, handed it over. 'This is it. A phone number and an address. Obviously they'd appreciate discretion when you go to call.'

'Of course,' she said.

'Is there anything else you can tell us, Mr Bailey?' asked Patel.

He frowned. 'I . . . don't think so. That's just about everything from yesterday.'

'Did she mention any other men?' asked Imani. 'Friends, boyfriends, even?'

'No,' he said. 'No one. She was very lonely, really. Quite isolated, I thought.' He sighed. 'I felt sorry for her. Sweet girl. Just married the wrong man.' He shook his head once more. 'Not alone there, sadly.'

Imani and Patel shared a glance. Imani stood.

'Well, we'll not take up any more of your time, Mr Bailey. If you do think of anything more, please don't hesitate to get in touch.' She handed him her card.

He took it. 'Thank you. I will.' He sighed. 'Poor girl. Times like this, makes you wonder why you bother.'

'I'm sure you did what you could to help her. We'll see ourselves out.'

Out on the street, Imani took a deep breath. She turned to Patel. 'What did you think?'

'What a depressing place. Suppose it would be, though.'

'Not much laughter in there.' She looked at the card in her hand. 'Fancy a trip to a refuge?'

He smiled. 'Who's doing the paperwork for all this?'

'Toss you for it,' she said.

His smile widened. 'Got a better idea. Tails, you do the paperwork. Heads, I do the paperwork. And I get to buy you dinner.'

'If it's tails, don't I have to buy you dinner?'

He shrugged. 'Only if you want to.'

She smiled. 'And I suppose now's the time you tell me you've got a two-headed coin.'

He returned her smile. 'You're too clever for me.'

34

By the time Phil drove up in his Audi, Wheeler Street in Handsworth, the home of the One True Church of God Pentecostal church, had been cordoned off.

Phil pulled up by the police tape, got out. Walked over to the nearest uniform, showed him his warrant card.

'DI Brennan,' he said. 'I'm expected.'

The call had come in just after he had left the university. He had sat in his car for what felt like years, trying to pull himself together after his abortive attempt to talk to Marina. His first thought was to take the rest of the day off. Find a pub somewhere and drink the daylight hours away. Then the night-time ones too. But he stopped himself from doing that. It wasn't easy, and it took a huge amount of willpower, but he managed it. He patched himself up, at least as far as facing other people went, talked himself into being as functional as possible, and drove towards the station.

He never got there. A call came in for him, reporting a disturbance at a church in Handsworth. Someone had barricaded themselves inside, taken hostages. And they would only speak to Phil.

'Who is it?' he had asked.

'Roy Adderley. Says you've been questioning him.'

Phil's heart sank. 'Yeah. On suspicion of murder.'

The sergeant on the other end of the phone laughed. 'I think this is what you might call an escalation of the situation.'

Phil drove straight to Handsworth. The afternoon was drawing to a close as he got there. The clouds threatening to let loose once more. The darkness of early dusk creeping over the city.

The uniform led him through the barrier towards the church. A mobile incident van had been set up in the middle of the street. He headed straight for it. Sperring was already inside.

'Here he is,' said the DS.

Another man was sitting with Sperring, a bank of CCTV and communication instruments before him. They all showed the outside of the church.

'You Phil Brennan?' said the man, rising.

Phil identified himself, shook his hand.

'Mike Battersby. Hostage Negotiation Unit. He's been asking to speak to you and you only.'

'Lucky me,' said Phil. 'What's happening in there?'

Battersby was tall, stocky and black. Dressed in a suit and shirt, no tie. 'Went in a couple of hours ago, from what we can gather. Closed the place up. Couple of cleaners in there, local community volunteers. Both women. Had a couple of jerry cans with him. Full of petrol.'

'Oh God,' said Phil. 'I can see where this is going.'

'You're not wrong. Poured petrol all over himself and got the two women as hostages. Won't let them go, won't leave, won't do anything until you talk to him.'

Phil sighed. This was all he needed, he thought, suddenly weary beyond belief. 'He given any reason for this?'

'Apart from the fact he's mental?' said Sperring.

Battersby gave him a sour look. 'Nothing. Wouldn't go into details until you got here.'

'How d'you contact him?'

'Mobile.'

Phil nodded. 'Okay then. Give him a call. Tell him I'm here.'

Battersby dialled. Waited. 'Mr Adderley?' he said eventually. 'I've got Detective Inspector Brennan for you.' He handed Phil the phone.

'DI Brennan here,' said Phil. 'What's going on, Roy?'

'Detective Brennan?' Adderley's voice was shrill, tinged with madness. 'I want to talk to you.'

'So talk.'

Battersby gave Phil a sharp look. That clearly wasn't the tone he was supposed to take.

'Not here.'

'Where, then? Shall we make a date? Cosy little bistro, bottle of wine?'

Silence on the line. Phil was aware that Battersby was gesturing at him. He ignored him.

'Just insults,' said Adderley eventually. It sounded like he had been crying. 'That's all I get. No respect. Just accusations. Insults.'

Phil sighed. 'Let the women go, Roy. Then we'll talk.'

'No. they stay here. If any of your armed police try to storm this church, I'll use my lighter. Then we'll all go up. Got that?'

'Got it. So what d'you want to do, Roy?'

'Come inside,' said Adderley.

'Into the church?'

'Yes.'

Beside him, Battersby was shaking his head vigorously, trying to attract his attention.

'Just a moment, please,' said Phil. 'I have to put you on hold.' He covered the mouthpiece with his hand, turned to Battersby. 'What?'

'No,' said Battersby. 'Under no circumstances are you going in there.'

'He wants to talk to me,' said Phil.

'Are you being deliberately stupid?' said Battersby. 'He's volatile, in an unpredictable state. He needs calm handling, not provoking. We don't know what he'll do next. He could kill himself and take the two women with him.'

'He could,' said Phil. 'But he might not. Could be bluffing.'

'You going to take that chance? I'm telling you. Under no circumstances are you to go inside.'

Phil listened, said nothing. Then put the phone back to his ear. 'You still there, Roy? Sorry about that. Should have had some music to play for you. Wind you up a bit more.'

Battersby shook his head again, turned away.

'You want me to come in?' asked Phil.

'Yes,' said Adderley. 'But just you. And unarmed.'

'I never carry a gun,' said Phil. 'Hate them. Not even firearm-trained. Okay. I'll be in. Put the kettle on.' He broke the connection.

Battersby turned to him, furious. 'What the fuck are you playing at? Didn't you listen to a single word I said to you?'

'Yeah,' said Phil, taking off his leather jacket. 'And don't worry. You'll get to try your way if my way doesn't work.' He walked towards the door.

Battersby looked about to explode. 'For the record,' he said, his gaze bouncing between Phil and Sperring, 'I want nothing to do with this. You're acting on your own. Against rules and regulations. Against my better advice. If anything happens to those hostages, it's entirely down to you. D'you understand?'

'Whatever,' said Phil.

'Boss?' said Sperring.

Phil pretended he hadn't heard him.

Just stepped out of the incident van, headed straight for the church.

Trying to wipe the image of Marina in her office from his mind.

35

Imani looked at the building again. A nondescript house in a nondescript street. Somewhere in Kings Heath. The houses were all big, Edwardian and Victorian, the majority of them turned into flats. The refuge seemed at first glance to be no exception.

She got out of the car, walked up to the front door. Patel stayed in the car. No men allowed. She rang the bell. A voice came through the intercom. Imani introduced herself.

'Right,' said the voice. 'There's a camera just above your head. Could you hold your identification up to it, please?'

She looked up, saw the camera, held up her warrant card.

'Thank you,' said the voice, and the door was buzzed open.

The hallway was bright and trying to be cheery. Homely. Pictures and posters. Some that looked like they'd been done by children. The woman who stood before Imani was medium height, blonde hair pulled into two long plaits. She was dressed casually in jeans and a peasant-type blouse. If Keith Bailey, the counsellor, was Fat Face man, this, Imani decided, was Fat Face woman.

'Could I see your identification again, please?' she said.

Imani had expected that, still held her warrant card in her hand. She passed it over. The woman examined it carefully, returned it.

'Thank you.' She gave a tight smile. 'Can't be too careful.'

'Quite agree,' said Imani.

'I mean, obviously we deal with the police on a day-to-day basis, but I've never seen you before, Detective Constable Oliver.'

'No, I'm with MIS. Major Incident Squad.'

The woman's eyes widened. 'Oh dear.' She braced herself for bad news.

'Is there anywhere we can go to sit?'

'Come into the office.' She walked along the hallway to the back of the house. There was a kitchen with a door off to the side. They went through it. Inside was a desk with a chair behind it, a couple of filing cabinets, shelves two old armchairs and not much else.

'Pull up a chair,' said the woman, sitting behind the desk.

Imani dragged one of the armchairs over, sat down. 'Sorry,' she said to the woman, 'I didn't get your name.'

'Haven't given it yet. Claire Lingard. I run this place.' She didn't smile as she spoke.

Imani wasn't getting much warmth from her. But that, she thought, was to be expected. This was a woman who would be naturally wary of everyone.

'Then it's probably you I need to talk to,' said Imani. 'Have you heard of a woman called Janine Gillen?'

Claire Lingard thought for a moment. Shook her head. 'No. Should I?'

'What about Gemma Adderley?'

'Rings a bell,' she said. She thought some more. 'Wasn't that the name of the woman who was found dead in the canal?'

'That's her.'

Understanding dawned on Claire Lingard's face. 'And that's what you're working on.'

'That's right. Janine Gillen was found dead this morning. We don't know yet whether there are links between the two, but it's a line of enquiry we're following.'

'So what has it got to do with us here?'

'Janine Gillen was found with your card in her purse. It was given to her by a counsellor at Relate.'

Claire Lingard smiled. 'Bet I know which one. Keith Bailey?'

'That's right. D'you know him?'

'Should do. I'm married to him.'

Imani's eyes widened in surprise. 'Oh.' Then she thought about it. Fat Face man and Fat Face woman. Yes, she could see that.

'Our work tends to overlap sometimes. When he gets someone he thinks can go no further with their domestic situation, or is in real danger, he gives them our number.'

'Is that how you get all your referrals?'

'No,' she said, sitting back, stretching. On her own territory now. 'There's lots of ways. They can look at one of the websites, Refuge, Women's Aid, the city council, even, and phone one of the numbers on there. Depending who they are, where they are and what their needs are, they'll get put through to whoever can help them best.'

'Their needs?'

'Birmingham has a very big Asian population. Muslim women who are forced into arranged marriages, or home slavery, or even FGM, may not feel comfortable going to a refuge with other cultures there. Especially because what they've experienced is so integral to their own culture. So we know who to put where.'

'Okay,' said Imani. 'So I'm presuming that the location of this place is secret?'

'The locations of all the refuges in the city are secret.'

'Right. So how would someone get here, then? Say they phone the helpline. What happens then?'

'Well, as I said,' a slight note of irritation crept into Claire Lingard's voice, 'they would be put through to the place or person that could serve them best.'

'Assuming it was this place.'

'Well, assuming it was this place, we would tell them to be at a prearranged spot and a car would come to pick them up. We'd give them a particular word that they would expect the driver to say so they would know to get into the car. Then they'd be brought here.'

'Right.' Imani looked round the room once more. It gave as much away about the refuge as its boss was giving away about herself. Virtually nothing. 'And then what?'

'The refuge is divided up into flats, so the women can lock their own door and feel safe. Once they're here, we sort out counselling, help with money, childcare, education, whatever's needed.'

Imani nodded, thinking. 'Could someone intercept the calls? Be there to pick the women up instead of your arranged driver?'

Claire Lingard's features hardened. 'Definitely not. Are you saying someone from here did it? Definitely not.'

'No, I'm not saying that. I'm just wondering if the system could be hacked in some way, that's all. Whether that was a way this person was meeting these vulnerable women.'

Claire Lingard relaxed slightly. Imani seemed to have said the right thing.

'I couldn't think of a way. But then I'm not computer-minded.'

Imani smiled. 'Me neither. Can barely work my iPad. Did you have any calls last night?'

'I wasn't on duty,' Claire Lingard said, features impassive. 'I don't know offhand.'

'Right. Do you keep a list of the names of the women who contact you?'

'If they give their names. Some give false ones. Some of them prefer not to give any name at all. We always ask for one, just so we know who we're talking to. It's up to them what they say. Remember, we provide a confidential service. But there's a transcript made of each call. Notes are taken. We can use those notes as a basis to assess their needs.'

'D'you keep recordings of the calls?'

'No, just the transcripts.'

'But you log the calls. Keep a list.'

'Yes, of course.'

'Could I have a copy of that list, please? And a copy of the transcripts?'

Claire Lingard sat back once more. 'I don't know. I'd have to talk to my superiors. I'm sure you understand.'

'Oh, I do,' said Imani. 'Definitely.' *She's a tough one*, she thought. *Harder to crack than a walnut at Christmas.*

'Thank you.' Claire Lingard spoke as if Imani was being dismissed.

Imani didn't move. 'Look, I understand about your client confidentiality. I really do. But I'm investigating two murders. And if there's a link between these two dead women and your refuge, it's best if we all know about it, don't you think? Then we can deal with it. All of us. Together.'

Claire Lingard realised what Imani was saying. She nodded, face held tight like a mask. 'I'll get a printout for you.'

She stood up and left the room.

On her own, Imani looked round once more. She saw something on the wall behind the desk that she had overlooked before. She stood up, crossed to it. A poem. She read the title: 'The Softest Bullet Ever Shot . . .'

Then the rest of the poem.

You hurt me and chained me
Humiliated and raped me
Spoke hate to me, taunted me
Tried to kill me inside
The bullet hit slowly
Fired year after year by you
Got right in the heart of me
Spread its fire all around
But I wouldn't let it
I found I was stronger
I ran and I healed and
I built myself up again
And now I grow stronger
And stronger and stronger
And the best thing of all
Is that you're out of my head
For ever.

'The title comes from a Flaming Lips song.'

Imani jumped, turned. Claire Lingard was standing in the doorway. Imani immediately felt shamefaced, like she was a schoolgirl who had been caught in the headmistress's office.

Claire Lingard smiled, entered the room, a bundle of paper in her hands.

'You wrote that?' asked Imani.

'I was a fan of the band. Had to get the title from somewhere.'

Imani looked again at the poem, then back to Claire. 'So you . . .'

She nodded. 'It was the album I kept playing. When I was in . . . somewhere like this. The poem was my therapy. Or part of it. Now I keep it there to remind myself of how far I've come. And why I do what I do. Every day.'

'It's beautiful.'

'And necessary. It'll stay there until I go. Or until it's not necessary. Whichever happens first. And I think I know. Unfortunately.'

Imani understood the woman now. And began to warm to her. 'But your story had a happy ending.'

'Keith? Yes, it did. I was lucky to meet him after what had happened. We understand each other. Know what we've both had to go through to be happy. But not everyone is so lucky. Here.' Claire handed over the papers. 'I didn't know how far back you wanted to go. Is six months okay for you?'

'That's fine, thank you.' Imani took them off her.

Claire Lingard stood there, seemingly thoughtful.

'Two women, you say?'

'We think so.' Imani gestured to the paper. 'Hopefully no more than that.'

'You looked at the husbands?'

'It's where we always look first. We're still looking. Nothing's off the table yet.'

Claire nodded.

They shook hands.

'Let me know what happens.'

'I will.'

Imani said her goodbyes and made her way back out to the car. Patel was asleep when she got there, the radio blaring. She rapped on the window with her keys. He jumped up, startled. She smiled, got in.

'What you got there?' he asked.

Still smiling, she turned to him. 'You know how you said you would do all the paperwork for this job?'

He looked at it.

'Aw, no . . .'

180

36

'**S** t-stay where you are. I'm ... I'm warning you ... '

Phil had opened the doors of the church, walked straight inside. He took it in immediately, made judgements, decisions, just as he had been trained to do. The building was old, originally a community centre. A concrete and plasterboard exterior gave way to a bare and uninspiring interior. No adornments, a minimum of religious trappings, just rows of wooden chairs, a slightly raised stage at the front and space for an electric keyboard at the side. A simple wooden cross was on the wall, a doorway to the left.

There had been an attempt at cheering the place up, with vases of flowers dotted round the windowsills. Stalks and petals were strewn on the floor. Phil surmised that the two elderly black women cowering in the front row, clutching each other in terror, had been engaged in flower-arranging when Adderley arrived.

'I said, I'm warning you ... '

Adderley stood on the raised stage, soaking wet, squinting. Two large jerry cans beside him, the floor wet also. A cheap lighter in his hand.

'Stay where you are ... '

Phil kept walking, slowing his pace only slightly. 'What's this about, Roy?'

'I'm ... I'm innocent ...' Adderley's eyes were almost closed.

The air stank of petrol; Phil could feel the sting of it in his own eyes, light-headed from the fumes. He stopped walking, looked at Adderley.

'So simple,' he said. 'Just click and burn and it's all over . . . '

Adderley frowned: not the words he had been expecting, not sure if they were actually directed at him.

Phil continued. Tried to wipe that image of Marina away, the hopelessness that accompanied it. 'All that pain, gone. Forever . . . '

He started walking again.

'Stay back . . . '

Phil spoke louder this time. 'I said, why did you want to see me? Why me?'

'Because. Because you think I did it . . . '

'So? You think this is going to change my mind?'

'I'm innocent . . . ' Screamed at him, a cry of pain torn from Adderley's body. Then softer, 'I . . . I didn't kill her . . . ' He looked at Phil once more, focusing through the stinging fumes. Noticed how near Phil was to him. 'Stay there, stay back . . . ' He moved his thumb over the lighter. 'I'll . . . I will . . . '

Phil stopped walking. 'So if you didn't kill her,' he said, 'why all this?'

'To make you . . . make you listen to me . . . '

Phil sat down on the nearest chair. 'You want to talk to me?' He folded his arms, crossed his legs. 'Talk.'

Adderley stared at him, suspecting some kind of trick.

'Come on, Roy,' said Phil with a sigh. 'Can't wait all day. I'm sure these ladies have somewhere they'd rather be.'

The two cowering women looked up at him then. Phil saw a flicker of hope in the eyes of one of them.

'I'm waiting, Roy. Convince me that you didn't kill your wife. The one you used to regularly beat up.'

'I . . . I . . . '

182

Adderley looked at the two women. It was clear that they knew him. Phil was sure that disapproval was now mixed in with their fear. Adderley dropped his head, shame on his features.

'She ... she wouldn't do what she was told ...' he said weakly.

'So you assaulted her. Repeatedly.'

'I ... She had to learn that a ... a wife's place is in the home. She ... she had to—'

'Really? You mean when she wouldn't do what you told her, when she demonstrated independent thought, you hit her, is that it?'

'It says in the Bible, a woman must ... must submit to her husband.'

Phil stood up. Adderley flinched, held the lighter aloft once more.

'You sick bastard,' said Phil. 'You weak, pathetic little man.' He began walking forward again.

'Stay back ...'

Phil ignored him. 'What about your new girlfriend? Does she know her place?'

'Don't ... don't bring her into it ...'

'Oh, she's a good girl, is she? Does as she's told?'

'It's different, different ...'

'Right,' said Phil, still walking. 'Of course. It's different. It would be, because you're making this shit up as you go along, aren't you? Whatever it takes to justify what you do. Blame it on the Bible. Women are either saints or whores, is that it? Nothing in between? That what your book tells you?'

'I ... I ...'

'And when women, when human beings, don't fit into those roles, you get angry, is that it?'

'I ... I didn't kill her ...'

183

Phil had reached the two women. He looked down at them. 'You can go now,' he said. He looked at Adderley. 'Can't they?'

Adderley said nothing.

The women hadn't moved. 'He's not going to do anything,' Phil said. 'He's not going to hurt you. He never was. Just go. Now.'

The two women, dazed and confused, as if they were being told to leave a car crash that they thought had been fatal for them, got to their feet and moved hurriedly down the aisle and out the door.

Phil turned to Adderley. Smiled. 'Alone at last.'

Adderley kept brandishing the lighter. 'Stay . . . stay back . . .'

'Why? You scared of me? Because I'm bigger than you? Because if you hit me, I'll fight back?'

'I . . . didn't kill her . . .'

Phil reached the small stage. He looked at the jerry cans once more. One of them seemed to be quite full. He stepped up on to the stage. 'You know what? I don't fucking care.'

'Don't . . . don't swear in the house of the Lord . . .'

'Fuck you,' said Phil, still walking. He suddenly felt tired. Beyond tired. 'I don't care. I don't care about you, or your God, or your dead wife, or whether you think you're innocent or guilty or whether you were fucked by your uncle when you were a kid. I don't care about any of it.' He stood right beside Adderley. The man seemed to visibly shrink before him.

Phil reached down, picked up one of the jerry cans.

'I don't care whether my wife hates me because I can't make her feel safe, or that I'll never see my daughter again . . . I just want some peace, that's all . . .'

He held the can over his head, upended it until it was empty, soaking himself completely. His eyes were stinging.

He threw the can to one side, looked at Adderley. The man

was cowering away from him now, trying to reach the back of the stage, look for the door behind them. Phil grabbed him.

'Where you going?'

He grabbed the lighter. Adderley screamed.

'Thought this was what you wanted,' said Phil.

'Don't,' sobbed Adderley. 'Please don't . . . '

'Come on, Roy, don't be like that.' Phil pulled Adderley close to him. Above the smell of petrol, he realised that the man had pissed himself. 'This is what you wanted . . . '

He held the lighter high, moved his thumb back . . .

The armed response unit burst in.

Phil heard noise, confusion, shouting. He was grabbed, pushed to the floor, the lighter taken forcibly from his hand.

He didn't resist, didn't complain. Said nothing.

Just lay there smiling.

37

Imani had taken Patel back to the incident room and, introductions made, the two of them and Elli settled down to work.

'This is the list Claire Lingard gave me,' said Imani, hand on the pile of paper. 'From Safe Haven. They log all the calls, take a few details, that sort of thing. They're rough transcripts of the conversations. It's a long shot, but let's see if we can match some of the names with missing persons. Start with last night, go a couple of months back.'

It was hard going, as Claire Lingard had predicted. Sometimes all that had been given was a first name, and they had no way of knowing if it was false or not. But they started with Janine – not a false name; at least they knew that – and worked back from that.

'Let's look at the ones that say they want to come to the refuge,' said Patel. 'That should narrow it down a bit.'

They read. Cross-referenced.

It made for depressing reading. Imani knew that the other two were thinking the same thing. So many sad, blighted lives. So many men who hated women.

Patel shook his head, leaned back, rubbing his face and sighing. 'My God . . . Never stops, does it?'

'Tip of the iceberg,' said Imani.

They kept going.

'Here,' said Elli eventually. 'Found something. It's Gemma Adderley. Look.' She pointed to the date on the transcript, then to the missing persons report on the screen. 'They match, give or take a day or two.'

'Brilliant,' said Imani. She looked at the other two. Knew they were experiencing what she was: that copper's thrill of knowing you were on to something. 'Keep going.'

They did.

'I think . . . ' said Patel, after a while. 'Have a look at this. This woman here. Gives her name as Mandy. Then here ...'He looked at his laptop screen. 'Missing persons report for the beginning of September. Amanda Harrison. Small Heath address. Still flagged as open. Never found, never turned up. Anywhere, never mind Safe Haven.' He looked at Imani, frowned. 'So where is she?'

'Or where's the body?' said Imani.

Elli shuddered. 'You think we've got a serial killer?'

Imani kept staring at the screen, the unsmiling face of Amanda Harrison gazing back at her.

'Let's not be hasty,' she said, 'But we could be on to something.'

'What would that be, then?'

The three of them looked up. An untidy, overweight man was standing before them.

'Detective Sergeant Hugh Ellison,' he said. 'From down in Digbeth. Just passing through.'

Imani stood up, positioned herself instinctively in front of the laptop. 'Detective Constable Oliver,' she said. 'What can I do for you?'

'Oh,' he said, trying to look over her shoulder at the screen. 'Just seeing how you're doing.' He gave up and looked round the room. 'Nice place. Well funded. Always liked it here.'

Imani looked at the other two. They seemed equally uneasy, as well as clueless as to why Ellison was there.

'Is there something I can do for you, DS Ellison?' said Imani once more.

'Oh ...' He shrugged, tried to make his enquiry casual. Failed. 'I headed up the Gemma Adderley missing persons case. Heard it was murder now. Just seeing how you were getting on.'

Imani hesitated. She was naturally disinclined to share information unless she was getting something in return. But there was something shifty and unsavoury about this man that made her even more reluctant to do so.

'Spoke to your CIO. Phil Brennan?' said Ellison. 'He can vouch for me. Worked with his missus, too. Just seeing how you're getting on.'

'We're—'

'Still at the evidence-gathering stage,' said Patel.

Clearly, thought Imani, he was feeling the same as she was.

Ellison nodded. 'I know you lot think that us in Missing Persons do nothing all day. Just fill in forms, do a few internet searches and leave it at that. But we don't, you know.'

'I'm sure no one thinks that,' said Imani.

Ellison nodded, looked round the room once more. 'Well,' he said, 'I can see you're busy. I'll leave you to it.'

'Thank you.'

'But if you find anything, I'd appreciate being kept in the loop. First dibs, and all that.'

'I'll see what we can do.'

'Oh, by the way, can I get a lift back to Digbeth? Any cars going that way? Mine's in for an MOT. Had to walk up here. Don't want to do that again.'

'Sorry,' said Imani. 'Not my department, I'm afraid.'

Ellison, clearly unhappy, turned and walked out. None of them were sad to see him go.

With a mixture of anticipation and dread, they went back to work.

38

'Oh my God ...'

Marina was at home. Josephina had been picked up from school and they had survived another day. Now her daughter was playing in her room and Marina was sitting in the living room, the files on the arm of her chair, notebook and pen beside them, the local news in the background. The sounds and pictures filling the empty space in the room.

Suddenly the TV had Marina's full attention. The reporter was talking about a siege at an evangelical church in Handsworth. The camera showed the scene, and there, caught fleetingly in shot standing by an ambulance with a blanket around his shoulders, was Phil.

Marina stared, open-mouthed.

The reporter continued talking. Told the viewers of the siege by an unnamed man, and his two hostages. It was understood that the actions of a lone police officer had defused the situation.

'Phil ...' Marina kept staring. 'You're soaking ...'

The camera had moved on now; DCI Cotter, her name displayed on the screen, was talking about the bravery of the officer.

Marina kept staring in shock.

The news changed, went back to the studio. Marina kept staring. She didn't know what to think, how to feel. Seeing Phil on her TV was the last thing she would have expected. And to see him the way he'd looked – bedraggled, spent – made it even harder.

Immediately she wanted to go back to the home gym. Another session on the bag – pound it, pummel it, get rid of all the conflicting emotions she was harbouring. Ache and tire them out of her system. But she couldn't. She had Josephina to look after. It was bad enough that her daughter was being deprived of her father's company without her mother being absent too.

She looked down at the folders once more, unable to concentrate. That made her feel angry. She had been making good progress on them, had reached some interesting conclusions about the two cases and definitely needed to speak to Imani first thing in the morning. But Phil's appearance had put paid to that. So she just sat there, staring at the screen.

Phil. He had looked so alone, so . . . forlorn. And the way he had been in her office earlier . . . She felt her heart break just thinking about him.

I miss him, she thought. *I miss him being here, being with us . . . I miss . . . I miss how it used to be.*

So do it, she told herself. *Go back. Be a family again.*

She shook her head. *No. She'll take it away. I know she will. She'll wait until we're happy again, until we've let our guard down, and then, wham. She'll be there. And everything'll be gone. And I can't let her do that.*

Then another voice in her head: *She has taken everything away from you. She's taken your happiness. Is that what you want? To keep going on like that?*

Marina sat still. Said nothing, thought nothing

Her chest rose and fell with her shallow breathing. Then tears – heartbreakingly small – began to fall silently down her face.

Something had to be done, she thought. They couldn't go on like this.

She looked at the TV once more. The news was continuing. DCI Cotter was back on again, this time talking about the death of a young woman in West Bromwich.

Marina looked at the files once more, her own notes. She dried her tears.

Yes, she thought, something had to be done. And something would be done. But right now she had work to do. Cotter's appearance on TV had reminded her.

She picked up the folders. Began working again.

39

'What the hell do you think you were playing at?'

Cotter sat behind her desk. All traces of the smiling woman from the local news praising the brave actions of one of her finest officers had completely vanished. She was now flushed with rage and indignation.

Phil sat opposite her, still wrapped in the blanket. His clothes were drying on him. He smelt like he'd been swimming at a petrol station. He was exhausted beyond tiredness.

'He was bluffing.'

She stared at him. Not a good sign. Phil knew that shouting was one thing, but when his superior went quiet, matters had become serious.

'Bluffing. You've had a couple of hours to think about it, to come up with a convincing story, and that's the best you can do?'

'He . . . ' Phil shrugged. Even he had to concede that the gesture seemed futile. 'I called him on it. I knew he wouldn't do anything.'

'He had two hostages.'

'They could have got up and left at any time. He wouldn't have done anything. They were just scared. When I told them to leave, he didn't try and stop them. People can do a lot with fear. I just . . . ' he shrugged again, 'burst his balloon.'

Cotter leaned forward, her slow, patient voice at odds with

192

the unblinking, angry stare. 'You knew he wouldn't do it. Did you really?'

'Yeah.' He couldn't meet her gaze and instead pretended the blanket was slipping from his shoulders. 'Copper's intuition. He's not the type. Doesn't fit that kind of profile.'

'And what about you, Phil? What profile do you fit?'

He didn't know whether to answer or not. Suspected that whatever he said would be wrong.

Cotter sat back, still regarding him levelly. 'Phil, you were overheard. We had a long-range mic trained on you.'

Phil said nothing.

'Talking about your wife and daughter. And then pouring petrol all over yourself?'

He shrugged.

'You ignored the hostage negotiator's advice,' said Cotter. 'You were abusive and confrontational over the phone while you knew the suspect had hostages and was in a volatile state of mind. The negotiator in question, fearing the worst as a result of your actions, then refused to have anything to do with the operation once you'd entered the church.'

'I got the hostages out, didn't I? And Adderley?'

'The response team did that. You were ready to set him on fire, and yourself too.' Cotter stared at him. 'I should sack you right now for what you did. On the spot.'

Phil sighed, head down. 'I agree.'

Cotter leaned forward. 'So why shouldn't I? Give me one good reason.'

'I'm ... I'm a good detective.' He felt his voice starting to break.

Cotter picked up her pen, twirled it in her fingers. It seemed to be occupying all her attention. She spoke again. 'Can you remember one of the first things I said to you when you came to this department?'

Phil thought. He knew exactly what she was going to say. 'Not offhand, no.'

Cotter didn't call him on it. 'Then I'll remind you. I was told you had a certain reputation for unconventionality in your previous force. I was prepared to tolerate that as long as it got results and didn't make my department look bad.' She leaned forward, eyes unblinking once more. 'But I also told you I would not tolerate any maverick or reckless actions. Especially from an officer whose competence I now have serious doubts about.'

Phil nodded, eyes downcast.

'Phil, take some time off.'

He felt himself beginning to shake. 'I don't need to take time off. I'm fine. I'm . . . focused.'

She shook her head. 'No, Phil, you're not. I asked you to be focused on this one but not fixated. You weren't. As a result of your fixation, an innocent man has now . . . ' She shrugged. 'Well, you were there this afternoon; you know.'

'Innocent?' said Phil, finding his voice belatedly. 'He's got a history of violence and he's a wife-abuser. He's not innocent. And he still has no alibi for Janine Gillen's murder.'

'No,' said Cotter, 'perhaps not. But this is a high-profile case. We're getting a lot of media attention. They're linking the two murders, calling him the Heartbreaker now, for God's sake. The pressure to get a result is increasing. And I need someone who can handle it. I want you to go home, take some time off, think about things. Talk to someone. See a doctor. And when you're feeling better we'll talk.'

Phil opened his mouth to argue, but didn't have the strength to form words. In any case, he knew they would be useless.

'I'm sorry, Phil. You're no use to me as you are. Please get yourself well again.'

Phil, broken, stood up and left the room.

40

Cotter waited until the reverberation from the closed door dissipated before letting out the breath she hadn't been aware she was holding. Phil Brennan. One of the best DIs she had ever worked with. Jesus. When they went off the rails, they really went off the rails.

She could see the incident room through the half-glass panelling of her office. The nearly empty board that was the touchstone of the whole investigation. Photos of two dead women and not much else. She shook her head.

With Phil regrettably gone, she needed help with this one. And fast. She couldn't just draft in a new DI. High-profile or not, there wasn't the budget for that. She would have to promote from within. Fair enough. She knew who that would be. But would it be enough?

She thought of something Imani had said to her earlier. And the more she rolled the idea round in her head, the better it sounded. Might be just what the case needed.

She picked up her mobile, scrolled through her contacts, dialled a number.

'DCI Cotter here. How are you?'

She waited, listened to the response.

'I know. Yes. Listen. Are you interested in some work?'

'Funny you should say that,' said Marina on the other end of the line.

41

*Y*ou? No. I don't love you. I mean, I like you, but not like that.
Not that way.

He was gone, lost to reverie and memory once more.

His first real job. Some dead-end agricultural supply company. Everyone passing through on the way to other things, hopefully better, sometimes not. His work colleague, Charlotte. Always looking at him flirtily, that back-over-the-shoulder look she did, hair sprayed out, eyes dancing with promise, lips red and wide. Always getting too near him to ask him something, bending over him, letting him see down her top, knowing he was doing it. Smiling all the more.

So he had asked her out. One night after work, all of them round the corner at the pub, making their meagre cash go as far as possible.

And she had laughed.

Let's not spoil everything, she had replied at first, laughing at him. *Let's just keep it as friends.*

He had tried to grab her, just playfully, but she had twisted away every time. Not unpleasantly, always smiling. Sometimes waggling her finger in mock-admonishment. Like it was all a game to her.

Just a fucking game.

And still day after day she persisted. That smile, those eyes, the bending down ... He wasn't to blame for the way he felt. It was all her fault. He was innocent. She was doing it deliberately, leading him on. Stringing him along for weeks. Cock-teasing.

He couldn't help it, he had to respond. He thought about her when he wasn't at work. Woke up thinking about her. Went to sleep thinking about her. Talked to her when she wasn't there, imaginary conversations in his head. All different kinds. Sometimes they would be sitting on the sofa after work, just chatting. She'd be thanking him for the dinner he had made, praising his culinary skills. Sometimes they would be out together. Strolling through the park arm in arm, or in the cinema, where she was thrilled and astounded by his knowledge of foreign language films. And sometimes in bed. Where he would make her pay for all the times she had led him on and not gone all the way. He liked those scenarios the best.

So he asked her out again. But this time it felt different. He had been living with her in his mind for all that time, built up a relationship. Asking her out was just a formality really.

What? No, I told you before. Let's just be friends.

And then he said it. That he loved her. And she gave her response. *Not that way.*

He had felt like walking out of the pub there and then, never coming back, never seeing any of those people again, the humiliation too much to take. But he didn't. He stayed. And he was glad he did.

Because he saw Charlotte get friendly with Guy Winterburn. Friendly in a way she had never been with him. Never intended to be with him. And when they left together, arm in arm, he thought his head would explode.

He had been let down again. By a woman. Always by a woman. All his life they had let him down, ridiculed him, patronised him, belittled him. And he had begun to hate them. But this time there was something else. Another man. He couldn't let them get away with it. He would have his revenge. Oh yes.

The next morning he woke expecting to have forgotten about his plans for revenge, put it down to the beer talking.

But he hadn't forgotten. They were there in his mind, sharper than ever.

Over the next couple of weeks, Guy and Charlotte became closer. She didn't flirt as much with him then, just smiled occasionally. Made no real attempt to talk to him.

Guy came to work on a motorbike. His pride and joy. The Heartbreaker didn't know anything about motorbikes. But he was clever. He could learn.

One night, after they had been to the pub, Guy had had a couple of pints and got on his bike to ride home. Charlotte, with her own helmet by now, climbed on the back with him. And off they went.

They never made it.

When Guy needed his brakes, zipping between two slow-moving buses and misjudging the space, they weren't there.

He lost his right arm and both his legs from the knee down. Charlotte lost an arm.

He never saw either of them again. Which was a shame, he thought, because he still had imaginary conversations with her. Only this time he was telling her who was responsible for the crash, who had looked up motorbike maintenance on the internet, who knew which cables to cut. Who really loved her the most.

He smiled. Perhaps he should forget about her. She had learned her lesson. Or had she? She was still there, in his heart; still needed purging. Like the rest of them. He had always thought of her in a good way, really. The turning point. The one who taught him about revenge. But she was still there . . .

Yes, he thought. *Another one. Make up for that aborted operation in West Bromwich. Yes. Another. Do it right this time.*

He had to get home. Needed to be in his room. Among the

198

boxes. Couldn't be away from them too long. And scanning the airwaves.

He had to find the next one. Things were moving quickly. The police were getting close. He couldn't let that happen. Not before he was finished.

PART FOUR

SAFE HAVENS

42

Imani couldn't believe what she was hearing.

No warning, no preparation. Not even being pulled to one side and given a heads-up. Nothing. From experience she knew that wasn't how things worked; there was always consultation. But not now, not today. That, she decided, was an indication of just how much pressure Cotter was under.

The morning briefing had started as always. Cotter at the front of the team in the incident room, standing before the murder wall, bringing out people to contribute as and when they were needed. The board was mainly white space at the moment, waiting for the details to be filled in. Pictures of the two dead women, names and information beside them. Lines linking them to their partners, photos of them too. Different-colour lines linking them to Safe Haven. And that was that. For the time being.

Marina Esposito was next to Cotter. They hadn't had time to say hello, so Imani could only assume she knew why the profiler was there. The second difference that she and everyone else noticed was the absence of Phil. And Cotter wasn't about to gloss over that.

'Thank you,' she said, while the team settled themselves, notebooks before them, cooling takeout coffees and pastries beside them. 'As you're all no doubt aware, Detective Inspector Phil Brennan has unfortunately had to take some time off for personal reasons. We wish him all the best and hope he'll be back with us very soon.'

Imani saw Marina look towards the floor at the mention of Phil's name, keep her gaze rooted there.

Cotter continued. 'DI Brennan's absence gives us an opportunity to try a new approach to this investigation. Focus on several avenues that may not have been previously explored.

'Now, I'll come to the question of his replacement as CIO in a while. Before that, I want to introduce you to a couple of new additions to the team.' She gestured towards Marina. 'Some of you may know her already, but for those of you who don't, this is Marina Esposito. She works for Birmingham University and she's to be our consultant criminal psychologist.'

Marina looked up, seemingly unsure whether she should speak or not. She settled for a single 'Hello', then fell silent once more. That was apparently what was expected of her, as Cotter made no attempt to engage her in further conversation.

'Ms Esposito will be going through all the available data we have on the two murders so far and hopefully coming up with a profile of the offender that we can then work from. I'm sure you'll all extend to her every courtesy.'

No one replied.

'The other new face you see is DS Avi Patel from West Bromwich.'

Patel put his hand up, waved, smiled. The team responded in kind. They knew how to react and interact with one of their own, thought Imani. Much more comfortable on home ground.

Cotter smiled. 'Now we've promised Avi that we'll go easy on him since he's from out in the sticks, so I want you all to respect that.'

A few laughs.

'But don't be too surprised if you have to help him out with a few things. Electricity, cars, stuff that West Brom probably think is witchcraft.'

Louder laughs this time, a few jeers. Imani was sitting next to Patel. He was shaking his head, full of mock affront but grinning broadly.

'Moving on,' said Cotter, 'Forensics haven't as yet come up with anything we can use from either crime scene, but they're still looking into them. Similarly, we don't expect anything imminent from Pathology. The preliminary post-mortems have been done and further tests are being carried out. In the meantime, it's down to good old-fashioned legwork. And I'd like DC Oliver to address the team with her findings. Imani?'

At Cotter's gesture, Imani stood up, moved to the front beside the board. She turned to face the team, notebook open in her hand. This was the kind of thing Phil usually did, she thought, and he was good at it. She, however, was just nervous. She swallowed hard, tried to conquer her nerves. Not look at the negative expression on Sperring's face. She began.

'Thank you,' she said. 'DS Patel and I have been looking at similarities between the two victims. Both were in their late twenties, early thirties, both married, both with children. The important thing here, I believe, is that they were both in long-term abusive relationships. Elli' – she gestured towards her – 'has been cross-referencing information on the two women and we have discovered that they both contacted this place here. Safe Haven.' She pointed at the board, then turned back to the team. 'This is a glaring similarity and one that really needs exploring.'

She glanced at her notes. Realised she didn't need them.

'They both contacted the refuge with a view to moving in there.'

'Any similarity in their husbands?' asked Sperring.

'Not really,' Imani replied. 'Different kinds of men but the end result was the same. Like that Russian writer said about

205

everyone being happy in different ways but everybody's sadness being the same.' She glanced round the room once more, realised she might have slipped and let her university education show too much. 'Think I've got it the right way round,' she said with a self-deprecating laugh. 'Anyway. They both called Safe Haven. The refuge said they would send a car for them. Neither of them ever arrived.'

She pointed to the board again.

'Gemma Adderley disappeared a month ago. Her body was found two days ago in the canal at Saturday Bridge. Janine Gillen was found dead in Oakwood Park in West Bromwich. Both women had had their heart removed. That's too coincidental not to be the same perpetrator. We're currently working on a new theory. Looking for other potential victims. Women who called the refuge, were sent a car but who never turned up. We think he may have been intercepting calls somehow.'

'What about Janine Gillen?' asked Sperring. 'Was he disturbed?'

Patel cleared his throat. Everyone turned to him. 'I'll have a go at this one. I was the CIO on that case. There were no signs of disturbance. Apart from the obvious. Nothing seen in the surrounding area, nothing suspicious; no one's come forward with anything. At the moment we're thinking that maybe she realised what was happening and tried to get away. Or even changed her mind about wanting to go.'

'Or,' said Sperring, 'she recognised the driver?'

'Could be,' said Patel. 'We're looking into her background at the moment. Any similarities between the two women, mutual friends, stuff like that. Nothing so far, though.'

Imani took over once more. 'It'll be a long job. Lot of cross-referencing.'

'Can I just ask something?' said Marina before she could continue.

Imani shrugged. 'Sure.'

'You're looking for other victims. Or potential victims. Previous ones. D'you think he's done this before? Is there anything you've found so far to indicate that?'

Cotter jumped in before Imani could answer. 'It's a definite possibility. We're hoping that you may be able to shine some light on that for us, Dr Esposito.'

'Sure,' said Marina and fell silent.

'Safe Haven is run by a woman called Claire Lingard,' continued Imani. 'I've spoken to her and she's as concerned as we are about what's happened, offered to do everything she can to help, put all her resources at our disposal.' It hadn't quite gone that way, thought Imani, but it didn't hurt to embellish somewhat. Especially now that Claire Lingard was fully onside. 'Her husband's name is Keith Bailey. He's a counsellor for Relate.'

'Bet it's great to be at their dinner table of an evening,' said Sperring.

Some laughter.

Imani continued. 'These two might be an angle worth pursuing. Someone might have a grudge against one of them, or both of them: some disgruntled ex-husband blaming them for what happened to his relationship, something like that.'

'So is Roy Adderley definitely out of the frame for this?' said Sperring.

Cotter jumped in. 'He has no alibi for the time of Janine Gillen's murder. No. He's not off the table. No one is.'

'So that's where we are,' said Imani.

'Good,' said Cotter, standing up. Imani took that as her cue to sit. 'Thanks for bringing us up to speed, Imani.' Cotter looked round the team again. 'I think that's all fairly comprehensive. The focus of the investigation, as you can tell, is shifting. Bearing in mind what we've just heard, I'm coming to the question of the new CIO for this inquiry.'

Imani saw Sperring perk up at the words.

'Because of the sensitive nature of this investigation, because it now concerns murdered and abused women, I think it only natural that a woman should be put in charge.'

Here we go, thought Imani. Cotter stepping back into the fray herself. A quick glance at the faces round the room confirmed that she wasn't the only one thinking that.

'That's why I want DC Oliver to be the new CIO.'

Imani's heart skipped a beat.

'She's proved herself already with her discoveries and I believe she has the necessary qualities to take this investigation forward. I realise some of you may not be happy about this because of her relatively low rank, but I don't want that to cause any consternation. We're still working together on this and everyone's contribution is equally valid. I hope you'll recognise that she is in charge and treat her accordingly.' She looked straight at Imani and smiled.

Imani tried to return the smile. Managed only a grimace and a stare.

She was aware that everyone in the room was looking at her. Especially Sperring, and he wasn't happy. She was also aware of Patel's eyes on her and she noticed him wink. That went some way to make up for the expressions of the others.

'Right,' said Cotter. 'I think we've all got enough to be going on with. Can I just remind everyone that this case is high-priority. We need to get a result and quickly. The media have got hold of it, they're camping on our doorstep and whipping everyone up into a panic. They're calling him the Heartbreaker. But I don't want anyone here using that name, right? Not on this team, not in my hearing.'

She looked round. No one dared to contradict her.

'Right,' she said. 'Specifics. Another chat to Claire Lingard. Marina, you got enough to be going on with?'

Marina nodded.

'Good.' Cotter smiled at Imani again. 'Sensitivity. That's what we need. And a result.' She addressed the room once more. 'Let's go, people.'

They all got up from their chairs.

As Sperring passed, Imani was sure she heard him mutter something about shoving your sensitivity up your arse.

Patel appeared at her side. 'Congratulations,' he said. 'A promotion without being promoted.'

'Thanks,' she said. 'Hope I can do it justice.'

And just at that moment, with a sudden jangle of nerves, she wondered whether she actually could.

43

The ringing in Phil's head woke him up. He slowly pushed open his heavy eyelids, tried to focus.

Sleep hadn't come easy to him the night before. He had just slipped into a kind of alcoholic mini-coma. The fact that he had made it to bed surprised him. The last thing he could remember was sitting in an armchair in the living room, the usual balm of music and booze not working. Neil Young singing about how only love could break your heart certainly hadn't helped. Another bottle of bourbon had been devoured and all he had to show for it was a swirling head, a nauseous stomach and an acid-bitten throat.

He had started examining the events of the day – and the last few days and weeks – in the minutest detail. Wondering if there was anything he could have done differently, trying to see if there was a tipping point, an indicator of when everything had started to go wrong. And he always came back to the same one: Marina leaving. No matter which route he took in his mind, it always led back to the same place.

Marina left me. Because she thinks I can't protect her.

His eyes were open now but the ringing continued. He realised it was coming from outside his head, not inside. The front door.

He managed to throw the duvet off and slide his feet to the floor. Immediately the room began spinning and tilting.

'Oh God . . .'

He flopped back down on the bed again. Maybe if he waited, whoever it was would go away.

Another ring. They were going nowhere.

Trying again, he managed to get to his feet. The bedroom felt like one long swirling, rotating corridor that he had to brave in order to reach the other side.

A thought struck him. Was it Marina? Had she come back? Something quickened in his chest. Gave him the strength to grab his towelling robe from the back of the door, make his way down the stairs.

Better not be fucking Jehovah's Witnesses, he thought.

He opened the door, heart in his mouth.

'Hi. Sorry for calling early. Did I wake you?'

It took him a few seconds to focus properly, to lose the image of the person he wanted to see there and replace it with reality.

Esme Russell.

He sighed. 'Oh. Hi. Sorry. Slept in.' And to emphasise the point, a yawn.

Esme looked embarrassed. 'Oh. Right.' She glanced from side to side. 'Is this . . . is this a bad time?'

Phil could have laughed at her choice of words.

'Erm . . .' He tried for something witty, couldn't even find coherent. He shrugged. 'What can I say? You know what's happened.'

She nodded. Looked at him. Silence fell between them.

'Look, d'you . . . d'you want to come in?'

He opened the door wide; she nodded and entered.

Closing it behind her, Phil realised how bad he smelled. Stale body odour, stale breath and stale alcohol. And how bad he looked. 'Sorry,' he said, finding he had to mention it, show her he was aware of it. 'I must look and smell something awful.'

She smiled. 'I've experienced worse.'

'Yeah, but you work with corpses.'

She laughed, desperately trying to break the ice between them. 'True.'

'Come through,' he said, hoping that the living room was in a fairly reasonable state.

It wasn't. Newspapers, old takeaway containers, empty bottles. And that, he knew, was just from the previous night.

'Sorry about the mess,' he said, trying to bend down and pick up the worst of it, giving himself an even worse headache.

'Have you been subletting to students?' she said, trying to laugh again.

He laughed too. But not too deeply and not for long. 'Please,' he said, once he had cleared a space on the sofa, 'sit down.'

She did so.

'Can I get you a tea? Coffee?'

'Whatever you're having.'

He went to the kitchen and made a cafetière of coffee, trying all the while to pull himself together.

'Here we go,' he said, returning to the living room and setting the tray down on the table, hoping it would hide most of the booze rings left there.

She watched him as he poured, then moved along the sofa and made space for him next to her. Phil pretended not to have noticed, went and sat in an armchair.

'So,' he said, aiming for cheerful and missing, 'what brings you here so early in the morning? Haven't you got work to go to?'

'I heard what happened yesterday,' she said, taking a sip of coffee, setting it down beside her.

Phil nodded, said nothing. There was nothing he could find to say.

'I just wanted to say I'm sorry.'

'Thank you,' he said. 'But it's not your fault.'

'No, I know it's not, but I wanted to let you know that . . . you've got a friend.'

Phil looked at her from behind his coffee mug. The concern in her eyes, on her pretty face. She really was pretty. Extraordinarily so. Beautiful, even. But . . .

'Thank you,' he said. 'I really appreciate that.'

She nodded. 'I know we left things on something of a . . . well, I don't know what. But I just wanted to tell you that I'm . . . I'm here. If you . . . you know.'

Her head was bowed as she spoke. It had taken a lot for her to come and see him, he realised, a lot for her to open up in front of him. And he felt bad because, beautiful though she was, and clever and funny and perfect, she just wasn't the one he wanted to be with right now.

He looked at her again. And could sense that she knew it too.

The silence stretched between them until Esme broke it.

She drained her mug, stood up. 'I . . . I'd better go. Bodies to cut up, and all that.' She tried to smile. It didn't take.

He stood up too. It still hurt. 'Thanks,' he said. 'I'm not much company at the moment.'

'I . . . Well, you know where I am.'

She leaned in to him, unsure of whether to kiss him or not, and with Phil offering nothing in the way of guidance, settled for a peck on his cheek.

'Thank you,' he said.

She nodded, turned and left the house without once looking back.

Phil walked back to the living room, sat down in the armchair once more. His coffee was cold now. He could make another. But in the meantime, all he had to do with the day was pick up where he had left off the previous night.

Working out what the greatest thing was he had lost.

44

Claire Lingard was trying to behave as if it was just a normal day. But given what she did, there was no such thing as a normal day. Safe Haven was exactly that. Claire was proud of what she and her colleagues had achieved. The refuge, along with other such places in the city, provided a vital resource. Don't judge, just help. That was the mantra she instilled in all of her co-workers and volunteers.

Don't judge, just help.

She sat in her office, looked at the things piling up on her desk. Risk assessments. Legal documents. Social services papers. Shift rotas. All needing her attention. All vital to the running of the refuge. She sat back, closed her eyes. The events of the last few days, the murders, had made her think back to a time when she was someone else. Someone on the other side of the counter.

Help. Me.

Her old mantra, repeated over and over again. And that was what she had needed, what she had found eventually. But it hadn't been easy.

It had started at university. Exeter. Shaun, his name was. She had been aware of him for some time. With a Venn diagram of mutual friends, they saw each other at parties, bars and clubs. He was her total opposite, the total opposite of Graeme, her previous boyfriend, too. Graeme had been on the same course as her, English literature plus social sciences. Loads in common. Too much, ultimately. They stifled each other. Then she met Shaun.

A rugby-playing IT and electronics student. Couldn't have been more dissimilar. But in the way opposites attracted, they fell for each other. Hard.

At first it was purely physical. Rough, animalistic sex. Like their bodies couldn't get enough, devouring each other in every way possible. Then, as the initial spark faded, as it always did, something else took its place. A deeper, more abiding thing. Love, Claire would have called it. She presumed Shaun called it the same.

She was wrong.

After their finals, they prepared to set a course for the real world. Claire wasn't sure what she wanted to do. Shaun was. He had been offered a place at a huge electronics firm outside Reading. Good prospects, excellent starting salary. He was going to take it. He asked Claire to join him. With nothing else in her life, she did.

The first few months were wonderful. Like it had been at university when they had just met. Great sex, optimistic about the future.

But.

Claire began to feel more alone as Shaun started to work late. Not only that, but she was expected to have dinner on the table for him when he came in. At first she had done it – ironically, she thought. Shaun the breadwinner, Claire the little housewife. A game they shared. But gradually she began to feel that Shaun wasn't playing. This was what he expected of her.

All through university she had prided herself on being a strong woman. A feminist like women should be if they wanted any kind of decent life. She was ashamed at how far she had fallen from that.

One evening, down on her hands and knees cleaning the

toilet while Shaun was out God knew where, she realised things didn't feel right in her body. She was pregnant.

Shaun was delighted. As long as it was a boy, he said. She thought he was joking. He wasn't. Luckily it *was* a boy. She wanted to call him Graeme but Shaun wanted Edward, after his father. Shaun got his way. And then Claire was a stay-at-home mother.

She loved Edward, but it wasn't enough. He was often the only other human being she saw for days at a time. She had to do something. She had a degree. Time to use it.

She applied for a job with social services. Got an interview and, despite being underqualified, was accepted as a trainee social worker. She was elated. This was it. Her chance to do something for herself rather than exist day-to-day as Shaun's shadow. She told Shaun. He pretended to be pleased but she could tell he wasn't really. He went along with it at first. But things soon came to a head. One night there was no dinner made.

'Thought we could have an Indian,' she said. 'I've had a really rough day.'

But Shaun had had a rough day too. Didn't she realise that? How hard he worked? And what did she think she was doing, getting a job for herself? Wasn't his good enough for her? Didn't he bring in enough for all of them? Anyway, a mother should be at home with her son, not working and paying for childcare, letting some stranger bring him up. What kind of a mother was she?

And that was when he hit her for the first time.

Both of them were in shock. Shaun sobbed, begged her forgiveness, pleaded with her not to leave, to give him another chance. He'd never done anything like that before, didn't know what had come over him, would never, ever do it again.

So she forgave him.

But he did do it again.

The pattern was established. And Claire changed completely from that strong woman to a timid, quaking shadow, terrified of being late home, knowing he was going to ask her where she had been and who with. She dealt with abused women in her job. Was fascinated and appalled at how they could turn into doormats for some angry, weak man. And then she realised. That was her.

He told her to give up her job. She was scared, agreed that she would. But she couldn't. That was when he gave her her most severe beating. The one that put her in hospital. The one that got the police involved.

The female police officer who talked to her told her there were places she could go. Claire laughed. I know, she said. I refer people to them every day. The policewoman wasn't impressed. Told her it was time she went there herself. With her son. Because there might not be a next time.

Claire felt like an alcoholic at an AA meeting, acknowledging what she had become. She went to a refuge, taking Edward with her. She never went back to Shaun.

Gradually she regained her strength. Pressed charges. His barrister tried to tear her apart but she stood firm. He got three years. The only thing she felt as she watched him go down, in tears, was: I wish I'd done it sooner.

And that was what led to her new career.

She looked round her office once more, at the mounting paperwork on her desk that wasn't going to deal with itself. Her life was different now. So much better.

But the last few days ... She kept the flashbacks at bay, her life with Shaun. But murder on her doorstep had a habit of bringing them back.

She would have to try even harder not to let the past take hold once more. And not just for her sake.

217

45

'This is a surprise,' said Keith Bailey. 'Wasn't expecting another visit from the police so soon.' He leaned forward, frowning, serious. 'Have there been developments?'

DS Sperring shook his head. 'Not as such, sir. We're just talking to people again. Seeing if there are any more details we can get. That sort of thing.' Affable, easy.

Bailey nodded. 'Right, of course. So.' He put his hands on the desk, smiled. 'How can I help you?'

'Can you tell us again about your relationship with Janine Gillen?'

'Relationship?' Bailey frowned. 'She was my client. She and her husband at first, then just her. I told all this to the other officer, DC Oliver, was it?'

'Just double-checking, sir. Like I said, you might remember something while we're talking that you forgot yesterday. No doubt you've been thinking about this.'

'I've barely thought about anything else.'

'There you go, then. Your relationship. What was it like?'

'Fine. Professional, if that's what you're insinuating.' Sperring didn't reply. Bailey continued. 'She was a . . . broken girl. Like so many we get here.'

'What was her state of mind?'

'Upset. Distressed. Naturally, given what she'd been through.'

'And you recommended she go to a refuge.'

'I did, yes. She was at her wits' end with her husband, no way out and no future. She was scared of him. I thought the best course of action would be for her to remove herself from the family home. I gave her a card for somewhere to go.'

'Safe Haven.'

'That's right.'

'Your wife's place.' Sperring leaned forward, smiled. 'You on commission?'

'Sorry?' The natural good humour in Bailey's face turned to puzzlement. 'What . . . what are you trying to say?'

Sperring gave an expansive shrug. 'Just a joke, Mr Bailey. Sorry.'

Bailey sat back, eyed Sperring warily. He didn't speak.

'Do you have a list of all the women you've referred to Safe Haven?'

Bailey frowned. 'I'm sure I could find one for you, yes. Either Safe Haven or one of the other refuges, is that what you want?'

'Just Safe Haven for now.'

'Well, it's . . . it'll take some time. I can't remember offhand. I'll have to go and physically check through my files.'

'Thank you.'

'Although I should warn you, Detective Sergeant, that that list is confidential. My work involves dealing with a lot of vulnerable women. Women who have experienced some of the worst things another human being can do to them. They tell me things in confidence. If I were to hand it over . . . '

'It'll be treated as confidential by us.'

'I see people from all walks of life. Even yours.'

'You have my word.'

Bailey nodded reluctantly. 'I'll get it to you as soon as I can.' He looked around, towards the door. 'I'm expecting a client soon. Was there anything else?'

'There was, actually,' said Sperring, gaze not shifting from Bailey's face.

Bailey looked puzzled once more. 'Oh? What was that?'

'Did a bit of digging on you, Mr Bailey,' said Sperring.

Bailey looked at him in surprise.

'Background, that sort of thing. Just routine.'

'On me?'

'Fancy yourself as a bit of a property tycoon, don't you?'

Bailey tried to laugh. 'What?'

'You inherited a block of flats, didn't you?' said Sperring. 'Or at least a couple of old houses that had been turned into flats. That right?'

'That's correct.'

'From a . . . grandparent? Aunt? Something like that?'

'A friend of my grandmother. She left the houses to me in her will.'

Sperring smiled, nodding, as if his memory was coming back to him and he hadn't been looking on the police computer only an hour ago. 'Right,' he said. 'Bit of a kerfuffle at the time, though, wasn't there? Didn't her family claim that she'd been tricked out of them?'

Bailey stood up. 'That's ancient history, Detective Sperring. I don't see what it has to do with—'

'They went a bit further than that, though, didn't they? In their insinuations. Claimed you'd actually killed her. Forced her to sign the flats over to you, then poisoned her. Have I remembered correctly, Mr Bailey?'

Bailey stared at him, mouth open. 'Oh, come on, Detective Sperring. That's absolute bullshit. Her family had had their eye on those flats for years, so naturally they were angry when they never received them. They tried their best to smear me, but it didn't work. They took me to court and lost, it cost them a lot of money, and that was that. What has any of it got to do with Janine Gillen's death?'

Sperring shrugged. 'Don't know. Perhaps nothing.' He

smiled. 'Just wanted to check you were the same Keith Bailey, that's all.' He stood up. 'Now, about that list.'

Bailey stared at him, seemingly undecided about what to do. Eventually he said, 'I'll get it sorted for you. It may take me a few days to go through the records.'

'Sooner the better, Mr Bailey. Thank you.'

Sperring left. No handshake, warm or otherwise.

Outside, it had started to rain once more. Sperring walked towards his car. His questions had been legitimate, valid. It was a murder inquiry, after all. But his dislike of liberals was well documented. If he had managed to annoy the *Guardian*-reading hippie in the process, just a little bit, then so much the better. That made him think about Phil. He smiled. He actually missed the leftie bastard.

Shaking his head, he hurried on, out of the rain.

46

'These are the phone transcripts from women who called Safe Haven.' Elli pointed to the pile on her right. 'Next to that, a list of missing women fitting the profile of the two victims. Goes back a year. Trying to cross-reference.' She gave an uneasy smile. 'Not a simple task.'

Marina looked at Elli. She had met her before; Phil had introduced her socially. She had intrigued Marina then and continued to do so. Small, Asian, with multiple piercings and tattoos, and her own idiosyncratic dress sense. Tolerated, Marina knew, because she got results. She could see why Phil liked her.

'What does that mean?' She pointed to Elli's chest.

Elli looked down. Smiled, blushing a little, but also proud to get the chance to talk. 'My T-shirt? It's Hank Pym.'

'Right.'

The design showed various superheroes of differing sizes, with a suited, shadowed man at the centre.

'That's him there. All the rest are his incarnations. He's a superhero who's not content with having just one secret identity. Down there at the bottom, that's Ant Man. He can shrink. Then Goliath – tall, obviously. Then Yellowjacket, then Giant Man. Biggest of the lot.'

'And who's the robot behind him?'

'Ultron. Evil. He created him too.'

'So how does he get these . . . powers?' Marina wasn't really interested, but she wanted to get Elli talking.

'Pills, initially. Pills to make him feel small, pills to make him feel big.' She laughed. 'He'd make a good case study for you, I reckon.'

Marina smiled too. 'I could build a career on him. If he was real.'

If Marina's final words upset Elli, she didn't let it show.

'Right,' said Marina, 'onwards. What have you turned up so far for me to work with?'

Elli looked at the desk once more. 'Just what was said in the briefing, really. I can fill you in on what's been done in the investigation so far, if you like.'

'I know a bit of that. I've already done some preliminary work on the two cases. Imani asked me. Haven't had a chance to talk to her about it yet.'

'Yes, but Phil—' Elli froze, eyes panicked. 'The previous CIO thought we should concentrate on Roy Adderley, the husband of the first victim. Phi— He thought that—'

'You can say his name, you know,' said Marina.

Elli looked embarrassed. 'Sorry.'

'Don't worry about it. He's my husband. And he was in charge of this investigation until recently. Don't feel you can't mention him.' Marina wished she felt as calm and composed as her words and the delivery of them made her sound.

Elli nodded, head down. She didn't continue.

Marina leaned forward. 'Elli? You were saying?'

'I . . . It's not really my place to talk about this,' Elli said.

'But he works here. You can mention him.' Hoping that her voice wasn't shaking as much as she thought it was. Hoping that the heaviness inside her wasn't showing.

'It's just . . . ' Elli looked round, checked to see no one was eavesdropping. 'He's been . . . really out of sorts recently. Not himself. I know he's been suspended, but don't judge him harshly for that.'

Marina smiled. 'I won't. I don't.'

Elli nodded. They sat in silence.

Marina opened her mouth, almost spoke. Closed it again. *I'll regret it if I do*, she thought. She wanted so much to talk about her situation, about Phil. And here was someone new, someone who would listen.

No. She was here to work, and that was what she would do. But she had to admit to herself that every time she heard Phil's name, something broke inside her. Something she hoped wouldn't stay broken for ever.

'Do you . . . ' Elli was looking once more at the desk, 'do you think that's it? Or will the two of you get back together?'

Marina was floored. The last question she'd been expecting from someone she didn't really know. But then Phil had told her he suspected Elli was somewhere on the spectrum, so it wasn't so out of the ordinary.

'I . . . ' She didn't know how to answer. 'Never say never, eh?'

Elli nodded.

'Now come on. Back to work. We've got a murderer to catch.'

47

'Back again?' said Claire Lingard, attempting a smile. 'Keep this up and we'll have to get a room ready for you.'

Imani smiled in return. 'Sorry to trouble you again. Could I have a word? Couple of things I wanted to go over.'

Patel had once again been left in the car. He was very understanding about it, which Imani appreciated.

'Sure,' said Claire Lingard, 'come in.'

Imani stepped through the doorway. The refuge was beginning to feel familiar. And, bare and institutionalised as it was, it had something about it. She could imagine how some women came to call it home.

Claire again led her to her office. Once inside, with tea on the way, she sat in an armchair, beckoned Imani to join her.

'I keep these two chairs for when someone wants to talk. The desk can get in the way of that sometimes. Well, quite a lot of the time, actually.'

'I can imagine,' said Imani.

'So has there been any progress?'

'We're examining a few leads,' Imani said diplomatically. 'In fact that's what I wanted to talk to you about. Plus get a feel for the place, how it works. That sort of thing.'

Claire smiled. 'You thinking of volunteering? You wouldn't be the first policewoman we've had here. On either side of the counter.'

'I'm sure. So tell me . . . how does it run?'

'You mean financially? Local council funding, mainly. We get a grant, donations. We're a registered charity.' She looked at Imani. 'That wasn't what you meant.'

'Not exactly.'

The tea arrived. The woman who brought it in was small, round, with her hair scraped back to make her as sexless as possible. She smiled nervously, as if she was asking for permission to do so.

'Thanks, Alice,' Claire said as the woman made her way to the door.

'She looks familiar,' Imani said, once the door had closed behind her.

'The case is public knowledge so I don't mind telling you. Husband was a banker. Tried to hire her out for sex to his friends. Used to hurt her if she refused. Eventually she hit him back. He's up on his feet now, and the police thought it would be safer for her to come here. Been with us a while now.'

'Yeah, I remember that. Not my case, though. How's she settling in?'

'Well. Still needs a lot of help, therapy and such. The risk now is she gets too dependent on us. Too institutionalised. Still, goes to show that class isn't a barrier to domestic abuse.'

Imani sipped her tea.

'Did the list I gave you help at all?' asked Claire.

'Thank you, yes. We've got someone going through it at the moment. Hopefully we'll get somewhere with it.'

'Glad to help. So what can I do for you now?'

Imani put her tea down on the small table between them. Noticed the box of paper tissues, the bottle of water and two glasses for the first time. She could imagine Claire having a heart-to-heart here. Since the woman had dropped her guard, realised that Imani was here to help, she had become a different person.

'Can you take me through the procedure after someone calls you?'

'It's watertight, the whole thing.' Claire stiffened slightly.

'I'm sure it is. But he's reaching these vulnerable women somehow, so we have to look at every angle.'

The word 'vulnerable' once more struck a chord with Claire. *Must be the key to unlocking her*, thought Imani.

'What d'you need to know?'

'Take me through it. Someone phones the refuge. They're desperate, at their wits' end. They need to leave their husband, need to come here. What happens next?'

'I thought I'd told you this.'

'You did, but I need detail now.'

'Well, they'd be assessed on the phone, as I said, and then if they had to come here we'd start to make arrangements. If they phoned during the day it wouldn't be a problem. We'd find out where they were, give them a location to wait in. A café, somewhere like that, if there's one local to them. But somewhere they'd feel safe.'

'Then you'd send someone from here to get them.'

'That's right. Or if we were busy, we'd ask them to get a taxi. Give them a number of a firm we trust. Or even the police. If they haven't any money and they're in immediate danger. Or – and again, this is if they don't have money but have a little time or need to travel some distance to reach us – we get them to contact social services, get a travel warrant arranged.'

Imani was writing it all down in her notebook. 'And that's all during the daytime.'

'Right.'

'What about night? Out of office hours?'

'That's when the emergency service comes in.'

'And how does that work?'

'The line's manned by volunteers, usually. The call will come through to here. Then it's a judgement call, really. The procedure's the same. Go to a safe place, wait to be picked up.'

'Now, would this safe place ever be a street corner?'

'No. We'd still aim for a café, somewhere like that. If everywhere's closed, then somewhere well lit. People about. Street corners are usually too conspicuous.'

Imani nodded. She wanted to drink her tea but didn't want to lose the momentum of the conversation. 'And then it's the same – a volunteer driver goes to get them, or a taxi.'

Claire nodded.

'And the driver would be a woman?'

'Yes.'

Imani frowned. 'Could the call be intercepted?'

Claire shrugged. 'I . . . don't know. I would have said not, but . . . in theory anything can be intercepted, can't it? Look at all those celebrities with their hacked phones.' She looked right at Imani, a half-smile playing on her lips. 'And I'm sure you lot have done enough of it.'

Imani laughed. 'Believe me, you have no idea the red tape you have to go through to set up an intercept or a wire tap. And then you run the risk of it not being admissible in court. Not worth the hassle, usually.'

Claire smiled, drank her tea. Imani closed her notebook. 'Thanks, Claire, I really appreciate it.'

Claire looked surprised. 'That's it?'

'Just about. Could you give me the name and contact details for the volunteer who would have taken Janine Gillen's call? And the driver she would have called?'

'Sure.'

She went to her desk, looked through some records on her computer screen, printed out a sheet of A4. 'Here you go.'

Imani thanked her, made to leave. As she reached the door, Claire put a hand on her sleeve, stopped her.

'Please,' she said, and there was something in her eyes, something that went beyond professional interest and looked like real hurt, 'please tell me. When you catch him, please let me know.'

Imani gave what she hoped was a reassuring smile. 'I will,' she said.

She turned and left the refuge, feeling Claire Lingard's troubled gaze on her back all the way to the car.

48

Roy Adderley opened the door of his house, pushed it closed behind him. The noise made him jump. Reminded him of the cell he had until recently been locked up in. He imagined all doors would carry the echo of that one for a very long time.

It felt like he had just got it out of his system from the last time. Back in his old, godless, violent life. Following his release then, he thought it would never go away, the clanging behind him as a door slammed shut, any door, anywhere, but he had gradually overcome it. With God's help, of course. Or so he told himself.

He walked into the living room, reliving the last few days over and over in his mind. Like a film he couldn't get up and walk out of because he hoped against hope that every time he saw it, it would have a different ending. A better ending.

A temporary moment of madness. Police bail. Own recognisance. The terms he was allowed home on. He closed his eyes, breathed in, out. Tried to forget.

'Roy? Is that you?'

A short, fat silhouette came down the darkened hall towards him. Something in Roy Adderley's heart sank. Trudi was here. On seeing him, she ran towards him, jewellery rattling cheaply against her flesh. She flung her arms round him, pulled him close to her.

Adderley's first instinct was to push her away, and he put his hands on her, ready to do that. But he managed to stop himself. Unable to respond in any way, he just stood there, allowed her to hug him.

'God, I've been so worried about you ...'

Her voice all cranking and screeching. He flinched at the sound of it. Noting his unresponsiveness, she pushed her body closer in to his. He could smell her sweat mixed in with her perfume, feel her hot, wet skin pressed up against him.

What had he ever seen in her? Why was he even with her? This ugly whale of a woman, with her fake blonde hair, fake nails, fake tan, fake everything. Even faking her orgasms, probably, just so she could move in with him. Find somewhere stable to live. He knew her type. The Bible was full of them. Jezebel. He knew a better name for her.

Whore.

She pulled away from him, let her eyes rove all over his face. She looked concerned. Or scared. He couldn't tell which.

'What have they done to you? Oh Roy, you look terrible ...'

Then she was hugging him again, stroking his face, and he felt like he wanted to throw up.

He'd had enough. He pulled himself away from her, walked into the living room, looked round.

'Where's Carly?'

'Social workers came for her. They wanted to take her away. She's at her grandma's for now. They won't let her come back here and they want to see you. Oh Roy, what are we going to do?'

Roy closed his eyes once more. Now this. No Carly. He opened his eyes, looked around. The room was different. Different things in it, different smells. Perfume. Sweat. Stale air. Trudi's smells. Trudi's things. A trashy magazine on the arm of

231

the sofa. A coffee mug leaving a ring on the glass-topped table. An open packet of cigarettes, an empty Coke can acting as an ashtray.

He turned to her. 'What have I said about smoking in the house?'

She stared at him, dumbstruck, like he had just said something that needed translating.

'Mm? What have I said?'

She looked quickly at the offending cigarette packet, back to him. 'I . . . Sorry, Roy, I was worried about you. I've only had a couple. Didn't think you'd mind.'

Adderley felt anger rising within him once more. Like a huge red tidal wave, building and building, looking for a shore to crash down on.

'Well, I do mind,' he said, voice calm and controlled. 'If I didn't mind, I'd say you could smoke in here all the time, wouldn't I?' The last few words rising in volume, his control slipping.

She backed away from him, hurt and confusion on her face. 'I'm sorry, Roy, I was worried about you . . . '

He looked at her once more. Properly looked at her. Short, fat, ugly. How could he ever have let her into his bed? Ever allowed her to tempt him into sex? That was what she had done. Tempted him away from his wife, who wasn't perfect but he was working on her, training her. And then look what happened. And what did he have to show for it? Nothing. Just this painted whore.

'They're going to lock me up,' he said, moving slowly towards her. 'Put me on trial and lock me up again . . . '

'I'm . . . I'm sorry,' said Trudi, now with no idea what was going on but not liking it. Not knowing who this stranger was in front of her. She reached out to him once more. 'Come on, come and sit down with me. I'll—'

'Get your filthy hands off me.' The words hissed at her. 'Whore.'

She just stayed where she was, too scared to move.

'I was weak,' he said. 'I should have resisted. God told me to. And I didn't listen. If I'd only listened to him, then none of this would have happened, would it?'

Moving towards her all the time.

He pointed a rigid finger at her. 'You. Your fault. All of it.'

'Me? Wh-what have I done? What have I ever done except be there for you, Roy?'

'Shut up.' He looked round, saw the Bible on the shelf. The one that Gemma had tried her best to tear up. God's word was stronger than that. He took it down.

Trudi kept backing away, inching towards the dining table, talking all the while. 'Remember when you used to come and confide in me, tell me that Gemma wasn't being a good wife to you? Remember?'

'Shut up . . . '

'You did, Roy. You talked to me all the time about her. About what she was doing wrong. And you remember what I said, Roy? Do you? Course you do, you must do.'

'Shut up . . . '

'I said I wouldn't be like that. I'd make you happy. That's what I said. And I did, Roy, didn't I? You told me I did . . . '

'*Shut up . . . *'

He swung the Bible hard at the side of her head. The force of the blow spun her round. She landed face down on the dining table, hitting it with a thud, the impact breaking her nose, sending blood pooling.

She moaned, tried to get up.

Adderley hit her again. Then he dropped the Bible on the table beside her, picked her head up by the hair.

'Whore,' he said, smashing her face into the table once more.

'Jezebel.' And another smash. 'This is all your fault, all yours ...'

Smashing away, screaming at her all the time.

'They're going to put me away again ... again ...'

She died long before he stopped.

Adderley stared down at her lifeless, pulped body, and as the angry red wave broke and dissipated, leaving him suddenly exhausted, he finally realised what he had done.

49

Phil wasn't going to answer the phone. Probably just a sales call. Or one of his colleagues asking how he was. Saying they were all behind him. That he didn't deserve what had happened. Well, he did. He'd thought about it and had come to the conclusion that this was exactly what should have happened to him.

And then another thought: *Marina.*

He picked up the phone. 'Yeah?'

'Phil Brennan?'

The voice was familiar, but not too familiar. Heavy, Brummie. Words spoken through a lifetime of booze and fags.

'Yes?' Getting impatient now.

'Hugh Ellison. Digbeth. DS Ellison.'

'Oh. Right.' Phil carried the phone over to the sofa that Esme had previously been sitting on. He had showered since she had left, forcing his body under the hot water, standing there until it ran cold. Then dressing in whatever was to hand. A Neil Young and Crazy Horse T-shirt, old jeans. 'What can I do for you?'

'Just heard about what happened.'

'Right.' *Should have let it ring*, he thought.

'I went in there, the incident room. Just to see if there was anything I could do. Help, you know.'

'Right . . .'

Phil was becoming slightly confused now. Why was Ellison telling him this?

'They weren't very friendly, I must say.'

'Well, DS Ellison, I don't know what to say. I'm not in charge any more ...'

'They've got your missus back working for them.'

Phil's stomach flipped. And again.

'Right,' he said, mouth suddenly dry. 'I see.'

'Just giving you the heads-up.'

Phil felt that ache, that yawning chasm opening up inside him once again. That sense of vast emptiness. The feeling that he wanted to be anywhere else but where he was at that precise point in time and space. That there was somewhere else – someone else – that would fill that void for him. He knew what it was. Work. Marina. And now to make everything worse, Marina had taken his place at work. It felt like an almost physical blow.

'Why ...' He struggled to find his voice. 'Why are telling me this?'

'Like I said, just letting you know.' Ellison sighed. 'Sounds like the women have taken over on this one. That black lass, Oliver? She's in charge, I hear.'

'Imani's the CIO?' Phil was genuinely surprised. But pleased, too. She was going places. 'Well, if it has to be someone ...'

'I'd have gone for your oppo, Sperring. But they don't want a bloke. It's political correctness gone mad, that's what it is. There'll be no place for the likes of you and me in this job soon. And they didn't want me anywhere near it. They made that quite clear.'

Phil's head was reeling. 'But ... I still don't understand. What's it got to do with you?'

'My case first, wasn't it? Taken away by the glory boys. Or girls, rather.'

The last thing Phil wanted to hear was some bitter old has-been copper whose career had stalled for whatever reason sounding off to him. Not today. Not when he felt like he did. 'Well, thanks for the call.'

'They've stopped looking at Adderley.'

'What?'

'New focus, and all that. Talking to the marriage guidance bloke. Looking at the refuge. Not what we would do.'

Phil wasn't sure who he was talking about. That just made him realise, guiltily, how closely he had become fixated on Adderley. It was like he was hearing about a totally different investigation. 'Right,' he said.

'That's the way it's going now,' said Ellison.

Probably needed it, thought Phil. *After the blind alley I led everyone down.*

'Well,' he said, 'nothing to do with me. And nothing to do with you. Not any more.'

'Yeah, well. Just wanted to let you know about your missus.'

Phil hung up. He'd heard enough. Ellison's call had left him angry.

And, he reluctantly admitted to himself, more alone, more bereft, than ever.

50

'Can I come in this time?'
    'If you behave yourself. And be quiet.'

Imani and Patel had rolled up outside the address they had been given by Claire Lingard. West Bromwich Library. The building was old, late nineteenth century or early twentieth, all ornate red brick and curling stone. It looked like it had been built by philanthropists, belonging to a time when reading was considered a valued part of social improvement. It was shabby-looking, soot-blackened, but still stood out in a street of charity shops, kebab houses and closed-up store fronts.

Patel looked at her, smiled. 'This is going to be a bust, you know. Tenner says she never got the call.'

'You and your bets,' said Imani, returning the smile. 'Of course it is. Or at least we think so. But here's one for you. How's he doing this?'

'Well,' said Patel, stretching back in his seat, puffing out his chest, 'I do know about electronics and stuff.'

'You're a bloke. Of course you do.'

He smiled, puzzled. 'I never know whether you're bigging me up or putting me down.'

'And that's just the way it should be. Go on.'

'Well, I had a mate who used to work on details like that. Said it was really easy to hack a phone. Divert calls, listen in. All of that. Had another mate who used to be a journalist. Started off on a national tabloid. A Sunday one. Said one of the first things he was shown was how to hack a phone. Common practice.'

'We know that.'

'So maybe this guy could be a journalist.'

Imani shrugged. 'Keeping an open mind.' She took the keys from the ignition. 'Come on.'

They entered the library, walked up to the desk, showed their warrant cards, introduced themselves. 'We're looking for Sophie Shah. Can you tell us where we can find her, please?'

The woman behind the counter looked nervous.

'It's nothing serious,' said Patel, with what he hoped was his most charming, winning smile. 'We just need to talk to her about something.'

That seemed to reassure the woman slightly. 'I'll go and see if I can find her.' She went off to do so.

Imani and Patel looked around. The building was even more impressive from the inside, all porcelain tiling and curved arches, high ornate ceilings, large double doors of glass and wood. The shelves were more modern; the space dwarfed them, made them seem slightly out of place.

'Should have shelves going to the ceiling,' said Imani. 'That's what this place needs. Ladders against them for the librarians to scoot along on.'

Patel nodded, not really interested.

A woman walked towards them. Small, neat, either light-skinned Asian or dark-skinned Caucasian. Her face was blank, unreadable. 'I'm Sophie Shah. Claire Lingard said you'd be coming. Didn't expect you this quickly.'

She led them to the staff room, depressingly like every other staff room, and sat down on a sofa that might have been on its last legs but wasn't giving up without a fight. She perched on the edge, palms together, knees together. She didn't offer them any refreshment.

'What can I do for you?'

'You work as a volunteer for Safe Haven, is that correct?'

She nodded. 'When I can.'

'And you sometimes pick up women who need to be taken there?'

Another curt nod. 'I do.'

Imani nodded herself. Sophie Shah had a hard carapace, she thought. She must have been through something to make her that way. And the fact that she volunteered at the refuge was a massive clue as to what that might have been.

'Were you working on Tuesday night this week?'

'I was on call.'

'And did you receive a call from the refuge?' Patel this time. She looked at him, gave her answer. 'No.'

'Nothing at all?' he asked.

'I said no.' Slight tetchiness in her voice.

Patel continued. 'It's just that someone called the refuge that night, needing to go there urgently. And you didn't get the call?'

'No.' Irritation threatening to spill over into anger now.

Patel went on. 'Would they have called anyone else?'

'No, I was on call that night. And I didn't hear from them.'

Patel sat back, sighed. Sophie Shah caught the movement. 'I'm sorry I can't be any more help.' She sounded anything but.

'Okay then,' said Imani. 'If you think of anything else, please let us know.'

They stood up. Sophie Shah did likewise.

'We can see ourselves out,' said Imani, heading towards the door.

In the corridor, Patel turned to her, shook his head. 'Bit of a man-hater, that one,' he said.

'Detective Patel.'

They turned. Sophie Shah was standing in the hallway behind them. Neither of them had heard her leave the room.

'I know it's none of my business what you think of me, but yes. When men treat me the way they have in the past, I do hate them.'

Patel frowned. 'Yeah,' he said, 'I understand that. But not all men . . . '

She laughed. 'Not all men. There's a hashtag on Twitter, Detective Patel. You know what that is?'

'What, Twitter? Yeah, course.'

'Right. Well, I know this isn't a scientific test, but there you go. Not All Men, it's called. It's where men – and women – report non-sexist activity. Fine. Good. There's also one called Everyday Sexism, where women report their daily harassment. By men who don't even realise how horrible they're being most of the time. Guess which one is used the most?'

Patel said nothing.

'Think about it. About what someone might have gone through. What she might have endured. And then laugh and call her a man-hater.' Her voice began to quaver.

'Thank you for your time,' said Imani.

Patel didn't reply. He couldn't find any appropriate words.

They said nothing more until they reached the car, drove away.

Then Imani received a call asking them to return to the station. Urgently.

Marina Esposito had something to tell them.

51

'**R**ight, listen up.' Cotter, standing at the front of the incident room, made sure she had everyone's attention. The lights were down low. 'This couldn't wait until morning. I want you all to go away thinking about it.'

Imani stood on one side of her, Marina on the other. *We probably look like the worst girl band in history*, Marina thought.

But it was just nerves making her think such things. She had enjoyed the day, getting back on the horse, feeling the blood pumping, doing what she should be doing. What she believed she was meant to be doing. This case had just reminded her.

'Okay,' said Cotter. 'I'm going to hand you over to Dr Esposito. She's come up with some preliminary findings that you all need to keep with you. I believe this is how we're going to catch this guy.' She looked at Marina. 'Over to you.'

Marina took her place beside her laptop. She had rigged a projector on to the murder wall. An appropriate place for the team to focus on. She looked round. Felt energised. She had arranged with the departmental secretary, Joy, to have her lectures and seminars covered. More importantly, Joy was also picking up Josephina. And Joy's boyfriend was a tae kwon do black belt. She was sure her daughter would be safe there for a while. And Josephina loved Auntie Joy.

She began her PowerPoint, feeling as if she was addressing a room full of students.

'I've narrowed down the variables and come up with a pro-file of the person who I believe is our perpetrator. This is where we start. White, male, mid-thirties.' She looked round the room, tried a smile. 'I'm sure you've all watched enough films to reach the same conclusion. Intelligent, articulate. Likeable, even. Or at least doesn't pose a threat. Knows how to blend in, adapt. A good predator is an expert at camouflage.'

'Doesn't that rule out Roy Adderley?' asked Sperring.

'Not necessarily. Apart from the fact that Sperring has no alibi for Janine Gillen's murder, he may be playing a double bluff. Being too obvious, attracting our attention. The old hiding-in-plain-sight thing.'

She looked round the room. No more questions.

'Right. Evidence for this. He has to persuade a vulnerable young woman to get in the car with him. There's a password the driver has to give and he knows it. Must have got it through hacking the phones – not my department, I'm afraid – but he still has to be plausible.'

Next screen.

'Does he work alone?' The words appeared as she spoke them. 'Answer: yes. What he's doing is a very personal act. Intimate, even. Something that has meaning only to him.'

Key pressed again.

'And how do we know that?' The words once again appeared. 'Hearts. He takes out their hearts. Cuts them from their bodies.' As she spoke, the word *hearts* appeared on the screen. By chance, it covered the photo of Gemma Adderley's face.

'And that's where the intimacy comes from. Because that act isn't accidental. It's not an afterthought. It's specific, it's tar-geted.' She looked round the room once more. Continued. 'Taking the heart is an attempt to bond with the woman he's killed.'

'Can I just ask . . . ?' Sperring.

'Yes, Ian?'

'His victims. You say there's a bond. Does he actually know them?'

'Not as such,' said Marina. 'Not personally. Or rather, not necessarily personally. We don't know that for sure. But it's the type he knows, or wants to know. The type, or even the archetype. These women all had one thing in common. They were all abused by men. But not just any men. Not randomers in the street or work colleagues or trolls on Twitter, no. Very specific men. Their partners. The men who were supposed to love them. Protect them, even.'

Marina stopped talking. An image of Phil had entered her mind. With a pang of regret, she let it go, continued with her presentation.

Another click, another slide.

'He targets these women when they're at their most vulnerable. They've all suffered. And he makes them suffer some more. Or he certainly did in the case of Gemma Adderley. She was in agony for a long time before she died. He knew what he was doing.'

Marina clicked on to the next slide. 'This is a man who's been grievously hurt by women. Or believes he has. Now by this I don't necessarily mean physically. I don't think he'll bear any visible scars. It's more emotional. He's suffered in terms of his relationships with women. Or believes he has.'

'He's had his heart broken?' asked Imani.

'Exactly,' said Marina, continuing. 'And it's that, I believe, that makes him want to take their hearts. The hearts of damaged, suffering, vulnerable women. This is the important bit in understanding what he's doing, and why. These hearts are his . . . ' She searched for the right word. 'His trophies. His mementoes. But of what? Of what happened to him. Of what he

244

believes women have put him through. His agony. His pain. Transferred on to them.'

She had their rapt attention now.

'He's a man on fire. He's burning. With rage. With hatred. And it's all directed towards women. Vulnerable women. Women he thinks of as weak. Who probably are weak, at their lowest ebb. But he's clever. He's cunning. Let's not forget that, not lose sight of it. And he hides his rage very, very well.'

'Like most men,' said Imani.

The women in the room laughed. The men looked either angry or uncomfortable.

'Like some men,' said Marina, smiling. 'But this one is cleverer than most. Or thinks he is. What he does takes planning. A lot of planning. And a lot of technical expertise. But with Janine Gillen he made a mistake. So he's not infallible. Let's not lose sight of that. Which leads us on to the next question.'

Another click.

'Gemma Adderley's body was found near Saturday Bridge, by the canal. Or rather in the canal. What does that tell us? Lots. And that's without even going into forensics. The first question we have to ask about this is did he intend us to find the body? And find it as quickly as we did? Or is he getting too clever, starting to make mistakes? And the answer?'

She shrugged.

'The location was specially chosen. Not so much for its geographical location in the city centre. Although, again, we have to think of the logistics of getting a body there and leaving it without being noticed. But that's not the concern here. I believe he left her body where he did because it meant something personal to him. This was a place where something significant happened to him. Something involving a woman. A woman who hurt him in some way. And he works through this – exorcises it, even – by leaving a dead, heartless body there to mark the spot. It wasn't a location chosen at random. But did he mean for us to find the body, and as quickly as we did? Did this methodical thinker miscalculate, or was it all part of his plan? Either he was panicked while leaving the body – somebody saw him, although no one's come forward – or he was in a hurry and didn't have time to secure it in place. The other option is he left it for us to find deliberately. So the answer: I still don't know. It depends where he is in the cycle. We'll come to that later.'

'So how many times has he done it?' asked Sperring, looking impatient.

'I'm coming to that too, Ian,' said Marina as calmly as she could. 'Now.' Another click, another screen. 'Let's look at Janine Gillen. She was a mistake. I don't mean choosing her was a mistake. She very definitely fits into his victim profile.'

She noticed that most of them were sitting forward now. Good.

'He went to pick her up, charm her, use his schmooze, whatever, and it went wrong. So he killed her there and then. Botched job. Now, the question we have to ask here is why did it go wrong? Well, again there are a few possible answers. Maybe she got cold feet, decided she didn't want to go to the refuge after all. Wanted to stay and sort things out with her husband. But she'd seen him, and more to the point, could identify him, so she had to be killed. One possible explanation. Another is that she recognised him already. Maybe she knew him.'

Sperring, Marina noticed, was leaning forward in his seat, listening intently. He nodded. To himself, thought Marina.

'Or maybe,' said Imani, 'she had been told it was going to be a woman and wouldn't get into the car with a man.'

'Maybe,' said Marina. 'Whichever you decide, one thing is certain. This is where he went wrong. No doubts, or shadows of doubts, like with Gemma Adderley. He went wrong.

'I believe that his pattern up until this point was to abduct the women, keep them alive, torture them, subject them to God knows what, and then eventually kill them. And afterwards take their hearts. To do with ...' she shrugged again, 'whatever he does with them. Whatever his ritual is. But he couldn't do that here. It went wrong. And the thing is, we might not even have recognised this as one of his if he hadn't done that one thing. That one thing he had to do – take the heart. His compulsion, the thing that drives him to do this in the first place, wouldn't let him behave any other way. Right, Ian.' She pointed to Sperring. 'The bit you were asking about. How many other victims.'

Another click, another screen. 'Answer? I don't know. But given what I've seen and read about Gemma Adderley, I'd say she definitely wasn't the first. Why? Because serial killers – and there should be no doubt that we're dealing with one of those – have a cycle. They go through phases. The initial phase is the getting started. Finding their voice, so to speak. Their ... thing, for want of a better word. The one indefinable thing that motivates them. They might make a few missteps on the way. Sometimes they're caught before they have the chance to set out. But if they get past that stage, they move on to the next one. That's where they realise what they want and how to achieve it. When they refine their methods, their approaches. Hone their skills. This is their most successful phase.'

She paused, hoping this was all going in.

'The next phase is one of ... well, boredom, really. They've achieved what they want. But they want more. This type of killer is, among other things – all of them sexually motivated in some way – an egoist. A narcissist. They want the world to be aware of what they're doing. How brilliant they are. Or how brilliant they think they are. And that's when the trouble starts for them.'

Another click.

'That's what I believe has happened here. To Gemma Adderley. And in a way, the answer to the question I asked earlier is the same. Did he let us find her body because he wanted to, or did he make a mistake? It's a moot point. He wants to let us find the body, say. He wants us to know how brilliant he is. It's also his downfall, leading to the next part of the cycle. The one where he makes mistakes. Janine Gillen is proof enough of that. And that makes him easier to catch. In fact, it's when most serial killers are caught. And usually for the stupidest of reasons. But it can also make him more desperate, quicker to lash out. Not so choosy with his potential targets. There's even the temptation to go out with a bang. A big blaze of glory. All these things have to be considered.'

She looked round the room once more.

'So to sum up, I believe there are other victims out there. Ones he's hidden, managed to cover up. And we have to find them. Then we'll know what we're dealing with. But more to the point, this Heartbreaker, as the media's calling him – and I apologise for saying that – is going to kill again. And it's up to us to stop him.'

52

He stared at his boxes. Lined along the walls, all around him. Every one a specially – lovingly – prepared final resting place for his darkest, bitterest, most disappointing and hurtful memories. Individually thought out, the trappings to match the memory, the shelf positioning matching the severity of pain. It was a room of loss, of failure, of harm, but also of hope. For the future. Strip the damage and the anger away, store it up here. Emerge a new man. A happy man. A perfect man.

But that wasn't what he felt now as he looked on his work. All he felt inside him was rage. And fear. One feeding and stoking the other.

The police were circling ever nearer. He could feel it, sense it. He had tried to enquire as to where they were with the investigation, what they were doing, how much progress had been made. There was a limit to what he could ask without giving himself away, though. And he was careful to skate along that line. As careful as he could be.

How could he stop them? Or at least hold them off until he had finished what he had set out to do? He didn't know. He had to think. Think hard.

Anger and fear roiled inside him once more. No. He couldn't be stopped. Not now. Not yet. He hadn't reached the point he needed to. Become the person he wanted to become. The good person. No.

So what, then? How could he stop them? Could he kill them? No. That wasn't part of what he was doing. His work didn't extend to something of that nature. That would just be murder. Pointless, senseless murder. And that wasn't what he did. Who he was. Murder was for lesser people. For those who couldn't help themselves. Who solved arguments not with rational discourse but with brutality. Not at all like what he was doing.

This was a calling. An experiment. And a successful one too. It was working. He was becoming a better person the longer it went on, the nearer he came to achieving his goal.

But . . .

Something would have to be done. If not killing, then . . . what? He walked round, stared once more at the empty boxes, more empty ones than filled ones. So many memories still to be locked away . . .

He knew what he had to. Escalate his plan. Find the next one straight away. Tonight, even. Weigh up the risks, of course, but keep moving. Only that way could he—

He heard a noise from outside. A voice.

Cunt.

Time to go back, he thought reluctantly. Time to put his emasculated mask in place once more, rejoin the rest of the world.

For now.

53

'Where you going?'

'Just out. For a bit.'

'Where?'

'Just . . . ' Ellison sighed. He hated being questioned like this. 'Just out. Seeing someone from work. That's all.'

Helen stared at him. God, he hated the woman. Didn't know why he'd married her. There she sat, in the same chair she was always in, her arse wedged in permanently, too fat to get up and do anything. The house was a tip. She never cleaned. And he was always having to bring in takeaways because she wouldn't – or couldn't – cook. Christ. What had he done to end up with her?'

'Who?'

And he hated her voice. Probably that most of all. Even above the sound of the TV, some inane chat-show thing, she could always find the right frequency to screech into his brain.

Hate wasn't a strong enough word for what he felt about her.

'You don't know them. No point in telling you. Christ, it's like living with my bloody mother.'

'Don't swear. I won't have you swearing in this house.'

'Fuck off,' he mumbled under his breath.

'When are you coming back?'

'Later. I don't know.'

'Don't be too late. There's that murderer on the loose. It said so on the news.'

'I'm sure you're safe from him.' Too bloody right, he thought. Bastard would want his head examining going after her.

She kept talking but Ellison wasn't listening. He slammed the door, breathed in the damp evening. It smelt of freedom.

He walked to his car, plans for the night already taking shape. He kept a few things in the boot for such occasions. Playthings. A dress-up box. A few drinks first, to get him in the mood, then that.

Fun.

He got in the car, drove away.

54

'God, what a day . . . '

Claire was opening a bottle of red when Keith walked into the kitchen. 'Want a glass?'

'Lovely,' he said.

She poured one for him, handed it over with a kiss and a smile. 'Cheers,' she said.

He returned both the words and the smile.

She walked into the living room. He followed her.

'Where's Edward?' she asked, looking round before sitting down.

'Went to a friend's after school. Something involving computer games, I think. *Call of* . . . I don't know. Something.'

She nodded, took a sip. 'More violence. Anyway.' She put her glass down, leaned back in her chair. 'Had the police back in today,' she said.

'You too? Lot of it about.' He didn't look at her while he spoke.

'Oh.' She looked surprised. 'What for?'

He shrugged. Kept his voice light. 'Oh, Janine Gillen. Had anything slipped my mind, had she said anything, all that. The kind of things you see on TV but real. All the clichés. What about you?'

'Same, really. Nice girl, though. DC Oliver?'

'Oh yeah. Spoke to her yesterday. Knows her stuff. Had a

different one today. A bloke. Sperring.' He forced a laugh. 'Old-school. More at home in *The Sweeney*, I think. The dinosaur type.'

'Lovely,' she said.

'Anything planned for tonight?' he asked.

'Just want to chill,' she said. 'What with everything that's been going on and that. See if we can find something on Netflix?'

'Great,' he said, and picked up the remote, pointed it at the TV in readiness.

'So when can I see them, then?' She had got used to living in only one flat in the building. She sometimes forgot that the rest of the flats lay beyond the door Keith had just come through.

He looked up, startled. 'Sorry? When can you . . . '

'The flats.' She smiled. 'Surely they're ready for inspection by now. I mean, you've been doing them up for ages.'

'The flats? Soon,' he said, 'when they're ready. Really good and ready.'

'And then we can start renting them out, thank God,' she said, taking another mouthful of wine. 'Making a bit of money.'

He stood up. Smiled at his wife. 'Why don't I cook dinner?'

She had her head back, eyes closed once more. She opened them at his words. 'You sure? We could get a takeaway. Save us both cooking.'

'It's not a problem,' he said, sounding like it really wasn't. 'You just sit there, find something for us to watch and leave it to me.'

She grabbed his hand as he walked past. 'You're like a little island of tranquillity in a sea of . . . I don't know.'

'Rage?' he suggested.

She laughed. 'Rage. Yeah.'

He dropped her hand, walked away.

55

Josephina was playing contentedly on the floor with her Polly Pockets, making up elaborate worlds for them to inhabit. Marina had picked her up from Joy's, where she'd inflicted *Frozen* on them for what felt like the three hundredth time, complete with singing and dancing. Marina had laughed, wished life could be as simple and as happy as that all the time.

Now she stood at the window, gazing out at the darkened street, sodium light illuminating only patches, making hidden shadowed swirls out of everything else. And for the first time in a long time, she wasn't scared by what those shadows might be harbouring.

She had actually wished Phil was there to talk to about her day. She was pumped, energised by what she was doing again, and wanted to share it with someone. But not just anyone. Him.

So now she stood looking over the city, or her part of it. Watching the lights both near and far, trying to imagine all those lives out there. All those people behind locked doors living their secret, private lives. The joy and hatred, the boredom and excitement, the life and death. All going on around her.

She felt she had absented herself from it, gone into her castle, pulled up the drawbridge behind her. Walls of stone and brick, imaginary and real, to cut her off from the rest of humanity.

And now here she was, thrust back into the middle of it again. Hunting a killer.

In the midst of life we are in death. The old Bible quote. She smiled to herself. Roy Adderley would be familiar with that one. But for her it was different.

In the midst of death was life.

She kept looking. Seeing the shadows, seeing beyond the shadows. Knowing what to look for, but tired of looking. Wondering whether she could live the rest of her life waiting for someone to jump out at her. Wondering what alternatives she had.

Wondering about Phil. Where he was now. What he was doing.

And for the first time in ages, she allowed herself to acknowledge something to herself, admit something and listen to it. She missed him. Really, really missed him.

And more than that.

She wanted him.

Now all she had to do was decide what she was going to do about that.

56

Darkness had fallen. Roy Adderley hadn't noticed. The street lights had come on outside. He didn't care. All he cared about was his world. And his world was right here in this tiny little living room.

Or dying room.

'Trudi, Trudi, I'm s-sorry . . .'

He cradled her head, or what was left of it, in his arms, blood and other matter covering his sleeves, hands and chest. Her body lay lifeless, half on the floor, half on him. Tears and snot all over his face.

As soon as he realised what he had done, the anger had left him. He had held her body, tried to bring her back to life. But it was no good. There was nothing left of her. Not even a face.

He had prayed. Continuously. First for the breath to return to her body. Then, when he realised that wasn't going to happen, for forgiveness. Both prayers had been met with a resounding silence. Not even the ticking of a clock to mark the passage of time.

And now it was dark. And Trudi was still gone. Her heart, that seductive, Jezebel's heart, the one that had enticed him away from his wife, was no longer beating. He had heard it stop. Seen it stop. *Made* it stop.

God had a plan for Roy Adderley. But this wasn't it.

And now Roy Adderley was crying. For him, for her.

Forever.

PART FIVE

LIVE BAIT

57

He stood before his shelved boxes once more. Waiting for the hours to pass, hoping that there would be one tonight. *Needing.* That desperate yearning inside him, that ache for ritual, for closure. But she had to be the right kind of victim.

There had to be one. *Had to be.* His plan had to move forward, get back on track after the recent setback. And with the police circling, the sooner the better.

He kept staring at the box he had chosen. A jewellery box. It was empty. But soon it would be filled. And then he could move on.

Because this was going to be a special one. A really special one. He had someone – and a memory – reserved for this one. And it would be a huge turning point in who he had been, who he was now, and what he would become. Critical, in fact. So he had to get it right, make it work. Ensure everything was perfect.

The box, to start with. He had had this one in mind for a while. Had brought it down for just this memory. It was covered in shells, like something a child would make. And in fact a child *had* made it. That seemed right, somehow. Apposite. Especially for the memory he was going to summon up.

He was twenty-one. Her name was Hannah. And she was beautiful. Long blonde hair, which he didn't usually go for, quite tall, curvy. Very well proportioned. The kind of figure that got stared at on the street. That got her into places – from buses to nightclubs to stadium gigs, to anywhere she wanted – for free. And she would dress to match this. Cut-off jeans, halter tops. Everything clung, was accentuated, exposed. But – and he wouldn't have believed it if he hadn't got to know her so well – she wasn't aware of any of it. Her looks, her figure, anything. She wasn't scheming, calculating, didn't get men – or women – to do things for her. She didn't need to. She was pleasant and honest. Happy being who she was, with her place in the world. She smiled a lot. And when she did, it felt like she'd made your day.

Like most people, he fell in love with her. But unlike the rest, he actually got to do something about it.

He met her at a nightclub. She was with her friends, politely fending off unwelcome enquiries, happy to accept drinks from boys she either knew or liked.

He thought he had no chance.

And then he bumped into her on his way to the lavatory. An actual bump. He apologised for not seeing her. She said it was her fault entirely, and they got talking. Soon they were seeing each other, then they were an item.

And he couldn't have been prouder.

At first things went well. He was always happy to be seen out with her, to show her off like she was an item of jewellery or designer clothing that someone like him wouldn't have been expected to be able to afford. But the thing was, he loved her. Really, really loved her. Probably more than she loved him, if he thought about it. But he never did. Never, ever did.

And then it happened. She found out she was pregnant. She had put off telling him, asking him out somewhere special, somewhere that meant something to them both, to break it to him. An Italian restaurant on Queensway. No one else they knew went there, preferring the chain restaurants. But they liked it. Or he did. Made him feel more sophisticated, less of the herd.

Listen, I've got something to tell you. It's ... really difficult and there's ... Oh God. I'm pregnant. Leaning in close, ensuring no one would be able to overhear.

He just stared at her. Unable to speak. She stared back, waiting.

Eventually he found his voice. *How ... how long?*

A couple of months. I wasn't well. Did a test. Then another. Then when I was sure, I went to the doctor's. And yes, I'm pregnant.

He looked at her over the weak flickering light cast by the candle in the Chianti bottle. Her eyes, normally so full of life, of joy, now seemed full of fear and uncertainty. As if childhood had come to a sudden horrific end and she was realising what it was like to be an adult.

He smiled at her. *It'll be fine,* he said, taking her hand in his. *We'll manage. Don't worry.*

They talked some more – lots more – about what was happening. He would stand by her, she needn't worry about him, he would be there for her. He told her all that.

And when he left her, he began to think. He was going to be a father. Have a child of his own. In the days that followed, he planned in his head what course his life would now take. What he would do to provide for Hannah and the baby. He kept calling her, but she never seemed to be around. Probably sleeping, he thought. Until she called him about a week later.

How's my little mother to be? he said, laughing.

Silence.

Hello?

I'm ... I got rid of it.

He stood there, unable to take in what she had said. *You ... you ...*

I got rid of it. Had an abortion. The words harder now, slightly more shrill.

Got rid of it? he said. *But ... but we talked about it. What we*

*were going to do. How we were going to make ends meet. Manage.
Our future. With our child.*

A sigh on the line. *That's just it. We don't have a future. I've
done a lot of thinking. And I realised a few things. I don't want a
child. I don't want to be a mother. Not yet, anyway. Not for years.
And . . .* She paused. Another sigh. *Not with you. I don't love you.
I don't think I ever did. But you were kind to me and you liked me.
You treated me well, which is more than a lot of guys have done. So
thank you. But I don't . . . I'm sorry . . .*

She put the phone down.

He tried to call her, to see her, but he wasn't able to do
either. It was like she had disappeared from the face of the
earth. Gone. And taken his child with her.

He had heard from her years later. Facebook. Married with
three children. Happy and smiling. Her figure no longer as it
had been, but she didn't seem to care. She seemed totally content with who she was now.

And he hated her for it.

He snapped back to the present. Looked at the shell-
decorated box once more. Felt that gnawing yearning in his
guts again. Soon, he thought, soon. It had to be. Tonight.

He stood back, checked his watch.

Waiting. He hated waiting.

But it wouldn't be long.

Until he found a heart to atone for the crimes Hannah had
committed against him. To be finally free of her memory.

58

You'll be wondering why I called you all here . . .

That was what Marina wanted to say, but she knew she shouldn't because she didn't know these people well enough yet. And also it seemed too flippant a thing to do. Plus she hadn't actually called the meeting.

But she couldn't help it. She felt if not happy, then giddy. That was the best word she could find. Giddy. Back at work, doing what she loved, all of that. But there was something else, something overriding all of that. She didn't feel scared any more.

She was in the Six Eight Kafé on Temple Row and it was stupidly early. Or at least it was for her. The other two people with her seemed more used to the hour. Imani Oliver sat opposite her, but this time she was joined by DCI Cotter.

Joy had once again rearranged her lectures and Josephina had gone to the early breakfast club at school. Marina had hated to do that, to let her go, but she had no choice. She had looked over the security arrangements at the school, satisfied herself that no harm would come to her daughter and said goodbye. Josephina seemed quite happy to be there early: more time to play with the friends she couldn't often see after school.

A pre-briefing briefing, Cotter had called it on the phone. Marina was intrigued. And also pleased: clearly she had done something right the previous day.

'Thanks for coming,' said Cotter, once everyone had ordered what they wanted and sat down, small talk opened and stowed away once more.

Cotter had gone for coffee and a piece of cake. While Marina had nibbled at her almond croissant, Cotter's cake lay untouched. Not just untouched, avoided.

Marina took in the DCI's trim, gym-honed figure and surmised what she was doing. She remembered reading about Aleister Crowley, the infamous occultist. He believed that the human spirit could conquer any kind of temptation. One of Crowley's particular vices was drugs. She had read that he used to sit in his chamber surrounded by bowls of heroin and cocaine, fighting the urge to partake of them, nurturing his strength of spirit. She imagined Cotter doing something similar with that slice of cake. The fact that Crowley died a hopeless drug addict was the one part of the story she didn't want to dwell on.

'I've been doing some thinking,' said Cotter, 'and I wanted to run something by you both. See what you thought.'

Marina exchanged a glance with Imani, said nothing. Having been hooked, they waited for Cotter to reel them in.

'Imani, how d'you feel about being a Judas goat?'

Imani frowned. 'Sorry?'

Marina understood immediately.

'If he's intercepting calls to the refuge and picking up his victims that way, we need someone on the inside. Someone who can play the part of an abused woman.'

'And you think I can do that?' Imani's eyes were wide.

'Yes,' said Cotter. 'You phone the refuge tonight – Marina can coach you, make you sound convincing. Then, once you've been accepted, you'll be given a place to be picked up. When he arrives, we'll be waiting for him. What d'you think?'

Imani looked between the two of them. Marina could understand her trepidation.

'You're sure you'll be there?'

'We'll have prepared hours in advance. The whole team will be behind you. Armed response, the lot. All we have to do is wait for him to turn up, then bang. We've got him.' She took a sip of coffee. 'You game for that?'

Imani looked thoughtful. Marina could tell that whatever reservations she had were being tempered by the excitement of the opportunity. 'Sure,' she said.

Cotter smiled. 'Good.'

Imani frowned again. 'One thing. How d'you know he'll be listening tonight?'

Marina leaned forward. 'May I?' she said.

Cotter gestured: the floor was hers.

'From everything I went through yesterday, he'll be restless. He messed up with Janine. Botched it completely. That means he's only conducted an incomplete ritual with the heart. No preparation time to do whatever he does. And he'll hate that. He'll want to get back on the horse as quickly as possible. Because that incomplete ritual will be burning him up. He won't be able to think properly, concentrate on anything, until he's done it.'

'Sounds plausible,' said Imani.

'And also,' continued Marina, 'because of where he is in his cycle, he's much more likely to make mistakes and be in a hurry.'

'So that should, theoretically, make him easier to catch,' said Cotter.

Marina nodded.

'Or it might make him more dangerous,' said Imani.

'He'll be more prone to making mistakes,' said Marina. 'That's a certainty.'

'Well,' said Cotter, 'it's a calculated risk. A chance we'll have to take. We'll be there, we'll be ready for him. Worst-case scenario, he doesn't show. Best case, we've got him.'

'What about the refuge? Do they know?' asked Imani.

'Not yet,' said Cotter. 'Perhaps you could deal with that, Imani. You seem to be building a rapport with the woman in charge there.'

'Will do.'

A faint smile flickered on Cotter's lips. 'Take DC Patel with you again, if you like.'

Imani looked at her coffee. 'Yes, ma'am.'

Cotter looked towards Marina as if seeking a co-conspirator. Marina gave a professional smile in return.

'Right then,' said Cotter, looking at her slice of cake, 'let's finish up and go to the morning briefing, let the rest of the team know what's happening.'

They drank up, made ready to go. Marina looked at the piece of cake.

'You not eating that?' she asked Cotter.

Cotter looked slightly shamefaced. 'I'll . . . take it with me. Have it later.'

Marina smiled. 'Course you will,' she said.

59

At first, Roy Adderley was going to go as he was. Dressed in the clothes he had been questioned and held in, covered in Trudi's dried blood and bodily fluids. He felt it was important to do that. A pilgrimage. Wearing his version of sackcloth and ashes.

But wiser counsel prevailed. A calmer, saner voice. And he knew who it was who had spoken to him. The thoughts, the words hadn't come from inside himself, from his own inner man or conscience. No. It was God. Jesus. The guv'nor.

He had sat all night on the living room floor. Crying at first, then praying, then crying some more. Then another bout of frantic praying. Until at last he had nodded off, come round with his head slumped down on to Trudi's. And with the wakening, acceptance of what he had done. He had sat unmoving, waiting for the coming of dawn, silently mouthing prayers and sections of scripture he knew by heart – even inappropriate sections, just as long as he said something – preparing her soul for the journey across. It was, he felt, the least he could do for her.

And then, job done, as God spoke to him, he listened, nodding in places, taking in the words, receiving his instructions and the reasoning behind them. Eventually he stood up, let Trudi's head fall gently to the floor, walked to the bathroom and got into the shower.

Now he was ready to go. Sunday-best suit, polished shoes, even a collar and tie. Hair neat and parted. Shaved.

Ready.

But it was a still to be a pilgrimage. That aspect hadn't changed. He was still going to walk. And walk he did. All the way into town, his shoes pinching his toes, hurting and rubbing his heels. His collar chafing at his neck, half strangling him, cuffs too tight round his wrists. But it was fine. All part of his suffering.

He called in to a petrol station on the way, selected a bunch of forecourt flowers. He didn't know what they were. Wide-headed, different-coloured bright petals. They looked fragile, as if they wouldn't survive the journey. But they would have to do.

And he walked on.

Until he reached his first destination.

Saturday Bridge was still cordoned off, the forensic teams not yet finished working the area. The white tent was still in place, the canalside path unpassable.

Adderley walked as far down the slope as he could, as near to the tent as he could get. Nobody made any attempt to stop him. Nobody even noticed him. There was a very small collection of wilting flowers at the side of the tent. Cellophane-wrapped and dying. Adderley knew who they were from. One bunch from Gemma's parents, one from them on behalf of Carly. He laid his pathetic, over-coloured flowers next to them, stood up, looked around.

He tried to work out what he was feeling. Remorse? Sadness? Loss? He didn't know. He was tempted to tell himself that he was feeling too many conflicting emotions to actually settle on something he could recognise. Something would hopefully reveal itself, define itself to him. Tell him what to say, how to feel. But that wasn't the truth. Because what he really felt – truthfully felt – was numbness. A void where there should be emotion of some kind, any kind. An absence of thoughts where prayers and eulogies should have been. His wife's body had been found there, mutilated, tortured and dead. And he could no longer feel anything for her.

He turned and made his way back up the path, on to the main pavement once more.

The route was memorised in his head. Besides, he knew where he was going. The inevitable place. Where he was always bound to end up.

The main central police station on Steelhouse Lane.

He stood on the street now, gazing up at the building. Behind the courts, it shared a lot of the same Gothic style, looking like an urban idea of an old Hammer horror film. But the cars, vans and uniformed officers wandering around in front dispelled that idea. Still, it looked appropriate to Adderley. As though some kind of old-style, truthfully physical justice went on in there.

At least he hoped so.

He found the main entrance, walked up to the desk. There were a couple of people before him so he calmly waited his turn. Eventually he stood before the glass partition. The desk sergeant looked up at him, waited expectantly for him to speak.

And the words deserted him.

'Yes?' said the sergeant, trying not to let irritation and weariness slip into his voice.

Adderley moved his mouth, hoped that the exercise would eventually produce words. It did.

'M-my name's . . . Roy . . . Adderley. Adderley.' He cleared his throat while the desk sergeant waited.

'Good,' said the desk sergeant. 'And what can I do for you, Mr Adderley?'

'I want to report a murder.'

The desk sergeant looked taken aback. 'Oh yes? Whose?'

'My girlfriend. And I'm only going to talk to Detective Inspector Brennan.'

'I'll see what I can do,' said the desk sergeant.

'No,' said Adderley. 'I'll only speak to Detective Inspector Brennan.'

'Fine. Okay. I'll get him. In the meantime, can you tell me, do you know who killed her?'

'Yes,' he said.

'Who?'

'Me.'

And Adderley gave a smile so radiant it was like he felt the sun streaming from his face.

60

'So,' said Imani, 'how d'you like it in the big city?'

Patel, in the passenger seat, laughed. She had hoped he would. They were driving back into the city centre, negotiating the roundabouts down from Balsall Heath through Edgbaston.

'It's not that different, you know,' he said. 'We've got mosques in West Bromwich.' He pointed to one through the right window. 'We've got roads, just like this one, we've got . . . oh, everything you've got here.'

'Including crime.'

'Well, that happens everywhere.' He looked out of the window, then back to her, still smiling. 'Scenery's prettier here, though.'

Imani tried hard to keep her eyes on the road, but glanced at him in mock surprise and admonishment. Or at least she thought it was only mock. She wasn't sure.

'Any more sexist comments like that, Detective Constable Patel, and you'll be walking back to Steelhouse Lane.'

He looked away from her, seemingly genuinely embarrassed. 'Sorry,' he said. 'Just trying to give you a compliment.' His words sounded clumsy, his body shifting like he was itching all over, hands gesturing impotently. He looked like someone trying not to lose their balance and fall downstairs.

'I know you were,' she said. 'Or I think you were.'

'I was,' he said. 'Honestly. That was all.'

Imani said nothing more. Just looked out of the opposite window and smiled to herself, hoping he wasn't watching her reaction.

She turned on to Bristol Road, heading into the city.

Patel had stopped talking. Imani risked a glance at him. He was looking out of the window, away from her. Something seemed to be on his mind, troubling him, furrowing his brow. It was a nice brow, she thought. Too handsome to look troubled.

She stopped herself. What was she thinking? Did she really fancy him? Well, yes. That much was obvious. And he fancied her. She knew that. Didn't have to be Psychic Sally to work out what he was thinking and feeling.

But why was she falling for it? It wasn't like her. She had spent a large part of her career fighting against the lazy, institutionalised sexism that was inherent in the police force. Batting away the wandering hands of senior officers, wondering whether to ignore or complain about the jokes directed at her. Knowing that she shouldn't have to stand for that kind of treatment, but that if she complained too much, stood up for herself, someone, somewhere, would be marking her down as a troublemaker. And if that happened, no matter how brilliant she might or might not be, her career would be less than stellar.

But Patel seemed different. Not like the usual rank and file, not treating her the same way. He had accepted her promotion to CIO, shared her concerns about domestic violence and even demonstrated that to her. It couldn't all be bullshit.

She found herself smiling once more. Risked another glance at him. He was still staring out of the window. She did like him. Admitted that much to herself. Even though she had told herself she would never end up with a copper. Because she knew what they were like. Not just from experience. Not just from working with them. Because she was one herself.

'Maybe . . .' Patel started, then stopped just as quickly.

'Yeah?' she said. Keeping her eyes on the road, negotiating the Queensway underpass.

'Well, I dunno,' he said. 'This investigation. I'm enjoying it. Better than we get in West Brom, you know what I mean?'

'I know,' she said. 'But we are the Major Incident Squad, don't forget. We don't do run-of-the-mill.'

'Yeah, I know that. But . . .'

Imani waited. 'Yeah?'

'I was thinking . . . maybe I should put in for a transfer.'

'To Birmingham or MIS?'

'MIS.' He looked at her, then quickly away. 'If, you know. If you think I'll be good enough. If you'll have me.'

'Well . . .'

'I mean, how would you like that? If I was on your team?'

'Don't know,' she said, trying and failing to keep a teasing tone out of her voice. 'We only take the best, you know.' She looked at him. 'You the best?'

He smiled. 'Oh yeah.' And there was a cockiness, a swagger she hadn't seen before. Not unattractive, she thought. He nodded. 'I've got some moves. Just wait and see.'

'I'll bet you have,' she said, and smiled all the way back to the station.

61

'Change of plan,' said Cotter, striding into the incident room and beckoning Imani and Marina towards her. They looked at each other, confused. The three of them huddled together in a corner.

'I've spoken to Claire Lingard, ma'am,' said Imani. 'She's ready to go tonight.'

'Well,' said Cotter, 'it may not come to that.'

The two of them looked at her quizzically.

'Roy Adderley's just walked in and confessed to the murder of his girlfriend.'

Marina and Imani stared at her. She continued.

'We've sent uniforms round to his place, and her body's there on the floor of the living room. It looks like he beat her to death.'

'Jesus . . . ' Marina stared.

Cotter turned to her. 'Could it be him? For the other two? Could it?'

Marina, put on the spot, shrugged. 'It's possible. As I said, he could be hiding in plain sight. So I'd say all bets are off.'

'Where is he now?' asked Imani.

'Interview room one.'

Imani looked at the door, back to Cotter. In a hurry to go. 'Who's handling it?'

'Well that's the thing,' said Cotter. 'He'll only speak to one person. Phil Brennan.'

Marina's mouth fell open. Before she could reply, Cotter continued.

'That was the deal. Phil's on his way into the building now.' She turned to Marina. 'I'm sorry.'

Marina recovered some of her composure. 'No, it's . . . it's all right. Had to happen some time. If that's what . . . It's fine.' She was breathing heavily.

'So if we can get him to admit to the killing of—' Imani stopped in her tracks, eyes drifting to the door.

'What is it?' asked Cotter.

The other two followed her gaze. DS Hugh Ellison was once again in the incident room. He spotted the three of them and began walking towards them.

'Doesn't he have any work to do in Digbeth?' said Imani.

'You've met him?' asked Cotter in surprise.

'Came in yesterday. Wanted to know if there was any progress on the Gemma Adderley case.'

'I worked with him on that,' said Marina. She gave an involuntary shudder.

'He's as slimy as they come,' said Cotter. 'We'll have to disinfect this place after he's gone.'

He reached them. They gave no indication that they had been discussing him.

'DS Ellison,' said Cotter, unable or unwilling to keep the dislike from her voice. 'What brings you here?'

'Is it true?' he asked. 'He's come in? He's admitted it?'

'Who are you talking about?' Cotter's face was blank.

'Adderley. Heard he'd copped for it.'

'Roy Adderley is in for questioning, yes. I'm afraid I can't say any more than that.'

'Oh, come on,' said Ellison, lip curling nastily. 'I worked that case. I'm not some sodding reporter that you're trying to fob off. Has he copped to it or not?'

'No,' said Marina, sensing that Cotter was becoming angry, jumping in to save a confrontation. 'He's come in but he hasn't been questioned yet.'

Ellison turned, looked at her. Didn't bother to disguise the leer on his face as he gave her a head-to-toe appraisal. 'Hello, Marina. Good to see you again.'

She nodded, not trusting herself with words.

Ellison reluctantly took his eyes off her, turned back to Cotter. 'So when and where?'

'When and where what, DS Ellison?'

'When's the interview? I want to watch.'

'That's out of the question, I'm afraid. We're—'

'Oh, come on,' he said, in what he clearly assumed was a charming voice but which came out thin and wheedling. 'I was there at the start, I should be there at the end. Want to hear him admit it.'

'Sorry, but no. You're not part of the investigating team. I won't allow it.'

Cotter held firm. Ellison stared at her. She returned his gaze. Hard, steely. He glanced at Marina.

'You're letting her watch,' he said petulantly.

'Dr Esposito is a valued part of my team,' Cotter said. 'She's allowed to.'

He stared at Marina once more, mouth open to speak, then closed it again, apparently thinking better of it.

'So that's it, then, is it?'

'I'm sorry, DS Ellison. I can't allow it.' Cotter reached across, shook his hand. 'But thank you for making time in your busy schedule to come in. We'll let you know what happens.'

Realising he was getting nowhere, he made to leave. But

before moving off, he turned back again. 'Nice to see you again, Dr Esposito.' He made the words sound like an insult.

The three of them watched him go.

'I'm going to wash my hand now,' said Cotter. She turned to the other two. 'Horrid little man. Used to work Vice. And from what I hear, wasn't averse to helping himself to freebies. He's with MisPers now. I think it was either that or early retirement.'

'Oh well,' said Imani. 'I'm sure it's the force's gain.'

Cotter gave a smile of relief. 'Glad we're all on the same page as far as he's concerned. Now. What are we going to do about Roy Adderley?'

62

'Good to have you back, boss.' Sperring was the first to greet Phil as he returned to the station.

It felt strange to be back. He had only been away for a relatively short time, but the experience of walking into the building again was disconcerting. He had been suspended from an inquiry once before, at the behest of his then DCI, but that DCI had had a hidden agenda which Phil had then gone on to expose, so he had been reinstated immediately. This time was different. He would have done the same as Cotter in her position. Now he was back, uncertain as to when his next appearance here would be, and under what circumstances. So just do what he had to do and get it over with.

To say he'd been surprised by the phone call was a massive understatement. Not just at being asked back so soon, but the manner of the invitation. The one thing that hadn't surprised him was hearing what Adderley had done. He felt vindicated in his actions.

He reached the interview room. No other members of his team – should he keep thinking of them as his team? – were about apart from Sperring. And for that Phil was grateful.

Especially where Marina was concerned. Just knowing she was in the same building was disconcerting enough. Enough to put him off what he was here to do. Enough to send him spiralling downwards once more.

Focus. He had a job to do.

'Thanks, Ian.' Phil looked at his DS, then at the door. He didn't know if he should say anything further, or indeed if he could think of anything further to say. Sperring made the decision for him.

'Just go right in, boss. He's waiting for you.'

Phil managed a smile. 'I'll soften him up for you to take over.'

Sperring managed to return the smile. 'I'll be watching.'

Phil entered. Adderley sat alone at the table. Phil motioned to the uniform standing by the door to leave, then crossed to the table, sat down opposite.

'Just the two of us,' he said, hoping that he would quickly fall back into the rhythm of things. 'How quaint.'

Adderley was wearing a suit, but his tie and belt had been taken from him. He stared at Phil. 'You look terrible,' he said, face filled with compassion.

'So do you,' said Phil, automatically. Before Adderley could speak, he continued, 'That what you brought me in for? To say that?'

Adderley frowned slightly.

'Oh yeah,' said Phil, 'I should say before we go any further that anything you say to me doesn't count. I'm suspended.'

Adderley shrugged.

'And also,' said Phil, 'anything I say to you doesn't count. This isn't an official interview.'

'I don't care about any of that,' said Adderley, his voice strangely, almost disconnectedly, calm, his gave level. Too level. 'I know what I've done, I know what will happen to me. That's not what this is about. I wanted to talk to you. Just you.'

Phil shrugged, kept his face impassive. 'I'm here. So talk.'

Adderley stared at him for a long time before speaking. Phil waited, his face giving nothing away. Adderley's expression was bland but his lips were moving, like he was having a secret conversation. Or saying a prayer. Eventually he smiled.

'This . . .' He gestured round the room, his arms stretched out expansively. 'This. Is all your fault.' Dropping his arms, looking straight at Phil. Waiting.

'No it's not,' said Phil, suddenly feeling back in the swing of interrogation, muscle memory taking over.

Adderley nodded, still smiling, face gravely serene. 'Yes it is.' His voice low, sure. 'Yes it is. You see,' he leaned forward, explaining a point, making sure it was understood, 'nothing would have happened. Nothing at all. If you'd left me alone. Nothing.' Leaning back, nodding to emphasise his point.

Phil folded his arms. 'Bullshit,' he said. 'It would have happened. All of it.'

'Really?' More amused than anything else, letting a lesser intellect have their fun before spoiling it with a killer argument.

Or at least that was the impression Phil received. And even though he shouldn't have let it, that rankled.

'Oh yeah,' he said. 'So you say you didn't kill your wife. Well, the jury's still out on that one. But you would have ended up here anyway. Maybe not like this, maybe not on this day. But you would have been sitting here, looking across the table at me, or someone like me. It would have happened eventually. Definitely.'

'Really?' Adderley still smiling, still not taking in Phil's words.

Denial, thought Phil. Work on that. 'Yeah. Because that's what you're like. This . . .' he gestured round the room, 'is who you are. A criminal.'

'A criminal. I see.'

Phil leaned forward. 'Not only that, but a coward.'

Adderley flinched, blinked. Phil, sensing a glimmer of breakthrough, of victory, kept going. Ramped it up a notch.

282

'A coward,' he continued, 'who's terrified of the world. And what he thinks it's done to him, or could do to him. Who hates and fears it because it makes him feel powerless. So what does this coward do? What do you do? You bottle up all this hate and fear inside you. And because you're too pathetic to let it out any other way, you take it out on someone else. But this person has to be weaker and smaller than you. And if this person also has the bad luck to love you, even better. It makes all your hate and fear hurt them more. All that rage you pummelled out, transferred to Gemma. Your wife. And what was her crime? To fall in love with you.'

Phil sat back, not bothering to disguise the disgust he felt at Adderley. *Something to be said for being suspended*, he thought. *I can say what I like. Or rather, what I feel.*

The endorphins were firing up, the righteous anger coming out. The old Phil, back again. He was actually starting to enjoy himself.

63

'**G**ood, isn't he?'

Sperring turned. He was in the viewing suite, watching Phil interview Adderley. And he was pleased with what he had seen. His boss had his old fire back, not like the angry, moping individual of recent times, shooting off his anger and despair at the most misplaced of targets. This was Phil back to what he did best.

'Didn't hear you come in,' said Sperring, hiding the fact that he had actually jumped on hearing Marina's voice. 'He is. Much as I hate to admit it.'

Marina gave a tight smile, moved closer to him, looked at the screen.

The room was small, almost a store cupboard, with a desk, an old chair and a monitor. But sometimes, especially if there was a big case on and an interview was going to blow it open, it took on TARDIS-like dimensions, somehow accommodating all the officers who wanted to see and be part of the outcome.

'Has he confessed?' asked Marina.

'To his girlfriend's murder,' said Sperring. 'That's all.'

'So why did he want to see only Phil?'

'I think we're coming to that.'

They continued to watch the screen, Sperring throwing surreptitious glances across at Marina, trying to work out what she was seeing, how she was feeling.

She looked proud, smiling a little, even.

'Hope he's back soon,' said Sperring, not taking his eyes off the screen. 'Properly.'

'So do I,' Marina said, the words coming out on a sigh.

Sperring took his attention away from the screen, focused on Marina. 'Why not wait till he gets out? Have a word?'

Marina looked round, suddenly flustered, like she was trapped and couldn't find an exit. Startled by her own words. 'I'd . . . better go. I . . . I've got work to do.'

'Marina . . .'

'I've got to go.' She turned, made for the door.

Sperring put his hand on her arm. 'Just wait. What's the matter with you?'

Marina stared at the hand, hard, until he released her. 'Look, I just don't want to bump into him.'

'Why not?'

'Because I don't feel . . . I'm not ready to see him yet, that's why not.'

Sperring shook his head, gave a bark of a laugh. 'Jesus. Why can't the pair of you behave like grown-ups and talk to each other? What's so bad you can't sort it out between you?'

Marina turned away from him, not wanting him to see her face. 'You don't understand.'

Sperring moved to her, turned her round to face him. 'I do understand.'

'He . . . If she comes back, he won't be able to protect me. Or our daughter. It's better if we're apart.'

'Better for who? Look, Marina, I've been working with him all this time. I know exactly what he's been going through, I've had it every day. It's been like hauling round the Incredible Sulk. It's hit him hard. And I'm sure it's been hard on you too.'

'Yes.' Looking straight in his eyes. 'It has.'

'All the more reason to talk, then. Sort it out.'

She broke the connection, turned away from him. 'I'm not ready . . .'

'Oh, Jesus Christ.' Sperring shook his head once more. 'Honestly. You two. Like dealing with a pair of kids sometimes.'

She glanced at the screen once more. Sperring thought she looked torn: part of her wanting to go, part of her wanting to stay. He said nothing, waited to see which part would win.

'I really have to go,' said Marina.

Sperring knew there was nothing more he could say.

'Whatever you think's best.' He couldn't look at her.

He heard her leave the room, close the door behind her with a soft click. He went back to watching the screen.

He wasn't alone for long. The door opened once more and Cotter entered.

'Has he got a confession yet?'

'Only for the girlfriend,' said Sperring once more. 'Not the wife. Think he's going in for that now.'

Cotter nodded, watched. 'So now we get to it,' she said. 'Now we see once and for all if it's him or not.'

The atmosphere in the room was suddenly tense.

64

P hil was back in the groove now, like he had never been away. Like he had never lost his focus.

Or Marina.

'So you killed Trudi,' he said, ploughing on in to Adderley. 'That much you admit.'

Adderley nodded.

'But what about Gemma? Your wife?'

'No. I didn't kill her.'

Phil gave a sad smile, shook his head slowly. 'No point in lying now, Roy. You're here. You're going down for this. You may as well admit it. You've got nothing to lose.'

Adderley leaned forward, eyes wide, unblinking. 'I didn't kill her.'

'Just admit it,' said Phil once more, but he could sense – reluctantly – the truth in Adderley's words.

'I didn't do it. I didn't kill Gemma. Or that other woman.'

'So where did you go the night I watched you? Where did you drive off to?'

Adderley shrugged uncomfortably. 'Just . . . drove.'

'Where to?'

Another shrug.

'Okay,' said Phil. 'Let's say I believe you about Gemma and Janine Gillen. Just tell me where you drove to and we'll leave it at that. Satisfy my curiosity, if nothing else.'

Adderley was clearly unhappy at being asked to deviate from what he wanted to say. But Phil was insistent.

'Tell me, Roy.'

'I . . . had sex.' His head dropped with shame.

'You had sex. What, someone you knew?'

He shook his head.

'A prostitute? That what you mean?'

Another nod of the head. Much more reluctant this time.

'So where did you go to pick this woman up? Balsall Heath, round there?'

Adderley mumbled something under his breath. Phil leaned closer to hear it.

'What was that?'

'I said, it wasn't a woman.' Adderley looked up. Shame burned in his eyes.

'A man?' Phil was stunned. 'You visited a male prostitute?'

He nodded once more.

'So that's it. Right. Why you hate women so much. Even why you turned to God. You feel like you should be doing one thing, living your life one way. But your family, your . . . I don't know, culture, whatever, tells you you should be doing something else, is that it?'

Adderley looked up, eyes filled with tears, face twisted with self-loathing. 'You know nothing. Nothing about me. I'm not gay. I'm not. That was . . . an accident.'

'You've done it before, though. That wasn't your first time.'

Adderley stared.

'And you always felt bad afterwards, right? Always felt sorry for yourself. Ashamed. You probably prayed, promised it wouldn't happen again.'

Adderley's head dropped once more, shoulders shaking as he sobbed.

'But eventually you felt the urge to do it again. That right?'

Adderley looked up, angry this time. 'No. That's where you're wrong. I wouldn't have done it again. Because I've got God's help. He keeps me strong. He helps me when I'm feeling ... tempted.'

'So you didn't kill Gemma.'

'No. I didn't.'

'But you would have done. If she'd stayed with you.'

'I wouldn't.'

'You would. You would have made it impossible for her to leave, no matter how much she wanted to. Scared her so much that she had to stay. And all it would have taken would have been one blow too many, and it would have been her you beat to death.'

Adderley said nothing.

'Or it could have been the next one. After Trudi. Maybe Trudi wouldn't have waited around to find out what you were like. One slap from you and she'd have been off. But you'd have found another. And you'd have killed her. It was going to happen, Adderley. The way you are, you were always going to kill someone. It was only a matter of time.'

Adderley's face looked like it had been repeatedly slapped, Phil's words having their effect. He wiped the tears from his cheeks, then sat still, his lips moving in silent, secret conversation, eyes closed. Eventually he opened them and that same stupid, beatific smile appeared on his face again. Back in control. Or what passed for his control.

'It's all your fault,' he said once more.

Phil shook his head, about to start again, but Adderley beat him to it.

'It is,' he said, 'and that's all right. Really.' Nodding now, still smiling. 'You know why?' Leaning forward, as if about to let Phil in on some great secret. 'Do you? Mmm?' He sat back, arms out. 'Because I forgive you.'

'Oh, for fuck's sake . . .'

'And Jesus forgives you. I forgive you. And Jesus forgives you.'

Adderley put his arms down and fell silent. Staring straight ahead, nodding to the words of a voice only he could hear, the vapid grin still in place.

'That it?' asked Phil.

No reply from Adderley.

'You've said your piece now, yeah? You've brought me all in the way in here when I could have been sitting on the sofa with a cup of tea watching *Homes Under the Hammer* and *Deal Or No Deal* just so you, a murderer, wife-abuser and repressed homosexual, can forgive me.' Phil gave a short, harsh laugh. 'Brilliant.'

Adderley said nothing, but the smile, Phil noticed, became more fixed.

Phil hadn't finished, though. 'Well, that's nice. How fine and dandy. Lovely.' He leaned forward once more. 'But it's you who should be worried about being forgiven. Don't you think?'

'God will forgive me,' said Adderley. 'Jesus has redeemed me.'

'I'm not talking about God,' said Phil. 'Let's put him aside for one minute. And I know that you religious types can twist anything to make your holy book say the things you want it to say, so let's also put aside the bit about "Thou shalt not kill". Not to mention the lying down with other men your lot seem to have such a problem with. That's for you to deal with in your own time. Of which you're going to have plenty.'

Adderley stared at the wall. Phil continued.

'No,' he said, 'not God. Much nearer to home. And a lot more real. I'm talking about Carly.'

Adderley flinched, as if expecting a blow.

'Carly. You must remember her. Little girl, very trusting,

very hurt now, of course. Hopefully she'll recover, but it's going to be a long road. Living with her grandparents, last I heard. Her mother's parents, of course. But then she has to, because you sent her mother, the one good and positive thing in her life, away from her. Forced her away from you. You should have been loving Carly, protecting her, nurturing her. Instead you made her home a battlefield. You terrified her. Now, when she has nightmares, it'll be your face she sees.'

Adderley shook his head, hoping to dislodge Phil's words. 'No . . .'

Phil kept on. 'You couldn't bear the fact that your wife and daughter were leaving you, so you killed Gemma, made it look like a madman was on the loose.'

'No . . .'

'Then you killed Janine Gillen. Why, Roy? What for?'

Adderley stared at him, eyes imploring. 'I didn't kill Janine! I didn't! I never even knew her, honestly! Why . . . why would I lie? I killed Trudi, why would I lie?'

Phil sat back. He had been in enough interrogation rooms, heard enough confessions to know when someone was telling the truth. Adderley wasn't the killer. The Heartbreaker. But that didn't let him off the hook.

'Fair enough. You didn't kill Janine Gillen. But you sent your daughter and her mother off into the arms of a madman, who abandoned Carly and tortured and killed Gemma.' He pointed at Adderley. '*You* did that. You. Not me. I don't need to be forgiven. Just you. You should be asking Carly to forgive you.

'And then there's Gemma herself. Gone. Dead. Her parents now have to bury their daughter. D'you think that's right? That parents should be the ones to bury their children? D'you think they'll be forgiving you any time soon?'

Adderley's bottom lip started trembling.

'Ask Trudi's parents for forgiveness while you're at it. Tell them what you've done to their daughter. And her two sons. They knew their mother was with you because you'd put a roof over her head, give her a safe place to bring up her kids. What about them? Going to their mother's funeral? Will they want to forgive you?'

Phil sat back again, finished. And in that moment he felt more alive than he had for a long time. More sure of who he was and what he was supposed to be doing in the world. Confident of himself and even of his future.

Adderley stared straight ahead, his face impassive. An alabaster death mask. Tears formed and rolled from his eyes.

Phil stood up, made for the door, turned back.

'There's a special place in prison reserved for the likes of you. A special wing. It's where the rapists go. The child-abusers and killers, the wife-beaters and murderers. Even in prison there's a hierarchy. And you're going to be the lowest of the low. The scum. Hated by everyone, staff and inmates alike. That's your life, what you've got to look forward to. Where you'll get . . .'

'What?' Adderley's voice was small, tremulous. 'What? What will I get?'

'What's coming to you. What you deserve. See how many of your new friends want to forgive you.'

Adderley's head dropped, shoulders heaving. Uncontrollable sobs.

'I'm going now,' said Phil.

Adderley looked up. 'Why? B—because you have to?'

'No,' said Phil, his voice calm and ice cold. 'Because I can't stand the fucking sight of you.'

He left the room.

Sperring was waiting outside the door.

'All yours,' said Phil, and walked away.

65

'I t's back on.'

Cotter strode into the incident room. Imani, Patel and Marina all looked up.

'Adderley didn't kill his wife. He's not the Heartbreaker. And yes, I know I said never to use that word in here. But we're back with Plan A. Let's go.'

66

Marina was back in the incident room, working through a pile of files, at the temporary desk they had assigned her. Trying not to think of Phil, of how he had been when she had just seen him. Trying and failing.

He had looked like the man she'd fallen in love with. Strong, in command. And handsome. Very, very handsome.

She tried to put all that to one side, concentrate on what she was supposed to be doing. She couldn't think about him at the moment. Maybe they did need to talk. In fact they definitely did. But not here, not now. She had work to do. Finding matches between the killer's victims and previous missing women.

Even though some on the team had taken to calling him the Heartbreaker, Marina refused to do that. She hated the way serial killers – or multiple murderers, as she preferred – quickly had a nickname attached to them. And it always stuck. Something dramatic, heroic or romantic, even. Very Hollywood.

In Marina's experience, multiple murderers were among the most banal, boring people she had ever met. Worse even than golfing enthusiasts and UKIP candidates. They killed because there was something lacking in them. Because their hard-wiring was twisted. There was nothing romantic, dramatic and certainly not heroic about them. Their brains were like hotel breakfast-buffet eggs, fried or scrambled, and their motives a collection of sad, and often harrowing, life experiences that went beyond psychological causes and explainable, dramatic tropes to become tiresome clichés. They had all suffered abuse as children. Not all abused children went on to abuse, but all adult abusers had once been in that situation. They had probably also suffered some serious head trauma that had sent their neural pathways down different routes. Combined with an already twisted pathology due to the abuse, that created a serial killer. Sorry, multiple murderer.

Marina knew all that. But it didn't help get her any nearer to finding him. So she hoped the list that Elli was going through could provide some help.

'Marina?'

Speak of the devil. Marina got up, crossed to Elli's desk. 'How you getting on?'

'I think I've come up with a shortlist of other potential victims. Women who've gone missing under similar circumstances.'

Marina felt that thrill she always felt when a discovery was about to be made. 'Show me.'

Elli pointed to the screen. 'Okay. I started on the list of missing persons, narrowed down by the parameters you gave me. Age, background, marital status. Missing in the last few months. That was a start. Then I narrowed it down further. Had these women ever been for marriage guidance counselling? Had they ever been involved in incidents of domestic violence, even if it was only reported and not taken any further? Then I checked the geographical area. And this is what I came up with.'

She pointed to the screen. Marina saw several files, all profiles of missing persons.

'Five matches,' said Elli. 'Here we go. Bethany Worth.

Known as Beth, it says here. Twenty-nine, married with two kids. Lived in Stirchley with her husband, Peter. Been missing for seven months now.'

'Domestic violence?' asked Marina.

Elli nodded. 'Police called to reports of a disturbance last April. She was found on the kitchen floor, bruising about the face, holding her ribs. An ambulance was called, taken to A and E. Patched her up, let her go. Tried to take the husband in for assault but she refused to press charges.'

Marina nodded. 'Right. And she's been missing since then?'

'Shortly afterwards. May. I've managed to get hold of her file. The husband was questioned but had an alibi. Cast-iron. Away in Glasgow for work. The investigation got nowhere. Still open but on the back burner. Apparently she had relatives in the north. The supposition was that she'd gone to stay with them.'

'Children?'

'Left behind. Lot of name-calling, bad mother, all that.'

'Right. She fits. Next one?'

'Ludwika Milczarek. Polish. No children. Lived with her boyfriend, Marek Chociemski. Both immigrants. Had a flat in a high-rise in Handsworth. She worked as a cleaner and barmaid in a local pub. Doesn't say what he did.'

'Working off the books, probably.'

Elli nodded. 'Apparently Chociemski didn't like Ludwika working in the bar. Accused her of flirting with other men, according to the police report. When she came home, he used to question her then beat her.'

'That's all on the report?'

'It's what she told the investigating officer. Said she didn't flirt with anyone. That he was out drinking nearly every night and God knew what he got up to.'

'Did it go any further?'

'She was given information about refuges by the uniforms, and that was that. Said she didn't want to take things further because she was scared of being deported.'

'And then she disappeared. Nearly a year ago.'

'Right.'

'And the boyfriend?'

'He kind of disappeared too. For a bit. Came back on to our radar a few months later, living with another girl, causing another domestic disturbance. Didn't seem too upset at the loss of Ludwika.'

'And of course the police didn't exert themselves looking for her?'

Elli shook her head. 'Says here they did everything possible. Checked the airports, ports, all of that. Released a description in the Polish community. But no. I doubt they knocked themselves out on it.' Her hands played over the keys. 'Right. Next one.'

'Just a minute. Thinking.' Marina looked at the screen. There had been photos attached to the reports and she was scrutinising them, trying to see if there was any common factor between them, any similarity that would trigger something in the killer's mind. She couldn't see it.

So what did that mean? There was a trigger, there must be. Had to be. She looked at the pictures again. Nothing. Young women. Some white, some black. Hurt, vulnerable young women. That was his trigger.

'Go on,' said Marina.

Elli put the next one up on the screen. A young black woman. Pretty, Marina thought. Hard eyes. But looked nothing like the first two.

'Elizabeth Thompson. Thirty-one. Three children. Used to stay with their grandmother a lot. She went out. Had a number of gentleman friends.'

'A prostitute?' asked Marina.

'Doesn't say so, not in so many words,' said Elli, 'but that's the implication. Had a boyfriend, though.'

'For that I think we can read pimp,' said Marina.

Elli nodded. 'He's the one that beat her up. And then she disappeared.'

'I bet the boys in blue went to town on him.'

She scanned the report on the screen in front of her. 'Oh, yes. Or at least they tried. Turned up nothing. Had to let him go. Now.' She pressed more keys. 'Number four. Gail Simpson.'

Another pretty black girl appeared on the screen.

'Different kind of background. Kings Heath. Middle class. Husband's business went bust, started drinking.'

'And got a bit handy with his wife.'

'Looks like it.' Elli gave a grim smile. 'But you know one of the golden rules of policing? Or at least one of the great unspoken ones.'

'Tell me.'

'Don't fuck with the middle classes.'

'So nothing was reported.'

'No domestic violence reports, no. Or if there were, they've been dropped. No trace. But they went for marriage guidance counselling. Seemed to be doing pretty well, according to the husband's statement. And then she disappeared.'

'Anything from marriage guidance about them?'

Elli nodded. 'Apparently Gail was scared of her husband. Wanted a list of refuges. Case is still officially open, but . . . ' She shrugged. 'And the last one that fits the profile. Jusna Kamdar. Originally from Pakistan, but had been living in the UK for ten years.'

Marina nodded. All vulnerable women with low self esteem. All isolated in some way. Her hypothesis about what his triggers were was strengthened.

'Disappeared three months ago. Recently married. But apparently unhappy. Her husband was a distant cousin who came over from the old country.' Elli looked up. 'We know what that means.'

'Arranged marriage?'

Elli nodded. Shuddered. 'Hateful. And she was having marriage guidance counselling. But not her husband. He wouldn't go.'

Marina frowned. 'Was she Muslim? Wouldn't she try to go to a Muslim refuge?'

'By all accounts she didn't want to be Muslim. Hated it. Saw herself as a Western girl. Went to university. But couldn't escape her family's clutches. Poor girl.'

'And disappeared,' said Marina.

Elli nodded. 'All of them.' She pressed another button. Another screen appeared. 'These are the notes from Safe Haven. Phone calls corresponding to the dates these women went missing.'

'So they all called Safe Haven and then all disappeared? And no one noticed because ...' She shrugged. 'How can you? What are you looking for?'

'Seems that way.'

Marina straightened up. 'Brilliant work, Elli. Really, really brilliant.'

Elli smiled.

'I'll go and tell Cotter. Confirm her worst fears for her.'

'Rather you than me,' said Elli.

But Marina was already out of the door.

67

Marina didn't reach Cotter. Not straight away. She went barrelling round a corner and ran straight into the last person she wanted to face.

Phil.

They both stopped dead, stared at each other. It seemed as if all those around them in the building, the building itself, the brightly lit corridor, the hubbub of voices and clacking of computer keys, echoing footsteps and ringing laughter, just melted away. There was only the two of them. Alone.

No running away now. Marina felt her body go into fight-or-flight, adrenalin pumping round her system. She couldn't help it: it was a physiological response. But even as it happened, she allowed her mind to take over and tried to override her body's response. After all, here was a man she loved, a man she had pledged the rest of her life to. A man who had seen her naked on every possible level.

And from the look in his eyes, she was certain that Phil was experiencing something similar.

'Hi,' she said, for want of anything else.

'Hi yourself,' he said, trying for nonchalance, attempting a smile. It died on his face.

'So,' she said, after an expanse of silence that seemed to last years, 'how are you?'

He shrugged. 'Fine,' he said, voice aiming for lightness, missing.

She nodded. 'Good. I . . .' Should she tell him? Admit it? She didn't know. But she couldn't stop herself. 'I saw you. In the interview room. From the observation suite.' She gave a laugh, forced and high. 'God, whoever named it that had a sense of humour. Cupboard, more like.'

'You saw me?' he said, not joining in with her brittle laughter.

She stopped laughing. Her face became serious once more. 'I . . . yes. I watched you.'

He nodded, head down, eyes averted. Said nothing.

'You were . . . good.'

He gave a smile, a short laugh, as if he had just won a pointless, pyrrhic victory. 'Thanks.'

'You . . .' She didn't know what to say next, felt she was talking for talking's sake. Just to be saying something, just to be communicating. 'You really nailed him. Good work.'

Phil nodded once more. Then he stared at her. And in the moment of their eyes connecting, she felt naked all over again.

She quickly looked away.

'Just what I do,' Phil said, distractedly. Like his words no longer mattered after looking into Marina's eyes. Like he had seen something there that made more sense than words.

She looked at him once more. Really looked at him this time. Saw beyond his usual battle armour of leather jacket and plaid shirt, took in the stubble, the messed hair, the black rings round the reddened eyes.

'You look terrible,' she said, the words out before she could stop herself.

His eyes widened slightly, as if he was taken aback a little. But only a little. She felt like he agreed with her.

301

'You don't,' he said, gulping the words like a drowning man struggling for air. 'You look wonderful.'

Her hand went instinctively to her hair and she smiled involuntarily. She felt herself blushing. 'No I don't. I'm ... I'm at work ...'

'Anyway,' he said, filling the void so she didn't have to respond further, 'you're not the first person to tell me I look terrible today. Getting used to it now.'

She looked like she was about to ask him who else had said it, so he continued talking, silencing her.

'You're back, I hear.'

She nodded. 'Yes.'

'On my case.'

She nodded again.

'Well, what was my case. Until recently.'

'That one, yes,' she said, as non-committal as possible, not going into detail, not picking up the thread from his words.

They stood in silence again. Staring at each other, looking away.

'How's Josephina?' asked Phil eventually.

'She's ... good. Yeah. She's safe.'

'Good.' He nodded. 'I'm glad. Safe. No, really, I'm glad. And you're safe? You feel safe? You can do this?'

Marina sensed something building within Phil, and while she couldn't blame him, she didn't want to go into it. Not here, not now. 'Please, Phil. Time and a place.'

He moved closer to her. 'Is there?' he said, voice a ragged whisper. 'When? Where?' As though everything he had stored inside, kept bottled up, was threatening to spill over. 'You tell me, because ... ' He sighed, stepped away from her once more, shaking his head, face twisted.

'I'm sorry,' Marina said. 'I really am.'

No response from Phil.

'Look,' she said, 'we need to talk. Properly talk.'

He looked up. 'You didn't want to talk a couple of days ago. What's changed?'

Marina sighed, shook her head. 'Look, Phil, we can't go into this here and now. I've got work to do.'

Phil nodded, composing himself. Glancing round to see who was walking past, suddenly aware that, no matter what they might be feeling, they weren't actually alone.

'Right,' he said, nodding once more. 'How's ... how's it going?'

Marina frowned. 'How's what going?'

'The investigation.' Phil's voice small, his eyes blinking, unfocused.

Marina was glad to be on safer ground, to have something she could actually talk to him about without him getting angry or upset. Well, not too angry or upset. 'It's bigger than we thought. We may have found more potential victims.'

'Confirmation that we're dealing with a multiple murderer?' he asked.

She nodded. 'That's about the size of it.'

She looked at him again and she could see it in his eyes. That hunger. That need to be there, to be involved. It was part of him, a defining part. It was who he was.

But there was more to it that that. Yes, he wanted to be back on the team, leading the team, involved, in the thick of it. But there was something more crucial. He wanted to be doing it with Marina. She could see that in his eyes, and it was a whole other level of pain for him.

'Look,' she said, 'I'd ... I'd better go. I've got to ... ' She gestured down the corridor.

He nodded, as if in acceptance of the situation. 'Yeah. Good ... good luck.'

She didn't know what to do. Kiss him, hold him, touch him ... She did none of them. She just gave an embarrassed half-smile, turned and walked off.

She knew, as she went, that he was standing there watching her.

68

'You ready? You know what to say and how to say it?'

Imani nodded. 'You coached me well, master.' She was aiming for levity, but the tightness in her throat, round her chest, betrayed her.

Marina took her hand from the other woman's shoulder. Looked down at her, then stood back.

Night had fallen. The incident room felt overlit, a lighthouse against the darkness outside. Imani had asked to be alone, or as alone as possible, when she made the call. She had Marina with her. Cotter, Sperring and the rest of the team were waiting nearby, out of earshot.

Imani had practised all afternoon. One-to-one sessions with Marina, getting the words right, and more importantly, the inflections, the sense of what she was saying. The emotions behind the words.

They had found a room, just the pair of them. Closed and locked the door. Marina had looked tense, shaken even, Imani thought. But then she had just discovered five other potential victims of the Heartbreaker, so in Imani's mind she had every right to be a little distracted. A little upset.

'Okay,' Marina had said. 'How d'you feel?'

'Good,' said Imani, feeling anything but. Trying to take it one step at a time, not think about what she was about to face, just make sure she got through things as they presented themselves to her. Not rushing.

'Really?' said Marina. 'If it was me, I'd be terrified.'

Imani laughed then. 'Yeah, that too.'

They went to work. Going over the words, using the script Marina had written for her.

'You have to sound like who you are,' said Marina, 'who they want you to be. You have to be convincing. You ever done any acting?'

'Nativity plays at school,' said Imani. 'I think I was a shepherd once. Wore a tea towel and a dressing gown.'

'Well, this is a bit different. Let's do it again.'

They did it again, Marina playing the person from the refuge. And the more they did it, the harder Marina tried to make it for her. At first Imani just stopped talking, said that what she was doing wasn't in the script. But as Marina explained, there wasn't a script for the person on the other end of the phone. All she had was Imani and her voice. And that had to be convincing. 'You have to know who you are and why you're calling. You have to be desperate. You have to be in fear of your life.'

That was the part Imani had found the most difficult. She spent such a large part of her life trying to be in charge, to make sense of things, to appear competent and commanding, that to behave in the opposite manner was totally against her instincts. She said so.

'Lie,' said Marina. 'Come on, Imani, you encounter liars every day. You sit there looking across the interview room table knowing the person opposite is lying their arse off to you. So all you have to do is take a bit of that on board.'

'I know, but . . . ' She hadn't found the right words of encouragement from Marina yet, the one phrase that would unlock her reticence, show her the way forward.

'Be weak,' said Marina. 'Or appear weak. When he goes for it, when you're out there confronting him, bringing him in, you've got all the time in the world to be strong.'

That made sense. That was it. A couple more run-throughs and she was ready.

Now she sat in front of the phone, Marina at her side.

'Ready?'

Imani nodded.

'Go.'

Imani picked up the phone, made the call.

'Safe Haven.'

She hesitated as she had been coached to do. 'Hello? I . . . ' She brought a quaver into her voice, her breathing, like she was fighting tears. 'I need help.'

'I'm Alice. What can I do to help you?'

'My . . . I . . . my husband, he . . . ' And then she broke down. To her surprise, she found that she was actually crying real tears. This buoyed her. She kept going. 'My husband, he's . . . I think he's going to kill me.'

'Okay,' said Alice. 'What makes you say that?' Her voice calm, professional, yet warm too.

'He . . . hits me. For the slightest thing. When I'm late, when I'm . . . out. He says things to me, he's always angry with me . . . '

And on she went, finding her strength, her voice. Or the voice she was pretending to have. The more she talked, the easier it became. And the more convincing she felt she was.

Marina, listening in on the other line, knew it was working, gave her a thumbs-up in encouragement.

But Imani didn't need it. 'Please,' she sobbed into the phone, 'please. I just need . . . I need to get away. Please. You have to help me . . . '

On the other end of the phone Alice said, 'Would you like to come here?'

307

Imani's eyes lit up. But she kept in character. Didn't want to lose it now, in the final few lines. It would be like a survivor at the end of a disaster movie slipping and falling on the way to the helicopter.

'Yes,' she said. 'Yes please . . .'

'Right. Whereabouts are you?'

Imani told her the name of the place the team had agreed on, and a fake name. Alice gave her directions where to go to meet the car.

'How . . . how will I know it's the right car?'

'You'll need a password. Ask the driver for it. The password's clementine. You got that?'

Through her sobs, Imani said she had.

'We'll see you soon.'

She put the phone down. Sat back and breathed a huge sigh of relief. 'Jesus, that was hard work.'

'You did brilliantly,' said Marina.

Imani smiled. 'Lot harder than playing a shepherd.'

Marina laughed. More out of relief than anything.

Cotter re-entered the room. 'We on?' she asked.

Imani stood up. 'We are.'

69

He couldn't believe it. The first night back listening in and here it was. Perfect. *Perfect.*

He could have leapt up, danced round the room with joy, but he controlled himself. Because he wasn't finished. The Heartbreaker still had something important to do. He watched the screen again. Saw the number being called. When it was just about to be picked up, he intercepted.

'Hello?' he said, his most passive voice.

'Hi,' said the voice, 'it's Alice from Safe Haven. Is Jan there?'

'She's . . . just nipped out. Shouldn't be long. Can I help at all?' As non-threateningly as possible.

'Oh, we need someone picked up and she was on call tonight. Don't worry, I'll try someone else.'

'It's no problem. As I said, she shouldn't be long. I'll tell her you called. She'll only be a few minutes. Shall I take the details?'

'You sure it's no trouble?'

What did I just fucking say, you thick fucking bitch?

'Absolutely. No trouble at all. And she'll be there. She won't keep your new charge waiting.'

'Well, if you're sure . . . ' Alice gave out the information about where Jan was to go. 'And her name's Melanie.'

'Melanie, right.' Talking like he was writing this down. 'Same, what is it, password, secret word, whatever as last time?'

'Same one.'

'I'll let her know.'

He said his goodbyes and hung up.

Same password as last time . . . He laughed to himself. Alice obviously thought she was being clever by not giving out the password. But in fact all she had done was confirm it for him.

He stood up, stretched. Eager to get going, excited that at last he was back in action. And this time there would be no mistakes. No fuck-ups. This time he would do things properly.

70

Claire Lingard was sitting at the dining room table, having commandeered it as her home office desk, papers spread out in front of her. She hated the idea of having a home office, wanting to compartmentalise her working hours and her leisure hours, her family hours. But unfortunately there were times when she had no choice but to combine the two, and this was one of them. She disliked working from home at the best of times, and completing grant forms counted as one of the worst.

Her phone beeped beside her. Grateful for any distraction, she picked it up, checked the screen. A text message from Imani: *It's on.*

She put the phone down, looked at it. Should she reply? If so, what should she say? She didn't know the etiquette of this kind of operation. She picked the phone back up again, answered.

Keep me posted.

That should do it.

She put the phone back on the table, took a mouthful of wine, looked at it.

A murderer. An actual murderer. Preying on the kind of women she helped on a daily basis. She still couldn't quite get her head round it. A murderer. Not in a film or a book, but here. Real. In her life. She shook her head. Took another drink.

Maybe it shouldn't be so hard to believe, she thought.

Murders did happen. Some of the women she had worked with were testament to that. But that was always an enraged, maddened husband or partner. This was different. A deliberate killer choosing his victims, targeting them. Killing them. A Hannibal Lecter. Here. On her doorstep. That was the hard part to work out.

The door opened.

'Hiya.'

Keith. Back from working in one of the other flats. Rubbing his hands together, shaking the dust from his clothes.

'Not in here,' she said.

'Sorry,' he replied with an apologetic grin. 'I'll go to the bathroom.' He set off down the hall, stopped, turned, came back. 'Oh, by the way. Just to let you know, I'm popping out for a bit.'

'What, now?'

'Yeah,' he said, scratching the back of his neck, face pulled into an awkward expression. 'Call from Brendan. Needs a chat.'

She sat upright. 'Brendan? What's wrong?'

'Dunno. You know what he's like. Him and Cath having problems, probably. Just needs a sympathetic shoulder.' He gave a small laugh. 'Or at least an ear. He does most of the talking.'

'But . . . didn't you see him the other day?'

'Yeah, I know, but . . . ' He gave a helpless shrug. 'What can you do?' He turned away, began walking towards the bathroom once more.

'But you've had a drink,' Claire called after him. 'You won't be able to drive.'

'Just one glass of wine,' he said. 'A small one. With dinner.' He laughed. 'Officer.' He came back into the room. 'I'll be fine. Don't worry.'

He pulled on his jacket, kissed Claire on the forehead and left.

She looked at the door to the other flats, the ones he was renovating. Where he spent all his spare time. Doing them up, preparing them to rent out. Bring in a bit of money. Or if everything went to plan, a lot of money.

She nodded to herself. Then looked at her phone, back to the door. She gets that text, he leaves. Coincidence? Of course. Of course it was.

She kept looking at the door. Unable now to concentrate on the grant forms.

Had she ever seen the flats? The work Keith had done? No. Wait until they're finished, he'd said. See them all at once. She'd be impressed.

She kept staring at the door.

Just a coincidence, that was all. Just a stupid, ridiculous coincidence. Not Keith. Not her husband. Rubbish. She couldn't believe it. Didn't want to believe it. Because if that was the case, if he was . . .

No. He couldn't be. No.

On her doorstep . . .

Claire kept staring at the door.

71

'Where to this time?'

'Just out,' said Ellison, pulling on his coat. He turned to look at his wife, still in the same chair, the TV turned up as if she was deaf. He hated her. 'For Christ's sake, woman, what business is it of yours?'

'I'm your wife, Hugh. I should know where you're going. Every night it's like this. I have to sit here while you go out.'

'You don't have to sit there. You could get up and do something.'

'Other husbands take their wives out places. Other husbands ask their wives if there's anywhere they want to go and take them. Not you. Oh no. Out with your friends.' She gave a snort of derision. 'Friends.'

'Yeah, friends,' said Ellison, turning from the front door, walking back into the lounge. 'Work friends. Colleagues. That's the only way to move up in this job. Networking. You know that.'

'Oh yeah,' she said, almost standing. 'I know that. There was a time when you used to take me with you. When there were parties and nights out with other coppers and their wives. Remember them? I know all about networking.' She stared at him, a cruel, unhappy look in her eye. 'I know all about the kind of networking you do.'

Ellison felt his hands shaking. He stuck them in his pockets so he didn't do something with them that he would later regret. 'What are you talking about?' he mumbled. 'You're talking rubbish.'

'I know your networking. I know who your friends are. Networking on their backs, is that what they do? Your friends?'

He stood over her, hands itching to come out of his pockets. He had never hated any woman as much as he hated her.

'You're a miserable, ugly cunt. Go fuck yourself.'

She was too stunned to reply.

He turned and walked out.

Trying to feel good about himself, about how he had behaved and what he had said. Trying not to hear the tears coming from behind him.

72

The Moseley Road Baths was a historic landmark, looking more like a church than a swimming pool.

An ornate Gothic Renaissance building with terracotta stone, red bricks and an imposing bas-relief coat of arms over the main entrance, the baths had been standing for over a century and was part of the city's rich Victorian and Edwardian heritage. But it had seen better days. Some of the square leaded windows were broken; moss and mildew grew on the brickwork. If it had been in a more secluded setting rather than a main road in Balsall Heath, it would have made an imposing haunted house.

Imani stood in front of it, checked her watch. Ten fifteen. The car was late.

It had been a struggle to organise things so quickly without making the driver suspicious. If indeed it was the Heartbreaker. Operations like this were usually planned well in advance, with areas chosen only after risk assessments had been done, negotiations conducted with all departments and permission granted from on high. But the speed of this one meant that no such action could be taken.

They had done the best they could given the time they had. The Moseley Road Baths wasn't a bad location. Somewhere public, somewhere it would be possible to make a scene if things went wrong. Hopefully.

Imani stood by the bus shelter before the baths. She shivered, even though the night wasn't particularly cold. But it had started raining again. Pouring. She was glad of the shelter to keep her dry.

The rest of the team hadn't been so lucky.

They were secreted all about the area: the junction with Edward Road, Moseley Road itself, even the back alley opposite. With an armed response unit stationed nearby, waiting for the word. The cavalry. Avi Patel had been elected personal back-up. Out of all of them he had the most recent firearms training, so he was armed. He was across the road, hood up, sitting on the bench of the bus shelter opposite.

'Anything yet?'

Imani heard his voice in her ear. She was in radio contact with all of them, but they were trying not to use it in case the Heartbreaker was watching, saw her talking to herself and put two and two together.

She sighed. 'No,' she said, trying not to move her lips. 'I'd let you know if there was.'

'You sound like a ventriloquist,' he said, laughter in his voice.

'Get off the line, Avi,' she said. Not unkindly.

She waited.

Just because you can't hear them, she told herself after a while, *doesn't mean they're not there. Just because you can't see them doesn't mean they're not there.* Her team were close. She knew they were.

Knew it.

But that still didn't stop her from shaking.

She waited. A bus came along, stopped. She made no move to get on it. It pulled away again, the driver giving her a less than friendly look. She waited some more.

Two youths walked down the street, coming towards her. Hoods up, gangster roll. Probably in their teens, she thought. Sixth-form kids trying to look tough. They saw her.

Please, she thought, *please don't start anything. Please don't make me start anything . . .*

They approached the bus shelter. One of them, the taller of the two, eyed her up, letting his gaze wander all over her body. Instead of playing meek, like her body language was doing, as Marina had taught her, she hardened her stare in return. Gave them cop's eyes. They looked away. Kept walking.

Imani sighed.

But whatever relief she felt was cut short. Her phone rang.

Heart pounding, she pulled it from her coat pocket, answered it.

'H-hello?' Still keeping in character.

'Hi,' said a cheerful male voice. 'I'm your pickup. I'll be there shortly. Traffic's terrible tonight.'

'Oh,' she said, as non-committally as she could. 'Right. Thought you'd be a woman.'

'Couldn't come. Sent me instead. I'm her husband.' Then, before Imani could answer, 'You there? Outside the baths?'

'Yeah,' she said. 'I am.'

'Could you just cross the road for me, please?'

Her heart skipped a beat. 'What?'

'Sorry,' he said. 'I'm on my way but the traffic's been terrible, like I said. If you could meet me over the other side of the road, I'd much appreciate it.'

Imani looked round. No cars slowing or stopped. Just the hiss and swish of passing vehicles in the rain. She scanned the nearby streets. No sign of a parked car with someone in it, even hidden in shadow.

'What's . . . what's the password?' she asked.

'Oh,' he said. 'Clementine.'

She nodded, even though he couldn't see her. Or maybe he could.

'I'm genuine,' he said, and gave a little laugh.

She nodded once more, thinking. Was there something familiar about that voice? Had she heard it before? Coming over her mobile in the rain, it was hard to tell.

'So can you meet me over the road? It's not far to go.'

Imani looked over at Patel. He was standing up now, looking across at her. Aware that something was happening, waiting for an order. She felt good knowing he was there. Safe.

'Oh . . . okay. Where will you be?'

'You see straight over the road from where you are? There's a road. Lime Grove. Dead end, leads nowhere. I'll park down there. That way I can just scoot round and get you to the refuge quicker.'

She looked across the road. Lime Grove was a narrow, shadowed, tree-lined lane with an old redbrick building on the corner and industrial units behind. It was a dead end, like he had said, mainly used for fly-tipping. *Dead end*, she thought. *Only one way out.*

'Right,' she said. 'I'll be there.'

'Good. Don't worry, soon have you out of the cold and the wet.'

He hung up.

Imani looked round. Patel was ready to go, but she didn't want him to accompany her. Too suspicious. Too obvious. She didn't know what to do.

She heard Cotter's voice in her ear. 'Imani, what's happening?'

She didn't want to talk, to say anything aloud in case he was watching, in case he saw her lips moving and suspected a trap. She tried speaking with her mouth closed.

'Got to . . . move . . . '

'Move, move where? Was that him, Imani?'

'Yeah.'

'Where do you have to move to? Tell me, Imani.'

'Just ... round the corner ...' She picked up her phone again, called Claire. Just to check that protocol was being followed. That there was no chance her driver would change the pickup spot.

Engaged.

She tried the refuge. Same story.

'Imani? What's happening?' Cotter again.

'Got to go over the road,' she said. 'Meet him there. Get Patel to cover me, follow from a distance.'

Without waiting for a reply, she picked up her bag, stepped into the road.

73

Sperring stood up. He had been crouching behind a railing at the side of the Moseley Road Baths. He had heard everything that was happening.

'Ian,' said Cotter.

'Here, ma'am.'

'On my signal, get ready to move. Imani's gone down Lime Grove. Wait a few seconds, then we follow. I'm not going to delay any longer. We can't have him driving her away.'

'He's changed the plan already,' Sperring said. 'Made her more vulnerable.'

'I'm well aware of that, thank you,' she said.

He heard her next call, to Patel. 'DC Patel. Go after her now.'

'Right, ma'am. She's just gone down the street. Lost visual contact with her.'

'Then go. I'll call the backup team, get them in place. Stop him from coming out.'

Sperring watched as Patel walked away from the bus stop and, moving as quickly as he could without drawing attention to himself, slipped down the darkened side street.

'Right, DS Sperring. Go. Now.'

Sperring made to cross the road but didn't make it. Another bus hove into view, slowed in front of him, stopped.

'Christ,' he said, ducking to the side of it.

Checking for traffic, visibility cut down because of the rain and the dark, he crossed the road. He was just at the entrance to the lane when he heard a sound. It could have been a car backfiring, but he knew exactly what it was.

Then he heard it again.

'Shots fired . . .' he shouted, and ran as fast as his overweight frame would take him.

A car screeched towards him, headlights on full, temporarily blinding him, making him stop, put an arm to his face. He moved to one side but the car did the same. To the other side; the car followed him once more.

He threw himself into a metal railing and the car sailed past him. Rounded a corner and away, before it reached the main road.

He watched it go, trying to make out the registration number. The rain and the dark stopped him. Plus the fact that it had been obscured by something – mud, or paint.

He looked round. At the far end of the lane there was a lump on the ground. Not the usual mattress or full bin bags that got dumped. He knew what the shape was immediately. He ran towards it.

'Get an ambulance,' he called, 'now.'

As he spoke, he hoped it wasn't too late.

The body of Avi Patel lay there, the life bleeding out of him.

PART SIX

HEARTS TO HEARTS

74

Phil was awoken by a knock on his front door. Not the bell; a knock.

His first thought: *Marina. She's back*.

He got quickly out of bed, pulled on his dressing gown, made his way downstairs. Then stopped, halfway down. Through the bevelled, coloured half-glass of the front door he could see a silhouette, and it wasn't Marina.

The small amount of hope he had been holding in his heart dissipated immediately and he resumed his downward journey, trudging now, in no hurry to answer.

Another knock.

Better not be UKIP canvassers, he thought. He was in just the mood to let them know what he thought of them.

He stopped again. What if it was the woman who had called before, the one claiming to be Fiona Welch?

Looking round, he tried to find a weapon. Couldn't see anything.

Another knock. Accompanied by a voice this time: 'DI Brennan . . .'

He relaxed. Not Fiona Welch.

He made his way down, opened the door. There stood DCI Cotter.

'Morning, ma'am,' he said, defensiveness creeping into his voice. 'To what do I owe this pleasure?'

Cotter looked directly at him. He saw the strain on her face, the dark circles beneath her eyes. He took in her rumpled, creased clothes. It didn't look like she had slept in them. It looked like she had been too busy for that.

'Can I come in?' she said.

He stood aside, let her in. Closed the door behind her.

'Coffee, please,' she said once inside, and Phil, unquestioningly, went into the kitchen and put the kettle on. He emptied the cafetière of the previous day's grounds, filled it once more.

'Black,' she said. 'And strong.'

He told her to go and sit in the living room, busied himself in the kitchen. He had slept well. His body and mind were fizzing with misplaced energy after the interview with Adderley, the accidental meeting with Marina. He had thought of using alcohol to help him relax, as he had the previous nights, but decided against it. Instead, he had gone for a run, pounded the streets of Moseley, earthing all that muscular and mental electricity as he went. He had returned home exhausted but strangely refreshed. He had eaten a decent meal – not takeaway junk – and listened to a couple of Band of Horses CDs. After that, sleep had come relatively easily.

Coffee made, he took two mugs into the living room. Cotter placed hers on a side table, barely glancing at the design on the mug: Hammer Films' *Countess Dracula*. A little in-joke between himself and Marina.

He took a mouthful of coffee, found it too hot, put it down. He waited for Cotter to speak.

'I'll come straight to the point,' she said eventually, her voice sounding as worn out as she looked.

Phil waited once more.

Cotter almost laughed. 'I can't believe I'm about to say this to you, DI Brennan.'

DI Brennan. Not Phil. That didn't sound good.

She took a mouthful of coffee. Liked it. Took another one. Replaced the mug. 'I've . . . got a proposition for you.'

Phil imagined the worst. This was obviously some way to get him to leave quietly, without any fuss. A way of brushing his recent behaviour under the departmental carpet, avoiding any unwelcome or difficult questions. Hush money. Or at least a hush pension.

'Go on,' he said.

'I . . . want you to come back.'

Phil wasn't sure he had heard her correctly. 'You . . . what?'

'I want you back.'

'In the department? MIS?'

She nodded. 'Yes. Well, need you back would be more accurate.'

'I thought Imani was in charge?'

Cotter looked at him levelly, holding his gaze for an uncomfortable length of time, then glancing away.

'What's happened?'

She looked up once more. 'This investigation needs a new CIO. I want it to be you again.'

'What?'

'Just what I said.' She was snapping, her voice rising in anger. She sat back, composing herself. 'Sorry. Lack of sleep.'

'What . . . what's happened?'

Cotter sighed, took another mouthful of coffee.

Told him.

'Twenty-four hours,' said Cotter. 'That's it. No more, no less.'

Phil sat back in his armchair, coffee long gone cold. He had listened to everything Cotter had said, made no comment, taken it all in. And now this. He still said nothing.

Cotter waited for his response.

'The Assistant Chief Constable wasn't happy,' she said, by

way of explanation. 'And that's putting it mildly. After everything that's happened in the last few days, with you, with DC Oliver, with DC Patel . . .' She sighed. 'It was a tough ask. I had to go out on a limb for you. He only did this grudgingly. After that, it's handed over to another team and they can start afresh. And no doubt we'll be tainted throughout the West Midlands. Untouchable.'

Phil nodded, eventually spoke.

'Why?' he said.

'Because it's been one cock-up after another,' she said.

'No,' he said, leaning forward. 'Why did you go out on a limb for me? Why d'you need me back so soon, so badly? Why me?'

'Because you're good. Because you know the case. Or part of it, and it won't take you long to come up to speed on the rest.' She leaned forward also, her coffee forgotten. 'I need you on this. And I need an answer quickly.' Seeing he didn't speak straight away, she sat back again. 'Twenty-four hours for you to come up with something. To break the case. That's all. Then it's taken off our hands. For good.'

Phil smiled. 'So, damned if I do, damned if I don't, is that it?'

Cotter reddened. 'It was the best I could do, under the circumstances.'

He thought some more. 'And . . . Marina. She was the one who asked you about this? About me?'

'She suggested you, yes. She saw you yesterday. Talked to you.'

Phil neither confirmed nor contradicted her words.

'Can you work with her?'

'I've always managed to do so in the past,' he said.

'I mean can you work with her now,' said Cotter, irritation and exasperation taking over her voice, 'after everything that's happened recently between you?'

Phil shrugged. Aimed for nonchalant; didn't know if he'd managed it. 'If she doesn't have a problem, then I don't either.'

Cotter looked relieved. She reached for her mug, realised the coffee had turned cold and the colour of a dredged canal. Left it where it was. She stood up.

'So,' she said. 'Shall I wait for you?'

'What?'

'You're giving the morning briefing. We've got to go.'

Phil stood too. He was trying to keep his face as blank as possible, devoid of emotion, but inside it was a different story. He was squirming, champing at the bit to be going.

He was ready for the front line again.

75

He'd *known* it. Known it was too good to be true. Or should have known, should have suspected at least.

He'd recognised her voice. Not entirely, not enough to turn and run, just enough to proceed warily, with caution. As soon as he'd called her, as soon as she spoke, he felt something wasn't right. He should have just turned then, driven away, tried another night. But he had stuck with it. The need, the hunger inside him had been so strong that he couldn't fight it. It went far beyond desire, anything so rational as that. He *craved* another victimised woman, had to have her, no matter what.

No matter what.

Now he looked down at the bed where Imani Oliver lay stretched out. He had secured her wrists and ankles at each corner of the bed, spread-eagling her body tightly over the metal mesh frame as he had done with all the others. She wouldn't be going anywhere.

After securing her, he had begun cutting off her clothes. At the start, embarking on this course of action, it had been something that had to be done, an expedient task. But as time had gone on, this part of his work had taken on aspects of the ritual, become a mini-ritual in its own right, even.

First the top half, the scissors – huge and sharp, dressmaker's scissors – gliding smoothly through the fabric like an ocean-going liner through a becalmed sea. Sliding all the way from neck to waist, shoulder to wrist. Then repeated again for the bottom half, waist to ankle. Then the clothing removed, folded and destroyed. Like her old shell, her old identity, being removed, revealing the real person, the woman he wanted to see, beneath.

She was naked, yes, but that didn't mean he was going to do anything sexual to her. Play with her, anything like that. He wasn't some creepy pervert, doing this because he enjoyed it, derived some twisted pleasure from it, he told himself as he cut. This was work. It had a purpose. And yes, he would look at her naked body lying there when he had finished, and yes, he would feel some arousal within himself at what he saw. But that was obvious, to be expected. He was a red-blooded heterosexual male. It was only natural. That didn't mean he would do anything about it. He wasn't an animal.

He had gagged her, too. Not that he thought anyone could hear – the soundproofing on the walls should have seen to that – but it wasn't worth taking the chance. Besides, he had left the first couple of women without their gags and couldn't bear the absolute drivel that came out of their mouths. So the gag it was.

He stared at her, ignoring the growing erection he could feel in his trousers, focusing his mind on the body before him. But he couldn't stop himself from travelling back to the previous night, going over what had happened once again, trying to work out what had gone wrong and how he could put it right.

He should have just driven away. As soon as he saw that policewoman walking towards his car, he should have just turned and gone. But he hadn't. And he knew why. He had thought about it enough times. At first, he was ashamed to admit, he had sat there unable to move, paralysed by indecision. If he drove off, she might see him, recognise him. If he stayed where he was, he ran the risk of her having already identified him. So he did nothing. Waited.

But he had learned something from his previous attempt. He had come to this meeting armed. An untraceable gun. There were gangs all over Birmingham. Easy enough to get if you knew which pub to go into, who to ask. That had been simple. And the other thing he had with him had been just as simple to obtain, in its own way. An electric stun gun. Easy. Bought from a mail order company in America, no questions asked. Sent to a false American address, then forwarded on to him. People offered that service. Again, if you knew the right people to talk to.

What he held in his hand as Imani Oliver approached looked like a large door handle. He waited until she came right up to the car before extending his hand and pressing the trigger. One point two million volts coursed through her, changing her expression from near triumph – she had recognised him and was about to speak, alert the rest of the team – to extreme agony.

Then he had to move fast. He was out of the car, catching her prone body, bundling her into the back seat. And that should have been that. But as he got back behind the wheel, his heart froze. Another police officer was running straight towards him.

He had reacted so fast it was like he hadn't thought at all. He picked up the gun from the passenger seat, leaned out of the window and fired at the approaching figure. Once. Twice. Three times. The man spun round, twisted and dropped. He didn't want to waste any more time. Throwing the gun down beside him, he drove away as fast as he could. Avoiding the main road in case there were more of them, taking the side streets like he had planned, until he was away and free.

It was only when he got back to the flats, running on adrenalin, that reptilian part of his brain having taken over, that he stopped to think. Had he just killed a man? An innocent man? Well, a police officer, but still. Someone who had no business to be there, who wasn't part of his plan. And he had sat there in the car, Oliver still out of it in the back seat, and wondered why he wasn't feeling the remorse, the doubt, the guilt he had expected to. He felt nothing, didn't even need to rationalise his actions to his conscience. Collateral damage, he had thought. Either wounded or dead, that was all he was. A necessary casualty for the greater good. *His* greater good. If he hadn't been there trying to interfere, he would still be alive. But he had been and he wasn't. So that was that. And yes, he had decided, that was something he could live with.

He stared down at the body on the bed once more. Wondered what to do next. She had come round a couple of times but he had successfully stunned her once more. Now she lay there staring at him, eyes wide in terror, pleading silently. Would the ritual still work? Even though she wasn't who she had claimed to be? Could the programming still be done? He didn't know. He would have to wait and see.

He stared at her some more. Tried to form answers in his head. Something came. He smiled. Why not? he thought. Why not give it a go? If she wasn't in that state of release to begin with, he would just have to work harder to put her there. Why not treat it as a challenge and relish it? He nodded. Yes. That's what he would do. It wasn't perfect. But he would give it his best shot. Whatever happened, things would work out better than the last one.

But that was something to look forward to later. There were things he had to do first.

He looked down at the prone woman. Smiled. Knelt beside her.

'Soon,' he said, whispering close to her ear. She tried to pull away but he ignored her. 'Soon.'

Then he stood up, and, mask in place once more, left the room.

Imani Oliver would keep. She wasn't going anywhere.

Ever again.

76

'It's good to be back,' said Phil, scanning the tired, drawn faces before him. 'Just wish it was under better circumstances.'

He looked round the room. It felt like an age had passed since he was last there. But it also felt like no time at all. He glimpsed Marina standing off to the side, slightly apart from the group, not wanting to be directly in his eyeline. He felt his stomach turn over, those familiar pangs once more. Tried to rationalise: she was his wife. The woman he'd shared his life with until recently. Why was he so nervous about being in her presence? He looked at the other faces again. No time to think about Marina now. This was work. And he had to treat it as such.

Apart from that private bubble of tension between him and Marina, in the rest of the team weariness was competing with tension.

'You don't need me to tell you what's happened,' he said. 'Or who we've lost. I know how you're feeling. But we have to pick ourselves up and carry on. These next twenty-four hours are crucial. For us, for Imani, for catching whoever did this. And I appreciate how tired you all are. But we still have to keep going. Right.'

He looked round once more. His words seemed to have perked them up. A little, at any rate.

'Also,' he said, that familiar tension once more creeping into his voice, 'we have the services of Marina Esposito for a few days longer. She'll be staying on to help us catch him.' He looked at her, wanting to say more but unsure what those words would be. She caught his eye; contact flared, then she turned away. He did likewise.

'Right. Let's get on with it. We need to move as quickly as possible. I appreciate you've all been doing that while I was sleeping, so let's have some updates. Where are we? Ian?'

'Preliminary ballistics report says it was a Glock automatic,' said Sperring. 'They're seeing if it's been used before for anything, but they're quite common among the gangs. The gangster's handgun of choice.'

'You think he's a gang member?' asked Phil.

'No,' said Sperring. 'But they also supply guns. Would be relatively simple for him to buy one off them.'

'Right. Time to get the confidential informants out. See if anyone's heard anything about someone buying a gun, or being seen with gang members when they don't look like they belong.' He paused. 'How many shots were heard?'

'Three,' said Sperring. 'And Patel had three shots in him. He's currently fighting for his life in hospital.'

'So we can assume – dangerous word – that Imani wasn't shot. He got her into the car some other way. I suppose, until we learn otherwise, we should be grateful for that. What about forensics from the scene? Anything?'

'Not yet,' said Cotter. 'The rain took care of most of it. The teams are still out looking, though.'

Phil nodded.

Sperring pushed himself away from the desk he had been leaning against. 'We've been looking for the car all over the city. Uniforms, patrols, everyone's been informed. A description's gone out, CCTV checks, the lot. So far we've come up with nothing. He was clever. Changed the location to what we thought was a dead end. Except there was another way out through that industrial estate and he knew it. Sneaky bastard. I saw the car but didn't get the make and model of it. It looked like a saloon, a Toyota Avensis, something like that. But I wouldn't want to say. And the registration plates were obscured too. There were dents along the side, though, so that makes me think it was the same car used to run down Janine Gillen.'

'Same guy, then,' said Phil. 'Not much doubt about that.'

'I don't think we'd be jumping to conclusions to think that,' said Sperring. 'The car was last seen heading towards the Kings Heath area. We're getting uniforms to concentrate their search there. See if it's been stashed, garaged, whatever.'

Phil nodded. 'Good. Thanks, Ian.' A thought struck him. 'Isn't that where this refuge is? Kings Heath?'

'It is,' said Cotter.

'Well, forgive me if this has already been done, but shouldn't we be looking into people there? See if there's any chance one of them was involved? Or even behind it?'

'We are looking into it,' said Cotter. 'We can't rule anything – or anyone – out at this stage. We called them and asked who was on duty for pickups last night. Someone called Jan Melville. The refuge called her and spoke to a bloke who said he was her husband. Said he would give Jan the message.'

'Let me guess,' said Phil. 'Jan Melville doesn't have a husband.'

'Exactly,' said Cotter. 'Claire Lingard's been great at helping us, but I think now's the time to look a bit harder at the rest of them.'

'What about Lingard's husband?' said Phil. 'The marriage counsellor. Would it be worth talking to him again?'

'I've turned up something about him,' said Elli, blushing as she spoke. The whole room turned towards her. 'DS Sperring asked me to look into his background.'

Phil looked at Sperring, frowned.

'I found out that he'd come into property a few years ago,' said Sperring. 'Some dispute about how he got it. Just thought on the grounds of that he might be worth another look. With everything that's been going on, it got pushed to the back burner.'

'Fair enough,' said Phil. 'What did you find, Elli?'

'Keith Bailey's not his real name. Well it is, but he used to be known as Michael Bailey. Keith's his middle name. He started using it after university. That's why it took so long to find this out. He's originally from Manchester. There was something when he was at university in Hull. An allegation of date rape. Well, two, actually. Nothing was proved, only alleged, and no charges were ever brought. That's it, really.'

'Nothing else in his background?' asked Phil. 'Sexual assault, robbery, anything like that?'

'Nothing,' said Elli. 'Well, nothing directly involving him.'

'What d'you mean?'

'Again, more digging,' said Elli. 'When he was a child in Manchester he was taken into care repeatedly. Abuse in the family.'

'Father?' asked Phil.

'Not according to this,' said Elli, pointing to the screen. 'Mother. Pretty bad stuff, too.'

The atmosphere in the room changed. A crackle in the air. The team were still tired, but a mental adrenalin and caffeine shot had just been administered.

'So how does a suspected rapist get to work as a marriage counsellor?' said Sperring. 'That's like Jimmy Savile working with school kids.'

'Which he did do,' said Phil. 'Bad analogy.'

'Person of interest?' asked Cotter.

'I'll go and see him today,' said Phil.

'I'd like to come too,' said Marina. 'Get a psychologist's view.'

Phil looked at her, not knowing whether to be excited or nervous. He was aware that Cotter was watching him, waiting for his response, so he continued. 'Good,' he said. 'Let's do it. But let's not jump to conclusions. Look what happened to me when I did that recently.'

'Can I say something before we all go?' asked Cotter.

Phil gestured that the floor was hers.

'Just before the briefing I heard that Detective Constable Avi Patel has died. They tried, he fought to hold on, but . . . ' Cotter looked close to tears. 'I know he wasn't with us long, but he was one of us. And he didn't deserve that. None of us deserve that. Will you join me in a minute's silence for our fallen colleague, please.'

They did so.

When it was over, Phil looked round the room. He noticed that plenty of eyes were glistening.

'Come on,' he said. 'Cases like this are solved by footwork. Paperwork. Database work. But by teamwork above all. We've taken big losses. We've got one of our own down and another out there. The clock's ticking. Let's find that bastard.'

77

Imani opened her eyes. Everywhere hurt.

All she could see was ceiling. Dark and soft, a single bulb hanging from a cord. It hurt to move her neck, but she did so. Plastic sheeting on the floor. Stained. She looked to the side. Walls similar to the ceiling: thick padding with soft peaks. No windows. She realised what it was: soundproofing. Her heart skipped at that, panic racing through her body.

She tried to calm down, think logically as she had been trained to. She looked round once more. Took in her surroundings, herself. She was naked. That much she knew. Could feel cold air on her body, making her shiver. She felt vulnerable. Alone and afraid.

She pulled on her arms, testing her bindings. Firm. No give at all. Metal handcuffs, chains. She managed another look round. She was secured to an old metal bed frame. Solid, heavy. She tried jumping her body up from it. No movement. Secured to the floor. She felt uncomfortable. Metal chain link digging into her back. Tried to move away from it. No good. She was tied too tight.

She tried to shout, but whatever she had been gagged with, something hard and unyielding, was too tight for her. No sound would come, just little whimpers at the corners of her mouth. She hoped she wouldn't vomit, because that would be that. She didn't need to worry about him; she would just choke to death.

She closed her eyes, tried to focus on her breathing, concentrate.

Don't panic, don't panic, don't panic . . .

Think, Imani, think. How did she get here? The car. Walking towards it. A flash of recognition as she saw the driver and . . .

Nothing. A searing pain in her chest, her whole torso, like something simultaneously sharp and painful yet dull and probing had been forced into her body, reaching bone deep and shaking her until she passed out. She surmised what that had been. Electricity. Some kind of stun gun.

She had woken up again later, felt the same kind of impact when she tried to move. And then finally here. Wherever 'here' was.

But she knew who he was. *She knew who he was.*

And that knowledge was both satisfying and dangerous. Because she wanted to let the rest of the team know – needed to let the rest of the team know – but couldn't. And because she knew what was coming next. She had seen the other bodies. It was only a matter of time.

Don't panic, don't panic, don't panic . . .

Calm. Calm. Think. Think.

She couldn't scream, couldn't move. What could she do? Smell. She did so, analysing the contents of the room. Not good. Human waste, only to be expected. But something else. Like old copper. A butcher's shop smell. Dried blood. Dead flesh. No, not a butcher's shop. An abattoir.

Oh God . . .

Think. Think.

He had been furious when he realised who she was and had administered a severe beating. On and on it went, like he wanted to just keep hitting her. The rage in his eyes horrific. Even worse to be on the end of. She knew it was just because he had been duped, but a beating administered out of desperation and anger was still a beating, and in her shocked state her body had taken about as much as she could bear before it collapsed, her mind shutting down again too.

And waking up once more to find herself here. Alone.

She listened. Nothing.

She pulled at her wrists again. They wouldn't budge, the metal cuffs too tight.

She had to get out, she had to—

Avi. Oh God, Avi . . .

She remembered then what had happened to him. She had heard the gunshots from inside the car, sounding like a sonic boom up close. Glimpsed his body jerk, spin and fall. No time to scream, shout. Warn him. Her body closing down, pain-addled from the stun gun. She had passed out then.

She just hoped he was okay. That someone had called an ambulance, got him to the hospital in time. That someone had saved him.

She pulled harder on her metal cuffs. Got only a pain in her wrists. She lay back on the metal frame, sighed. She wondered how many women had died on this bed. Been tortured, hurt, had their hearts removed . . .

Stop it. *Stop it*. That wasn't helping. *Concentrate. Come on. Focus. Don't lost it, don't* . . .

Think. The team. Cotter. Sperring. One of them. All of them.

She prayed that someone had worked out who had taken her, where she was. That they were coming for her now. She felt her spirits rise at the thought.

She clung on to that thought as she lay there. Desperately, as if her life depended on it.

Because she couldn't think about the alternative.

She really, really couldn't think about that.

78

Phil and Marina drove in silence. Not because they had nothing to say to each other but because they had too much.

Phil pulled the Audi in to the kerb in front of the Relate offices.

'How appropriate,' said Marina.

Phil was unsure whether she was joking.

He locked the car; they walked towards the centre. Still neither of them spoke. As soon as they entered, Phil felt something change within him. He didn't know if Marina was feeling it but reckoned she probably was. A dropping-away of professionalism. A sense of the true function of the place. It wasn't lost on either of them.

They walked to the desk. The woman sitting behind it smiled. Tolerantly, putting them at ease. Phil introduced himself.

'DI Brennan to see Keith Bailey, please.' He showed his warrant card.

The receptionist's eyebrows raised. 'Oh,' she said. 'I thought you were a couple. Sorry.'

Neither of them spoke.

'D'you have an appointment?'

'We don't,' said Phil. 'But it's important.'

Realisation began to dawn in the woman's eyes. 'The police have been in to see him a couple of times already this week.' She was frowning, thinking the worst.

Phil headed off her thoughts by giving her what he thought was a disarming smile. 'Just routine. If you could . . . '

'Yes,' she said. She checked a register in front of her. 'I'm afraid he's busy with a client at the moment.' She gestured to a room behind them. 'Would you like to wait?'

They did so, sitting down on two spectacularly uncomfortable chairs. Still they didn't speak. Phil looked round the room. Shelves full of books, all on the subject of healing relationships. Coping with infidelity. Sexual problems. Keeping relationships together. Marina was also looking.

'Nothing about being hounded by a homicidal woman,' she said.

Phil didn't reply.

At his side was a large hard-bound scrapbook. He picked it up, opened it. It was full of handwritten letters and testimonials. He flicked through them, read a few. All told variations of the same story. They stated the gratitude couples and individuals felt for the counselling they'd received. How their relationships, their lives, even, had been saved. All of them, over and over, pages and pages. Some with more detail than others. All the same outcome.

Marina looked also. 'Like online reviews,' she said. 'They only put the good ones up.'

Phil looked at her. Properly, for the first time that day. She was almost smiling but it was a tight, controlled smile. 'Cynic,' he said.

'Oh, come on,' she said. 'You're the same as me. You don't like counsellors either. Isn't it always the people who are most messed up who decide to be life coaches?'

'But this seems to work,' he said, gesturing towards the book. 'Counselling.'

'Yes,' she said. 'I'm not saying it doesn't. But there are other ways.'

Phil didn't answer. 'The receptionist mistook us for a couple in trouble,' he said eventually.

'Not much of a mistake,' said Marina.

Something dark shuddered through Phil at her words. 'Is that what we are?' he said. 'In trouble?'

Marina looked at him. Straight in the eyes. Her gaze was completely naked, nothing hidden. 'What d'you think?'

'I asked first.'

She shook her head.

'Just answer,' he said. 'Please.'

'I think . . . we've got things to talk about. Things we need to talk about.' She looked at him, waited for his answer.

He thought. 'We've got a problem. But it's not the usual kind that couples have.'

'No. But it's still a problem. It still stops us from being together.'

'Does it?' Phil turned to her. His voice more intense, urgent. 'Because it needn't. We're stronger together. You know that. Why can't you see that?'

Marina was facing him fully now, voice also hushed but intense. 'You want to do this now? Really? Here and now?'

'We have to do it some time. We can't keep ignoring it. If we've got to work together, we should at least know where we stand with each other.'

Marina shook her head. Said nothing.

'You think this is good?' asked Phil. 'A good way for us to live? To bring up our daughter?'

'Well, it's better than pretending nothing's the matter, isn't it? That we don't have a crazed psychopath just lurking around somewhere, waiting to attack us, to . . . I don't know, kill us? Kill our daughter? We don't know who she is. Or what she wants. So I'm not taking any chances.'

Phil nodded. 'So that's it. Do her work for her, yeah? Split us up. Make us miserable.' He leaned in even closer. 'Have you ever stopped to think that this might be what she wants? The two of us at each other's throats, separated. It would be so easy for her to move in, don't you think? Do whatever she's going to do.'

Marina said nothing. Phil continued.

'You can't live your life like this. Neither of us can. We have to—'

A throat being cleared. They both looked up.

Keith Bailey was standing there watching them. They didn't know how long he had been there. Long enough, Phil imagined.

'Detective Inspector Brennan?' he asked.

'Er, yes . . . ' Phil stood up.

'You wanted to see me?'

'Yes, I . . . I did.'

He looked at Marina. 'And this is?'

'Marina Esposito,' said Marina, also standing.

'You're not police.'

'I'm working with the police. Psychologist.'

Bailey's eyebrows raised. He smiled. 'Really?'

Phil looked round the waiting room. 'Could we go somewhere . . . '

'Of course,' said Bailey. 'Please follow me.'

They did so.

Neither looking at the other as they went.

79

Keith Bailey ushered them into a room, closed the door behind them. It had two easy chairs facing a third, a small table with a box of paper tissues. He gestured for Phil and Marina to sit in the two chairs. He took the single one. Crossed his legs. Looked at them.

'Now,' he said, concerned, 'what can I do for you? Is it about Janine? Have you found her killer?'

Phil started. 'We just have a few questions, Mr Bailey.'

Keith Bailey frowned, confused. 'What about?'

Phil ignored the question. 'Where were you last night, Mr Bailey?'

Bailey looked between the pair of them, mouth open in surprise. Phil's features were impassive, Marina's likewise. Something she had picked up from her husband as they had worked together over the years.

'Erm ... At home.'

'All night?' Phil.

'Yes.'

'And could your wife confirm this?' Marina this time, leaning forward.

'Yes, she could,' said Bailey, then, in a louder voice, 'Can you tell me what this is about, please?'

'So,' continued Phil, taking out his phone, 'if we were to ring your wife right now, she would confirm that?'

Bailey, still looking between the two of them, relented. 'I . . . did pop out to see a friend. Brendan. Brendan Hewson. He's got a bit of trouble with his . . . Well, let's just say that when you're a marriage counsellor, your friends always seem to be asking for advice. Rather like a GP, I suppose.'

'Your friend Brendan.'

Bailey nodded.

Phil held up his phone once more. 'And if I were to call him now?'

Bailey looked confused, and slightly scared. 'He'd confirm what I said.'

'He would?'

'Yes. Can you tell me what this is about, please?' Angry now.

Phil replaced his phone. 'I'll need his full name and address,' he said.

'I'll write it down for you.' Another look between the two of them. Neither of them returned it.

Phil was finding it hard to disengage from the conversation he had been having with Marina in the waiting room. But he was trying not to bring his personal baggage into his work and hoping he had succeeded. A quick glance at Marina. She was giving nothing away.

He kept going. Ploughing on through his questions. 'What kind of car d'you drive, Mr Bailey?'

'A Toyota. Avensis. Why?'

Phil stiffened, sat back. Beside him Marina did the same. Bailey looked between the pair of them.

'It's off the road at the moment,' he said. 'In the garage for repairs. Been there a while now.'

'How did you get to work, then?' Marina asked.

'My wife gave me a lift as far as the bus stop. Public transport the rest of the way.'

'Can we check with the garage, Mr Bailey?' Phil again.

Bailey looked at them both once more. Eyelids fluttering like a caged bird's wings. 'Can you tell me what this is about, please? I've asked you four times.'

'Keeping count?' asked Phil. 'It concerns the murder of a police officer and the abduction of another.'

Bailey tried to answer; Marina jumped in. 'And the abductions and murders of several vulnerable young women. Including at least one you had a connection with.'

Again he looked between the two of them. Settled on Marina, since she was the last to have spoken.

'You're a psychologist, is that right?' he asked.

Marina looked surprised at the question. 'Yes,' she said.

'What kind?'

'The criminal kind.'

'Oh.' Bailey looked surprised, then gave a tight smile. 'And are you here to psychoanalyse me?'

Marina kept her face still, stony. She leaned forward very slightly. 'I don't know. Are you a criminal?'

Bailey laughed. It seemed to break the tension in the room for him. 'Very funny. Good.'

'Are you going to answer the question?' asked Marina.

'Which question?'

'Your car,' said Phil.

'Oh, that.' Bailey sat back, scrutinising them once more. 'In the garage. I said.' Getting angry.

'I know you said that. So can we check with—'

Bailey cut Phil off. 'Of course.' He turned back to Marina. Pointed. 'You interest me,' he said. 'You being here. I didn't think this kind of thing happened outside of TV dramas.'

Marina ignored his words. 'What made you become a counsellor, Mr Bailey? A marriage counsellor in particular?'

Bailey smiled. 'Because I'm good at it,' he said.

'Are you?' asked Marina.

'Yes,' he said, warming to the theme. 'I am. Or at least I like to think so.'

'How did you find out that you were good at it? At advising people about their marriages? What made you go into it? Was there a specific incident? Some trigger?'

Phil sat back, didn't interrupt. Let her go.

Bailey gave a self-effacing shrug. 'I . . . It was just something I was always good at. Friends were always telling me their problems. I must have that kind of face. I was always sought out.' He laughed. 'Sought. Funny word, that, isn't it?'

'And an interesting choice, too,' said Marina. 'Implies that you had all the answers. Your friends had all the questions.'

He smiled. *What can I say?* Still trying to be self-effacing, but his body language spoke the words for him.

'Because,' continued Marina, 'most people come to do this kind of thing through personal experience. A bad marriage, rough relationship. A counsellor helped them, inspired them to retrain. Happens with Samaritans too. Nurses, even. An involved response. But you're not saying that. Your motivation was because you were good at it.'

'Yes. What's wrong with that?'

Marina nodded, as if his words confirmed her theories. 'Dare I say it, that's quite an arrogant thing to believe, don't you think?'

Whatever traces of affability had been on Bailey's face dried up. He stared at her. He didn't get the chance to respond. Phil spoke first.

'So let me get this straight. Your friends were coming to see you for advice about relationships,' he said, as innocuously as possible.

'That's right. Nothing wrong with that.' Bailey sounded hurt.

'Nothing at all,' said Phil. 'But I just want to be clear. Was this before or after the rape allegations?'

Bailey froze. Stared.

Phil kept at him. 'Before or after? Just clarifying.'

'You've done your homework.' A small, dry voice.

'We have. University, wasn't it? Hull? Not just once. I mean, once and it could have – possibly – been swept away as a misunderstanding. Possibly. But twice? Two allegations? From different women? That's more than just coincidence, don't you think? That seems to me like a pattern emerging.' He turned to Marina. Making eye contact with her fully for the first time since they had entered the room. 'What would you say? Your professional opinion?'

Marina nodded. 'A pattern, definitely.'

Bailey still said nothing, just stared.

Phil continued. 'So what happened? What turned this fledgling, wannabe rapist into someone doling out relationship advice.'

'*Sought* for relationship advice,' Marina said.

'Thank you,' said Phil, making eye contact with her once more, 'Sought. What happened?'

Bailey still stared.

80

Hugh Ellison stared at his desk. The room seemed smaller and shabbier than ever.

He was finding it hard to concentrate. He knew he shouldn't be there. Somewhere else had a stronger call on him. The investigation into Gemma Adderley's death. That was where he should be.

That was his chance. His last chance, possibly, to be taken seriously, to get back on the ladder. If he could have just managed to squeeze a confession out of Roy Adderley, got him to admit what he had done, he would have been happy. Not just happy, vindicated. That would have shown the higher-ups what he was made of. That he didn't deserve to be stuck in this backwater, that he should be out and about, in MIS, high-flying with the other high-flyers. That was what he should have done. And it had been playing on his mind all morning.

Even if Adderley hadn't done it. Didn't matter. That wasn't the point. There was circumstantial evidence, a false statement He could have worked on that, built it up. For Christ's sake, the CPS had brought things to trial that had a much slimmer chance of a conviction.

But no. The case had been taken off him. Given to the golden boys. And girls. His stomach curdled at the thought. Bile rising. *And girls*.

Brennan had got Adderley to confess to his girlfriend's

murder but not his wife's. Well, great for Brennan. But Ellison should have been in the room with him. He should have been the one to get him to open up. To take the acclaim for that.

And then there was Brennan's wife. But that was a whole other part of his mind. He pushed her away from his thoughts: that wasn't what this was about.

But it was hard to do. He'd seen the way she had looked at him when he walked into their offices yesterday. They way all those bitches had looked at him. The black one, that dyke Cotter and Marina herself. They'd made him feel unwelcome even before he had spoken. Looked at him like he was a piece of shit. And having to turn round, leave the room while he knew they were all watching him had been fucking humiliating.

Fucking humiliating.

That hurt too. All wrapped up with everything else. Turning him into a ball of spite and rage.

He sat back, sighed. Tried to bring himself under control. Thought of last night. Smiled.

That had been good. Revenge. Sweet, sweet revenge. He felt his body tingle once more at the thought of it.

Hadn't been so much fun when he got home, though. The arguments that had followed, the tears. The abuse hurled at him, all his years of failings laid bare. In the end he had walked out. Gone to a Travelodge. He didn't have to take that shit. Not from anyone. Especially after the night he had just had.

Sublime.

He sat there thinking of what he could do. How he could relive the delicious thrills of the night before over and over in his mind, keeping him going for the rest of the boring day until he was free to do something about it once more.

Living for later.

81

'You're a couple,' Bailey said. 'Together.'

Phil frowned. Not the answer he had been expecting. 'Nicely deflected,' he said with a grim smile. 'Are you going to answer the question?'

'You're a couple,' continued Bailey, 'but ... you're *not* together. Am I right?' A small smile of triumph.

'You were listening to us talk in the waiting room,' said Marina. 'You'll already know the answer to that one. Try again.'

'Or try answering my question,' said Phil, his voice hard, flinty.

'You're separated,' said Bailey, continuing as if they hadn't spoken. 'Living apart, at least. But it's not ... ' He gestured towards them. 'There's eye contact. You looked at each other. That's good, that's a positive sign.'

Phil sighed. 'I've had enough of this. If you don't—'

'Eye contact,' said Bailey, 'yet your body language is all wrong. Look at you.' He pointed towards Marina. 'You're stiff, pulling away from him. Arm on the opposite side of the chair. You softened slightly when he looked at you. There was depth in that look. Softness and warmth. You returned it, too, didn't you?'

Phil stood up. 'Mr Bailey—'

'This won't take a moment,' said Bailey. 'Please sit down.' He smiled, attempting to regain control.

Phil looked down at Marina. She wasn't looking at him; she was studying Bailey. Recognising that she was up to something, Phil sat once more.

Bailey seemed to take the gesture as an indication that he had won a battle of wills. Emboldened, he continued. 'And your body language, Detective Inspector, it's just as indicative. You aren't pulling away. You're leaning in, reaching towards her. Attempting to draw her back. But she won't come back, will she? She's pulled away and she's staying away. I wonder why that is?'

Anger welled inside Phil. He could feel it rising, looking for escape. Marina reached across, placed her hand calmly over his. Startled, he sat back.

Bailey noticed the gesture. Smiled. 'Touching now. That's progress, isn't it? Very quick.' He laughed. 'You've only had one session with me. And it isn't even over yet.'

Phil was trying to stand. Marina increased the pressure on his hand, stopping him. He stayed where he was. For now.

'So why are you still separated?' Bailey made a play of stroking his chin, thinking. 'No, don't tell me.'

Neither of them answered.

'Not infidelity,' said Bailey. 'I think we can rule that out. Unusual, though. That's generally the reason.' He sat forward. 'This is becoming interesting. I think we can rule out work, because you work together. Or you are in this instance, so you know what the other one has to go through. Hmm ...'

'Something came between us,' said Marina.

Bailey's eyes lit up. 'I knew it.'

'Not hard to work out,' said Marina. 'Given that you've established we're separated and it's not one of the other two things.'

'Yes,' said Bailey, 'but what was it that separated you? That's the interesting bit.'

Marina glanced at Phil. He was staring straight ahead, looking like he wanted to attack the counsellor. She returned her attention to Bailey.

'Something threatening,' she said. 'Something big and threatening. Something we had no control over.'

Bailey sat forward. 'I'm intrigued.'

'Marina . . .' Phil's voice held a warning.

Marina ignored him, sat back, the ghost of a smile on her face. 'That's as much as you're getting.'

Bailey also sat back, thinking. 'Big and threatening . . . Must have been very big, very threatening to split you up.'

'Oh, it was. It is.'

'And it's still there? Still hanging over you? Stopping you from getting back together? Not infidelity, not pressure of work or lack of it, not illness, not money troubles, not falling out of love with each other. An outside influence. Big enough to split you up.' Eyes fluttering, his head went back.

Marina was aware of Phil trying to look at her. She kept her gaze firmly on Bailey.

Eventually his head snapped forward. 'Fear,' he said.

'Fear,' repeated Marina.

'Yes, fear.' Bailey nodded as if he had just solved Fermat's Last Theorem. 'You see, it doesn't matter what it was, this big and threatening thing; all I need to know about it is what it did. What it caused to happen between you. Fear. That's all. That's what split you apart. Fear.' He looked at them, jubilation in his eyes. 'Am I right? I am, aren't I?'

Marina glanced at Phil. He returned the look. Marina felt something comforting in it, something she hadn't allowed herself to feel for a long time. Hope.

Bailey noticed it too. He smiled. 'Fear. What's that? Really, what is it?' He leaned forward, making sure neither of them missed the importance of his next few words. 'Nothing. That's

356

what it is. Nothing. Fear is . . . ' He shrugged. 'What? Ourselves, or part of ourselves, holding back the rest of ourselves, the bigger and better parts. That's all it is. Feel the fear and do it anyway? A cliché, but it's true.' Still leaning forward, hands clasped together, eyes on the pair of them. 'You have to face your fear. Confront it. Only then can you . . . ' his hands became agitated; he turned one into a fist, hammered it down into the palm of the other, 'destroy it. Dismiss it. See it for what it is, get rid of it.' He frowned. 'What is it you fear? No, you don't have to tell me the actual thing. Just what it involves. The physical process of this fear. A fear so horrendous that it separated the two of you.'

'A sudden attack,' said Marina. 'One we're not prepared for.'

Bailey nodded, expression sympathetic. 'I see. Right. Of course.' He looked at her once more. 'But you can't live your lives like that, can you? It's not helping. What will you have if you do that? I'll tell you. Regrets. For not taking chances. For not conquering your fear, for not taming it, for letting it dictate and ruin your lives. So face it. Embrace it, even. And live.'

Marina nodded.

But Bailey wasn't finished. 'Because only then can you fully be yourselves.' He nodded, pleased with himself. 'Only then can you be the people you want to be. Should be. Deserve to be.'

He sat back. Finished.

Marina nodded as if she had taken it all in, was digesting his wisdom.

'Thank you,' she said.

'You're welcome.' Bailey was beaming.

'Just one thing,' said Marina, face innocently quizzical.

'Yes?' he said.

'What is it *you* fear? Is it those women who said no all those years ago?'

The smile faded from Bailey's face. 'What . . . '

'Are they still after you?' Marina kept going. 'Do they still haunt you? When you close your eyes, do you see them? And what are they saying to you? No, Keith, please don't, Keith, I don't want to, Keith . . . something like that?'

Bailey's eyes widened. He began looking round the room as if frantically seeking an exit. His face became a mask of fear.

But Marina wasn't letting go. 'Is that why you do this, Keith? Really why you do this? Not because you're good at it, or people *sought* you out, none of that. You speak to people at their most vulnerable, try to fix them. Am I right? Is that a fair description?'

Bailey didn't reply.

'Are you really just trying to fix yourself, is that it? Trying to find out what went wrong? With them. With you. Trying to find it and fix it?'

Bailey said nothing. He seemed close to tears.

Marina leaned forward, eyes locked on to his. Never leaving them no matter how hard he tried to pull away. 'Are you still trying to put the ghosts to rest, is that it, Keith? What other ghosts do you see?'

She sat back. Glanced at Phil. He nodded.

'What do you know about the murder of Detective Constable Avi Patel last night?'

Bailey shook his head.

'What do you know about the abduction of Detective Constable Imani Oliver?'

Bailey clamped his eyes shut.

'Or about the murder and abduction of Janine Gillen, and Gemma Adderley, and—'

Bailey stood up. 'Get out. Get out now . . .' gesturing, pointing frantically at the door. "How dare you, how . . . fucking dare you . . .'

Phil opened his mouth to speak again. Bailey jumped in first.

'You want to talk to me, you do it through my solicitor. Now get out.'

He grabbed Phil, tried to hurl him towards the door.

Phil and Marina stumbled through, heard the door slamming behind them. They heard a further noise as Bailey slumped down against it.

As they walked away, they were sure they could hear sobbing.

82

Phil and Marina got back into the Audi. Neither spoke or even looked at each other as they left the building.

Phil put the key in the ignition, made to turn it. Stopped. Looked at Marina.

She seemed to consider looking away, but something stronger won. She turned, looked at him too.

'You were great in there,' he said.

She smiled. 'You weren't so bad yourself.'

Their eyes were locked. Eventually Phil pulled away. Her gaze made him feel naked.

'What d'you think?' he said.

Marina frowned. Puzzled. 'About what?'

'Him. Keith Bailey. Reckon he's our guy?'

'I'd say he goes straight to the top of the leaderboard. Evasive, narcissistic, delusional . . . all the boxes ticked.'

'Still wouldn't answer a direct question,' said Phil. 'Hardly a criminal mastermind.'

'Doesn't need to be,' said Marina. 'He's got away with it until now.'

'Right,' said Phil. 'Back to the station. Get the wheels in motion. Talk to Cotter. See about bringing him in.'

'You going to charge him?'

Phil hesitated. 'I'll talk to Cotter. Last person I charged, well . . . that didn't go too well, did it? I have to make sure all the t's and i's are crossed and dotted.'

Marina nodded. 'No time for that. If it is him and he thinks we're on to him and he's got Imani, then we should move quickly. Like I said, he's coming to the end of his cycle. If it seems like he's not going to get the chance to complete it, he might step things up a gear. Or two.'

'Tell that to Cotter, then. Back me up.'

Marina smiled. 'Always.'

Phil turned, looked at her. And before he knew what was happening, his arms were round her, hers around him. They held each other tight, neither speaking. Phil's hands stroked Marina's body through her coat, feeling the familiar contours. Slow. Reverential. Privileged to be doing it, savouring it, like it was an experience he thought he would have again. She was doing the same with him. He knew what she was thinking.

They pulled apart slightly, looked at each other. And there was that gaze again. That naked gaze.

'I've missed—'

'Sshh,' said Marina. 'Talk later.'

She moved her face closer to his. Opened her mouth.

They kissed.

Deep. Hard. A kiss of life. Their mouths breathing a new cycle of existence into each other.

Eventually they pulled apart. Smiled at one another.

There was so much Phil wanted to say. So many emotions threatened to spill out of him. Marina sensed this. Put her finger to his lips.

'Later,' she said. 'Let's catch a killer first.'

Renewed, Phil turned on the ignition. The stereo came on. He drove away, The War on Drugs singing about how they were lost in the dream.

83

They're closing in. That was all he could think. Those three words. *They're closing in.*

He had pulled himself up off the floor after they had left – the angry-eyed copper and that bitch who though she was so clever, so fucking, *fucking* clever – and tried to get himself together. He paced his room, measuring the footsteps. The width. The length. Thinking, thinking all the time.

They're closing in. *They're closing in.*

He wanted to scream, to shout. To rend his clothes and grind his teeth. There were things inside him that were too big to stay inside. Feelings. Emotions. The way his mind was working, his heart. They should be let out, *needed* to be let out. He imagined them as if they were Hollywood special effects in the final reel of a film, shooting from his body, wraiths and ghosts, memories and previous lives. Filling the room, the city, the world. Exorcising himself. Ridding himself of them. So he could go on. Complete the ritual he had set out to do. Be the perfect man he knew he could be.

But that wasn't going to happen. Not here, not now.

Because they were on to him.

He knew that. Knew it from the way those two had talked to him. He had been playing her and she had been playing him. The bitch. Rage welled up inside him once more at the memory. He had reached her – both of them, but mainly her.

He knew their problems. Not that it had done him much good. Because she had turned it back on him. Got inside his head. And no one had ever done that before. Never even come close.

It was only a matter of time before the police arrived. Before his house was raided, his workroom, his ritual room. Before he was stopped. He knew it. Could sense it. He had to do something about it.

But what?

Pacing. Pacing. Thinking. Thinking.

He could cry again, tears of rage and self-pity. But he had done that and it had got him nowhere, so it was time to think. *Think.*

He weighed up his options. What to do?

Run. Take what he could. Get out. No. Not an option. They would find him. He wasn't equipped for escape. Besides, his work wasn't finished. And that was the important thing. His work.

So he had no choice. Not really. He had to go back. Home. The ritual room. Complete his work.

Just move the schedule forward, that was all.

But what about the woman? The police detective? Would she do?

She would have to. She wasn't perfect; he had been duped into taking her. But he would have to make her perfect. Or at least as perfect as he could manage. She would have to do.

He would *make* her do.

He grabbed what he could, left his room. Ignored everyone on the way out.

Headed home.

He had work to do.

84

Imani had never known such agony.

She stretched and pulled her hand once more, felt the flesh and bone grinding against the metal cuffs, knew from the wetness round her wrist, the ragged, pulpy squelch she felt, not to mention the pain that accompanied it, that the only thing she had done was drive the metal further in.

She had tried to escape, but he had been too clever for her. The cuffs were tight round her wrists. If she kept on doing what she was doing, pulling at them, she risked disfiguring her hands. She had tried squeezing her thumbs into her palms, pressing them into the flesh as tightly as she could and pulling against the cuffs like she had seen in films. No good. The hero or heroine always happened to be double-jointed or could shrink their wrists or something. Imani could do nothing like that. Except pull as hard as she could, try to wriggle her hands free. It was no good. She couldn't do it.

Then she had tried to grip the chains that held her, attempting to twist her fingers round the links, pull against the bedstead. She had hoped that the bedstead, being old, would be weak in places. It was up to her to find those weaknesses, exploit them. There was rust on the frame. At least she assumed it was rust; it was dark brown in colour. But the more she pulled and heaved at the metal, the more she realised that the bed wasn't going to give. And it wasn't rust. It was dried blood.

She flopped back on to the metal mesh. Felt the sharp edges rip and tear at her once more, work their way into fresh wounds. But tetanus was the least of her worries.

Imani sighed. She had always been so self-sufficient, so driven. Refused to let anyone else dictate how she lived her life. She had never felt so helpless as she did now.

She felt herself giving in to panic and self-pity once again. She had held it off so far, tried to concentrate, focus on escaping. But the longer she spent there, the more she realised she wasn't going anywhere.

Possibly ever again.

No. *No. Don't think like that.* They would be looking for her. The team would be looking for her. They had to be. They had to be . . .

She looked round once more. She had lost all concept of time. With just that one bare bulb shining down remorselessly on her face, she didn't know how long she had been there or whether it was day or night. It shone on and on, like its own special kind of torture. She was hungry, that much she did know. But that was it. She couldn't even trust her own body any more.

She sighed. Thought once more of Avi.

Oh God, Avi . . .

No. No. Don't think about him. He was all right. He was sure to be. She had enough to think of without worrying about him too. Right now he was probably tracking down where she was, joining the team in hunting for her. Finding her.

Yes. That was it.

She sighed once more. Shook her head. Felt tears well at the sides of her eyes. No. She wouldn't give in. No. They were looking for her. They had to be.

She thought of all the cases she had worked on. All the times they had been hunting some missing person, knowing that the longer the hunt went on, the less likely they would be to find them. Alive, at any rate. Knowing all too well that moment that a hunt for someone missing turned into a hunt for a murderer.

She just hoped it wouldn't happen to her. But she knew that every victim of every crime thought that.

She tried not to give in to tears.

85

Claire Lingard hadn't gone to work. She had got Edward ready for school, taken him in, then come back home. After everything that had happened recently, a killer migraine had put her back to bed. After a few hours' sleep, however, the worst of it seemed to have passed and she felt able to get up. If not strong enough to go to work, then guilty enough to try and do something productive with the remains of her day.

Head still throbbing, she moved slowly round the flat, like she was a reluctant ghost, haunting it.

And saw the door to the other flats.

With that, she remembered the night before.

She had heard Keith come in. Creeping round, trying not to wake her. She heard him showering, coming to bed. She had checked the clock: past three a.m. And she was sure she had heard him in the flats before that.

'Bad stomach,' he had said when she had moved, looked at him. 'Been up for hours. Don't worry about it, go back to sleep.'

But she hadn't gone back to sleep. At least not until the safety of the morning had crept round the bedroom curtains.

So where had he been? With Brendan, he had said. Until that time? Was he seeing another woman? Or was he the serial killer, even? She felt ridiculous thinking such a thing.

And now she looked at the door to the other flats. She was sure she had heard noises from there last night.

It couldn't hurt . . .

She went back into the bedroom. Found Keith's clothes. Taking a deep breath, she started looking through the pockets. Trousers, jackets, nothing. The bedside table drawer held nothing out of the ordinary either. She went into the room Keith used as a study. And there, hidden amongst documents and files, she found the keys for the rest of the flats.

Not hidden, she told herself. No. Just . . . buried under all these papers by mistake. That was all. A mistake. Yes.

She took the keys and walked towards the door that joined them to the rest of the block. She'd never ventured further. A whole two houses that had been converted into flats. Keith had told her it wasn't safe. Too many loose or rotting floorboards. She had taken him at his word, stayed in the downstairs one they lived in, treating it like a bungalow. But now, fingers trembling, heart and head pounding, she put the key in the lock, turned it. Opened the door.

And stepped into the hallway.

She found the light switch, flicked it on. And sighed. Relief. She didn't know what she had been expecting to find, but this wasn't it. Building supplies lined up against the wall. Lengths of wood. Coving. Skirting. Pots of paint piled at one side. An opened tool box. All pointing to ongoing work being done.

She looked around. Except, she thought, that it didn't look like much had actually been done. Not considering the time Keith had been taking.

She tried to dislodge the thought from her head. He said himself he wasn't good at DIY, that he was learning as he went. He was probably going as fast as he could.

She walked on. Everywhere was less than half finished. As if any attempts at renovation were cosmetic, just there to show that something had been done.

She came to a door. Tried it. Locked.

Her heart skipped a beat. Why a locked door? Why here? She rationalised her anxiety, tried to calm herself down. Maybe this was where Keith kept his expensive tools. An extra deterrent if the flats were broken into.

She took the key ring out, tried the keys on it until, hands still trembling, she found one that fitted. She turned it, felt the lock open. Slowly she pushed the door.

She looked round before she entered. Like she was expecting to see someone there, some friend of hers, or Keith himself, even, laughing, telling her that there was nothing to worry about. But there was no one there. No reassuring, consoling voice.

She stepped into the room.

Found a light switch on the wall. And frowned at what she saw.

A desk and chair. On the desk, a laptop, one she had never seen before. It was set up with some unfamiliar equipment: a headset, earphone and mic. She had no idea what any of it was, what it did. Then, with a shudder that almost threatened to tear her apart, she understood.

This was where he must have intercepted the calls to the refuge. This was how he did it.

Claire's legs felt weak, her head spun. She needed to sit down, grabbed the chair and almost fell into it. As she did so, she touched something and the screen of the laptop lit up. Numbers scrolled there. She looked closely, recognised one.

Safe Haven.

Oh God . . .

She didn't know what to feel, how to think. It was as if she had realised her whole world was built on a lie – a succession of lies – and it was crumbling away. She stared at the screen feeling like she had been physically attacked.

She didn't move for a while. Couldn't move.

Then she noticed another door, at the end of the room.

Oh God . . . Oh God . . . Oh God . . .

Standing up, like her body was hollow, being controlled by a puppet master, she made her way to the door. She'd found this room, she thought; what could be worse?

Numbly, she tried different keys until she found one that fitted. Turned it. Opened the door.

Stepped in.

And realised just how much worse things could be.

86

In front of Claire were shelves. All round the room, rows and rows of them. And on those shelves were boxes. She looked closer. Beside some of the boxes were other things. She walked over to one, picked up the things beside it. Photos. She looked through them. Keith when he was much younger. With another woman. Pretty, long curly hair. Not at all like Claire, she noted. Underneath the photos were a couple of sheets of writing paper. Taped to the first one was a lock of hair. It matched that of the woman in the photo. The paper had writing on. Keith's handwriting. She started to read:

I found you. Or someone like you. Near enough like you. You didn't think I would, did you? Not after the way you left it with me. Well, I did. And I told her – or you – everything you'd done to me. I got you back for all the hurt . . .

She read on. And wished she hadn't.

Feeling physically ill now, she let the papers drop to the floor. Her head was spinning. She was nauseous, as if she was going to throw up or faint. She grabbed the side of one of the shelves to steady herself.

The boxes. There were still the boxes.

She didn't want to open them. Really, really didn't want to open them. But knew she had to. Like Pandora, she didn't know what she would let out, but she knew it wouldn't be good.

She reached for the nearest one. Dark carved wood. Took it off the shelf, flipped the lid open.

There was a heart. In formaldehyde.

She was physically sick then.

She dropped the box, the heart and the liquid going all over the floor, mixing with her own vomit.

Tears in her eyes, pain in her heart – pain like she had never experienced before – she spun round, desperately trying to get away, knowing there wasn't really anywhere for her to go.

She ran through the room with the laptop and radio equipment, back out into the hall. She flung herself against the wall, sliding down to the floor, sobbing all the while. Eyes screwed tight shut, knowing that all her worst fears were confirmed. She didn't think she could have felt worse if she'd been diagnosed with a terminal disease.

Eventually she opened her eyes. And saw another locked door ahead of her.

Oh no, no, no, no, no . . .

She put her head back down, closed her eyes once more. She didn't know what horrors that room would contain, what could possibly be worse than the room she had just been in.

Get out. Now. That's what I need to do. What I should do. Get out.

She looked at the locked door once more. There was a smell emanating from it. Creeping under the wood, around the frame. It wasn't good.

Claire stood up. Keys in hand. She had to do it. Had to see what was behind it. She had no choice. She knew that now.

She found the right key. Opened the door. And entered.

Jesus . . .

Imani Oliver was chained to an old metal bed frame, gagged and naked. She stared at Claire, eyes wide with shock, infused with just the slightest bit of hope.

'Imani . . . '

The room stank like an abattoir, old blood and animal waste. Claire wanted to be sick again, but seeing the other woman there in the state she was in, she knew she didn't have time for that, couldn't think about herself. She got the key ring out once more, went through the keys looking for the one that would fit the handcuffs. Couldn't find it. She threw the useless keys to the floor, undid the gag.

'Thank you . . . ' Imani was gasping in air, trying to speak at the same time. 'Thank you . . . Oh God, I thought . . . I thought . . . '

Tears welled in the corners of her eyes. She struggled not to give in to them.

'Get a . . . get your phone. Call Cotter. Tell her . . . tell her . . . '

Claire understood. She took her phone out of her pocket, made ready to call.

'I'll have that.'

A voice from behind her. She turned.

There, looking like someone she had never seen before, a malevolent stranger, was Keith.

87

Keith tried to grab the phone from Claire, but she moved out of the way.

'Don't do anything stupid,' he said. 'Well. Anything more stupid than you've already done.'

'Keith, I . . . ' Claire stopped. She had no words.

'You dared to enter my trophy room,' he said, face contorted with rage.

She had never seen him like this before. It was his features, his body, his clothes. But his expression . . . it looked like a demon had entered him, possessed him.

'You . . . *fucking* . . . dared . . . to go into my trophy room . . . '

'I . . . Keith, what have you done?'

'That room isn't for you. It's for me. *Only* me. You've . . . defiled it. Spoilt it. Spoiled the ritual . . . '

He kept moving towards her. She backed away. Glancing down as he advanced, she noticed he was holding something in his hand. It looked like an overlarge door handle.

Imani saw it too.

'Claire,' she managed to call, 'that's a stun gun he's holding, be careful . . . '

Keith turned to her. 'Shut it, bitch.' Spitting the words. He turned his attention back to Claire. 'And you . . . ' Pointed at her with his free hand. A long, accusing finger. 'You are going to do what I tell you.'

Claire found her voice. 'Why did you do it? Why? I can't ...'
She shook her head. 'I don't understand ...'

'No,' he growled, 'you don't. You wouldn't. You're too ...' He
searched for the word. 'Thick. Unambitious. Useless. You think
because you wrote poetry that made you special? Fuck you.'

Despite the fear she was experiencing, Claire was still hurt
by his words. 'Keith ...'

'Fuck you.'

'Keith, this ... this isn't you. You're a good man. A kind
man. Why ...'

His eyes flared. 'I'm not good, I'm not *kind* ...' He said the
words like they were alien, hateful objects in his mouth. Then,
having rid himself of them, he smiled. 'But I will be. Soon.'

'What d'you mean? What are you talking about?' Real
incomprehension in Claire's voice.

'Perfection. All the damage women have done to me, all the
hurt, the broken hearts ... soon it'll be gone. Cleansed from
me. And once my rituals are completed, I'll be perfect. The perfect man.'

'I don't ... Keith ... please—'

Claire's words were cut short. Her phone rang.

She froze. So did Keith. He stared at it. She knew what he
was about to do, and in the split second before he moved, she
answered the call, put the phone to her ear.

'Hi, Claire? DS Sperring here. I just wanted to check
someth—'

'He's here!' she screamed. 'It's him, he's here, in the flat, in
here—'

The phone fell from her hands. Pain like she had never experienced passed through her. Like a thousand dull blades ripping
her flesh, hitting every nerve in the process. She screamed. Fell
to the floor.

Unconscious.

88

The phone in Sperring's hand was screaming. Then it abruptly stopped.

He stared at it, then looked round the incident room. He hadn't expected that.

He put the phone to his ear, tried again.

'Claire? Claire Lingard? This is DS Sperring. Hello?' He waved at Cotter as he spoke, tried to attract her attention.

A voice answered. 'What d'you want?'

He could guess who it was. 'I'm Detective Sergeant Sperring. Where's Claire? Is she all right?'

The only answer was breathing. He could hear a raised voice in the background, whimpering and gasping.

'Keith Bailey, is that you? Am I talking to Keith Bailey?'

Nothing.

'Hello?'

The voice came back, speaking slow and low. 'Why don't you just fuck off and leave us alone?'

The phone went dead.

Sperring stood up. Cotter had reached his desk.

'We've got trouble,' he said.

89

It didn't take long for the circus to roll up.

The road in Kings Heath was cordoned off, police tape unrolled at either end, makeshift barriers erected, uniforms posted on duty. The mobile incident room had been set up outside the flats. Phil and Marina entered.

'Oh God, not you again.'

Mike Battersby, the hostage negotiation expert, looked up. Did a double-take. Phil gave him a nod of acknowledgement by way of greeting.

Battersby stood up, finger pointing. 'Right,' he said. 'I don't care what you say, you are not having anything to do with this negotiation. You go nowhere near it. You got that?'

Phil held his hands up in mock surrender. 'Fine by me.'

Cotter interjected, leading Phil away by the arm. 'I'm sure DI Brennan has plenty of other duties to take care of.'

Battersby resumed his seat.

'Where are we?' Phil asked Cotter.

She told him about Sperring's call.

'Anything else? Any movement from inside? Attempt to contact him?'

Cotter shook his head. 'Waited until you got here.'

'And you're sure it's him? Keith Bailey's the guy we're looking for?'

Cotter looked quickly round as if being overheard. 'We don't know. We can only assume so at the moment. But it seems like a strong assumption. I think we have to proceed as if he is and that he has Imani in there as well as Claire Lingard. And hope that Imani's still all right.'

'Right,' said Phil. 'Think it's time for a phone call, don't you?'

Cotter nodded.

Battersby dialled the number of Claire's phone. Put it on loudspeaker. They waited. Each ring seeming to get louder. Eventually it was answered. No one spoke.

'Hello?' said Battersby.

No response. Just breathing.

'Hello, is that Claire Lingard?'

'Who's this?'

Phil recognised Bailey's voice. Nodded at Cotter, confirming it.

'This is Detective Sergeant Battersby. Mike Battersby, if you prefer. What's your name?'

'If you're calling this number then you already know who I am.'

'Keith Bailey?'

A snort. Laughter?

'Right, Keith. Listen. I just want to know who you've got in there with you and whether they're all right.'

'I'm not talking to you. I don't want to talk to you.'

'Why not, Keith?'

'Because you're going to try and talk me out of it. Try and make me let them go when I haven't finished yet.'

'Haven't finished what yet?'

'My work.' Said as if it was the most obvious thing in the world. 'What I have to do. You don't think I do this for fun, do you?'

'I don't know, Keith, you tell me.'

'You don't know. You don't know . . .'

They felt he was about to explode. Cotter sat forward, ready to order in a response team.

'Well, you'll have to help me, Keith,' Battersby continued. 'If you talk to me, I can—'

'Oh, fuck off,' said Bailey. 'I don't want to talk to you.'

'Well, Keith, I—'

'Is she there?'

Battersby looked confused. 'Who's *she*, Keith?'

'The psychologist. The one I spoke to this morning. Is she there?'

All eyes in the room turned to Marina. She stepped forward, moved close to the microphone.

The room held its collective breath.

90

'I'm here, Keith,' said Marina.

'Yeah. Thought you would be.'

Marina sat down to be nearer the microphone. Battersby moved along to let her in. Phil noticed – with dark relish – that he looked somewhat put out by that.

'What d'you want to talk about, Keith?'

'What I wanted to talk about earlier. I think you know. I think you would have talked about it – properly talked about it with me – if I'd said. Wouldn't you?'

Marina looked round slightly, as if she had missed a couple of pages in the script they were following. 'I would have talked about it?'

'Yes.'

'In your office?'

'Yes. If you'd known what I'm doing. And why I'm doing it.'

'Okay then, Keith, if you want to talk to me about it – all of it – then tell me all of it. I know what you're doing. You're taking women and killing them, is that right?'

'No,' he said. 'Well, yes, I suppose it is if you look at it in purely reductive terms.'

'And what way should I look at it, Keith? Just to get a handle on it, so we can talk about it.'

'It's not *what* I've done. It's *why*. You should know that.'

'Right. Well, as I see it,' she said, 'they're surrogates for women who've hurt you in some way, is that it?'

'Yes.' His voice cracked slightly on the word.

'And this is to make up for it?'

'Yes. For what those bitches did to me. All of them.'

'They hurt you, those women, did they?'

Behind them, one of the uniforms rotated his finger at the side of his head. Sperring knocked it away. The uniform dropped his head, stood in shamefaced silence.

'Yes. All of them.'

Beside Marina, Cotter scribbled a note: *Did he know all the women he killed?* Marina shook her head, continued.

'These women. The ones you took. You didn't know them, did you? They just represented the ones who had hurt you, didn't they?'

Silence.

'Keith?'

'Yeah. I said yeah.'

'So they let you down. The women in your life. They hurt you.'

'Every time.' His voice cracking once more. 'And they enjoyed it. All of them. That's the worst thing. They enjoyed it. Or just . . . didn't care. Treated me like I was nothing.'

'Surely that wasn't the case every time?'

'It was. Always.' The words sounded pained, forced out.

'What about your mother?'

Silence on the line. It lasted so long Marina thought he might have gone. 'Keith?'

'Don't mention my fucking . . . that fucking . . . '

'Right,' said Marina, responding to his raised voice by making hers even calmer. 'I see. Right. So you did what you did because of the hurt that had been done to you.'

'Yes.'

381

'But why these particular women?'

'Because . . . because they were damaged,' he said, as if that explained everything, desperate to be understood. 'Hurt. Like I was. Just like I was.'

'Did you think you were mending their broken hearts? Was that part of it?'

'I took their hearts. And gave them to the women who had hurt me. Used their damaged hearts to help heal me. Don't you see? You should understand that.'

'I do, Keith,' said Marina, nodding, even though he couldn't see it.

Bailey continued. 'When I've done that, it's complete. That's the ritual done. For each one. The ritual gets rid of the ghosts. Makes them go away. And when they leave me, I become a better person. Well, obviously you can see that.'

'Yes,' said Marina. 'But what about Claire? Where does she fit in?'

'What d'you mean?' His voice hard once more. Wary.

'She's a good person, Keith.'

He made a sound like a wounded animal. Marina ignored him, kept going.

'She loves you, Keith.'

'No,' he said, the wounded howl tailing off. 'She doesn't. She can't.'

'Why not?'

'Because she doesn't know me,' he said, again desperate to be understood. 'Not really. She thinks she does. We all think we know someone else, love someone else. But we don't. None of us do. Because all we see is the mask. All she knows is my mask. She doesn't know what's behind it. She just fell in love with a mask. How stupid . . . '

'But Keith,' said Marina, genuinely engaged with him, 'don't we all wear masks?'

382

'W-what d'you mean?'

'It's simple. We all wear masks. All of us. Every day. You know Kurt Vonnegut? The writer?'

Nothing.

Marina continued. 'He said we all had to be careful about the masks we choose to wear because in time we become them.' She looked up. Phil was staring right at her. She continued, eyes locked with his. 'Or they become us. You know, if we want to be brave, we pretend to be brave. If we want to be good, we act good. Or happy. Or anything. We find a mask for it.'

She saw Phil smile. Nod.

'And gradually,' she said, feeling encouraged by what she was saying, genuinely feeling she was making a breakthrough, 'gradually we become that thing the mask represents. Don't you think?'

Silence from the other end. Then slowly a scream built up. Deep and wailing at first, then ragged. Anger and pain vying for dominance.

'Shut up,' screamed Keith, 'shut up . . . '

Marina looked round quickly. She was losing him.

'I thought you would understand. You of all people . . . '

'I do, Keith, I do,' she said. 'Listen. There's something I need to know. Have you got Imani Oliver there with you? Detective Constable Oliver?'

'What?' Screaming again. 'What the fuck do you want to know about her for?'

'I just—'

'Her. That's all you were interested in. All this time. Her. Not me. You, you fucking liar. You fucking bitch liar . . . '

'No, Keith, I'm not. I swear I'm not. Please, listen to me . . . '

'Bitch . . . '

'Keith, please. What have I just said to you? What have we just talked about? If I wasn't listening to you, then what was all that for?'

'You . . . you just . . . ' He had calmed down slightly but she knew he was on a knife edge and could go either way. She had to be careful what she said next.

'We talked, Keith. And I meant every word. I'm trying to understand what you're doing. Why you're doing it. That's what you want, right? You want me to understand?'

Silence.

Marina continued.

'Listen, Keith. If you've got Imani Oliver there, why not let her go, eh? She's not part of your ritual. She's not damaged or hurt. Nothing like that. She's no good to you. You can't use her. Why not let her go?'

Silence. More heavy breathing. Then: 'Fuck you.'

The line went dead.

Marina sat back. Exhausted.

91

'**Y**ou should have been closing,' said Battersby. 'All the time. Closing.'

Marina stared at him in disbelief. 'Sorry? Are we selling second-hand cars or something?'

'In hostage negotiation you're always moving towards that. Always trying to get the hostages out safely. Not . . . ' he threw up his hands, 'indulging him in his fantasies.'

Marina squared up to him. 'I was not indulging him. I was talking. He wanted to talk to me, not you. Maybe you'll get your chance later. *Close* him then.'

She turned to Cotter before he could answer. 'Alison, have you thought about what I said?'

When the phone had gone dead and Bailey had refused to pick up again, Marina had asked Cotter to go somewhere private, have a word. They had stepped outside, hidden round the back of the unit, away from long-range media lenses. There she had put her idea to the DCI.

Cotter, inside now, was shaking her head.

'But it's the only way,' said Marina. 'At least with such short notice.'

'No,' said Cotter. 'I won't hear of it. It's too dangerous.' She threw a glance at Battersby, then back to Marina. 'And you're not even trained.'

'It'll work,' said Marina. 'I go in. Claire comes out. I wear a wire. While this is happening, Phil leads a team in from the back.'

Cotter turned away. 'No. We've already got the stigma of this being some kind of maverick operation as it is. I can't allow a civilian in there.'

'After everything I've done, I'm hardly a civilian.'

'It's too dangerous.'

'It's the best chance we have. Otherwise this could drag on for ...' she shrugged, 'God knows how long. And we don't know what the situation is in there. What state Imani and Claire are in. I could provide information about that.'

Cotter sighed. 'It should be a member of my team.'

'Well, unfortunately, he doesn't want to talk to anyone on your team. Only me. That makes me an asset. Use me.'

'Marina's right,' said Phil.

They both turned, unaware that he had been listening.

'She's already established a bond with him. I think this is the best chance we have.'

Cotter looked at Marina, reluctantly relenting. 'Would you be armed?'

'No,' said Marina. 'No point. If I take a gun in there, it just makes it more dangerous.'

'But you wouldn't be protected. You wouldn't be safe.'

'Yes I would.' She spoke the words to Cotter but her eyes were on Phil.

Phil tried hard to hide his smile.

Cotter said nothing, thinking. Marina kept talking.

'And I'd be able to relay information back. Tell you which part of the building he's in.'

'We can do that with thermal imaging.'

'But you haven't got the equipment here yet. God knows how long it will take to arrive, or what he could do before then.'

'This is completely against protocol. If it goes tits-up, it could be the end of all our careers.'

'And if we do nothing,' said Marina, 'if we wait, it could be the end of Imani and Claire's lives. Which is more important?'

Cotter said nothing, looked at Phil. 'And you,' she said, 'how do I know you won't go in there and mess it up like last time?'

'Because I won't,' said Phil.

Cotter looked between the pair of them. Sighed.

'Do it,' she said.

92

The phone rang. They all looked at it. Waiting.

The tension in the room was palpable. Claire wanted to scream again, just to hear her own voice, to remind herself she was still alive. After Bailey had hung up, no one had spoken. Claire had pulled herself into a corner, arms round her bruised torso, gasping as the pain slowly subsided. Imani lay silently on the bed, spent. Bailey had put the stun gun down on a table, switched it for an automatic. Now he strode up and down, talking to himself, hitting himself in the temples occasionally, as if his head was hurting and it would alleviate the pain.

That was when the phone rang.

'Answer it . . . ' Imani.

'Shut up, shut up . . . ' Hitting himself in the side of the head once more. 'Shut up, I'm thinking . . . ' Still pacing.

Claire had never seen him like this. Unravelling. She no longer recognised the person before her.

'Please,' she said, Imani's voice giving her the courage to speak, 'please just answer it.'

Bailey stopped moving, stood still in the centre of the room, threw his head back and gave a silent scream. The phone kept ringing.

Something had to be done, thought Claire. Ignoring the pain, she leaned forward, made a movement towards the phone. Bailey saw her, snapping out of his pose straight away, and beat her to it. Before he realised what he had done, the phone was to his ear.

'Hello? Hello? Keith? Is that you?'

Marina's voice again.

He groaned by way of response.

'Listen,' said Marina. 'I've got a proposal for you. Why don't you let Claire and Imani go and I'll come in instead?'

Bailey looked round, as if expecting a trick. 'What, I . . .'

'I think it's a good idea,' Marina continued. 'We can keep talking, like earlier. You can explain your work to me. How does that sound?'

He didn't reply.

'I won't be armed,' said Marina. 'I'm not police. Nothing like that. Just you and me. Talking. What d'you say?'

Keith closed his eyes. Thought. Just him. Alone with Marina . . . the two of them . . .

Then another thought struck him. He smiled at it. Felt excited by it.

Marina was damaged. Marina had been hurt. By her husband. Even better.

Yes.

Perhaps she was the one. The one to finish on. She could finally set him free.

Yes . . .

He nodded to himself at how clever he was.

But another thought entered his mind. A darker one. What if she was lying? Or what if it didn't work? He didn't have time, something like that? He would need insurance. A way to prevent that happening.

He looked round the room, worked out who was expendable, who was not. Who was useful, who was not. He made up his mind quickly.

'Claire can go,' he said into the phone. 'The other one stays.'

He hung up.

93

Marina put her arms up, let the technician thread a wire across her body, prior to pulling on a stab vest. Phil stood beside her, his own stab vest in place, anxious.

'You sure about this?' he said.

'As sure as you are,' she replied. 'You agreed with me.'

He leaned in closer, cutting off the rest of the activity in the trailer. Just the two of them. 'Well, yeah, it made sense.'

'So why are you asking if I'm all right with it?'

'Because . . .'

'Because it's me,' said Marina.

'Well, of course. I mean—'

'Do I ever stop you from doing what you're supposed to? Am I asking if you're all right with wearing a stab vest and leading a team in through the back?'

'Well, no, but—'

She turned to him. The technician had finished. 'Well what?'

'I just . . .'

'What?' said Marina. 'You want to keep me safe?'

'Course I do.'

She stretched out her arms, felt her muscles coil and uncoil. Spring-loaded, ready to punch out. She had changed into her gym kit and training shoes, the Lycra sculpting her body, helping her to move as freely as she wanted to.

'I don't want to lose you,' he said.

A smile spread slowly across her face. 'You won't,' she said.

94

The day was fading, dark creeping in, when Marina approached the front door of the house.

She felt alone, the distance between the incident room and the house seemingly immense as she walked, but she knew that was only an illusion. Time hadn't slowed down or speeded up. It only felt that way.

She was scared. She had agreed to do this, told Phil she was fine with it and smiled at him, but it was bravado. Out here, in this open space, she felt so alone. Like she was walking away from safety towards ... what? Danger? Uncertainty? Both. She was doing this because it was the right thing to do. Facing her fear, trying to conquer it. Because there was something bigger at stake. But there was also that gnawing thought that she might enter that house and never emerge. She saw Josephina's face becoming more distant with every step she took.

She would see her again. She kept telling herself that. She had to believe it. Had to.

And Phil. He would be there. It was going to work. Ignore the fear, don't give in to it. She would be fine.

She would be fine ...

She reached the door. Put her hand out to knock but didn't get the chance. It swung open slowly. Marina felt the telescopic sights of rifles on her back. She knew there was an armed response team waiting nearby, hoped they wouldn't be foolish enough to take a shot at him while she was in the way.

Claire Lingard was pushed roughly outside. She was holding herself, wincing with pain. Marina didn't have time to talk to her, ask her what had happened or even steady her. A hand holding a gun appeared.

'Get in. Quick.'

She did so.

The door closed behind her.

In the shadow she could make out the features of Keith Bailey.

'Hello, Keith,' she said. More for those listening in than because she was pleased to see him.

'Get through there,' he said, waving the gun at her.

She began walking. 'Down here?' she said. 'Down this hallway?'

'Move.'

She kept walking until she reached a set of stairs.

'Upstairs.'

She did so. Moving slowly, deliberately, trying to make her trainered feet reverberate as much as possible, hoping that whoever was listening would be able to count the steps.

'Left,' he said at the top of the stairs.

She turned left. *This bit's easy*, she thought. *He's doing my job for me. Hope the rest is the same ...*

But she doubted it.

'Stop.'

She did so.

'I want to show you in here.' He opened the door wide, ushered her into a room with a laptop, kept walking, opened another door. The room was filled with shelves, boxes on shelves. 'This is where I keep them,' he said. 'The hearts. This is where the ritual takes place.'

Marina was suddenly terrified. More scared than she had been in a long time. The enormity of what she had agreed to suddenly sank in and she hit a new level of terror. The plan had been one thing. Now it was just her in a room of body parts with a dangerous maniac holding a gun. She knew he was waiting for a response from her. She had to find the right one.

Don't look appalled, she thought. *Don't show him you're scared.*

'And does it work?' she asked. 'The ritual?'

'Yeah, yeah, it works.'

'It gets rid of the ghosts?'

He nodded. 'It was doing, yeah. But that last one ... that wasn't so good. I had to act quickly. In a hurry. That didn't feel right.'

'I see,' she said, quelling the screams she was hearing inwardly. 'But you're nearly finished now.'

He gave a smile that was the most frightening thing she had seen in a long time. 'Oh yes. I'm nearly finished.'

He waved the gun at her once more, gesturing for her to leave the room.

'Which way?' she said out in the hall, relieved not to have seen what was inside the boxes.

'Down there.'

'Left?'

'Just keep walking.'

She did so until they reached another room with a closed door.

'And this,' he said, reaching for the handle, 'is where the magic happens.' He gave out something that could have been a laugh and entered.

Marina followed him. There was Imani, chained to a rusty old bedstead. Again Marina felt screams within her. She tried to keep them down. Like increasing nausea, they were getting harder to swallow each time.

She turned back to Bailey. 'Come on, Keith,' she said, hoping her voice didn't sound as shaky and breathless as she thought it did. 'You've got me now. You don't need Imani as well. Let her go.'

Bailey, still smiling, was advancing towards her. 'I don't need her?'

'No,' said Marina, backing away. This was all getting out of hand too fast. She had to calm down, try to talk. Engage him. Give Phil and the team time to get in place. To make an entry.

'Come on, Keith,' she said, trying not to move any more, though his approach was hindering that. 'Let's . . . let's just talk. That's what you wanted, right? So let's talk.'

'We've talked, Marina. Haven't we? We've talked a few times now. Have you anything else to say? Anything I want to hear?'

'I must have. That's why you asked me here.'

He laughed. 'Is it?'

Marina was aware that Imani was trying to tell her something. She was looking at Marina, nodding in the direction of something with her eyes. Marina was confused at first, didn't know what she was looking it. Then she saw it. And understood.

She gave a small nod of acknowledgement. Kept moving.

'It's the end, Keith,' she said. 'Surely you realise that?'

Nothing. Just grinning.

'Why not let it go? Now?'

He giggled.

'There's other ways of getting rid of those ghosts, you know,' she said. 'Other therapies you can use. Ones that don't involve hurting people.'

Nothing. Just the slow advance.

'Come on, Keith. I know you don't enjoy hurting people. I know that's not what this is all about. You're not like that, are you?'

Bailey stopped, and for a single, blessed second, Marina

thought she had got through to him. But all he did was tuck the gun in the waistband of his trousers and replace it with a knife. He studied the blade, watched it glitter in the overhead light.

'It's too late for that,' he said, looking back at her. 'Much too late . . .'

95

'Here, boss. Look at this.'

Behind the flats that Bailey was holed up in, there was a row of garages, all with metal pull-over doors. Sperring had managed to open one of the doors and was standing inside. Phil turned to see what he had found.

'Toyota Avensis,' he said. 'Looks like it needs a bit of attention, too.'

'Good work,' said Phil. 'Best not touch it, though. Leave it for Forensics.'

He moved away. They were heading towards the back of the flats. They made their way past the garages and over the wooden fence, then edged up the garden, checking all sides.

Phil's team was augmented by a response unit. They were used to this kind of thing, knew how to effect a decent entry. They were carrying a battering ram, a heavy metal tube filled with concrete, handles on either end.

Phil glanced at Sperring. His DS was looking straight ahead. Determined. 'You okay? You ready?'

'Course I am,' Sperring said, not breaking stride. 'Why wouldn't I be?'

'Just thinking of your knife wound.'

He stopped walking, looked at Phil. Gave a grim smile. 'Take more than that to stop me,' he said.

Not the only one wearing a mask, thought Phil.

They reached the back door. Phil stood aside, let the guys with the battering ram get set up.

'In three,' called the lead officer. He held up three fingers. 'One, two . . . '

The third was silent, just the folding down of his index finger.

The battering ram hit. One blow was all it took. And they were in.

'Upstairs,' shouted Phil. 'That's where they are.'

He found a staircase, took it two at a time, Sperring hurrying behind him.

He reached a landing. Looked left to right. Tried to orient himself from Marina's words. Turned left. Ran. Opened one door. A laptop. Some other equipment. Tried another. Boxes on shelves. Getting nearer, he thought. Tried another one.

That was it.

The door swung open. There stood Bailey, one arm round Marina's neck, the other holding a large and vicious-looking knife at her throat.

'Too late,' Bailey said, and began to push the knife in.

96

M arina felt what he was doing. She screamed and tried to push him away. Bailey stumbled backwards. His knife hand moved to steady himself but his other arm remained firmly round her throat. Marina also stumbled, but only as far as the table. Then Bailey had her once more, shoving her forward, the knife back in place.

'Let her go,' said Phil, trying to remain calm but failing.

'A stand-off,' said Bailey. 'Who has the power now, Mr Alpha Male Detective?'

'Let her go,' repeated Phil, calmer and more controlled this time.

Bailey gave out something that might have been a laugh. 'No,' he said. 'I won't. Because I have one more ritual, one more sacrifice to make. And you're not going to stop me.'

'And then what?' asked Phil. 'After you've done that, then what will you do?'

'I'll be complete, of course.'

'Complete. Right. But you can't escape, can you?'

'Can't I?'

'Look around you. Look outside. You're going nowhere.'

Bailey smiled. It had no connection with anything humorous. Or even remotely sane. 'Oh, I always had an escape planned. Of a sort.'

'Tell me.'

'You wouldn't understand.'

'Try me.'

'Well, it's very simple, really. Once I've achieved perfection, where could I go?'

Phil stared at him.

'Go on,' said Bailey. 'Answer the question.'

'I thought it was rhetorical,' said Phil, noticing that Marina almost smiled at that. 'Okay, where could you go?'

'Nowhere. I could go nowhere. Because once I've achieved perfection, there's no point in me being here. I'll use the knife on myself. Stop my own heart. Make my escape.'

'That's not an escape,' said Phil. 'That's getting away with what you've done. Not answering for all the murders you've committed. That's the coward's way out.'

Bailey just shook his head. 'We'll see, shall we?'

Phil took his attention away from Bailey, brought it to Marina. 'You okay?' he said.

She nodded.

'It's all right,' he said. 'Don't be afraid.'

And then Marina did something that took Phil completely by surprise. She smiled. 'I'm not,' she said. 'I'm not afraid of anything any more.'

'Well, you should be,' said Bailey, voice raised, not wanting to be ignored. 'Because I decide what happens next.'

'No you don't,' said Phil. Hoping his voice had conviction even though he didn't know what he was going to do.

Bailey laughed. 'You're not even armed,' he said.

'No,' said Marina. 'And I don't need to be.'

She stamped down hard on his instep. Bailey let out a cry, his knife hand loosening. She brought her head forward, then jerked it back sharply, making contact with the bridge of his nose. He screamed, stepped backwards, letting her go in the process.

Marina turned. Blood was pumping from Bailey's nose. He still had the knife.

'Bitch . . .'

He telegraphed a thrust with the blade and she neatly side-stepped it, bringing her leg up hard, her foot making contact with his thumb, bending it backwards. He screamed and dropped the knife. Staggered backwards.

Phil had made his way round the pair of them, picked up the stun gun from the table. He lifted it, ready to use it, but Marina brought her arm back and punched Bailey hard in the face. He went down. Just to make sure he wouldn't get up, Phil knelt and emptied the charge into him.

The voltage coursed through Bailey's body. He screamed, passed out.

Phil stood up, looked at his wife.

She turned to look at him.

And all hell broke loose in the room.

Police officers poured in. Picked Bailey up, dragged him out. Paramedics ran over to Imani on the bed.

But Phil and Marina were oblivious to it all. The calm at the eye of the storm, they stood there holding each other, letting everything happen around them.

Holding each other tight. Not letting go.

'I'm not afraid,' whispered Marina. 'Not of anything. Not any more.'

Phil smiled. Whispered back.

'Neither am I.'

They held on to each other like their lives depended on it.

PART SEVEN

BROKEN HEARTS

97

The rain was nearing torrential levels. Leaching what little colour was left out of the day, turning everything to a dull grey monochrome. The Sandwell Valley stretched down the hill and away, and Phil had to admit it probably looked beautiful in the summer. But this wasn't the summer. Now the trees just looked threadbare and apologetic, denuded and exposed.

The crematorium was behind them. He and Marina sheltered in the porch, keeping away from the rest of the mourners. They were both dressed in black, Phil with his Crombie overcoat pulled tight about him.

They didn't need to be there. Marina had said as much. It wasn't like they'd worked with Avi, or known him well. But Phil felt they should make an appearance. Avi Patel was, to all intents and purposes, one of their own.

The family had filed in before them, the parents still unable to believe that they were saying goodbye to their son. Phil found that shocked tableau depressingly familiar. He had seen it enough times. And it never got any easier.

Marina pulled in close to him. He still wasn't used to feeling her warmth near him again, didn't take it for granted. Almost a week since the events in the block of flats in Kings Heath. Since they'd caught Keith Bailey. Since they had come back together.

*

There had been the paperwork to take care of, but Cotter, seeing how close Phil and Marina were with each other, not to mention how exhausted they both looked, had sent them home.

Imani had been taken to hospital, Claire Lingard was receiving treatment, and Keith Bailey had been driven away to spend the first of many nights in a cell on his own.

'Where's Josephina?' Phil had asked.

'Joy's picked her up from school.'

Phil took his phone out.

'I already called,' said Marina, placing a hand on his wrist. 'She's fine.'

Phil returned the phone to his pocket.

'What about us?' he said, looking straight at her. 'Are we fine?'

Marina smiled. Phil saw tiredness etched in her features. 'We need to talk. About the future, about us. About that psychopathic threat hanging over us.'

'We do,' said Phil. 'Let's go home and do it.'

Leaving Josephina with Joy, they went home. It felt strange having Marina back after so long alone. For her part, Marina was appalled at the state Phil had allowed the house to get into.

'I was in a bad place,' he said. 'I didn't think anything mattered. If you weren't here.'

She smiled. 'I've always loved your honesty.'

He returned the smile. They put their arms round each other.

Kissed.

The next morning the sun came up, streamed through the bedroom window.

'Feels like a new start,' said Phil.

And Marina had to agree.

*

404

Things progressed smoothly after that. Keith Bailey was sent for psychiatric assessment. Marina made it clear she would be on hand for advice, but that was as much as she wanted to do with him. It was already looking like he might not stand trial, for reasons of insanity. He had admitted to other victims; all they had to do was find the bodies.

'That could go on for ever,' Phil had said to Cotter in the office a few days later. 'Depending on how much he wants to string us along.'

'Don't I know it. Still, at least there should be some anxious families who can put their minds to rest about their missing loved ones. Not in a positive way, though.'

'Closure,' said Phil. 'I hate that word.'

Cotter had nodded. Looked at him. 'So, DI Brennan, I believe you've had a change in your personal circumstances.'

'Things are looking up,' he said. 'Yeah. One step at a time.'

'Good. Well, with that in mind, are you ready to resume your place in the team?'

He grinned. 'I would love to.'

Claire Lingard had found it difficult to go back to work. She had found it impossible to stay at home. She had gone to her parents' place out in Oxfordshire, taken Edward with her. They had told her she could stay as long as she needed to.

One day while Claire was sitting in an armchair by the huge woodburner in the oak-beamed living room, trying to lose herself in a book, there was a knock at the door. She made no move to get it. Heard her mother talking to someone on the doorstep.

'Someone for you, Claire,' her mother said, coming back into the room, worry in her eyes.

Claire's stomach turned over. *He's found me. He's out. Oh*

God . . . She knew it was irrational, but she couldn't help but think that way. Not after what she had been through.

But it wasn't him.

'Hi, Claire.' Imani Oliver followed her mother in.

Claire stood up. She didn't know whether to hug Imani or shake her hand. Or just keep her distance. Keep contained. Imani made up her mind for her. She came over, took her in her arms. Claire had no option but to return the hug. Yielding as she did so, her defences dropping. Eventually they stood apart, looked at one another.

'How are you?' asked Imani.

Claire couldn't answer.

'Sorry, stupid question. Shouldn't have asked. I just wanted to see you.'

Claire nodded. She understood. When people went through an intense experience – good or bad – they could only talk about it with someone who had experienced something similar. As good as her parents had been, Claire hadn't been able to bring herself to open up to them about what had happened.

'I know,' she said. 'I was wondering how you were too.'

Imani nodded.

They sat on the sofa next to each other. Claire's mother excused herself, left them alone.

'It's . . . hard,' said Claire. 'Every day. You just can't . . . I just keep thinking back to . . . to what happened. What he was like. You know, whether I should have known, picked up on something. Some sign.'

'It's not your fault. Don't blame yourself. He had that mask firmly in place. He wore it well. There's no way you or anyone could have known.'

Claire just shook her head. 'I'm sure everybody's saying I must have known. Blaming me as well. But I . . . I . . .'

Imani placed her hand over Claire's.

'Sorry,' said Claire, starting to well up.

'It's okay,' said Imani.

Claire looked up, wiping her eyes. 'Sorry, I haven't asked about you.'

'That's all right.'

'How are you?'

Imani shrugged. 'Physically? Fine, really. No lasting damage.' She held up her bandaged wrists. 'Everything's on the mend.'

'And mentally?'

Imani tried to smile but couldn't. 'That'll take a little longer, I think.'

'Yes,' said Claire. 'You were very brave.'

'I was doing my job.'

'And it was a brave thing to do. The bravest thing I've ever seen.'

Imani looked straight at her. 'There's different kinds of bravery. You should know that.'

'I just run a refuge,' said Claire. 'There's no bravery in that.'

'You think not?' said Imani. 'You know what you had to go through to get there. Now you help other women to do the same. That's bravery.'

'I'm not sure I can go back there,' Claire said.

'Get yourself sorted first. That's the main thing.'

They talked on, well after day turned to night. So long that Imani accepted an offer to stay over.

Talking was good for both of them. There would be much more of it.

Together they had found their own personal refuge.

Hugh Ellison had heard what had happened. How Phil Brennan had been a hero once again, taken down that serial killer with the help of his wife. His *wife*. A psychologist, for fuck's sake. Confronting a killer. He felt sickened every time he heard

407

about it. And since it was still the main topic of conversation in the station, he heard about it a lot.

He sat on the pull-down bed in his studio apartment just off Hagley Road in Edgbaston and stared at the TV. His wife had finally kicked him out. Drinking in the Ivy Bush, meals from the chip shop next door. His life. And how he hated it.

He lay back on the bed. Thought again about the only thing on his mind. Phil fucking Brennan and Marina fucking Esposito. That case should have been his. *His.* He should have been the one to crack it, to find the real killer. He had gone over and over it. Marina should have done more when she was helping Carly. Should have gone further. All the brilliant stuff she came up with later, she should have done that with him. He hated her for it. *Hated* her.

But he knew what to do about that.

He checked his watch. Late. Good. It was time.

He took one last slurp from his bedside bottle of Bell's and made his way out. Drove to Balsall Heath. He knew where he was going. Rang the bell. She answered. Stared at him.

'Back again,' she said, and stood aside, allowing him to enter.

He was back where he always went to feel better about himself. To let off steam. The place his wife had continually complained about. Where he'd been when he told her he was out with friends. Networking, he had said.

He threw something at her.

'Put this on.'

She caught it, looked at it. 'Not again.'

'Just do it.'

She sighed, bracing herself. 'That's extra, you know.'

'I always pay, don't I?'

'For what you want to do, you should.' No attempt at seduction, no niceties. They both knew what he was there for. And what she was there for too. 'And go easy, will you? Bruises have just healed from last time.'

She walked away from him, pulling the long black curly wig on as she went. She reached the bedroom. It stank of stale bodies and cheap air freshener. She stood in front of him, bracing herself. Closed her eyes.

'I'm ready.'

He drew back his fist. 'Right, you fucking slut,' he said, building himself up for what he was about to do. 'Treat me like that, will you? Look at me like that, will you? I know what you're like. What you're really like. I know what you want.'

Rage built to a peak and he let go with his fist. It connected with her face, spun her round, knocked her down on to the bed. He was quickly on her.

'Right, you bitch. You're going to get it now. *Marina*.'

This was better. Now he was in charge.

Now he felt like a real man.

The rain was drying up as the service in the crematorium finished.

Phil and Marina had sat at the back, away from everyone else. They weren't family and they weren't strictly speaking colleagues. Just there to pay their respects.

The mourners filed out. They nodded and spoke. Phil noticed Esme Russell among them. She nodded at him, didn't speak. The family invited them back for something to eat. Phil declined. Waiting a decent amount of time, they made their excuses and left. Drove back to the city.

'We seem to go to a lot of these, don't we?' said Marina.

'Funerals? Line of work we're in, I suppose.'

Marina nodded. She drew in a deep breath, let it go. 'And I suppose also . . . that one day it'll be one of us.'

'You think?'

'Some things we just have to accept, don't we? It's what we do. Who we are. We've got someone after us who might strike at any time.'

'Or,' said Phil, 'might not strike at all.'

'True, said Marina. 'But you know what? You're right. We're stronger together. If it happens, it happens. But we won't go down without a fight.'

He turned to her, smiled. She returned it.

They drove on in silence.

'So where are we going?' asked Phil after a while.

'You speaking philosophically or geographically?'

'Both,' he said.

Marina smiled. 'How about lunch?'

He laughed. 'That'll do nicely.'